CW01209484

BLOOD BETRAYAL

BLOOD BETRAYAL

ERIC RICHARDSON

Troubador Publishing Ltd
Unit E2 Airfield Business Park,
Harrison Road, Market Harborough,
Leicestershire LE16 7UL
Tel: 0116 279 2299
Email: books@troubador.co.uk
Web: www.troubador.co.uk

ISBN 978-1-80514-429-8

British Library Cataloguing in Publication Data.
A catalogue record for this book is available from the British Library.

Printed and bound in Great Britain by 4edge Limited
Typeset in 10.5pt Garamond Pro by Troubador Publishing Ltd, Leicester, UK

Dedicated to my sensitivity reader
– Ted Bundy

Intellectual honesty is a crime in any totalitarian country; but even in England it is not exactly profitable to speak and write the truth.
– George Orwell, *Fascism and Democracy*

The author could not be arsed to list all the multiple trigger warnings in what you are about to read and takes no responsibility for the content of the book. The author believes this novel should be compulsory reading for all university students as in a world devoid of toxic role models he altruistically gives you Nic Hunter.

Behind every great fortune lies a great crime.
– Honoré de Balzac

Nothing on earth consumes a man more quickly than the passion of resentment.
– Friedrich Nietzsche

PROLOGUE
THE LAST CHRISTMAS

"*Duw helpa ni*," muttered DCI McBride of Dalston CID as he brought the Ford Scorpio Granada to a halt and turned off the wailing sirens. Foot heavy on the gas and lights flashing, he'd made it over from Hackney to West London in record time. This wasn't his patch, but he'd pulled strings using his rank and the fact that if anyone should have this case, it was him. The atrocities that had happened here tonight were linked to him like a ball and chain. It had been cleared by the top ranks of Scotland Yard between the Yard's Deputy Assistant Commissioner and the Assistant Chief Constable. It overruled traditional practice, as this was far from conventional. A mother and her babies had been brutally murdered. When the husband and father heard of these horrific crimes, it would send shockwaves through the underbelly of London. The ramifications of this incident would create a bloodbath across the capital. From what he'd been told over the radio by PC Hutson, who was at the scene, the weapon that had been used to carry out the atrocities looked like a sawn-off shotgun.

Flicking his seatbelt off, he opened the car door. He flinched as a cold gust of wind hit him in the face, cursing under his breath, "*Gwaed diniwed*."

It was 11.30pm on 6th December 1989 and snow was falling on Curzon Street, Mayfair. Struggling to ease his large frame out of the car, McBride took the last bite of his bacon-and-egg roll. His fingers dripped egg as he locked the car and pocketed the keys. At fifty-two he'd been with the Met for over twenty years after transferring from Butetown Police Station. This was due to the level of corruption he'd witnessed there as a PC. He thought the Met would be different. Little did he know that his move from Cardiff was like going from the frying pan into the deepest fires of hell. Dante's *Inferno* didn't go to this sepulchral depth. There were epidemic levels of corruption, extortion and witness intimidation in East London, and no more so than by his own colleagues in the force. This dirty misconduct reached to the highest echelons of the Met. A firm within a firm. A police force where racism and misogyny were systemic. In Dalston, where there was a large population of Caribbeans, Cypriots, West Africans and Turks, the Met thought the best way forward was to employ glow-in-the-dark white men. Many officers started a progressive trend where they assaulted random, and yet always black people, then in a cunning twist, turned the tides and arrested their victims and charged them with assaulting them. It never failed to get convictions. With these crime-catching statistics, due to their 'intelligent policing', they met Home Secretary David Waddington with pride. The real menaces that the Met largely chose to ignore, as many were taking bungs from them, were the untouchable gangsters making millions per year, leaving a body count behind them to rival Auschwitz. A crime family that had been around for decades which had gone from controlling the East End into having their tentacles all over London. A gang

McBride intended to bring crashing to the ground if it was the last thing he did.

McBride being many things – never married and with no family and friends – corrupt he wasn't. The DCI took his job very seriously. Born in Blaen-Y-Maes, Swansea, he and his Mam had moved to Tiger Bay when he was ten. He didn't speak with the harsh Cardiff twang, more the spit-inducing South Walian accent, further pronounced by his unfortunate underbite. McBride's Mam worked as a cleaner to keep a roof over their heads. He had no recollection of his Da, who'd gone back to Glasgow before he was born. His Mam told him on many occasions his Da was a no-good waster and better off out of their lives. They lived hand to mouth in a flat infested with vermin and plagued with black mould. His Mam worked her way into an early grave. Not long before she'd informed him his Da had died years ago of a heroin overdose while living rough on the streets of Haghill. He saw the police force as a way out of the life he'd been born into. Ninian McBride would be somebody. To spare him from a lifetime down the pits in Nantgarw Colliery, where at aged thirty-eight he would die an excruciating death of pneumoconiosis, coughing up bloody phlegm and wheezing like Muttley.

"It's bloody nobbling, mun," mumbled McBride as he stepped onto the road shuddering with cold. He turned into Curzon Place. Snowflakes swirled around him, and in less-tragic circumstances this would've been a Dickensian magical scene, had it not been for the heavy presence of police cars, personnel and ambulances. Rubbing his greasy hands on his shirt, he just added to the stains that were already there. McBride didn't see the necessity of washing his clothes; he had police work to do. His personal hygiene didn't factor at all in his life. When he was in uniform in Cardiff, he'd been reprimanded about his lax approach to cleanliness. Complaints had been made of having to endure sitting near to him at the station, where he reeked. When he moved to CID in London and was plain clothed, he thought things might improve. Unfortunately, they didn't, and McBride wore the same brown cords, frayed shirt and crumpled Mackintosh.

As he waddled along, McBride couldn't help but be impressed by the majestic architecture and regal beauty of Mayfair. The street's Christmas tree sparkled with festooned tawdry lights, the smell of pine needles heavy in the air. McBride made his way to the main door of the building that was 9 Curzon Place. An impressive black-brick Georgian townhouse. It was four stories tall and included a basement which housed five luxurious apartments. The slaughter he was here to investigate had happened on the top floor. Doing a little tap dance as his feet hit an icy patch on the pavement, he cursed between gritted teeth, letting out a ghostly plume of cold breath followed by a noisy belch. McBride ran his fingers through his scraggy beard, unlodging food debris that was festering in his matted bristles. He surveyed the scene in front of him. There were four police cars and three ambulances parked outside. Crime tape marked out the area – 'POLICE LINE – DO NOT CROSS'. As he approached the doorway, he flashed his warrant card so the uniformed plebs knew he was the man in charge. The porch was white-marble pillared with gold torch snufflers. Overhead a lantern set off a soft tawny glow. A brass lion door knocker hung on the front door. They say it acted as a guardian to your home, but not tonight; there'd been no paladin knight visitation, but a demon hellbent on bloody slaughter. McBride was met by a stout female PC.

"Guv, the pathologist and SOCO are upstairs."

Barging past, McBride huffed and puffed his way up the spiral staircase. The Chief Inspector was greeted at the door of Flat 5 by PC Hutson, who looked very green around the gills.

"PC Hutson, guv. Glad to have you here. This is the most shocking thing I've ever seen."

"You don't say. Sometimes we as the police have to deal with things other than catching diplomats' wives stealing silk scarves. Serious crime, like."

PC Hutson, who'd come from the local police station, West End Central on Saville Row, no doubt didn't deal with the daily carnage that he did in Hackney. He noted forensics dusting for fingerprints and bagging evidence and thought, *good luck on that.* London's major faces' fingerprints were probably all over the flat. Only last week intelligence had seen Terry and Patsy Adams entering the building.

"Which rooms?" asked McBride.

"Female victim was found in the second room on the right, just down the hallway, and the babies in the next-door bedroom," said Hutson as he gestured in that direction and followed his superior.

Offering just a grunt in response, McBride made his way down a black-and-white-tiled hallway with mirrored walls. The hall was furnished with a King Edward chair and a walnut desk. It was a hive of activity with assorted police personnel. McBride barely acknowledged them, just giving the most cursory nods. He walked past the first door. It was open and revealed a lounge elegantly decorated in cream and pale gold. There were plush sofas and chairs around a glass coffee table. An elaborate chandelier hung from the ceiling. The bare Christmas tree was surrounded by unopened bags from Harrods probably full of Christmas decorations. He'd always wondered what this flat looked like inside. It was almost surreal to literally be walking through it. "*Sy'n dweud nad yw trosedd yn talu*," muttered McBride.

This place reeked of death, and not just of tonight's bloody slayings. This house had a gruesome history. In the 1970s, when the building housed twelve flats, before they were knocked into five by a property developer, the singer-songwriter Harry Nilsson owned Flat 12, a flat which had been interior decorated by Ringo Starr. He'd let the flat out to Mama Cass of the supergroup The Mamas & the Papas. In 1974 she died there of a heart attack, although conspiracy theories surfaced that she had choked on a ham sandwich. Later he rented the flat to Keith Moon, the party-animal drummer of the rock band The Who, a man with a penchant for playing live drugged up on Ketamine, used by vets to castrate horses. In 1978 he died in Flat 12 from an overdose of clomethiazole. It was ironically a drug he'd been prescribed to alleviate his alcohol-withdrawal symptoms. Some would say coincidence, but others a curse. Believing in the latter, Nilsson sold the hexed apartment to Moon's guitarist bandmate Pete Townsend.

McBride moved towards the bedroom and walked in. It hit him like a steam train coming at him at full speed, the coppery smell of blood. And there was so much blood. Innocent blood. Doctor Albert Fish, the pathologist, evaded pleasantries. An arrogant man with a bulbous nose and close-set eyes. The only other person in the room was the police photographer, a portly man in his late forties, who took pictures of the macabre scene from all angles.

"I see CID are quick on the scene, but this really isn't your patch is it. Not enough bodies in your neck of the woods," said Fish, his jowly cheeks flapping as he munched on a sweet.

"We've got plenty in Hackney. As yew know it keeps the body-bag industry afloat, it does. This case yere is of special interest to me, it is. I'm Senior Investigating Officer on it; no one else has any business heading this investigation up."

"I've declared life extinct on all three bodies."

"Well done, yew. Must have been a difficult one to work out, like."

Fish just gave the inspector a cavalier flick of his hand while rolling his eyes on his smug face.

The site before McBride was one of sheer horror. The female victim was lying on the floor by the foot of the king-size bed covered in blood, her long blonde hair dripping with crimson liquid. She was in her early twenties, extremely pretty, angelic almost, with a petite body and large, pert breasts. Her open blue eyes were haunted with terror. No doubt her final thoughts would have been what would happen to her babies. Whose eyes was she looking into pleading for her life when the trigger was pulled? The victim wore a pink camisole and knickers. They were now saturated with scarlet gore and splattered with intestines. Bits of her ribs, now pulverised, stuck out of her torso. The fatal wound tinged with burn marks. McBride stifled the urge to shut her eyes, as if by doing so he could put her out of her pain.

"*Duw duw cariad*," said McBride.

But the inspector had seen her before, when she'd been very much alive. A woman as beautiful on the outside as she was on the inside. Her name was Suzi Hunter. McBride looked around the decadently furnished bedroom. He noted the silk bedspread was ruffled, as if someone had pulled on it, and the dressing table had been upset. Expensive bottles of perfume and jewellery were strewn across the floor. She'd tried to fight back. A tailored suit was laid out on a Baroque armchair. Feeling his blood boiling, knowing exactly who the suit belonged to, McBride turned his attention back to Fish.

"All right, what yew got, butt?"

"It looks like a sawn-off-shotgun wound at close range to the stomach. There are some flame burns, and the wound is so big you could fit Tyson's fist through it. But I can't confirm anything at the moment," said Fish as if he was discussing the weather.

"Anything else?" asked McBride as he moved nearer to the body.

Fish grimaced at the stench coming from the DCI. Some of the dead bodies he'd encountered in his career had smelt better.

"Judging by the stages of mortis, I would say she's freshly dead; a few hours tops."

"Hutson, come in yere now, like," shouted McBride.

Obeying his superior, Hutson stepped into the bedroom from the hallway.

"Who called it in, PC?"

"The lady who lives in the apartment below. Mrs Burlington-Befrey. She's the only resident in the building. The bottom two flats are up for sale and the basement is owned by Phillip and Wendy Paddock – you know, the ones who do the *Morning Medley* show on TV – but it's in darkness and we got no answer. She heard a bang that she thought was a car backfiring at approximately 10pm, then a few minutes later she heard a further two bangs in quick succession, prompting her to think they were gunshots. She didn't call for over half an hour. She was hiding under the bed with Boots."

"Boots? Who the bloody buggary is Boots, PC?"

"It's her cat, guv. A seal point ragdoll."

"Not being funny, mun, but I very much doubt the cat did it, I don't; but if yew want, I can go downstairs and try to eliminate Boots from the inquiry."

"Sorry, guv. I just thought I'd give you as much detail as possible. When she did make the 999 call, she was barely making any sense. She said that she was probably just being silly. Mrs Burlington-Befrey is a recluse. She hasn't left the building in twenty years. A PC has been to see her and taken a statement."

"Bloody useless," said McBride. "Like a sheep's fart in a

jam jar. Do we know how the perp got into the building and apartment door?"

"It looks like the locks were picked on both occasions, so I think we can rule out that she knew the attacker."

"To be honest, like, Hutson, let me do all the thinking around yere."

"Understood, guv," said the PC, trying not to sound too miffed. "The strange thing is, nothing seems to have been stolen, and there are expensive things everywhere. There's a top-of-the-range alarm system, but it's been disarmed or maybe not switched on."

"*Bydd hyn yn achosi gwaedbath*," said McBride distractedly, as he doubted the motive for the triple murder was robbery. Mat Hunter owned this apartment. Hunter was without doubt the biggest gangland boss in London, head of the Hunter clan he ran closely with his brother, Nic, and twin cousins, Sparky and Flint. Mat was said to be worth around £50 million. The gang were so wealthy they had high-ranking police officers in their back pockets feeding them intelligence. The Hunter crime syndicate had become untouchable. Mat had taken the gang from being the most feared in the East End to controlling much of the very lucrative West End. The Hunters were linked to numerous gangland murders and disappearances. The problem for law enforcement officers who were not corrupt and entangled in their spider's web of corruption was that the bodies seldom turned up. The gang became masters at covering up their lawlessness. If no body was found, there was no crime. They had become so powerful they could afford the best accountants, lawyers and barristers, having the finances and proclivity for violence to silence people with whatever method they chose. Cross them and you disappeared forever. The syndicate had dozens of henchmen with clump and shooter power around London and hundreds of snitches and snouts. They collected bent coppers like stamps.

Fuck-you money bought you eyes, ears and fists everywhere. The gangland boss collected secrets as ammunition about powerful people, people he may need services from in the future, those who were too high profile to use the preferred method of just torturing to death. Mat's criminal empire had done well for him. His assets included a six-bedroomed house in Brentwood and a sprawling villa in Marbella. Commercially, he owned many going concerns, including a large scrapyard in Hackney, businesses he needed to keep his dirty money clean, as the main reason for Mat's wealth was drugs. He was the biggest cocaine importer in the UK. The world was going mad for the narcotic. It crossed all social boundaries – politicians, journalists and bricklayers were hoovering it up their noses. London by 1989 was awash with the white powder. It was Scotland Yard Intelligence that Mat dealt directly with the Medellín Cartel. This meant he had a pipeline of cocaine coming into the UK with a street value of multi-millions.

The eldest Hunter was the brains behind the operation, then there was Nic the younger brother, a complete psychopath. Whereas Mat used violence as an indifferent necessary part of his life, Nic actively enjoyed inflicting pain. It was a high no different to the high he got from sex and drugs. He owned strip clubs and nightclubs. The first cousins were Chad and Nathan, aka Sparky and Flint. The twins had a special love for arson. Setting light to things and watching them burn was the ultimate high. The *pièce de resistance* was watching a human being burning to death screaming in agony as the amber blaze devoured their skin. At age six they'd set their neighbour's pet bunny alight after dousing it in cooking oil. It was their Uncle Len who had affectionately given them the nicknames. This was the new generation of Hunters, their fathers now living the life of Riley in the Costa Del Sol. But not before leaving behind carnage.

"That the bathroom bu there, is it?" asked McBride to no one in particular as he made his way to the doorway. Sticking his head around the corner, he saw the bath had recently been used. There were remnants of bubbles lining the bottom. A towel lay discarded on the floor. The waste basket held nothing more than make-up-smudged cottonwool. He went to turn tail, but something caught his eye near to the toilet. On the ledge above was a small plastic object obscured by a bottle of Chanel. McBride walked over and peered. It was a used pregnancy test. "*Annwyl Duw*," he muttered as he went back into the bedroom.

"The babies next door, or what?" asked McBride.

"Yes. You may want to brace yourself before you enter," said Fish with the hint of a grin on his face.

McBride made his way next door. He entered a child's room decorated in Winnie the Pooh wallpaper. There was a soft light coming from the mobiles above two cots. Moving further into the room, the DCI could see blood splatter dripping from Tigger and Piglet. The white sheets of the cots were saturated in blood. The babies had gunshot wounds to their tiny chests, their little bodies so small the wounds had nearly obliterated their torsos. Both little boys cuddled teddies. Blond-haired cherubs whose hair was now drenched in sanguine fluid. Lying on the floor next to the toybox splattered in blood was a card: Mr Potts the Painter. Suppressing the urge to be sick, McBride turned away from the carnage and took a moment to compose himself. Trying to hold down the butty he'd eaten earlier, McBride could feel a vomit infusion creeping up his oesophagus into his mouth. He was a bit sick in his hand, so he wiped it on the back of his cords; the rest he swallowed back down, letting out a foul-smelling burp. He turned to walk back into the hallway, looking back one last time at the grisly horror. The wife and babies didn't deserve to die in this heinous manner because they had an *diafol* as a husband and father. Suzie and the twins were innocent, just more bodies to be added to Hunter's never-ending list. If she'd never let him in and been pulled into his murky world... it was like Babes in the Wood meeting Vlad the Impaler. Walking back into the main bedroom, he noted that the photographer had left but Fish was still there.

"McBride, I'll let you know as soon as I can determine the cause of death and time," he said as he rummaged in his pocket until he found what he was looking for and proceeded to stuff into his mouth the Liquorice Allsort he'd freed from the paper bag.

"I'm not being funny, mun. I'd hazard a guess it was around 10pm tonight, and I don't think they were poisoned by cyanide, I don't."

Not rising to the bait, Fish replied in an irksome tone while swallowing the sweet, "You'll have to wait for the results of the autopsy."

"Yew may want to run a pregnancy test. I think yew'll find there were four deaths yere tonight, butt."

McBride made his way out the door and back down to the main foyer, which was now an even bigger hive of activity. Walking out of the building, the atmosphere was sombre. No copper had any enjoyment out of murder, especially child murder, apart from those who'd managed to slip under the radar of what should've been protocol police checks. Heading back to his car, McBride was in heavy contemplation. The powers that be would be eager to solve this pronto. This would cause major ripples in the criminal underworld, not wanted by the force, especially those who were neck deep in *cachu*. This needed to be solved pronto, before Hunter put in place a bloodbath across London. Whoever was responsible for these barbarous crimes had better wish that the police got to them before he did. A triple life sentence in a hellhole locked in your cell for twenty-four hours a day would be preferable to the punishment he'd administer. It was one thing to try to take out Mat or any of his associates, Gangstercide being actively encouraged by the Met, but an innocent woman and her children slain. Even the underworld had a code of honour where civilians were concerned. But then again, there was a new breed of gangster – the Turks, the Yardies and the Albanians – who didn't adhere to these rules. But it made no sense. It would only make Mat more deadly. Other gangs knew the Hunters had the money and soldiers to crush them into oblivion. And make no mistake, he had no doubt that the crime lord would seek bloody retribution, and after what had happened, the old school rules wouldn't apply. He would take out the perpetrator and his family. One by one he'd track them down, and they wouldn't die quickly or quietly. It didn't add up. As he opened the Granada, he wondered whether Mat knew Suzie was expecting, or was that a loving conversation she was yet to have with him and would now never have. "*Bydd uffern yn cael ei ryddhau,*" said McBride. Shutting the car door and starting the car up, McBride made his way back to Hackney. He whispered, "*Gwelaf Yr Afon Tafwys yn ewynnu â gwaed.*"

ACT 1

SOLDIERS OF FORTUNE

All empires are created of blood and fire.
– Pablo Escobar

We know that no one ever seizes power with the intention of relinquishing it.
– George Orwell, *1984*

"Fuck me," said Den Hunter, choking on the dense fumes the thermic lance was making. The orange fiery rain sprinkled down around them as the lance cut through the reinforced concrete of the vault floor, fizzing like a giant sparkler. He was happy that he and his brother Pat were wearing the full protective kit – head shield, goggles, gloves. They were very much seasoned professionals in their line of work.

"We can't use this; it's just not working. Gotta go to the next plan," said Den as he turned his ruggedly handsome face, gasping for breath as the smoke engulfed them.

How could they have come so far to give up now? The thermic lance had cut through half of the concrete. They just needed to get through the other half to gain access to the vault which held a safe full of gold.

"Right, Pat, ovah to you, bruv. You're the explosives expert."

Checking his Rolex Sea-Dweller 4000, Pat got the explosives

ready. It wouldn't be an easy feat. It was a small, enclosed area, and it needed to be dead right. He drilled holes in the underside of the vault floor and packed the gelignite in tightly, an explosive more stable than dynamite, which could suffer from sweating nitro-glycerine. This meant it could become extremely touch sensitive, whereby even a gentle touch could detonate it. He expertly taped up the explosive to the floor and pushed the detonator. The duo stood back while there was a controlled boom. A 12-inch-wide hole was blasted. Pat started to clear the debris with his hands.

"Grab the 'ammah and chisel, will ya, bruv. We need to widen the 'ole to get us lumps in."

Both were big, muscular men, well over six feet tall. Den slung Pat a hammer and he started to use the chisel. They hacked away, and when they finished, the exit hole measured 12 inches by 14 inches.

"We're in," said Pat as he swatted the air full of thick dust.

They made their way into the vault where the safe was kept. As Linda, Den's wife, had described it, it was a small room, with the safe taking up most of it.

"Right, Den, ovah to you to crack the safe. Not like those days when we used to use a chainsaw to open up the back of security vans like cans of beans. We're talking propah precision work. Fuck, the buzz on these jobs is betta than any drugs. All the adrenalin pumping frough me right now is fucking incredible. Every job; it nevah gets any less."

"You evah fink on these jobs our old man and Ray's looking down on us?"

"Nah, bruv. Where they are they're looking up at us surrounded by naked birds wiv 'orns on their 'eads."

Den stood in front of the large steel structure mentally sussing it out. Everything hinged on him opening the safe without setting off any alarms. Precision was everything, which was tricky when you had hands like shovels, but surprisingly he was highly dexterous. Running his fingers through his stubble, Den aimed the cobalt-blend power drill into the top of the safe. A small sweat broke over his forehead, dripping onto his boxer's nose. This had to be meticulous. He skilfully drilled into the safe. When he'd drilled just enough, he removed the drill, prompting steel curls of silver like confetti spilling up through the small hole. Den brushed these away. Now he could peek through the small incision and see the internal state of the combination lock. He took out a torch and peered through the tiny gap. While looking at the lock, Den manipulated the dial to align the lock gates so that the fence fell and the bolt mechanism was disengaged. It was the sound of success, but this job had been a scrupulous operation.

The job had taken them six months to plan and put into action. Many days had been spent in Ye Olde Mitre, located in an alleyway just off Hatton Garden. There they'd downed pints and chain smoked while waiting for a rental lease to come up on a shop near to one of the many jewellery shops of Hatton Garden, the jewellery district of London. The game they played was one of waiting and patience. The ploy had paid off when a shop became free to rent one door down from E Katz & Co Jewellers. The only premises between them was P. R. Deltoid Newsagent's. The shop had a basement that was at the same level as the jeweller's vault. Within thirty minutes of Savills putting the 'TO LET' sign outside, Den had made a call to their commercial property lawyer, Thomas Hewitt of Sawyer and Jedediah Solicitors. The property was leased to Den under a false name, Charles Lytton. The three brothers had got to work as soon as they had the keys. The windows were whited out and a sign went up saying 'OPENING SOON – MONA LISA OF PEARLS'. With larceny equipment, they'd drilled a tunnel under the shop to the vault of the jewellers. This had taken them a whole month. It was a painstaking operation. They tunnelled forty feet using jackhammers and picks up through the vault floor. Not to arouse suspicion, they only dug from close of business on a Saturday until the early hours of Monday morning.

Den's beautiful wife visited E Katz & Co, her five-foot-eight slim figure wearing Prada, her long blonde hair tied in a chignon. She went in with the rouse of buying a gold chain for her son Mathew. The jewellery owner, Mr Katz, who was mesmerised by her, insisted she called him George. What she was really doing was getting the ins and outs of the shop's diameters, her mathematical brain working out measurements. She made three trips to scout the place and work out dimensions, even managing to go down to the vault with George. On the third visit she picked a twenty-four-carat gold chain. Telling the jeweller that it was the perfect purchase, she gave him a warm smile that went all the way up to her piercing blue eyes.

The brothers heaped the debris and rubble into the back storeroom; there was around 8 long tons of it. They tunnelled under the vault, because the walls and ceilings were protected by vibration alarms and trembler switches which could sense any unusual vibrations or shockwaves and automate a trigger alarm directly to the police. Fortuitously, the tremblers in the vault floor were being switched off due to ongoing roadworks which had triggered numerous false alarms to Islington Police Station. All this information had been supplied to them by a moody security guard working for the jeweller's security company.

But it hadn't all been plain sailing. Once they had dug the tunnel, they realised that they had a major obstacle, this being three feet of concrete reinforced with steel between them and the vault. First the brothers had tried to use a 100-ton jack to force a hole into it. Two railway sleepers were placed on the floor to support it. Unbeknown to the brothers, there was an old well beneath the end of the tunnel. The strength of the jack thrust the bottom of the tunnel down into the well instead of lifting the vault floor skywards.

Once the job was done, Len, their younger brother, would drive them over to Castle Hedingham in Essex, where their wives were holed up in an abandoned farmhouse should anything go wrong. Linda and Lorraine, Pat's wife, were used to it; it was the usual drill – bags packed and tickets to Spain. All legal eventualities could be sorted out in just a few phone calls. But tonight everything had gone perfectly, so it was just a matter of Len getting them over to Essex, where they could lay low for a while. Then they could start to unload their ill-gotten gains with their fences. Should something untoward happen, Den would have to make the call he'd spent his life drumming into his eldest boy, Mat. The call that would tell him he was now in charge of their criminal enterprise, with Nic and the twins at his side. Den had no worries passing things on to Mat. He was razor smart and extremely ruthless – key characteristics to make it in this life. Nic was currently finishing up a stretch in borstal. Mat had also done a stint there too. Both had dealt with borstal like chips off the old block. They were his sons – vicious, brutal thugs who'd made themselves top boy. They went in with the pedigree of the Hunter name – a namesake steeped in respect. Respect earned by fear.

Stuffing the bags full of gold, the brothers were surprisingly agile for their big frames as they made their way back down the hole into the tunnel. From there they climbed back up into the rear of the shop, where they exited from the back door. Hatton Garden was deserted at 9pm, so different from the daytime, when it was a hive of activity. Incongruously, the glamorous neighbourhood stank; the rubbish bags were piled up, oozing rubbish. The refuge collectors striking was causing havoc across the UK. It was January 1979, and it was being called the Winter of Discontent. They made their way swiftly towards Greville Street, where Len was parked in a Ford Transit van.

"It's fucking freezing, Den, and just look at the state of Lundun. It's gone to the dogs. Makes me wanna just fuck off and go on 'oliday like Sunny Jim. 'E 'ad the right idea getting 'imself off to the Caribbean."

"Pat, you ain't the Prime Ministah like Callaghan is. 'E should be ovah 'ere sorting this mess out, not fucking 'bout on a beach in 'is Speedos. The Lib-Lab pact; what the fuck is that all 'bout? We're being called the sick man of Europe. Maggie; for a bird, she's clued up. She's worked out we're sick of immigrants swamping us, and since Powell no fuckah 'as tried to sort it."

"Agreed, bruv. Callaghan, in the name of God, fuck off."

Len was reading *The Sun*, the headline announcing '**CRISIS: WHAT CRISIS? RAIL, LORRY, JOBS CHAOS – AND JIM BLAMES THE PRESS**', the newspaper even having to apologise that due to the lorry-driver strikes they were short of print. 'Don't shoot the pianist'. Everyone seemed to be striking, even gravediggers in some parts of the country. The rubbish piled up and was left to decay. London looked like a dystopian post-apocalyptic nightmare. Len wouldn't be surprised if he saw spectral horses galloping over the horizon, bringing with them conquest, war, famine and death. Callaghan's government needed to get their act together. It really came to something when *The Sun* had jumped ship and was now flying the blue flag big time. There was only more doom and gloom on the front page. Prolific terrorists MAF had bombed the Vanguard offices in Pennsylvania; there were no survivors, including their founder, John Bogle. It was MAF's deadliest attack since 1971, when they cluster-bombed the Davos Congress Centre in Switzerland, where the European

Management Forum's annual meeting was taking place. MAF to date had not issued a statement as to why they'd first crucified their founder Professor Klaus Schwab upside down or why prior to that they had made him drink a gallon of (OPV) infused with (SV40) then covered his body with dermestid beatles. MAF cited the same reasons for the Vanguard attack as Davos. There could only be one New World Order and Great Reset.

Could things go more downhill? They were also experiencing the coldest winter in sixteen years. But far worse, West Ham had been relegated to Second Division. Even Lyall's signing of goalie Phil Parkes hadn't saved the Irons. Len was momentarily brought back to the present as Den knocked the side of the driver's window, holding up the swag bag.

"Job done," mouthed Den, which morphed into a giant shit-eating grin.

PC Kernick was looking forward to finishing his shift. A quick dash back to the police station and then he was on a home run. His night patrolling Hatton Garden had been without incident, although the smell like rotten cabbages had started to get to him. A smile formed on his lips; that meant no paperwork so he could get home all the quicker. He'd seen the perfect ring in the window of a jewellers, with a price tag that he could just afford. He planned tomorrow to buy the ring for his long-term girlfriend. Making an honest woman of her had become all the more pressing when she'd announced six months ago they were having a baby. He started to walk back to the station. As he reached the corner of Greville Street, he heard a noise that caught his attention. Some men were talking in whispered tones. Kernick advanced further and could see it was two men in workmen overalls with their heads in the back of a Transit. Grumbling to himself, but knowing that it was his duty to investigate, he advanced further towards the van. The lateness of the hour made him suspicious. Kernick startled the two men as they loaded bags into the back of the van.

"Evening, gents. Can I ask what you're doing here at this time of night?"

"Uh, yeh, we 'ave been doing building work in the new place on 'Atton. Been working 'round the clock to get it open. Jewish ownah is working us like slaves. You know what these oven dodgahs are like," said Pat with a false laugh.

"And who is the owner?" asked Kernick as he got his notebook and pen out.

"It's a, uh, Mr Streisand. Yeh, that's it. Ebeneezah Streisand," said Den.

"And the bags?" asked Kernick, not convinced by his answer.

"Just work stuff, really. You know, us buildahs need our tools for the job," said Den.

Something didn't feel right with this situation. His copper's nose was smelling something off here. There was an uneasiness with the men. They smiled but it looked forced. Their body language was guarded.

"Okay, I understand. Just unzip the bags so I can see what's in them, then hopefully we can all go home, because it's a cold one tonight."

"No problem," said Den as he reached into the van and pulled out a Berretta 92 semi-automatic pistol and shot Kernick through the forehead. The policeman's dead body fell to the ground, hitting the pavement, blood spurting from his head wound.

"Let's get the fuck out of 'ere," said Den as he and Pat jumped in the front of the van. Len swung the van off sharpish, leaving exhaust fumes in the air. All three brothers were synchronised in lighting cigarettes, inhaling deeply on the nicotine high, the flax paper burning rapidly with an amber glow in the dark, illuminating their troubled, etched faces.

"'Ow the fuck did that 'appen? We was on an 'ome run. Cunting pig 'ad to poke 'is nose in," said Den.

"Well, 'e won't be doing that again evah, will 'e," said Pat. Let's just get the fuck ovah to Essex. Girls won't be expecting this, that's for sure."

"It was always the case that somefink like this could 'appen," interjected Len. We need to just fink clearly 'ere."

"Soon as you see a telephone box, stop the van. I gotta call Mat."

Len swerved the van onto Old Street and parked opposite a telephone box. Den jumped out to make the call he hadn't anticipated on making tonight. Stuffing a load of 10ps in the slot, Den picked up the receiver and dialled his house. Mat answered after one ring.

"Son, there was an unexpected pig that 'ad to go on the list. You know what to do. Get ovah now wiv the twins to the farm'ouse. The stuff will be in the kitchen cupboard undah the sink. Once you 'ave it, torch the place. Nufink must be found."

"Undahstood," said Mat, who terminated the call. There was nothing more to be said.

Den jumped back in the van. "Right, Len, step on it. We got a flight to Spain to catch."

It was now full speed ahead down the M11 to Castle Hedingham. Once in Essex the wives would be waiting for them. Albeit, Den doubted they would be expecting the revelations to come. It wasn't like they would be slumming it; they would be leaving an Armageddonesque England. What awaited them in Spain were their luxury houses on the Golden Mile. Linda and he had travelled back and forth finding the perfect villa. They'd settled on a Pueblo-style one in Plaza Bocanegra. The more Den thought about it the better he felt. The UK was the pits at the moment. Callaghan completely out of touch, the shocking state of the economy always there like Banquo's ghost haunting him. Once they were across the Channel in Spain, they were safe. The UK police couldn't touch them. It was fast becoming the United Nations of organised crime. Costa Del Sol was known as the bit of Europe that had fallen off the back of a lorry. In 1978 a century-old extradition treaty between Spain and the UK expired. There was suddenly no chance of fleeing British criminals being sent home to face trial. The part of Spain nicknamed the 'Costa Del Crime' was seen as a safe haven – a sun-soaked destination for crooks. So they took to the blue sky and escaped the grey walls of a prison cell. It was better to be safe than sorry should the police be able to trace the murder and burglary back to them. All Den's UK assets would pass to Mat via his solicitor. Den was going to semi-retire, lie low and enjoy the laid-back lifestyle. He and his brothers would be sent their share through offshore accounts set up by their accountant, Jonathan Steerpike.

At eighteen Mat Hunter was by anyone's standards drop-dead gorgeous. He had his dad's body type, muscular and tall, at six-foot-two, and dark hair, but he'd inherited his mum's stunning looks, piercing blue eyes and full lips. But there was a deadness behind those eyes. This only seemed to make him more attractive to women. The sex tonight with his girlfriend Lisa had been, as always, explosive. He'd shoved Lisa down roughly on the bed and hiked down her figure-hugging trousers and pulled down her lacy knickers roughly with his hands. She teasingly tried to protest, but Mat knew she wanted him really badly, so he pinned her arms above her head, entering her with his rock-hard, large cock. Mat thrusted deeply as Lisa responded with her body meeting him, bucking wildly beneath him with orgasmic sighs. Mat threw her around the bed like a ragdoll, fucking her hard in every position. Lisa, in wild abandon, gripped his back, digging her talon nails in. She dug in so hard she drew blood as she came. Mat, now de-spunked, rolled over. He didn't bother to cuddle her. The reality was, he didn't really like Lisa; he was just addicted to the mind-blowing sex.

"Lisa, I gotta go out," said Mat. He'd just put down the phone to his cousins, telling them to get over to the scrapyard.

"Why at this time of night? I thought we were spending the night together, take advantage of having the house to ourselves. It's bad enough you've practically been by the phone all night."

"Like I said, somefink 'as come up, so I gotta go out. It's a bit urgent. Nufink to trouble yourself wiv; its business. Why don't you ask Casey ovah."

"That's charming, leaving me here on my own. We've got champagne and caviar," said Lisa petulantly, sticking out her chin.

Lisa had demanded that Mat bring bottles of Cristal and Beluga caviar. Tonight Lisa had pulled out all the stops to look a million dollars. Her long brown hair was styled, all flicks and big curls, just like Farrah Fawcett. She wore skin-tight turquoise satin trousers with a matching sequin boob-tube, teamed off with stiletto strappy sandals. Just before the phone call, Mat and Lisa had been sipping champagne and eating caviar. Mat watched with relish as Lisa tasted the black unfertilised fish eggs for the first time.

"It's lovely," said Lisa, trying not to gag on the crunchy, salty, taste.

Mat watched in perverse pleasure at Lisa's mouth involuntarily grimacing while at the same time trying to feign enjoyment.

"Lisa," said Mat, picking up his car keys from the cabinet, "I'm going out. It's not up for debate." Mat walked out the front door and jumped into his Mercedes-Benz 280 3.5 coupe. Putting the car in gear and his foot on the accelerator, he sped off to the scrapyard.

Lisa debated whether she should jump in her Porsche 911 that Mat had bought her and head home, but the idea of spending the night with her parents was beyond boring. Fuming, tapping her long red nails on the phone, she dialled her only friend, Casey. Mat owed her a bigger-than-usual shopping trip. She made a mental note to tell him not to let that creepy guy Sid mind and drive her when she was out. She knew Mat liked her to have a minder, and she revelled in this perk – she loved the attention that she was Mat Hunter's woman – but, come on, not a smelly old man. Lisa knew Mat wasn't a nine-to-five bloke, but tonight was supposed to be about *her*. *Everything* was about *her*. Lisa waited for Casey to pick up. There was no way she wouldn't be able to come around; in fact, she would be delighted. Unlike Lisa, Casey was fat and ugly, so she was no threat. Lisa despised attractive women; they were all a threat to her, trying to get their teeth into Mat. This wasn't unfounded thinking, as women flung themselves at him. Lisa had been going out with Mat since she was thirteen. He was a year older. She'd moved to Dalston from Kent with her family. Mat had seen her walk into school, and he wanted her to be his. Lisa was just perfection, with long dark hair coupled with a slender figure and blossoming bosoms, exotic hazel eyes and heavily pouting lips.

Casey answered on the second ring – not surprisingly, as her mother was morbidly obese and she barely got off the sofa.

"Hi, Case, do you want to come over. Mat's had to go out."

"I'd love to, Lisa. I'll be over in about twenty minutes. Just gotta get Mum her tea."

"Good. I knew you would. It's not like anyone else would have invited you anywhere. You won't believe the Tiffany necklace

Mat got me," said Lisa as she put the phone down. With that, Lisa poured herself another glass of champagne.

Mat had driven Sparky and Flint over to Essex once they had met at the scrapyard and picked up provisions. He stopped outside the deserted and remote farmhouse. Hissing Sid had done well. Like his namesake, he was lower than a snake's belly, but he had come up trumps again; he still had his uses even after all these years of working for the firm as a lackey. The farmyard was made up of a granary, stables and a haybarn, all in rack and ruin. Mat noted that a place like this could be made into residential housing. Some barn conversions here in a highly sought-after area; you could make a mint. He'd always wanted to get into property development, and there was no reason now why he couldn't. He had big plans for the firm.

"I'm gonna grab the bags from the kitchen," said Mat as he made his way towards the Georgian farmhouse. Like the rest of the smallholding, the house was dilapidated and left to decay, its windows smashed and missing panes. Many of the clay slates on the roof were long gone, now covered with strangling moss, the elaborate-style, cast-stone exterior crumbling and forgotten.

"We'll get the stuff out the back, do a propah clean," said Flint with a twisted grin on his face.

Like Mat and Nic, Sparky and Flint were big blokes, but they didn't have the looks their cousins had inherited. Whereas Den had married a beauty, Pat's wife Lorraine was homely looking. The twins, with their light-brown hair and grey eyes, were dulled-down versions of their cousins. Sparky and Flint had been fascinated by fire since they were toddlers. Once they'd grown out of playing with fire-engine toys and dressing up in fireman costumes, they'd made the natural progression to arson, setting fire to anything they could get their hands on. At the age of seven they'd outdone themselves, and after finishing their tea on a Saturday, they'd gone out to play on their MK1 Chopper bikes, before they'd come home to watch *Jim'll Fix It*. They'd written to him asking if like Evel Knievel they could ride motorbikes through a burning ring of fire. So far Jim hadn't responded, but when he did, they hoped their old man didn't come with them. He'd told them, "The gormless git makes me skin crawl. I'd like to smack 'im so 'ard in the mouf 'e chokes on 'is own teef, then I'd shove 'is face into the ring of fire and watch the cunt's boat melt off."

The boys hoped he'd do that after they'd done the stunt, then they wouldn't care. Armed with a box of matches, they made their way to their school, then they set it on fire. Giggling to themselves, they stood fascinated as they admired the fiery carnage they'd caused. Three-quarters of the building had been destroyed and was shut for months while it was rebuilt at a cost of hundreds of thousands of pounds to Hackney Borough Council. Sparky and Flint had been identical until at the age of thirteen, when there'd been an unfortunate accident when Sparky had set light to a can of their mum's hairspray, which exploded. The result was that Flint now had a burn scar on his right cheek. Now seventeen, they were heavily influenced by Nero.

Mat walked into the ramshackle kitchen. It had probably not been lived in since the 1950s. The hearth still had old grey embers in the fireplace. A copper kettle stood redundant on the stone slab shelf. Tarnished and thick with dust, saucepans hung from metal hooks. The grimy lemon oven door hung off its hinges. Blue lino was pulled up from the floor. The ceiling precariously hung down with collapsed lath and plaster. The solid oak beams were rotten with neglect. Moving quickly, he opened the cupboard beneath the sink and pulled out the bags. Turning his back on the neglected abode, Mat took the spoils back to the car and loaded them in the boot. There was one last thing that needed to be done. Even though Mat knew his old man and brothers would have wiped everything down, you couldn't be too careful, unlike Biggs's gang back in 1963 – after they robbed a Royal Mail train – who'd left an Aladdin's cave of evidence at Leatherslade Farm. Three hundred fingerprints and fifty palm prints. The twins proceeded to douse the kitchen with petrol from jerry cans, leaving a trail of petrol onto the farmyard. Flint took a cigarette from behind his ear and stuck it in his mouth. Taking out a box of Ship matches from his pocket, he grabbed a match and casually sparked it up. Flint then tossed the burning red phosphorus on the rainbow trail.

"Gonna be quite some fire display. Shame we can't stick 'round," said Sparky as he and Flint got into the car to head down the M11 to London.

Den and his brothers had turned up at the smallholding and told Linda and Lorraine the situation. This was one flop house they wouldn't be flopping in after the adrenaline rush they were on. They travelled to Stanstead Airport in an inconspicuous Ford Escort Mark II. Tickets and passports to hand, they boarded the flight. Once they landed, they drove from Malaga Airport via N-340, snaking along the coast through Torremolinos, Benalmádena and Fuengirola. There were no central reservations, and the N-340 was known as the most dangerous road in Europe. It was called the 'Road of Death'. But Len got them to Marbella safe; expert driving came with the territory. They spent the next night at Regine's Nightclub, where the jet-setters frequented, downing bottles of Dom Perignon. Len made a pass at Brigitte Bardot but got knocked back brutally, but what the hell did he care; there was a goer in a sequin bodysuit giving him the eye. "You don't know what you're missing, darling," he'd said nonchalantly as he swaggered off to sit by Den and Linda.

"No idea why we didn't do this soonah," said Len. "Blighty 'as gone to the dogs. Labour govahnment. What a joke. It ain't fucking working."

"Lorraine and I just wish we could've said a proper goodbye to our boys," said Linda, sucking daintily on a Sobranie cigarette.

"Darling, they'll be fine. It's not like Mum's gonna let 'em starve, and as soon as fings settle, they can fly ovah for an 'oliday. Gotta get the old woman on a plane now."

"Well, just as long as she doesn't bring those awful playing cards with her," said Linda.

Den saw a familiar face: Gordon Goody, a man with a blond bob, wearing Persol shades and a mouth that looked like he was perpetually gurning.

"All right, mate. 'Ow's the new bar going?"

"Going well, Den. Look it up if you're ever in Majorca. To what do we owe the pleasure?"

"Felt like a bit of sun, mate. Change of scenery. You 'eard from Biggs?"

"No, and I don't want to. He's an arsehole. No one likes him. Catch you later, mate."

"Yeh, you will do. We're gonna be 'round a while."

Lighting a Cohiba cigar, Den turned to Linda. "We should 'ave done this soonah, sweet'eart." As far as Den was concerned, Linda was the hottest woman in London. He could remember the first time he'd seen her. She was eighteen and he twenty. She'd been at the Marquee Club on Wardour Street to see Cream. Den, turning the Hunter charm on to nuclear level, had made a beeline for her. Linda wasn't just a pretty face; she was smart too, working as a clerk in an accountancy firm.

"Don't worry 'bout the boys. They'll be fine. I controlled the past. Now Mat will control the future."

Den noticed Adnan Khashoggi by the bar, all five-foot-four of him, dressed in a Dolce & Gabbana white suit with a black Stefano Ricci bow tie, a hideously expensive Vacheron Constantin 222 watch strapped to his wrist. Towering over him was a beautiful Saudi woman dressed in a Balenciaga dress imprinted with an uncharacteristically subtle design of baby embryos that had been beheaded, castrated and anally gang-raped. He nodded his head to him, thinking they could maybe do business. You never really left the life.

THE CASUAL INMATE

Nic Hunter woke up with a smile on his face. He'd been dreaming of his girlfriend Debbie, who had her 38DD boobs stuck in his face. He was giving her the old in-out real savage. If he died in his sleep, he would've been a happy boy. But he had another reason to be happy. This was his release day from Feltham Borstal, known as 'The Nutters' Borstal', the dumping ground for the most difficult and disturbed young offenders that other like institutions had failed and found impossible to deal with. Nic hadn't wanted to spend his time here, telling the judge at his trial, "I'd ravah do me time at the Scrubs like a man and not some fucking youf club."

"Morning," said Nic, yawning to his next-door dormitory mate, Dexy. "I woke up and I fought in the night I 'ad gone camping cos I was in a tent, me cock being the tent pole. Got me an 'ard-on the size of Mount Everest. Can't wait to get me 'ands on Debbie. I plan to be smashing the granny out of 'er by this aftahnoon. Give me right arm a break, like. Since I got in 'ere, it's practically gone dead. Am finking of getting me brief on it to take this shit'ole to court ovah it. Reckon I'd win."

"Wish I 'ad someone waiting for me like 'er. You're one

lucky fuck, 'aving her send you all of 'em pics. She's as fit as Linda Lusardi."

"I know. She's a right sort."

Nic thought Debbie was as near perfect as any girl could be – knockers like Dolly Parton and gagging for it. Complete marriage material.

"Giz us a look, mate," said Nic, grabbing *The Sun* from Dexy and going straight to page three.

"Love Linda Lusardi. You seen the nips. I could suck 'em to deaf. What I call prime wank-bank material."

"Surprised, Nic. The old wank bank ain't full yet."

"No chance, Dex; not even 'alf full. It's like the vault of the Bank of Englund in there. Been working on it since I was nine."

"Who was the first in the bank?"

"It was this bird who lived across the street. I fink me old man was giving 'er one. She used to wear these really short miniskirts. If I seen 'er walking down the street, I would, like, go ovah and tell 'er any old bollocks, like 'ow well I was doing in school, which was a load of shit 'cos I was suspended most of the time. Then I'd drop somefink so I could get a good look up 'er knickahs and she nevah wore none. Propah wank bliss. I couldn't run 'ome to me bedroom fast enouf. Me bruvah started shagging 'er when 'e was firteen. And then me and the twins soon enouf was all 'aving a go. Was like a conveyah belt 'round 'er 'ouse. She couldn't get enouf. Propah filfy bitch she was. We used to come in firty seconds – well, if she was lucky, like. I still wivdraw that one."

"What sort of bird walks 'round wiv no knickahs on?"

"One who is seriously gagging for it, Dex. Makes 'em feel wanted, dunnit. I look back at 'em as more innocent times."

Nic was doing a stretch for beating up his English teacher and hospitalising him. He'd been enraged with Orwell's *Animal Farm*. Pigs talking bollocks. It was nothing like the film he'd seen on pirate VHS. He'd had a few months extra added to his stretch due to starting fights in the food hall and pissing in the housemaster's tea in full view of him.

"What motah is Mat turning up in?"

"Aston Martin V8 Vantage. Propah quality. They're only gonna make 'bout forty of 'em. Not sure 'ow long 'e'll 'ave it. Gotta keep changing your motah so Old Bill don't get too familiar. Gotta get me one pronto; mind you, gotta pass me test first. Can see me in a Durango 95. Been driving since I was eleven. The old man taught us on the scrubland by 'is scrapyard. That's 'ow I was first nicked. Me and Sparky took the old man's car for a ride. We was twelve. This sheep shaggah, PC McDick, collared us."

"Was you driving badly?" asked Dexy, cracking up.

"Nah, was driving fine; but I was driving past the police station ovah and ovah again for a larf. Cunt saw us. 'Ad to do a double take. Our old men gave us the beating of our lives. They was down the Princess Alexandra in Canning Town playing darts and really pissed off they 'ad to come down the station to pick us up. It was like some sort of big tournament. Seems strange that the old man won't be 'round anymore, but, like, me and Mat be running fings togevah from now on. Look me up when you get out. Could put work your way; always looking for lads who can 'andle 'emselves."

"You're a legend, Nic. I'll do just that."

Nic and Dexy had become mates, looking out for each other's backs. They had bonded when Nic had been gobbing to the housemaster and Dexy had joined in. Dexy was five-foot-seven with a slim build, so they looked like David and Goliath together, but make no mistake Dexy could handle himself; what he lacked in height and bulk, he made up for in unadulterated savagery. Nic had gone into borstal as a thoroughbred, wearing the surname of an infamous crime family, but he still had to make it work to be the daddy. "Being weak, you may as well be dead" had been drummed into the brothers since they were toddlers. Once they reached the age of five, if they cried, they had the belting of a lifetime from their old man. Neither boy had shed a tear since.

"Real men nevah fucking cry."

At seventeen, six-foot-three and as psychotic as they come, most left Nic alone, but there was always one who tried to muscle in. This one was a black lanky lad from Peckham called Neville Brown who was in for stabbing a lollypop man. His defence was the man had dissed him. Neville explained to the judge and jury sincerely, "Ting is shots waz fired. He knows Ise need him to put up stick. Ise got places to go. Yuh dun know he a bloodclaat wastemon."

The baby Yardie had been found with a bag stuffed with £1,000. When asked where he'd acquired this money, he'd advised the arresting officers, "Mi go to bank wid mi life savings Ise been saving since Ise lickle bwoy."

To stop the walking afro in his tracks, Nic had seen to this attempted takeover of power by administering a napalm attack in the showers. This was a mixture of scalding water and sugar, which intensified the burning to an agonising extent. Neville, not being a grass, had told the screws, "Mi accidently set miself on fire."

He'd suffered third-degree burns to his back and buttocks and would be scarred for life. Nic and Dexy had taunted Neville from that day onwards. "There ain't no black in the Union Jack, just claret, white and blue."

Now that his old man and mum were in Spain, Mat was looking after his interests. Mat would control everything until he turned eighteen, and then assets would be given to him. Since his father and brothers had left, Albanians had tried to muscle in on their turf. Mat had ironed it out straight away.

Sparky and Flint had taken out three of the gang, executed in drive-by shootings, piston-style, on a Honda CBX, their bodies now buried off Dalston Lane in the remains of the abandoned St Bartholomew's Church. The criminal underworld was no different from any other infrastructure: there was a hierarchy you had to respect. But there was a new breed of criminals who didn't understand this. They'd be dealt with mercilessly. Nic couldn't wait to make his mark too.

Thinking about seeing Debbie properly, Nic could feel his erection growing again. All he'd had for the last twelve months was the allocated thirty-minute visitors' allowance once a week, which was over a table carved in graffiti from the ghosts of past inmates. Nic was lucky to get a fumble under the table, where all the time the screws watched them. Nic had met her three years ago, and it had been lust at first sight. Debbie had been outside the Rio Cinema with her mates. She was olive skinned with large brown eyes and plump lips. Inside he'd had to make do with her perfumed letters and scantily clad photos. The lads had called him a lucky fucker, as they made do with the smuggled-in copies of *Fiesta*. But inside beggars couldn't be choosers, unless you were a Hunter. Inside Nic had wanted to dip his wick for real. He tried it on with Mrs Arbourne the matron. All he'd got for his trouble was a clip around the ear. Nic had been seriously pissed off that the cheeky bitch had knocked him back. She looked like Deirdre on Corrie, but not quite as fit. He'd planned on doing her from behind, having to dig really deep into the wank bank. It was her loss.

Mr Tanner, the walrus-moustached housemaster, had tried to be the bane of his life. As a consequence, he and Dexy made his life as miserable as possible. They called him 'Mr Tosser', or mainly just 'Tosser'. Unlike Tanner, many of the screws were taking backhanders from his old man. He'd done his stretch with all the contraband given to him he could wish for – cigarettes, chocolate and, more importantly, the pictures Debbie sent him. After Nic had sorted himself out, thinking about his girlfriend, he got out of bed. It was 6am, and Tosser was doing the morning shower drill. Smirking, he walked past the housemaster, knowing he would never have to partake in this communal ritual again.

"Move it, Hunter and Dexter. Quick march now."

Both taking their time, they strode casually into the showers. There were already six inmates in there. He could see Neville was one of them. Nic turned the shower on, stuck his head underneath and grinned at his handywork. Once he had taken the allotted two minutes, he put the shower off and turned to Dexy.

"Shame that coon ain't like Cass. 'E's a top bloke," said Nic, gesturing to Neville, who was walking out of the shower room back to the dorm.

"Yeh, Pennant is a legend. 'E's a massive fuckah; biggah than you."

"Yeh, 'e's a general now, and rightly so. Make sure that cunt doesn't get any ideas when I'm gone 'bout being the daddy. You're the daddy now."

"If 'e tries anyfink, 'e will 'ave a front to match 'is back. I can still 'ear the coon screaming now when you dun it. Funniest fing I evah seen. Bet you can't wait to see the footie lads."

"Too right. Mat told me last time 'e visited that Gardnah, Leach and Cass went down the Blue Anchor wiv West 'Am balaclavas on, tooled up wiv coshes, and took on the F-Troop. Well, like, not really 'Ammahs balaclavas. They was bobble 'ats they 'ad cut eyes and mouf 'oles in. But it looked the dog's bollocks, and they cunted most of 'em."

"Right, Hunter and Dexter, back to your dorm. Quick march."

"You gonna miss me, Tossah, it being me last day and all."

"Hunter, we'll be seeing you again soon. You have no real desire to reform."

"You got more chance of Raquel Welch grabbing 'old of your 1-inch dick and giving you a blow job than seeing me again, Tossah."

Nic walked slowly towards the housemaster. When he was a few inches away from his face, he stopped menacingly, towering over him. "You said I'd learn to obey. You was wrong. You said, 'Shut your filfy 'ole, you scum' you'd 'ave me stinking 'ooligan guts for gartahs. You shit cunt 'aven't even made a chink in me armour. I was cured all right." Nic walked out of the room with a one-finger salute on both hands, his savage exoskeleton firmly intact.

Back in his dorm his West Ham kit bag was on his bed. He stared into the closet. There, hanging up, was the travesty he'd been forced to wear – denim dungarees and a shirt with collars so long and pointy they could take your eyes out. After drying himself off, he started with his hair; it was of cardinal importance. The wedge haircut had a long fringe grown low in a flick over one eye, with the sides shorter, layered and cut to a point at the back, the style perfect in Nic's view; posy enough, and yet the face slightly obscured gave you a menacing edge. The prison barber had tried to give him a borstal bad-boy cut, but Nic had made it clear that he did exactly as he told him, unless he wanted his throat cut with his own scissors. Nic had gone in there a serious lump, but with time on his hands inside, he had worked out at every opportunity. He was now solid muscle, with a rock-hard six-pack and huge biceps. Unzipping his bag, he pulled out his civilian clothes – Fred Perry tennis shirt, Fila red, white and blue tracksuit top, Lois jeans and Adidas gazelles – and put them on.

"Dex, 'ow do I look?"

"Like, you're off down Upton."

"Old Bill 'aven't worked out yet we ain't going to the matches in Dr Martens and Union Jack T-shirts. Can't wait to get down the chicken run. Once I get out of this shit'ole, gonna get as fucked up as possible and then get balls deep in me missus. Tomorrah gonna 'ave a puff and catch up wiv the droogs. Good job I've got a copy on pirate VHS, since the dick'ead director banned 'is own film. I mean, who does that? So, 'is family 'ad a few deaf freats, but, like, whose doesn't? Wivout that film, we wouldn't 'ave Darf Vadah."

"Yeh, 'e played that manservant who's a propah lump – picks up Alex like 'e's a ragdoll, wearing 'em red Speedos aftah 'e got the shit beat out of 'im by Dim and Georgie cos they 'ave turned their lives backwards and joined the pigs."

"*A Clockwork Orange* 'as taught me a lot, life-changing, like. I became a different person for the betta aftah watching it. Dexy, gonna leave you wiv me stash," said Nic as he took a carrier bag out from under his bed. Rummaging in it, he pulled out two packets of Regal cigarettes, Texan bars, packets of cola Spangles and two copies of *Penthouse*.

"Look me up when you get out. Gonna miss me, cell droog."

"Latah, mate," said Dexy with a genuine smile on his face.

Nic walked to the front office for processing before a screw unlocked the main door. It was a bright, cold, perfect day in April, and Nic's watch had just struck 1pm. Lighting a cigarette and puffing contentedly, Nic looked up at the azure sky.

Mat started his car outside the family home – 35 Colvestone Crescent – as he left to pick Debbie up in Homerton.

"I don't see why I have to come," said Lisa. "I don't want to sit in the car with that fat cow for an hour. You know I hate her."

"Debs isn't fat. She's just a biggah build than you."

"You fancy her, do you?"

"Leave it out, Lisa. Debs is me bruvah's bird. What the fuck is wrong wiv ya? 'Ave we really gotta go frough this again?"

"You always stick up for her, Mat. Just saying."

"Lisa, for fuck's sake, Debbie is like a little sistah to me. That's it. Now, I'm warning you, darling, you'd betta be'ave yourself today."

Lisa petulantly stared ahead of her. She was wearing a coral mini dress and gold Roger Vivier stilettos. She looked like she was on her way to Tramp nightclub, and not to pick up her boyfriend's brother from borstal.

"For once it's not 'bout you. Me bruv just dun a stretch. Nan is at the pub sorting out the party, and the twins are on a bit of business, so be nice that 'e sees some familiar faces when we pick 'im up. Nic will wanna let 'is 'air down. 'E's been locked up for momfs. You can do this for me, can't ya? If you gave Debbie a chance, you'd see she's all right and you could be mates."

Mat and Nic had tried to get the girls to like each other, but from the moment they met, it was handbags at dawn. Debbie had gone into meeting Lisa openly, but Lisa hadn't. At their first meeting, Lisa had met Debbie by looking her up and down with disdain. Debbie saw red, and the pair had to be separated physically before a slagging match became a full-on cat fight.

"You're wrong. We'll never be friends. She's got no class. Have you seen the clothes she wears? She thinks she's sophisticated, which is pathetic."

"This isn't up for debate. You'll at least pretend to enjoy yourself. Am I getting frough to you, cos I'm gonna be seriously fucked off if I'm not."

"Oh yes," said Lisa. "I can't wait for your Nan's buffet. I bet she's doing sausage on sticks and pasties. I mean, why couldn't you book somewhere like Daphne's in Chelsea?"

"'Cos Nic will want to be in the Crown wiv 'is family and mates 'round him. No way will 'e want to traipse up West to some posh restaurant. Like I said, it's not 'bout you, darling; it's 'bout Nic."

"Just please don't tell me there'll be a sign outside the pub saying 'WELCOME HOME, NIC'. Talking of which, have you seen a place up West you're going to buy? I see us living there."

Mat was going to hand over the deeds to the family home to Nic and then get a place up West. He'd, in bed after a marathon fuckfest, divulged this to Lisa, pillow talk that he could've shot himself for letting the grabbing harpy know. Mat had seen a place he liked in Mayfair. What Lisa didn't know was that he had no intention for her to move in with him. She was a selfish narcissistic bitch who did his head in. Whenever he had the urge to split up with her, she had this way of finding her way back in – always with her knickers down. Once he was in her and she was clamping down hard on his dick, he forgot about everything else. Her vagina was a wonderland that no man wanted to come back from. It gave real meaning to '*abandon all hope, all ye who enter here*'. The tension between Mat and Lisa was on a short fuse when they picked Debbie up from Oriel Road.

"Debs, 'ow you doing, darling," said Mat as Debbie opened the door wearing a peach jumpsuit, cleavage spilling out with abundance and reeking of Charlie perfume.

"I'm so excited. I can't believe Nic's finally coming out. It seems like 'e's been away forevah."

"Yeh, Nic's dun 'is time good and propah."

"I didn't sleep a wink last night, I was so excited. Been planning me outfit for weeks."

"Did you get it from Geekay Styles?" asked Lisa.

"No, it's from Chelsea Girl."

"Chelsea Girl. That's for kids. I shop at the boutiques on King's Road and Kensington High Street. I have a lovely pair of Halston culottes that would suit you. Shame you couldn't get one of your legs in them."

Face agog, Debbie rummaged in her handbag, took out her lipstick and reapplied another layer of mango frost. Mat drove off, but not before giving Lisa a you'd-better-behave-yourself look, which she reacted to by defiantly glaring at him, flicking her hair and then looking straight ahead. Lisa stood by her convictions. The girl was *déclassé*. Who on earth wore Charlie? She wrinkled her nose up in disgust, reached in her Bebe bag and brought out a bottle of Opium, which she made a big deal of squirting liberally. Now practically dying of perfume fumes, the rest of the drive, thankfully, was in silence.

Debbie was determined that Lisa wouldn't spoil today for her. She'd waited so long to be with her man. They were the real deal, and they could now spend every minute together to catch up and be a proper couple like they were before. Nic could spoil her, take her up West and stay in a five-star hotel just like the ones Mat took Lisa to. Or even better, a romantic trip away to Paris, shopping on the Champs-Élysées and staying in the Le Meurice. She knew Lisa had been bending Mat's ear about taking her there. It would be such a result if Nic took her there first. The thought put a little smile on her face. She couldn't wait for Nic to make passionate love to her like he did before he went away. The thought made her blush. He'd been her first and only love.

Mat parked his car on Bedford Road just in time to see Nic strutting towards them dragging on a cigarette and flicking his hair out of his eye. Lisa shot Nic a half smile, satisfied she'd done her best at greeting him as he approached the door. Nic threw his cigarette on the floor and opened the back door straight into the cleavage of his lady, where he got nice and comfortable – Debbie enjoying the closeness of having Nic back.

"Who's missed me?"

"Good to 'ave you back, bruv. Got a real treat in store for ya. We're 'eading straight for the Crown."

"Fucking sweet, bruv."

"Got you a little 'omecoming present," said Mat as he turned around and handed him a Wade Smith bag.

"Nice one. Missed me clobbah inside." He opened the bag and pulled the blue and white box open. Inside were Adidas Forest Hill trainers.

"Fucking the business, these are," said Nic as he held up the contrasting yellow sole unit with its three gold stripes, the three-hole bottom footbed designed by NASA. "Can't wait to get 'em in me trainah rotation wiv me Trimm Trab, SL 72 and Samba."

"I got Sid to go to Livahpool to get 'em. They're shipping 'em ovah from Germany. There's only four 'undred pairs available ovah 'ere. Gonna be a good crowd in the pub. Told Tommy not to let any cunts in like Junkie Jimmie and 'is skag'ead mates."

"Good load of junkie scumbags. Toerags will pinch everyfink that's not nailed down. Is Gardnah, Pennant and Leach coming?"

"Yeh, I got a gavering of the football lads coming."

"Sounds fucking blinding."

"Right, let's get you back 'ome before Nan sends out a search party."

Mat put the car in gear and turned the radio on. Pink Floyd's 'Another Brick in the Wall' blasted out.

"Fucking love this tune. Screws used to let us watch *Top of the Pops* on Fursday. It was the 'ighlight of the week. Seen the video. The Floyd is obviously Iron supportahs. Seen 'em 'ammahs?"

"Don't fink that's why the walking 'ammahs are in the video."

"Course it is, bruv. What uvah reason would there be. The Floyd is just making an important point. Every cunt should support the 'Ammahs. Yeh, and 'em Legs & Co wurf watching it just for—" It was then that Nic, who had momentarily forgotten, remembered he wasn't, after many months in all-male company. "Yeh, they're, like, really good at, uh, expressing 'emselves to show the seriousness of the music."

Nic walked into his local to a raucous welcome. The Crown & Castle was packed to the brim, folk giving him slaps on the back and telling him how much he'd been missed. The Jam's 'Eton Rifles' blasted from the jukebox. Mat had bunged Tommy, the landlord, a wad for a free bar. Nan's buffet was a sight to see – sausage rolls, pasties and ham sandwiches aplenty. Hand in hand with her man, Debbie was on cloud nine. Her only worry was that Nic would kick off. If any guy so much as glanced at her, he got beyond jealous. He'd beaten up boys in the past. One had both his legs broken and was wheelchair-bound for months. The last thing she wanted was for Nic to go away again. Debbie looked at the lavish buffet that Nan had laid on.

"Nic, I fink that the way to a man's 'art is frough 'is stomach. Men like women who can cook, don't they?"

"Uh, you what, babe? I ain't finking of shagging Delia Smif. Not me type, and she's a canary supportah. 'Er 'air bovahs me. It's like she's put a bowl on 'er 'ead and cut 'round it."

"No, silly. Nan's been giving me cooking lessons. She said that me cottage pie was as good as 'ers."

"Yeh, princess. Can't wait for you to cook for me, do what you was put on the earf for, wait on me 'and and foot. I love this pub. Me and Mat been coming 'ere wiv the old man since we was kids. 'E used to make us look at the display cabinet. The old man used to get really passionate and tell us all these stories 'bout the 'Oly Trinity – Moore 'Urst and Petahs. 'Ow Ted Fenton took 'em back into First Division."

The Crown & Castle had been a staple in Dalston since 1818, situated on Kingsland Road and Dalston Junction. The run-down Georgian exterior displayed a ceramic depiction of the eponymous crown and castle. It was a proper East End boozer, with a dartboard, fruit machine and snooker table. There was something very special there too, the glass cabinet dedicated to West Ham United. Inside was a football signed by the team of 1966 and a copy of the newspaper when on 30th July 1966, Moore's team defeated West Germany 4–2 in the World Cup. Tommy kept it under lock and key. Tommy Costello, the landlord, was a bald guy with a beer belly that looked like he had swallowed a beach ball. Rain or shine, he wore a sting vest. The display cabinet was always pristine, unlike the rest of the pub, which was all spit and sawdust. Nic could see his cousins had just walked in dressed in Lacoste tracksuits and Adidas Bermuda trainers.

"Darling, go see if Nan needs 'elp wiv the buffet. I need to go see the twins."

"Okay, babe. Don't take too long. Just getting used to 'aving you back."

Debbie sashayed off, but not before Nic gave her backside a squeeze. She was so getting it later. He could feel the beast stirring in his pants.

"Good to 'ave you back, cuz. Not been the same 'round 'ere wivout ya. Got an aftah-party planned for you latah back at ours. Make sure all your needs are taken care of."

"Right up for that, Flint. Didn't even bovah putting any kecks on. Gotta give the birds easy access. I'll be going out commando for the foreseeable future."

"We invited those sistahs you was giving a seeing to before you went away. That Nicola and Liz."

"Yeh," said Nic vacantly, having no idea what their names were but vaguely recalling they had decent racks. He really needed to figure out a way of getting rid of Debbie later. He really needed to let his hair down tonight and unemotionally fuck the living daylights out of as much random fanny as possible.

"A little present," said Sparky as he pressed a package into Nic's hand.

Taking the wrap to the bogs, Nic walked into the cubicle and locked the door. Opening it, he shook some of the white powder out then lined it up with his cigarette packet and snorted it off the cistern. Feeling like the king of the castle, Nic strutted back into the bar. Grabbing his girlfriend, he pulled her into the disabled toilet. Debbie was just breathlessly waiting for Nic to make passionate love to her. She'd fantasised about this for months, her bloke taking her sensually into his strong arms. Nic threw her unceremoniously up against the wall and roughly pulled her jumpsuit and knickers down and started thrusting his rock-hard cock up her. Debbie was panting in pleasure as Nic ripped off her bra. Debbie's boobs needed to be liberated – they'd been incarcerated for too long. He started to suck greedily on them, putting his all into getting as much of them as he could into his mouth. Debbie was gripping his firm bum as he thrust harder inside her, relishing every second. Her legs wrapped tightly behind him. Nic came and gave Debbie the orgasm of her life. Pushing her away, as he was done now and in a state of euphoria, pulling up his jeans, Nic strutted back into the bar. He had a party to get back to. Debbie was left with fanny batter and come dripping down her legs.

Nic walked straight into a welcome face.

"'Ow you doing, son? Sorry I couldn't get in to see you last week. Batty Betty 'ad a nasty fall in the market. I went 'round to see 'er wiv a marmalade cake. You know what she's like for gossiping. She was going on and on. I was there for 'ours. I told 'er I got to get back to watch *Quincy*. I nevah miss it now *Kojak* ain't on telly no more."

"Let's get you a drink, Nan."

"I'll 'ave an 'alf Guinness. Means so much to me 'aving you boys 'round me. You coming ovah Sunday? I'm doing roast beef wiv Yorkshire puds."

"Wouldn't miss is for the world, Nan."

"Lovely, son, and we can 'ave a game of 'Appy Families. You boys all loved playing that when you was nippahs. You liked 'Mastah Brisket the Butchah's Son' card."

"Yeh, Nan, sounds good. Can't wait for that," said Nic, thinking of nothing worse. Those cards were creepy as fuck, Master Brisket being the one they hated most and fought over who was going to destroy it. Sparky and Flint had, of course, done their best and set fire to many cards, but this didn't deter Nan. She seemed to have a never-ending collection. Nic took Nan's arm and walked over to the bar, where Debbie was now standing, her face still flush.

Lisa was beyond bored. She'd ordered a white wine spritzer and Tommy had given her a soda water and lime with a slice of lemon, smiling as he handed it to her as if she was going to be impressed. Then, just as Lisa thought things couldn't get any worse, she saw it: the cheese and pineapple hedgehog on the buffet table. It was mocking her. She sashayed over to Mat, who was chatting to Sid, who was playing on the fruit machine. Lisa stopped in her tracks and made eye contact with Mat and gestured for him to come over to her, chin stuck out, hands on hips, her cat eyes flashing with venom. Mat took his time finishing his conversation with Sid and strolled over to her.

"Mat, I can't stay here any longer. There's only so much Squeeze and The Jam that I can listen to."

Mat hissed in her ear, "Just smile, finish your fucking drink and pretend you're 'aving a good time before I lose me tempah."

"I can't, Mat. It's vile."

"Just drink it, Lisa, before I force it down your froat."

Lisa glared at Mat with pure defiance, smashing the glass down on the table and sending cigarette ash from the ashtrays everywhere.

"Right, darling, you're going 'ome," said Mat as he frogmarched her out of the pub, where he hailed her a taxi. The taxi driver pulled over and Mat grabbed open the door and pushed her inside. "You couldn't do this one fing for me, you selfish bitch." And with that he slammed the car door and walked back into the pub.

Lisa was left fuming in the back of the taxi. I mean, she had turned up. That should've been enough. But, oh no, Mat wanted so much more. How dare he treat her like this. And worse, that cow Debbie had clocked the whole thing. She'd seen the smug look on her face. She checked her diamond Graff watch. There was still plenty of time to go up West shopping. There was only one thing for it: putting a dent in Mat's credit card.

"Mickey," shouted Nic to the heavily tattooed man in a pair of tartan trousers. "Need to speak wiv ya, mate."

"Debs, I need to 'ave a quick word wiv Mickey. Go get us a plate. Pile it up. Don't get me any of 'em devilled eggs. I 'ate 'em. But make sure you get me pork pies and lots of 'Ula 'Oops and Frazzles. Oh, yeh, and loads of pickled onions."

"Okay, babes," said Debbie as she planted a kiss onto his lips and walked over to Nan, who was replenishing the crisp bowls.

Rubbing his lips with the back of his hand as he noted his girlfriend had been more than liberal with the lipstick, he wandered over to Mickey.

"All right, Nic. Fanks for the invite. Been looking forward to it. Work 'as been mental. I 'aven't stopped. Been so busy, finking of getting anuvah tattooist in to work wiv me, the demand's so 'igh. Like, there's been a surge in locals wanting 'cut 'ere' tattoos across their necks and 'love and 'ate' across their knuckles. And that's just the birds. Still doing an insane numbah of Iron shields for the blokes."

"Yeh, well, it's 'bout that I wanna talk to you 'bout. See, when I was inside, I 'ad this blinding idea for a tattoo all the way down me left arm."

Mickey was the local tattoo artist and had already worked on Nic. He had a West Ham 1975 shield on his chest, Alex DeLarge on his back, bowler hat on head and dagger in hand, and the numbers '655321' inked at the back of his neck.

"What you got in mind?"

"I want a couple of large 'ammahs bashing down on a lion's 'ead wiv, like, loads of blood running down me arm from the lion's 'ead. Then at me wrist I'll 'ave West 'Am these colours don't run wiv the '64 Shield. It's like one of 'em contraception fings. Got the idea when I bashed the 'ead in of a Bushwackah wiv a snookah cue and this childhood memory I 'ave," said Nic, momentarily trailing off in recollection.

To this Mickey took a sip of his pint while downwardly diverting his eyes as Nic had some sort of flashback.

Snapping out of his childhood memory, Nic continued in his usual brash tone, "It's the contraceptive of taking the piss out of 'em down the Den. The blood from the Millwall wankahs running, but West 'Am, we don't run from nufink. Make sure the Lion's 'ead is propah smashed in, like. Totally cunted."

"I get you, mate. A sort of concept tattoo, you mean. You finking blackwork or colour?"

"Colour, mate."

"That can be done no trouble. I'm visualising it in me mind. You've got somefink really unique 'ere. When do you wanna come in?"

"I'll pop in Friday aftanoon. Now I'd betta get back to me missus, mate."

Nic made another trip to the toilets, where he hoovered up two humungous lines of coke. Nic headed back to the bar. Another pint was in order. This new drug Sparky and Flint had been talking about when he was inside was the business. Shame it wasn't more widely available and so expensive. But what the fuck, thought Nic, money was no object.

The homecoming party got more and more rowdy. By eleven Nic was up for moving onto the house party. He just needed to get rid of Debbie.

"Princess, party is finishing up and I fink I 'ave outdone meself. I'm propah knackahed, so I'm gonna pop you in a taxi 'ome. Nan can share wiv ya. Then I'm gonna go 'ome and 'ave a good bedways in me own bed. Been sleeping on a lumpy 'ard mattress for momfs."

Debbie was a bit miffed, as she thought she'd be invited back to Nic's to spend the night with him. But things had gone so well today. Apart from Nic and her making passionate love, the highlight had been when she saw Mat dragging Lisa out of the pub.

"Ah, okay, babes. I guess you must be tired. It's been a big day for ya. What 'bout tomorrah night? You said you're gonna take me up West to one of 'em posh restaurants. Where're we going?"

"It's, uh, like, a surprise, Debs. I'll bell ya tomorrah and let you know what time I'm gonna pick you up. I've squared it wiv Mat, and 'e's giving me 'is motah for the night. As soon as I've 'ad a good kip. You betta look out. Be giving me missus a propah seeing to. Rule out the next day cos you're not gonna be able to walk. And make sure you wear some of 'em knickahs I likes."

"What, G-stings, babe?"

"Yeh, lacy black ones so I can, like, rip 'em off wiv me teef. Like I used to rip out 'em Tampax fings when we was kids."

The truth was Nic had no idea where he was taking Debbie. It hadn't even crossed his mind. He'd have to chat to Mat to see where he was taking Lisa these days. But satisfied he'd been romantic as fuck today, laying on the charm thickly, Debbie was happy, and why wouldn't she be? Nic gave Debbie a lingering kiss on the lips and then watched her and Nan walk out of the Crown to get a taxi home. Now the fun would really start. Back at Sparky and Flint's on Richmond Road there was going to be all the birds, booze and drugs he could contend with. Nic's attention turned to the door as he heard it open and saw Junkie Jimmy walk in with his girlfriend.

"Get the fuck out of 'ere, you junkie shit cunts," said Nic as he hauled himself at Jimmy and grabbed hold of his emaciated body and threw him out the pub door onto the pavement then yanking Stacey by the arm and seeing her go the same way.

"Now I'm in a good mood cos I've come out of the clink today, but next time I see ya I may not be, and I may 'ave to 'urt ya. I mean really 'urt ya. So, if I was you, I'd keep the fuck out of me way." Nic gave Jimmy a hard kick to the side of his stomach, which violently winded him. As he turned to go back into the pub, he realised that he needed a slash. Nic unzipped his jeans, took out his cock and pissed all over them. He then zipped himself back up and walked into the pub. Jimmy and

Stacey had all but crawled back to Sandringham Road, Jimmy to see if he could cadge some gear off some of the other junkies who inhabited their hive of villainy. Stacey had been told, stinking of piss, to service as many punters as she could. Junk didn't pay for itself.

White-privileged Jimmy Darke hadn't had any chance in life. To say he was dragged up was an understatement. Living on the crime-ridden Holly Estate – famous for its mile-long snake blocks that stretched across Queensbridge Road – with his parents, he'd been a latchkey kid since he was seven, his parents preferring to fritter all their benefits away at the pub. Once they'd paid for their alcohol and cigarettes, there was little left to buy much more, so since he was a toddler, Jimmy had survived on cornflakes and cold tins of beans. If the cupboards were bare, Mr and Mrs Darke thought nothing of sending Jimmy out to pinch from the supermarket, this pitiful kid shoving tins and packets into the pockets of his ill-fitting school uniform, shop assistants eyeing him suspiciously, which was very off-putting when you were trying to nick stuff. He had no friends at school, and even the teachers found him repellent and steered clear of him. He was called scumbag so many times it became a self-fulfilling prophecy. At the age of nine, left at home to his own devices, Jimmy had started to smoke his father's dogends from the ashtray and glug the dregs from the bottom of his Tennents Super cans. By the age of ten he finally made a friend called Kenny. The kindred spirits had bonded while rummaging for fag buts in a rubbish bin. Kenny's dad was a pothead, and it wasn't long until the two boys were bunking off school to smoke weed. He soon progressed to glue sniffing then amphetamines before falling in love with the brown. From the age of fourteen he'd suffered with cystic acne. This had never cleared up, and the white angry pustules were now bubbling on top of his heavily pockmarked skin. Jimmy, socially mobile at the age of sixteen, had moved out of the family home into a squat in Sandringham Road, where he met his first girlfriend, Stacey Tubbs. Her habit had cost her her hair, and all she had now were tufts of black shoots sticking out of a scalp riddled by dermatitis.

HAPPY BIRTHDAY

"The wanderah returns. We got business to discuss," said Mat while lying back in his chair with his legs on the desk.

Nic had met Mat at the scrapyard dressed in an Ellesse tracksuit and Stan Smith Adidas trainers. He would've come in sooner to discuss what business ventures he was taking control of, but it was now five days after his eighteenth birthday. His hangover had been brutal. He'd told Debbie he just wanted a boys' night out, as Sparky and Flint had arranged something.

"Just a few pints and football talk, princess."

The reality was quite different. He, Mat and the twins had started to party hard at Briefs Wine Bar in the Elephant and Castle, owned by their criminal solicitor Michael Relton. A lot of Old Bill went there, but they were as crooked as the faces that frequented it. Then to Soho to the Plaything, one of his old man's strip clubs. The boys had walked in like royalty. The hostesses fawned over them. The night had been hedonistic carnage from start to finish. Nic had stayed up partying for three days straight – there seemed to be a conveyor belt of women. Debbie was livid when Nic finally decided to grace her with his presence. He told her he and the boys had had a few pints at the Crown then gone for an Indian on Balls Pond Road and he had the worst food poisoning ever.

"Been on the twins' khazi wiv the shits, Debs. Fought me arse'ole was gonna fall out. No idea why me and the lads dun it. Everyone knows Pakis are dirty cunts. Nevah wash their 'ands, even aftah they've 'ad a shit."

Debbie had eventually come around after Nic started talking about how he hoped he wouldn't get food poisoning when they went to Paris.

"Just getting psyched up to get stuck into the family business. Debbie's gonna 'ave to know I gotta put the business first. She's practically 'ad me chained to the bed like some sex slave since I come out. But one fing being inside taught me is you gotta make the most of everyfink, so I've just gone along wiv it. No idea why these feminists got a problem wiv it. Just enjoy it. Like, why do they 'ave to be moaning about being violenced?"

"Violated. No idea, bruv."

"Me 'ead's in the right space now. Gonna concentrate on the business. Everyfink else will take a second seat."

Psyched up he may be, but the vast Hunter enterprise was very much in Mat's control, and he had no intention of handing too much of it over. He was the boss. At the moment he wasn't sure Nic could handle too much responsibility.

"I'm gonna 'and ovah to you all the strip clubs – fink you'll do a sterling job running all of 'em. You'll put your stamp on 'em, and as you know, gonna sign the deeds of the 'ouse ovah to ya."

"What's this place you got up West? 'Round 'ere not good enouf for ya?"

"Just fancied a bit of a change. Fell in love wiv it. It's in Mayfair. The way the story goes is that it 'as a reputation for people dying there. I'm not supahstitious; that's just for weak-minded cunts. Nufink bad is gonna 'appen there. Come ovah and see it wiv me Fursday if you want. Got an engineer coming ovah. 'E's installing a security system for me."

"Yeh, will do, bruv. So, for startahs I'm 'aving the strip clubs."

"Yeh, that's right, the clubs. Like, you know, there's two in Soho and one down the Cross." The truth was Mat wanted to get shot of the strip clubs. They were too much hassle; the girls were high maintenance. Mat despised them. They were just fanny for hire, a way to make more money for him – nothing more, nothing less. His brother was a loose cannon. He needed to prove himself. Nic had been more or less AWOL for months, but Mat would give him the benefit of the doubt for now. He had ambitious plans, and nothing was going to stop him. Not even his brother.

"Sounds sweet," said Nic. The Plaything on Dean Street in Soho was one he wanted to concentrate on. It was already doing well, but he knew it could do better. First he intended to do a rebranding.

"Gonna get straight on it if I can get Debs off me back. She keeps banging on 'bout me taking 'er to Paris, sightseeing togevah. It's not me idea of an 'oliday. Mine is spending all day in bed shagging the life out of 'er. I told 'er she can see me Eifel Towah from as many angles as she likes. If she wants to take pictures, I won't be charging."

"Yeh, Lisa keeps banging on 'bout Paris. Maybe the girls can go togevah."

"Yeh, that's, like, really gonna 'appen. Nevah mind that. May not be able to leave the country if Old Bill 'ave their way, as I'll be banged up in the Scrubs. McDick keeps taking me in on fucked-up charges. Must 'ave slung me in at least ten times since I've been out. Like I 'ave to be up to some nastiness. I keep telling 'em, 'Wasn't me. I was wiv me missus.' Some rookie

PC arrested me uvah day. Must 'ave been his first. 'E couldn't remembah what to say, so aftah 'I'm arresting you on suspicion of witness intimidation'– no idea what 'e was on 'bout – 'e said I freatened to gut some bird like a pig from 'er fanny to 'er froat. I can't remembah, like, but if I did, was probably when I was off me 'ead. I take no responsibility for what I say when I'm off me cunt. But anyways, I filled 'im in. I arrested meself. Old Bill be arresting me next for being Jack the fucking Rippah."

"McDick dun the same to me when you was inside. Nufink 'e could pin on me; just trying to make a statement. Finks the old man was be'ind the pig murdah and robbery, but they can't prove nufink. Old Bill must 'ave more mugshots of us than Mum's got pictures."

"McDick betta watch out I don't find out where 'e lives and pay 'im a visit 'e won't forget."

"McDick's not worf the trouble, and we don't need any unnecessary aggro from Old Bill. The ones who're not bent are on some sort of crusade to prove 'ow straight they are. Nevah act rash. Revenge is a dish best served cold."

"Not got the foggiest what that means. Why would I be serving pigs grub in the first place. I wouldn't shit on a piece of bread and give it to 'em," said Nic with genuine confusion. "Anyways, Dexy's been in touch. Just got out. Gonna make 'im 'ead of security at the clubs. Short bastard, 'e is, but still a menace. Takes people by surprise, as 'e doesn't look like your usual lump. E'll be a propah asset to the firm. 'E's got charactah."

"Sounds like you got it all planned. I've got big plans for the firm. We gotta expand out into the West End. That's where the money is. Got me eye on a casino on 'Alf Moon Street. We're going up in the world. Talking of which, taking you to Saville Row to get you a suit made in 'Enry Poole at the weekend, but in the meantime, 'ere's a little somefink," said Mat as he handed Nic a Deakin & Francis giftbox.

Nic popped the box open. Inside was a pair of platinum and diamond cufflinks in the shape of the letter 'N'. "Fucking sweet," said Nic, flicking his hair out of his eye.

"Gotta get you looking the part, like. I know you like all your sports makes, and we are 'Ammers frough and frough, but ICF time to distance yourself. We're not football 'ooligans. They 'aven't figured out that they're violent but get nufink out of it. It was a bit of a larf back in the day, but time to grow up now and leave that all be'ind you. We can use some of the lads as lumps for security, but they got to 'ave the smarts as well. We don't need liabilities, the ones who 'ave IQs ranging from fick as pig shit to certified brain dead. As you know, Pennant 'as got a four-year stretch in the Scrubs, and for what? 'E got nufink out of it. The only firm you're loyal too is our family."

"Yeh," said Nic uncommittedly, admiring his cufflinks but thinking just when did Mat start telling him what to do or how to dress. Just last week he had done a mega shop in Stuarts. Since he had come out, he'd noticed Mat no longer dressed in the clothes he used to favour, like Sergio Tacchini and Diadora. Now it was made-to-measure suits and John Lobb shoes. He was meeting Pennant and Leach for a pint that evening at the Britannia in Stratford. Only last weekend he'd had the new West Ham shield tattooed on his right bicep.

"That's not all," said Mat as he got up and walked out of the room. Moments later he returned with two Romanian Rottweiler puppies in his arms. "Gotta bit of extra protection for us. What you gonna call 'em?"

"Coopah and 'Enry," said Nic, completely enamoured with the dogs.

Nic scooped the puppies into his arms. "Gonna get 'em studded collars wiv their names on. You're gonna be propah rip-your-froat-out boys, ain't ya?"

"We're gonna rule Lundun, and drugs are the way forward. Bollocks to real criminals only rob banks or 'old up trains. What's the point of risking your life to rob somefink when you can make far more and not evah 'ave to touch the product. Pavement artists gonna be a fing of the past. It's getting too 'airy. The old man 'ad a good fing going wiv 'is connection in Afghanistan wiv the 'ash and brown. Gonna speak to 'is contact, Sherzia. See if we can up the game."

Den and his brothers had the foresight to not believe that narcotics were never to be touched either personally or professionally like the majority of their contemporaries.

"Sounds like a plan," said Nic indifferently while petting the puppies, wondering what was wrong with the set-up their old man had left them. Why mess with a winning formula? But seeing as he and Mat would be equally leading the Hunter syndicate forward in a far more enthusiastic tone, he said, "It's just come to me the new name for the Playfing. Gonna call it the Love 'Ole. Yeh, you're right. We're going places."

"The only place we're going is to 'ell, and that's if we're lucky, Nic, and get an 'aircut, will ya."

"What you on 'bout. It's me luscious glory. Nineteen eighty gonna be a top year for us. Tenf of May embedded in me brain, when we stuffed Arsenal. Undahdogs, were we fuck. The roar of the crowd firteen minutes in. Brooking flicked that 'eadah past Jennings. The goal set in fucking stone. Goonahs can't fucking touch us. No cunt can touch us."

WELCOME TO THE PLEASURE DOME

"I'm impressed," said Mat genuinely, who'd had reservations as to what Nic would do with the club after telling him of his rebranding name. Mat had thought it was some sort of ironic joke, but after subsequent conversations with Nic, he realised it wasn't.

"I'm 'appy, and it's turning over serious cuttah. Good job that corrupt cunt DCS Moody 'as gone down for a long stretch, as there's no way 'e was getting any dough. Bent coppahs do what we say, not the uvah way 'round. Dirty squad, leave it out. Fucking joke."

"Yeh, got 'imself a twelve-stretch. I bet 'e 'ad a warm welcome inside."

"I put me 'art and soul into this. It sets us apart from the uvah clubs, so the puntahs know they've come to an 'igh-class knocking shop wiv top-class gash. Raymond finks Revuebar is the only gaff in Lundun where 'e can show full frontal muff. Well, girls 'ere got theirs out large. In fact, I'm finking 'bout 'anding out fines if their snatch ain't out in full view. Raymond you should see the fucking state of 'im. Seen 'im coming out of the White 'Orse uvah day. It was, like, seventy degrees and 'e 'ad a long fur coat on. Fucking tragic."

"The girls be'aving?" asked Mat, smirking.

"I'm running the club wiv a zero-tolerance policy. Piss me off and you're 'aving a slap. I just tell 'em to see me as a werewolf in wolf's cloving. Nevah mind the brasses; I 'ad some cunts come in 'ere trying to sell gear the uvah night. They won't do that again. Dexy 'andled that. Only stuff being sold in 'ere is what I'm pushing."

"Yeh, seen 'im earlier on the door. Some bloke giving 'im agg and 'e ironed it out."

Mat took another look around the club. Pictures of the performers lined the walls pouting in cheesecake poses. Dispersed between them were Cornelis Makkink paintings. Exuberantly priced drinks were the name of the game. Buying a drink meant you paid for the girls' time, whether you were chatting at the bar or taken to one of the Love Hole's private rooms where prices for extras could be discussed in an opulent bedroom. The rooms played non-stop porn: *Behind the Green Door*, *Deep Throat* and *The Devil in Miss Jones*. The main room of the club was a sumptuous affair. Shows were performed on a stage in the middle of the club, the only prop a king-size bed draped in red satin sheets. The girls wriggled in blissful pleasure that was rehearsed and practised to perfection. The XXX-rated shows were taped on 8mm film and could be bought at an exorbitant price, but high from the alcohol and the heady atmosphere of sex, they sold like hotcakes. A DJ played in a booth on a Transcriptors Hydraulic Reference Turntable. There were alcoves furnished with red velvet sofas. Each had a glass table ready for the bucket to be filled with champagne. Red silk drapes with gold tassels hung over the gateways that could be pulled for privacy or left open for the more exhibitionistic personalities.

Nic had also added some flavour, courtesy of his favourite film. Allen Jones had made the furniture – triple-jointed female mannequins bent over in grotesque shapes to make tables and chairs. The pop-art figures adorned orange, purple and blue wigs. At both sides of the stage, mounted on large marble boxes, positioned on their knees, buttocks and breasts thrust out, were naked white mannequins wearing elaborate pink renaissance wigs. The only other colour on the sculptures were the silver chains tying their hands together behind their backs. Where Kubrick had failed, Nic hadn't taken no for an answer. This was in ode to the Korova Milk Bar. Quite incongruously on one wall was Alex DeLarge in giant poster-framed form with his double false-eyelashed eye following you around the room. He symbolised that everything was there for the taking, and Nic planned to take as much as he could from any mug who came in. If you wanted to party like Caligula, this was your Soho Shangri-La.

"You got the look right, Nic. Debauchery, decadence and degeneracy."

"Yeh, that's what I was going for, deb—uh, yeh, like, the three Ds, innit."

He had personally handpicked every performer, referring to himself as 'Fanny Finder General'. Every woman who worked there had to look like they had walked out of *Playboy*.

"What you 'aving to drink? I recommend a Milk Plus. It's one part Drambuie, one-part Souvern Comfort, then topped up wiv Tequila."

"Nah, you're all right. I'll just 'ave a pint."

"Suit yourself," said Nic, whistling like a dog for a scantily clad waitress to come over.

A waiflike woman with long auburn hair shimmied over to them with a plum lip-glossed smile.

"Darling, get us a pint of Carling and a Milk Plus." As the waitress went to walk off, Nic's head snapped around and said, "Make mine a pint."

"Been finking, once I got the clubs going, I could 'andle more businesses. I'm finking of doing a rebranding on Club

Vegas. Get the name right, and everyfink else falls into place."

"Concentrate on the clubs for now, then I'll start passing more your way, like. Your 'air's looking good."

"Yeh, 'ad a refink. I don't need the 'air wiv these looks," said Nic, sporting a short back and sides. Nic was now clothes shopping on South Molten and Bond Street. But at the football the terrace clobber came out.

ACT 2

THE UNFORGETTABLE FIRE

I assess the power of a will by how much resistance, pain, torture it endures and knows how to turn to its advantage.
– Friedrich Nietzsche

It is better for a man to have chosen evil than to have good imposed upon him.
– Anthony Burgess, *A Clockwork Orange*

Mat had decided to eliminate the enemy and anyone who went against his firm. They were small fry, no threat to them at all. But it was the liberty-taking in their manor that had really riled him up. A message had to be sent out loud and clear. Sid had seen them in the Railway Arms blatantly selling their narcotic wears – weed to be exact. They were brazen and made no attempt to hide what they were doing. They were the gypsies, and they were taking the piss, running riot through Dalston since they'd set up camp on Hackney Marshes. The bogtrotters showed no respect to land nor property, spraying IRA graffiti on any spare surface they could find. They didn't adhere to speed limits in their horses and traps. Nan had told Flint how upset Batty Betty had been. She'd been waiting for a Number 9 bus and there'd been a gang of traveller kids swearing and acting up, so she'd given them a ticking off. A teenager with an unruly mop of black hair had spat in her face and called her "a fecking gorger bitch".

Mat had no problem with the travellers' political affiliations, which were blatantly pro-Republican. In fact, the Hunters supplied weapons to the IRA. It was just business. They dealt directly with the chiefs; these nomads were shit feeders. Mat had been dealing with their IRA contact direct for the last few years; it had been a long-standing partnership for the firm. Len Hunter had been doing a stretch in Strangeways, where he'd formed a friendship with Donovan Sands, an IRA leader in for murder and possession of explosives. Len had confided in him that he had a Syrian source that could supply weapons in bulk to his 'noble' cause. Once back on the outside, Len had contacted Akbar Mustapha, who he'd become acquainted with some years earlier in the Ten Bells in Spitalfields. At a very handsome broker's fee, they became an intermediary between the Syrian paramilitary and the Provos. They supplied the IRA with handguns – Lugar P08s, Mauser C96s and Glock 17s, assault rifles AK-47 and machine guns FN MAG. They also supplied Semtex and top-quality black balaclavas. Mat continued with the lucrative arrangement, dealing with the top lads in Falls Park, Belfast. The Irish Republican Army was an organised criminal network with an ultimate agenda. Mat couldn't give a monkey's if Ireland was united or not; it was business. If the Ulster Volunteer Force asked him to supply weapons, as long as a deal could be struck, he would, although his old man had been gutted about Scott's on Mount Street – it was a favourite haunt of his in 1975.

"Love the fish pie there. Why the fuck did they 'ave to bomb it? I 'ad a reservation for me and the missus on Saturday. The selfish cunts. It's put me plans right fucking out, this 'as. Sid, get on the blowah. See if you can get a reservation at Il Portico."

"We will unite Mother Eyerland and free it from the tentacles of the British government's oppression." Callahan Tommy, Mat's contact, had told him.

"Yeh, mate. 'Ope you do unite and all that, like. So same shipment next momf, is it?"

The twins had been watching the gypsy camp nightly. There was a pattern they adhered to. As the women and youngsters went to bed around 11pm, the elders stayed up around the campfire, where they drank whisky and talked about the Cause. There were five of them in all – the decision makers. They only knew the name of the leader, Fergal Ryan, a burly man with a ruddy face. Sid had snuffled out that information for them while infiltrating the Railway Arms. Fergal had approached him and tried to sell him some puff at the urinal when he was taking a piss.

"A grand aul day to yous. Yous be looking for some weed, so you be? Tink I be the fella to help ya."

Sid had just stuck his dick back in his flannels and walked out. He had a person to see and a place to go. Namely, Mat Hunter at the scrapyard. Sid was the eyes and ears of the street and the bogs. As Sid walked out, Fergal muttered under his breath, "Fecking gorger eejit, scarlet for your mother for having ya."

The four men were parked behind the gypsy encampment in a Land Rover Defender. They proceeded to get out of the car. They pulled balaclavas down over their faces and gripped the Browning BSS shotguns, moving swiftly but having to dodge stinking piles of horse shit. The men were talking loudly around the campfire, which was larger than usual on account of one of the clan dying of emphysema, and in their tradition their belongings were incinerated. The non-elders, women and children were inside their caravans, which were now in darkness. The women folk needed a good night's rest, as they were usually up at 4am to start cleaning and cooking for their menfolk and sprogs – such was the idyllic traveller way of life. In return, their women got to wear, even in sub-freezing weather, fuck-me heels and cervix-flashing dresses. The men's voices boomed out, and yet they had little idea what they were talking about, their accents so thick. Only certain words were caught – 'Proddys', 'UVF' and 'Adams'.

The men had little time to react as they opened fire on them. Seriously maimed or dead, the men were slung on the bonfire, leaving trails of blood and viscera matter, strangely black in the moonless night. At least one was still alive, as they heard the excruciating screams emanating from the flames. This was coupled by the sound of horses stirring. In a flash a stallion bolted out of the darkness towards them. The rapid blowing of air came from his nostrils, making a loud bubbling sound. The horse stampeded towards them, his tail swishing in the eventide air. Nic blasted at the top of its head, which exploded, leaving just the horse's muzzle grotesquely hanging in the night shadows. The stallion stumbled around for seconds, almost trying to cheat death, then fell like a dead weight to the floor. As the carcass lay bloodied on the grass, a few horses gingerly came forward to examine their fallen equine. Mat gave them a signal and they moved back to the Land Rover, away from the funeral pyre. A young lad opened the door of one of the caravans. His head peered out of the door. He'd never seen the campfire that big. The flames, amber and gold, danced high as a kite. The smoky smell accentuated with another stench, that of burning meat – namely, very-well-done pikey. Tentatively peeking her head out of the door behind her son, a woman let out a blood-curdling scream.

LONDON CALLING

"You what! You bought Cyclops Wharf."

"Yeh, bruv. I'm finking of investing 'eavily in the redevelopment that's going on there. Fink you should too. I fink we're onto a winnah. You could make serious money. You need to start buying up land now so you can sell on to the LDDC."

"What's the LDDC?"

"It's the Lundun Docklands Development Corporation. You don't wanna miss out. It's gonna be one massive development. Lundun is gonna be the capital of Europe, the leading European state. I've got Caledonian and Globe Wharfs going frough, just waiting to exchange contracts. That MP Mellor the old man 'ad in 'is pocket, 'e gave me the tip-off. We're looking at 8 square miles of derelict land that can be regenerated into profitable progress."

"Yeh," said Nic half-heartedly, dunking his Banjo into his tea. "Fink I'm gonna leave that. The clubs, they're raking in serious cuttah, and to be 'onest, like, I can't imagine posh types spending money to live in the likes of the Isle of Dogs. I just don't fink it's a goah. And where's all the locals gonna live when they can't afford to buy 'ouses 'round 'ere when the yuppies move in?"

"I don't care where they live. Just 'ave a fink 'bout it. You could sell some of your assets to fund it. Sell a few of your clubs. You keep saying they're 'assle. Go and see our accountant, Steerpike. See what 'e can do for ya. 'E knows 'is stuff. The old man been using 'im for years. Not that I don't still check everyfink 'e gives back to me. I check everyfink 'im and any brief does for us. It's still Lundun, and the real estate can be prime, like. You need to see the biggah picture. The docks, yeh, was once the greatest in the world, but those times, they're ovah. Fatcher 'as no intention of evah making 'em a going concern again as an industry."

"Yeh, but Mat, that's me point; why would anyone want to? It's wasteland, like the scrubland we got next to us 'ere in the yard. Same principle, innit. No cunt would wanna live there."

"Nic, you're wrong. This will be the biggest social enterprise this century. It's gonna be one massive building site."

"No idea what this enterprise fing means."

"It means these areas will be exempt from property taxes. There'll be all sorts of incentives, like simple planning stuff and capital allowances. Believe me, the govahnment will buy up as much land as they can. It'll create a property boom. It's a once-in-a-lifetime investment. Up to you if you wanna come along wiv me into the big league."

"We're all part of this firm, Mat. Anyways, you're not really selling this to me."

"Nic, at least 'ave a fink 'bout it."

"More to the point, when you 'anding ovah to me more of what's mine? You know, like, this should be more of a fifty-fifty fing?"

Mat had tried to hold off on it, but Nic was asking incessantly now. "Gonna 'and ovah to you the nightclubs."

"Nice one. I got some rebranding to do, and I got the perfick names for 'em."

Mat didn't bother to ask what, as last month Nic had renamed Sapphires the Cock Socket.

PRINCE CHARMING

"I need your 'elp, Flint. I need you to get up the attic and bring down what's up there. Can't do it meself, wiv me arfritis. I need a good clear-out. They're begging for stuff down Oxfam. State of the economy. People 'round 'ere's 'urting, what wiv 'aving to pay 57p for a loaf of bread and 20p for a pint of milk. It was easier in the war."

"I got to go pick Sparky up, Nan. 'Is car's at the garage. But I'll pop 'round tomorrah and sort it out for ya. Don't worry 'bout the economy. Lisa will be 'eading up West, no doubt armed wiv Mat's cards, so she'll be kick-starting it for us."

"'Orrible mare, she is. I was at 'is place one morning last week. Mat was at work. Must 'ave been 'bout eleven. I 'ad the 'Oovah on. Next fing, lady muck comes out of the bedroom dressed in next to nufink and tells me to keep the noise down cos she's trying to sleep. Lazy article."

"I'll see you tomorrah, Nan."

"All right, son. Shove the radio on on your way out. It's Bruno Brookes. I nevah miss 'im."

Sticking Radio One on, Bruno announced it was 5th April 1982 and we were in an undeclared war with Argentina over their invasion of the Falklands. Then he seamlessly cranked up Blondie's 'Atomic'.

"I ain't investing in land in the Isle of Dogs. Fucking stupid idea. Mat's already got land down there the old man 'ad. I bet he can't even get a couple of quid for it, let alone buy up more. Mat's welcome to it. It's worth fuck all. The old man bought it cos 'e 'ad some MP ovah a barrel. 'Ad a picture of 'im wearing an Arsenal top. 'E should 'ave 'ad 'is brains blown out just for that, but 'e was, like, giving 'is mistress one doggy style wiv a dog's chain 'round 'er neck. Told 'im it would be worf money someday. What a load of bollocks. And this property portfolio 'e keeps banging on 'bout; Mat needs to be more concerned wiv 'anding ovah more assets to me, and not playing Monopoly. 'E'll be buying a fucking train station next. Like, yeh, I got the clubs, but 'e is sitting on so much more. I want a biggah cut of the deal 'e 'as wiv Sherzia for startahs. Winds me up a treat when 'e keeps saying ''is firm'. Not 'appy. We're all in this firm, and 'e's nufink wivout us."

"We told 'im too. We ain't interested. Mat is more than welcome to all the ball ache running fings. We're doing more than all right for ourselves. Gonna look at anuvah abattoir in Wapping," said Sparky. "Yeh, and we got somefink else in mind. Finking of branching out."

"What's that, Sparks?"

"Just anovah money-making venture. Can't let Maggie down, like, can we? Somefink we got that solicitor 'Ewitt looking at. It's just we may not be suitable people for this particular line of business."

"'Ewitt looks weird as fuck wiv all that stuff ovah 'is face. Fink it's something 'e's 'ad since 'e was a nippah. Some sort of skin condition. Anyways, like I was saying, Mat shouldn't be the only one running fings. I'm sure the old man would want it to be a bit more even. 'E needs to talk sense into 'im, but me Mum can't get 'im out of Charlie's Bar. 'Im and your old man been living in there."

"Can't believe they've been gone free years, but anyway, look what we found up Nan's attic," said Sparky, desperate to get his cousin to stop talking about Mat. It was always the same when they were growing up, fighting and bickering, but it didn't mean anything. Sparky reached behind his back and brought out a Flintlock Horse Pistol, the perfectly preserved weapon, complete with ornate sliver embellishment.

Nic reached out and took the pistol. "It's a fing of great beauty. This is a quality firearm. They knew 'ow to make 'em back then," said Nic. Weighing the gun in his hand, he pointed it at his cousin.

"I'd like to try it out wiv ammo. Gotta be decommissioned, but someone will 'ave some 'idden away somewhere."

"I can't exactly put an ad in the *Gazette*: '**NAFAN 'UNTER LOOKING FOR AMMO FOR HIS GUN**', can I? Couldn't see any up Nan's attic."

"Yeh, but some old codgah 'as got it up their attic. They keep everyfink. Like that bird downstairs from Mat. Probably can't get in 'er gaff, amount of stuff she's got in there. You know, that retard."

"You mean the recluse."

"Yeh, the old bird," said Nic, mesmerised by the pistol.

"Can see you as an 'ighwayman, Nic."

"Me too, living in 'em olden days wiv the Vikings as an outlaw. I reckon I'd like it."

"You gotta 'ave an 'ighwaysman's name. Somefink aufentic."

"It would be Big Nic. Nah, on seconds fought, who's that geezah on TV. That's it, Dick Turnip."

"Fink its Turpin."

"For fuck's sake, Nic Turpin then. I'd be a propah 'ighwayman too, not like that Adam Ant twat wiv chalk across his boat. What the fuck's that 'bout. I'd be on me 'orse riding 'ell for leavah escaping the 'angman's noose, not prancing 'bout in trousahs so tight e's given 'imself a wedgie. Stand and delivah your money or your life. Giz us your jewels, you saucy wenches, and while you're at it, get your kit off."

"Dick used to drink in the Nightingale on the Green down Wanstead. 'E met up wiv uvah 'ighwaymen there. They schemed togevah to rob rich people ovah in Epping Forest."

"What, that guy off the telly?"

"Nah, the real Dick. Some of these wenches you'd be robbing may be propah old boilahs."

"It goes wivout saying. 'Nuff said. I'd only tell the fit sorts to get their kits off. Any ugly bird, I'd be putting 'em straight and telling 'em to get their kit back on apart from their jewellery. I'll 'ave that."

"What 'appens if the fit ones say no?"

"That won't 'appen."

"'Ow come?"

"Caus they'll 'ave seen the size of me weapon."

"Fit ones take 'em a while to get all their stuff off. All 'em layahs of material, like, and bodkin fings they keep their tits wrapped up in. So you'll need an accomplice."

"Nah, I'd be working alone. I'm a greedy cunt, and all the fanny and cuttah it's for me. But I'd be one of 'em gentleman 'ighwayman. 'Elp 'em out wiv getting their kit off. That's where me lenf comes in 'andy – me cutlass."

"Look what else we found up the attic," said Sparky as he reached into his Fred Perry sports bag and pulled out two squashed teddy bears, the claret and blue football kits faded with time.

"Takes me back," said Nic with genuine nostalgia in his

eyes as he picked up Redknapp and Moore. "I can remembah Nan giving us these for Christmas. What 'bout Bickles and 'Urst?"

"Nah, we didn't find 'em. Fink they've gone. Just be careful 'aving a fag 'round 'em, cos who knows back in 'em days what kind of made-in-Taiwan, 'ighly inflammable shit they got stuffed wiv."

VIEW TO A KILL

"Let's 'ave anuvah game of Subbuteo, Mat," said Nic, dangling his legs off his bed.

"Nah, you keep cheating, bruv. Let's light 'em fags you pinched from the old man."

Passing his brother the loot, they both lit up, adopting the smoking stance of their father, cigarettes pressed between their thumb and index finger.

"Giz us a look at the dirty mag. Where'd you find it?"

"Dad 'id it on top of the bog."

"I wondah why Dad let us bunk off school today?" asked Nic.

"Dunno; don't care. 'Ate school; 'ate the teachahs. Don't see why we 'ave to go anyway; we're just gonna work for Dad when we're oldah. School can't teach us nufink."

"I don't fink Mum will let us leave school yet," said Nic, "cos we're only ten and eleven. We gotta read and write propah first and know 'ow to do our sums. She said knowing sums is very important in life."

"Yeh, I fink Mum is right, but I don't see why she can't teach us, like. She's dead clevah. She used to be an accountant."

"What's that, bruv?"

"It's making sure Old Bill don't get your dough."

"I don't want the pigs getting me dough. When I grow up, I wanna make loadsa money like Dad so I can 'ave a top car and season tickets to the 'Ammahs," said Nic.

"Yeh, me too, bruv, and a swimming pool and a bird that's as pretty as Mum or 'er," said Mat, pointing at the Penthouse Pet in the centrefold.

Putting out their cigarettes in an empty can of Tizer, Mat got out his football sticker book. "I just need Moore; I'll trade ya for Robson."

"I don't need 'im. Giz us Trev Brooking."

"Nah, it took me momfs to get that one."

Taking them out of their football talk, their dad barged through the door.

"Right, boys, we're going on a trip."

"Where we going? Is it on anuvah 'unting trip?" asked Mat.

"Just get your arses downstairs."

"We going to Lundun Fields. Shall we get our football?" asked Nic.

"Not today. We got work to do."

Not liking the sound of work, Nic asked, "Can we go to Wimpy first?"

"Nevah fucking mind Wimpey. I'll take ya there latah if you do good today. Now move your arses. Don't wanna 'ear any more backchat from ya."

The brothers followed Den downstairs and out the front door, jumping in the back of his Bentley S2 Continental. Den stepped on the accelerator and sped off, turning the radio on, which blasted out 'Smoke on the Water'.

"Dad, do we 'ave to listen to this purple fing, cos me and Nic don't like it. Can we 'ave some Beatles on?"

"Can't stand those four poufs. I'm bringing you up to be propah men, and this is propah music. You got a choice, eivah this or Sabbaff."

"We don't like 'em eivah."

"Shut your moufs. Like I told ya, I ain't 'aving me sons growing up as poufs."

"Is that like, Dad, when you tell us to chin someone first and not ask no questions."

"Yeh, that's what me old man taught me; it's dun me no 'arm."

"Is Grandad in 'eaven wiv Uncle Ray?"

"Uh, yeh, 'e's, like, in 'eaven. That's it. Somefink like that."

"Where we going, Dad?"

"Just shut it. You'll see soon enough. Don't make me 'ave to come back there and belt ya."

The rest of the journey the two boys whispered to each other, concocting all sorts of scenarios as to what was in store for them. Bringing the car to a halt, Den jumped out and opened the back door. Mat and Nic looked puzzled, arms folded and squinted eyes.

"Dad, why're we at the scrapyard?" asked Mat. "'Ave we gotta work 'ere, cos we're only kids."

"Yeh," injected Nic, "we should be in school. Mr Smif told me I was on me last chance. Said I was gonna be chucked out cos the caning weren't working."

"I told ya before. You take the beating like a man then tell the teacher to fuck off."

"We do that, but we just get anuvah caning. Our arses are propah stinging," said Mat.

"Just get out the car and follow me."

"Is Uncle Pat making Sparky and Flint work too? It's not fair if it's just us. Do we 'ave to sweep up or somefink?"

Den continued to walk on in silence. They wandered through the knacker's yard for automobiles, where laid the carcasses of crushed cars piled up like a metal fortress. Copper, lead or iron; there was money to be made in scrap metal. There were a couple of cranes standing immobile, the smell of rust heavy in the air. Den quickened his pace, and the boys followed him into a large warehouse that was stark, with little light, save one dim bulb dangling from the ceiling. They made shrugging motions to each other as they followed behind their father. As they walked in all wide-eyed, they were happy to see that Sparky and Flint were there. Before they had a chance to shout out to their cousins, they noticed something else. A gagged black man with dreadlocks was tied naked to a chair. There was blood pouring down his face and he was moaning incoherently behind the mouth restraint. A bloodied eyeball hung out of one of his sockets like a grotesque yo-yo.

"Winston, you're gonna tell us what we want to know; we can make this as painful as you want," said Len as he brought a baseball bat down on the captive's head, making a sickening cracking sound as blood erupted from the fresh wound. Den ripped the petrified man's gag off. The man coughed and spluttered blood as he tried to speak to no avail. Pat stood to the side of the man motionless, holding a Heckler and Koch HK36. The boys watched in morbid fascination.

"I'm a reasonable geezah. Enlightened, like. I don't mind you niggah spear-chuckah Sambos living 'round 'ere as long as you do what the govahnment brought you ovah to do. Jobs we don't want, like washing dishes and cleaning floors. But drugs, well, that's our business. We know you 'ave been dealing brown on our manor. We just wanna know where you're getting it from. Giz us the name, and we may be more lenient wiv ya. We may even let ya leave 'ere severely disabled, but you'll live. Who's your distributor?" asked Den as he smashed a claw hammer on the man's leg, breaking skin and leaving a bloody gash in his thigh. Winston winced in pain as blood gushed from his new wound.

Winston Brown had come to live in the UK from Trench Town, Kingston, Jamaica, in 1959, when the British government encouraged immigration to the country to fill existing job vacancies. Not that the Yardie had any intention of doing any legitimate work. In Jamaica he'd left a world of hurt filled with poverty, political corruption and crime. He'd lived on the infamous ghetto, Tulip Lane. Winston was a member of the Scare Dem Bad Gang. They abruptly disbanded one evening after the Jamaican Constabulary Force took out Desmond Noonan, another member of the gang – the only other member of the gang. Winston jumped at the chance of a brave new world and took the first boat he could with his wife, Latoria. The UK seemed to be a land of opportunity and benefits – namely, the Welfare State and NHS. They settled in Peckham, South London, on the notorious North Peckham Estate. They soon realised they'd come from one hell hole to another. But not to be deterred, Winston soon got to work doing the only thing he knew – crime.

"You see, we 'ave to make an example of any fuckah who finks they can deal 'round 'ere. Your kind don't seem to appreciate 'ow it works ovah 'ere."

"Merci, purlease, mon. Ise not di big mon. Ting is Ise don't know who di big mon is. Ise only met one time. He raghead," said Winston, with sanguine fluid and spit running down his chin.

"We need a fucking name!"

"Ise tell ya, Ise don't know di big mon's name."

"Does this jog your memory?" asked Den as he brought the claw-hammer down on the victim's arm, his humerus bone snapping out grotesquely from his skin, making Winston cry out in pain.

"It may bi Muhammad. He bi di big mon. Yeh dat's right. Muhammad. Ise remember now."

"That really narrows it down for us," said Len.

"On mi Neville and Nyoka's lives, mi children."

"You what? You probably got 'bout twelve half-caste bastards running 'round on your estate, and fuck knows 'ow many more in Jamaica, but well done remembahing two of 'em," said Den.

Mat and Nic momentarily took their eyes off the grisly scene and noticed that Sparky and Flint were eating orangeade Spangles and wondered if they were going to get any. Winston continued to babble incoherently.

"I vex man. I beg yuh lef mi. Mi should never lef di Yard."

"I can't listen to any more of this cunt's bollocks," said Den as he yanked his head up and roughly put the gag back on.

Pat turned swiftly and shot the captive at close range three times in the stomach. The wounds spewed blood, guts and intestines, splattering the floor and walls. Jerking manically as the consecutive shots struck him, his body jolted one last time as he accepted death and lay motionless. The boys noted that it was no different from when they shot an animal on their hunting weekends – even the metallic smell was the same.

"See, boys," said Len. "This is a weak piece of shit who needed to be put down. 'E 'ad the balls to start selling gear in our manor."

Den signalled the four boys forward nearer to the dead man. "This, lads, is what 'appens when you cross our family. No fuckah disrespects us. The 'Untahs are nevah the 'unted. Always the 'untahs. Undahstand?"

The four boys nodded their heads.

Den and Pat motioned for the boys to follow them out of the warehouse. The boys turned their heads back to get one last glimpse of the grisly scene.

"Dad, why did that geezah 'ave to be dun in? Why didn't you just beat 'im up bad like you did Mr Davis next door when 'e parked in your space?" asked Mat.

"'E was on the list, son."

"What list?"

"The kill list. Sometimes we need to do a cull. Nevah forget, only the strongest survive. There's this fing in life called natural selection. You're 'Untahs, an 'ighah species. Your loyalty is only to your family. You got each uvah's backs whatevah, then no one can touch ya."

"So, Dad, if they're on the list, they got to be dun in so we're not."

"That's right, son," said Den proudly.

Nic noticed Sparky and Flint were still sucking on their sweets.

"Giz us a Spangle," said Nic, holding his hand out.

"Can't, cuz. We've eaten 'em all."

"Ah, what! Dad, can we go to Wimpey?"

"Right, we'll do a pitstop at Wimpey then get you 'ome before your mum gets back from up West. She'll tie me up by me balls if she finds out you 'aven't been to school."

Den and his brothers had found out some days ago who the distributor was, and they now had the lucrative brown deal. They just needed to make an example of Winston, and this was something the boys needed to see. This was the first of many trips to the torture chamber at the scrapyard. From an early age the boys saw so much blood. They became anaesthetised to seeing such pain and human misery, and later inflicting it.

OUR HOUSE

The sun peeked through Debbie's venetian blinds, blazing into her hungover head like a pneumatic drill. Peeling her eyes open and seeing nothing but a blur, Debbie leant over to the other side of the bed, hoping that Nic was there, but all she found was cold unslept-in sheets. Her heart lurched. This was all too familiar now, but she never got used to the heart-wrenching feeling – it only got worse. The neglect stabbed her over and over again in the heart. Then in a flash her despair turned to anger. That no-good rat of a husband hadn't come home again now for the third night running, or was it the fourth. She couldn't remember, she was drinking so heavily. What had happened to the fairytale life she was supposed to have? How had it gone so wrong? At first it was fun. They partied all the time. Debbie loved to down vodka and wine and then mop it up with greasy food. Always statuesque, Debbie could take putting on a few pounds; it just added to her Jane Mansfield physique. It was non-stop debauchery, which had gone on for months, but they had each other, and even when hungover as hell they would just spend the next day in bed having heated sex. Then Nic started to go AWOL, not calling her and missing dates. Debbie hadn't been too worried at first, just a bit peeved. After being inside, he was just enjoying his freedom. So she brushed it to one side and put up with it.

After an argument with her mum, Debbie had moved into Nic's house. She was already spending a lot of time there, and after she made amends with her mum, she still continued to live there. Nic wasn't bothered. It was a big house, and it was *his* house; he could come and go as he pleased. Debbie was a good cook, so coming home to the likes of shepherd's pie was welcome. When he dropped his trousers, socks and kecks in a pile on the floor, Debbie dutifully picked them up and put them in the twin tub. It was like having a maid on hand, with extra benefits. After partying very heavily for a week, they'd woken up one morning and decided on the spur of the moment to get married. They were wed at Hackney Town Hall, with Dexy as their witness. Nic wore Emporio Armani Jeans, a Farah shirt and Adidas Munchen trainers, Debbie in a white ra-ra dress and Gina heels.

The strip clubs were a huge bone of contention for Debbie now that Nic elected to spend most of his time at them. When Nic graced her with his presence and Debbie was eager for him to make love to her, he would criticise her. "Debs, sort out your landing strip. It's getting well ovahgrown down there. You're letting yourself go. Like, I 'ad no idea where I was going. I fought I was battling me way frough commando-crawl-style in a forest in Nam. Get yourself down the fanny 'airdressah and get a skin'ead, cos I can't go frough that assault course again."

The only time she was guaranteed to see Nic was Sunday lunch at Nan's, which Nic insisted they do for her. She liked the fact that she knew he'd take her there, but it had now become a farce trying to act like everything was okay in front of that devious bitch Lisa.

Debbie was left alone to drown her sorrows and comfort-eat. One day she had no desire to drink; she felt nauseous just thinking about it and she was even off her food. This went on for days, the nausea so brutal she took to her bed. Knowing something was wrong, Debbie did a pregnancy test. Unfortunately, due to her erratic lifestyle, she often forgot to take the pill. She went to Medicare to get a test. Hurrying back to her house, Debbie peed on the plastic stick and saw the positive red lines. At first she was freaked out being pregnant at such a young age, but then she saw this as a way to keep Nic. When she told Nic, at first he'd been mad. "You're 'aving a giraffe. We don't wanna 'ave a crotch goblin at our age. I gotta concentrate on business at the moment."

Nic had eventually calmed down. He had money, and he'd always seen Debbie and him having kids in the future. She just needed to go to the gym and get her mouth wired up after the baby was born. Lisa was all into the new aerobics stuff. She'd turned up at the scrapyard in a gold leotard and silver leggings teamed with hot-pink legwarmers. The more he thought about it, the more he liked the idea. He'd be a great dad.

Nic shrugged, "Okay, babe. We're going to 'ave a nippah. But you're, like, the mum, so you gotta look aftah it. Giz us a boy who'll play for West 'Am."

"Ahh, babe," said Debbie, happy Nic had taken the news as well as she could've expected and trying to be playful, "what if 'e wants to play for the Lions?"

"Debs, we don't even joke 'bout fings like that in this 'ouse evah."

Nic started to spend more time at home and even bought a baby mobile that played 'I'm Forever Blowing Bubbles'. But the novelty soon wore off and Nic went back to his old ways. Debbie, alone, had to contend with the twenty-four-hour nausea, sometimes not getting out of bed for days on end unless she needed the toilet. Nic gave her words of encouragement, when she actually saw him. "You just gotta get on wiv it. It's not like you're the only one who feels sick when you're up the duff. Nan says eat gingahnut biscuits." Then he added as an afterthought, "Yeh, but not too many, like. You don't need to cane 'em or nufink."

When she reached her second trimester, the nausea stopped. It was then that she went back to drinking and eating with abundance. She didn't have to lie to Nic about the drinking, as he came home infrequently, and the weight gain everybody put down to her pregnancy. The messy state of the house was, however, a bone of contention. "You lazy bitch. You're pregnant, not ill. There's nufink stopping you from cleaning the 'ouse and putting the washing on. I'm the one who 'as to go out grafting every day."

"Work! You what! At your tart clubs. Do me a favour, will ya. They're sluts. Not like me. I 'ave dedicated me life to you. All I evah wanted was for us to settle down togevah and 'ave a family. I mean, what do you actually do at work?"

"I 'ave to manage 'em. It's 'ardah than you fink. Mat stitched me up when he 'anded 'em to me. If I could go back in time, I would 'ave fought more about taking 'em on." This wasn't 100% true. At eighteen Nic had lorded it up owning them. Nic's clubs made serious money, but he was also pissing it up against the wall with his hedonistic lifestyle. The strippers, at first. Nic wanted to fuck every one of them – and he did. Beautiful women with bodies to die for, but also damaged goods with a shed load of issues. It was all the back-to-back grief Mat hadn't told him about that riled him. It was just non-stop problems. The amount of girl fights he'd had to split up; they may look ultra-feminine, but he'd been almost impressed how viscous they were. It wasn't all pulling hair and scramming with their lethal nails. Some of them had very handy right hooks.

Debbie went into labour a month early. Her waters broke in Victoria Wine. She got a cab over to Homerton Hospital alone, unable to get hold of Nic. It was a difficult labour, but a baby boy was born, weighing just under 5 lb, with complications. After barely having a look at her son, he was whipped away into intensive care. The baby boy fought for his life, but as little as he was, he was a fighter.

At first Debbie had doted on Charlie, and Nic spent more time at home. But it wasn't long until Nic went back to his old ways and Debbie returned gung-ho to heavy drinking and started to neglect her son. Charlie was the apple of Nan's eye. To begin with Debbie had been glad of Nan's insistence on coming over to help out with Charlie. She took him out for walks in his pram – which Debbie seldom did unless it was to the off-licence to buy more booze – and cleaned the house, which was always a tip. Then Debbie, in her muddled, irrational state, became begrudged with Nan just turning up, as this ate into her drinking and eating time. The excuses came thick and fast as to why Nan couldn't visit, and in the end Nan gave up. At least they always came to hers for Sunday lunch, so she was guaranteed to see him. Rosie feared for her grandson. She'd seen bruises on his arms. Nan had tried to be diplomatic and asked Debbie about them.

"Charlie just fell ovah. 'E's clumsy. Just boys being boys."

Nan had given Debbie the benefit of the doubt. She'd never seen her lay a finger on the boy. Shouting yes, but never physical violence. But Nan couldn't help but think it looked like someone had grabbed Charlie's arms.

With everything she had to endure, she also had Batty Betty, a few doors down, constantly window-twitching, no doubt reporting her every move back to Nan, clocking how many Victoria Wine bags she was vacating a taxi with.

Debbie prized her head slowly off the sour, make-upstained pillow, surprised to hear voices downstairs. She tentatively got up her head pounding and her body shaking. It must be Nic. He'd finally come home, probably with Dexy. Grabbing a dressing gown, she crept barefoot and made her way to the landing to listen.

"Fing is, these brasses, they do me 'ead in. I don't need this shit. The problems I 'ave to deal wiv. The fanny earn good money. All they gotta do is stick their tits in some puntahs face. 'Ow 'ard can that be, right? So no more Mr Nice Guy. Gotta put me foot down wiv these slags. And then there's that bruvah of mine. Dun me up like a kippah. I want me lot, not dribs and drabs. Who the fuck does 'e fink 'e is?"

Charlie just gurgled back, "Daddy, Daddy", as Nic ranted and fed him Ricicles.

"You undahstand me, son."

Debbie crept into the kitchen, eager to see Nic spending time with Charlie. Forgetting her raging headache for a minute but unsteady on her feet and not seeing Charlie's Matchbox toy on the floor, she tripped and landed on the tiles.

"Well, look who it is. Muvah of the year," spat Nic.

Slightly disorientated, having smacked herself quite hard, Debbie, through pure willpower, composed herself and stood up unsteadily.

"So, you've finally come 'ome, you bastard. You're the devil, Nic. I 'ate you. You fink more of those 'orrible dogs than you do of us."

"You what, Debs? Why the fuck would I wanna come 'ome to a nagging fat bitch. Seen the state of ya. You've grown dreadlocks. When was the last time you took a showah. You make me stay away; that's why I don't come 'ome and miss out on seeing Charlie. I got enough 'assles at work. I don't need to come 'ome to earache from you. Your job is to look aftah our boy and the 'ouse and make sure me tea's on the table."

"I stopped bovering, seeing as you 'ardly evah come 'ome. Do you know the amount of times I frew your tea in the bin."

"Don't believe ya, Debs. No way you dumped it in the bin. You ate it, you greedy cow."

Heaving with anger, Debbie picked up the Breville sandwich toaster and threw it at Nic, missing him but making a dent in the kitchen wall. Jumping up, Nic grabbed hold of Debbie and pushed her forcefully against the wall. Shoving his hands aggressively in her face, he said, "You psycho bitch. You could 'ave killed Charlie. You're an unfit muvah and a lush. I'll nevah forgive ya if Charlie grows up an alkie 'cos you was feeding 'im 100 proof tit milk." Looking with rancour into her eyes, for seconds that felt like hours of anguish for Debbie, he watched her drop to the floor, whereupon she started to cry unstoppable tears. Charlie didn't understand all the shouting. Was it his fault that his mummy and daddy didn't get along? He began to sob, his little face pink, his hands clenched.

"Charlie, your muvah will get up when she needs to stuff 'er face. Now shut up. Stop crying, son. I can't deal wiv this. What's on telly," said Nic as he grabbed the remote. "Look, it's *Pipkins*. You like that 'Artley 'Are, don't ya?"

Nic headed for the front door, leaving a parting shot for his wife. "You make sure you sort yourself out Sunday. Don't you dare show me up 'round Nan's."

FOR WHOM THE BOW BELLS TOLL

"Ahh, Victor, so nice ya could come 'round. Couldn't believe it when I saw ya outside Mecca Bingo," said Nan affectionately as she opened her front door.

"Been looking forward to it, Rosie. Your lettahs, I always loved to get 'em. It made me feel I was still part of the community," said Victor, handing her a bunch of chrysanthemums.

"Me favourite. 'Ow did ya remembah?"

"Saw your Eddie enough times ducking into the Crown for a pint before he went 'ome to give you a bunch."

"Ahh, Eddie. Can't believe 'e's been gone all these years. And Raymond. It was one fing losing me 'usband, but me boy too. Not a day goes by when I don't fink of 'em. Now come on frough. We'll 'ave a nice cup of tea and a catch-up."

Victor took a seat at the kitchen table and Nan started to make the tea. She was pulling out all the stops. She had her best china set she'd taken down from her backless Welsh dresser. She'd made an effort with her appearance too. Always a fine-looking woman, she had put some pink lippy on and a touch of rouge on her cheeks. Her hair was in a messy bun. She pulled out a vase from the kitchen cupboard to put the flowers in and padded over to the sink to fill the vase, plonked the flowers in and took them to the dresser, where she gave them pride of place.

"I remembah that dressah. Maureen always wanted one. Makes me feel like times 'aven't changed. You used to put your shopping list on the 'ooks."

"Now, Victor, I got to put all me remindahs on there, like to return books to the library. Me memory is a bit up the spout these days. I just read one called *The Miracle of the Snowflake.* It's by Caferine Cookson. I read all 'er stuff. They're the kind of books your Maureen would 'ave liked. Remembah when I used to read to 'er when she wasn't long for this world. She used to love Charlotte Brontë. This one is set back in 'em Victorian times. A woman called Tilly Trottah finks she's been born special, and she's entitled to marry this local farmah cos 'e's got a bob or two. But 'e doesn't love 'er, so 'e marries someone else. This triggahs Tilly to 'ave a mental breakdown and ends up in the work'ouse where she dies of dipferia. And fings like remembah to take some cakes ovah to Batty Betty. She nevah was one for baking."

"Betty Short was always curtain-twitching to be up to much else. Age creeps up on us all. Talking of baking, what's that lovely smell?" asked Victor, sniffing the air.

"That's the Victoria sponge we're 'aving. It's been resting," said Nan as she poured boiling water from the kettle into the teapot and proceeded to take the sponges from the wired tray and place them on a plate. She then spooned on dollops of strawberry jam and whipped cream. "Betty's living on Colvestone Crescent, where Nic lives wiv 'is wife Debbie and me great-grandson Charlie. She's still wearing 'em awful 'ats."

"Looks 'andsome, Rosie. Missed stuff like this; fings I once took for granted. Maureen was a good cook, but Barbara, she could burn a sandwich, that one."

Rosie had been a friend of Victor's wife, Maureen. After Maureen had been diagnosed with breast cancer, Rosie had called around, bringing home-cooked food and dishing out her own brand of East End resolve. Rosie never failed to make Maureen giggle, even when she was weak as a kitten. She'd tell her raucous stories about what Eddie had been getting up to. Victor wouldn't forget her kindness. He knew Eddie and his brother Phil were on the take, but he spoke, as he found. Victor had been exempt from National Service during the war due to his heart problems and worked in the Clarnico confectionary factory. Eddie and Phil went underground when they received their conscriptions. The local bobbies just gave up on chasing them in the end. World War 2 was a time of rationing, so when Rosie turned up with butter and chocolate, it was much appreciated. Years later Victor moved to live in Bristol with his daughter Barbara. She was married to Colin, an optician, who had his own practice on Whiteladies Road. But he missed Dalston. It ran through his very core. The hustle and bustle of the Ridley Road Market, the vibrant Kingsland Road, where you could see many ethnicities going about their daily business. They didn't always get on, but it made for an interesting life. You could take the boy out of Dalston, but not Dalston out of the boy. Then a new practice opportunity had come up in Sydney for Colin. They'd begged Victor to move to Australia with them, but his heart wasn't in it, so he moved back to where his heart really belonged.

"Right, 'ere we go," said Nan, handing Victor a cup of tea and a helping of cake.

"Oh, that's magic, that is," said Victor taking a gulp of his tea.

Nan plonked herself down opposite Victor and took a bite of cake, cream oozing as she daintily wiped her mouth with a napkin.

"Fings 'ave changed 'round 'ere, but some fings 'ave stayed the same. Arfur's café is still there on Kingsland. Arfur, what an East End legend. Even frough the Blitz 'e didn't close 'is place down. Told Eddie if ya shut, your living is going. Arfur still does a lovely chipolata and chips. Course, 'round 'ere in the war we got it bad. Those Krauts wanted to bomb our docks, cut off our supply chains. Funny I remembah so much 'bout what 'appened back then but these days I'm forgetful wiv day-to-day fings."

"I remembah Arfur's. Sitting in there 'aving dinnah and 'earing the doodlebug, and everyone would duck undah the table, cos you nevah knew where it would drop. As soon as the noise stopped, you knew it was going to drop somewhere. When the all-clear went, it was all back to normal. We just carried on. Takes more than Mr 'Itler to keep us from our grub."

"We did just that; we got on wiv it. We got blasted out twice by two bombs. Do ya recall Victor, one in Nuttall Street? That was awful. Killed a lot of people. And anuvah that landed on the air raid sheltah at the Geffrye Museum. Arfur kept the café open all night so that everyone could 'ave a cup of tea. You would go down the sheltah and there was always different families, but we spoke to each uvah. In a funny way it seemed to bring people togevah."

"It did, Rosie, but there was a few bad apples. I nevah forget Sidney Nettle used to go to the sheltah in Rossendale Street. I remembah 'im getting caught red 'anded pinching a pack of Woodbine from some gal's 'andbag. 'E 'ad the nerve to say 'e'd dun nufink like it before; 'e didn't know what come ovah 'im. Shameless 'e was. Is 'e still knocking 'bout?"

"More's the pity, 'e is, Victor. Sid does some work for me grandsons. Some people, they're just born a bad lot, ain't they? But what do you expect? 'Is old gal was a dock-dolly."

"Rosie, in the war there was a camaraderie. It was such an awful time, but at the same time they was good times. I look back on 'em wiv fondness. Now it's all different. I don't recognise this world. It's all queer to me."

"You're right, Victor. We just got on wiv our lives as best we could. Saturday night down the Golden 'Art, Shoreditch, or The George, Whitechapel," reminisced Nan, touching her gold locket, something she did to feel closer to her late husband, a picture of him and her eldest son inside. "You could bet your last shilling someone would be singing 'Knees up Muvah Brown' in there. Then to The Windmill Featre, Soho. Everyfink seemed gay in many ways. Funny, I don't look back on the war as bad times eivah."

"I can recall your boys carrying their kids gas masks. They used to call 'em Mickey Mouse ones. You used to take 'em ovah to Befnal Green to that Repton Club to teach 'em boxing."

"I nevah could part wiv 'em. It didn't seem right evacuating 'em to some far-flung place like Norf Wales. I mean, they don't even speak the same language there as us, do they? I always fought me boys be betta off wiv their mum. When they got old enough, they used to make 'emselves useful too. Used to go up Kent to do a bit of poaching wiv their Dad. Became dab 'ands wiv a shotgun. Used to bring me back all sorts – rabbits and pheasants."

"Now it's all new 'ousing 'round 'ere gonna go up. Posh people from up West wanting to live 'ere. Calling it Docklands. Who would 'ave fought," said Victor, helping himself to another slice of sponge. "Cor blimey! People wanting to move to the likes of the Isle of Dogs wiv all their corrugated iron fences and waterlog problems."

"Mat me grandson is doing well out of that. 'E's been selling land to the corporation, that 'Eseltine set-up. 'E loves Maggie

Fatchah and us being part of that Europe fing that Edward 'Eaf made us join. Says it's good for smoovah import and export cos 'e's involved in all that. Not sure what exactly. It goes ovah me 'ead. I preferred it before. Don't like 'em continentals telling us what to do. I mean, this is Great Britain. I don't want foreigners in Strasbourg and Siberia poking their noses in. There was nufink wrong wiv the way we was before."

"You couldn't Adam and Eve it. I mean, us belonging to somefink the Krauts are part of. Most of 'em are still left-wing lunatic Nazis, ain't they. I mean, 'ow can we be sure they won't start up a Fourf Reich? What's your uvah grandsons up to, Rosie?"

"They're all doing well. Nic, Mat's bruvah, 'e owns these gentlemen clubs. I fink it's men talking politics ovah cigars and whisky. The twins, they've got a few successful businesses. One is a big abattoir ovah in Dagen'am. What they really want is to buy their own crematorium. Apparently, there's lots of money to be made in private cremations. Nevah fancied being cremated meself. I've got a plot next to Eddie and Raymond at St Mark's Church when me time comes. We've a lovely vicar. Favah Tobias from the diocese of Llandaff."

"It's because Maureen's buried there is one of the reasons I couldn't go to Australia. Going to the other side of the world made me fink I was deserting 'er."

"I've always kept an eye on 'er grave since you went away. Put out fresh flowahs and do any weeding."

"You're a good woman, Rosie. What 'bout your sons out in Spain?"

"I've been out to see 'em a few times for an 'oliday. They 'ave really settled ovah there. It's a different way of life. Nevah fought I would see a real palm tree. Wasn't sure at first 'bout going on one of 'em aeroplanes."

"That's the fing; Spain, it's not too far, but Australia, it's the uvah side of the world. 'Ow would I get to watch the Irons on the telly?"

"Look at this," said Nan as she took a picture down from the wall. "Linda took this picture. Must 'ave been Christmas '65 or '66. I'd given the boys teddies as presents and knitted 'em all footballs kits. They loved those teddies; took 'em everywhere wiv 'em and called 'em aftah their favourite playahs. One was called Moore, but I can't remembah the uvahs."

It was such a shame when the twins set fire to theirs, thought Nan.

"Where does time go, eh? In Bristol I loved watching the Irons play on *Grandstand*, and they're doing good back in Division One, but when they play at Upton, I felt so 'omesick."

"You're back now, where you belong. You'll come for Sunday lunch?"

"Don't put yourself out. I've become a dab 'and at making beans on toast."

"Don't be daft; it's no trouble."

"Why don't I take you out one evening to one of the old 'aunts for a few drinks?"

"That sounds lovely. Now 'ow 'bout a nice game of 'Appy Families?"

"Ahh, yes, that be nice," said Victor, having clear recollection of the creepy card game Rosie used to spend hours playing with Maureen.

NADSAT KICKS

"We're not, like, sure why we've been called up the school again," said Den as he turned to look at Linda who was sitting on the chair next to him wearing Emilio Pucci, her long blonde hair loose and her wrists laden with expensive bracelets.

"Mr Hunter, I'm sorry that this is such an inconvenience for you, but let me be clear as to why you have been called to the school yet again. On this occasion your sons were caught in the female changing rooms engaging in inappropriate behaviour with two girls."

Den just stared ahead before shrugging and saying, "That's just normal kids stuff, innit? We all dun it."

"I can tell you with great authority, I certainly did not. Mr Hunter, they are thirteen and fourteen years old and have no business in the girls' private spaces. These adolescent years are very difficult and challenging times. It is sacrosanct that girls and boys feel safe in changing areas and lavatories. Can you imagine a girl had walked in and taken a shower in a place where she should feel safe to do so without male, prying eyes. It is of the utmost importance that strict boundaries are drawn and kept in the name of decency."

"I'm confused now. So Mat and Nic was in the showah wiv these bir—girls," said Den beginning to smirk then dropping it to a faux-serious face after seeing the steely expression on the headmistress's face.

"No, Mr Hunter, they were not, but that's not the point. They shouldn't have been in there in the first place."

"So, like, did these bir—uh, girls make a complaint or somefink?"

"No, they didn't, Mr Hunter, and they have been reprimanded for encouraging this disgusting behaviour."

"I don't really undahstand the problem then."

"The problem is your sons are out of control. I was warned by your children's primary school that they were, well, let's just say rambunctious."

"No idea what that means."

"For want of a better word, they are spirited boys. But they cannot go through life thinking that laws do not apply to them."

"Why, you bringing Old Bill into this?"

"I mean, Mr Hunter, the laws of this school. The fighting, swearing and setting fire to things."

"Nah, that would be the twins."

"Excuse me, Mr Hunter?"

"The fire fing. That weren't me boys. That's their cuzins, Spark—Chad and Nafan."

Mrs Rutherford prided herself on her competence and efficiency, but even she was getting befuddled by the four boys and who was responsible for what. It was never-ending. The cane didn't work. They were constantly together like they were four brothers.

"That may as well be, but this is a very serious situation. My teachers have voiced concerns that so far the abuse had been verbal, but they are worried it could turn to physical violence. Both of your sons are big for their age and can come across as intimidating, and quite frankly their behaviour is quite unacceptable. The lack of

respect for their teachers, calling them by the unmentionable 'C' word."

"Not sure what you're on 'bout. The little cunts talk fine at 'ome. No idea why they're acting up at school."

"I have no choice than to suspend them yet again."

"We can't 'ave 'em."

"I beg your pardon, Mr Hunter."

"We're off to Spain on 'olday tomorrah," said Den, who'd booked himself and Linda into the Marbella Club Hotel while they were villa-hunting. There was no way they wanted the boys under their feet. They'd been perfectly fine when they had left them before.

"Are you contemplating leaving the boys on their own in the house to fend for themselves?"

"Uh, no," said Den, backtracking, as the last thing he needed was Social Services sniffing around. "Me Mum, yeh, she's moving in when we're away, to look aftah 'em."

Mrs Rutherford noted that the wife, as per usual, said nothing and looked straight ahead, occasionally looking at her Chopard watch as if it was such a tiresome inconvenience for her.

"We'll 'ave a word wiv em aftah school. Tell 'em that they need to, like, respect the girls' bogs and all that."

"Mr Hunter, there's no after school. They are suspended with immediate effect."

"How long we gotta 'ave 'em for?"

"The suspension will be for two weeks. Hopefully, for all our sakes, we can start afresh when they return," said Mrs Rutherford as she took her glasses off and let them hang around the chain they were on. "The general consensus is that Mathew is very bright. If he works at it, he could go to university. He just needs to apply himself. He's especially gifted at mathematics."

"Mat's coming to work for me. I'm dead against 'em universities. Kids go in normal and come out messed up in the 'ead,

like brainwashed. Can't fink for 'emsleves. I ain't brought me kids up to be weak-minded. Got no jobs but go and join picket lines for 'em that does. Come out fickah than they went in. No way that's 'appening. What 'bout me youngest?"

"Let's just say, Mr Hunter, with Nicholas there is room for improvement in all areas. Now can you take your children home. I have seen enough of their recalcitrance to last a lifetime. Never in all my years of teaching have I seen anything like this total and unashamed disregard for authority."

Den and Linda walked out of Mrs Rutherford's office to where Mat and Nic were slumped on plastic chairs, ties loosened and shirts hanging out.

"Right, you little fuckahs, get in the car before I belt ya. What's the first rule I taught ya? Don't get caught. Me and your Mum ain't got time for this."

The boys followed behind, smirking. As if experiencing some sort of telepathy, they were both thinking how good it would be if the twins were suspended too. Home alone, they could do whatever they wanted. As for the girls they had been fingering in the girls' changing rooms, they'd made plans to meet them outside the Rio later. Then hopefully they'd take them over to Hackney Marshes and get their legs over. The pair of them were right goers and had very much grown out of trainer bras.

DANGER ZONE

"Be a lovey, will ya, Nic? Take the plate of chicken out to the table and start to dish up. Twins got me a lovely bird. Cooked beautifully, it 'as. The skin's golden brown. Cooked in the oven, not like these days. I mean, putting a bird in one of 'em microwaves and browning it up wiv Marmite. 'Ave you evah 'eard of such a fing? I won't 'ave one of 'em fings in me kitchen."

"Nan, looks 'andsome. I 'ad the shits last night. 'Ad a Kebab from one of 'em Turkish places on Arcola Street. You buy one and you get a side of the shits for free. If I was sobah, I wouldn't touch it, but I was off me nut."

"You wouldn't catch me eating that foreign muck. Probably 'orse meat you got. Any'ow, that's what I'm talking 'bout. Victor is 'ere. Don't use that kind of language. 'E will fink 'e 'as come to lunch at the zoo."

"Victor seems like a nice bloke. Looks a bit like a garden gnome."

"Victor's 'air and beard went white ovahnight when 'is wife passed away. You go dish up. All the veg is on the table. I'm just bringing the gravy to the boil. Such a big bird, we'll 'ave chicken sandwiches for tea with mayonnaise. Propah British food; get your tummy sorted in no time," said Nan, spooning the stuffing onto the plate.

"Reckon I'll be right as dodgahs aftah this, Nan. So, what's Victor looking for 'ere? What's 'is angle?"

"Nufink, Nic. You can 'ave a friend that's of the opposite sex. It's called companionship. Victor's a gentleman. Won't let me put me 'and in me pocket, and 'e opens the door for me."

"Like me, Nan. I'm always opening the back door of me car for birds. I still don't get it. What's in it for 'im? Is 'e trying to get 'is leg ovah. Or as 'e 'ad 'is wicked way wiv ya?"

"No, 'e's not, and I'm warning you, Nicolas, on your best be'aviour today."

"Just a sec, Victor. Just got to put me teef in," said Nic in a high-affected voice.

"Not everyone 'as sex on their brains all the time."

"Neivah do I. I fink 'bout football too. Sometimes bouf at the same time. But it's like a primal instinct in blokes, innit. That and twatting a bloke in the face for no reason. It's in our 'ardwiring, unless you're one of 'em arse bandits, and even they got an angle."

"I leave all that bedroom business malarky to you youngstahs. Can't fink of anyfink worse wiv me arfritis. Seen too many dangly fings in me life."

"Nan, I don't need to know 'bout that. It's making me feel a bit uncomfortable, like."

"You know exactly what I mean. One 'usband, four sons, four grandsons and one great-grandson. It's enouf for any woman. Now take the meat in before it gets cold."

"Right," said Nic, walking into the front room talking in a high-affected voice. "What do you want, bruv, leg or breast?"

"I'll 'ave bouf."

"You greedy git. Ain't Lisa got enouf of that for ya?"

Lisa just glared at him. She didn't find Nic funny at all. She hated coming to Nan's for Sunday lunch, but Mat told her it was non-negotiable. And even worse was the ritual of all going to the pub after, looking united as a foursome.

"What 'bout you, Lisa?"

"Nothing for me. Meat is fattening. I know how to control my food intake, unlike some," said Lisa, shooting Debbie a glare which was met by a look of pure hatred.

"Not even a bit of stuffing, or is Mat giving ya that?"

"I don't want anything, Nic. I'm just having vegetables."

"Suit yourself. You one of 'em weird vegetation fings? What 'bout you, Debs?"

"Just breast for me, please."

"Ain't you got enough of that already?"

"Nic, stop talking in that silly voice and just put the meat on me plate. It's really annoying."

"Put me meat on your plate. Can't ya wait until we get 'ome? I'll come ovah there in a minute and wash your mouf out wiv Gumption. Stop showing me up in front of Victor. I'd 'ave given you a good seeing to before we left the 'ouse if I fought you was gonna do this. Nan, did you 'ear that? Debbie wants me to put me meat on 'er plate," said Nic as Nan walked through the door, gravy boat in hand. Victor had never felt so much relief when she took the plate off Nic. He'd been wondering what he should ask for.

"Victor, 'ere's a nice leg for you."

"Fanks, Rosie. This all looks very tasty."

"Want a fill-up, Victor?" asked Mat, holding up one of the bottles of Mateus Rosé he had brought, noting that he was draining his glass quicker than Debbie.

"I won't say no, son," said Victor, holding out his glass.

"Is there anything else to drink?" asked Lisa, staring at the offending plonk.

"No, Lisa, it's this or nufink," said Mat, moving to pour her a glass. Lisa smacked her palm down on top of the glass in defiance. It wasn't as if she'd get anything near to her standards at the Crown after this ordeal.

"Victor, you go to the matches now you're back 'ome?" asked Mat.

"I went down the Boleyn to see 'em play Birming'am City."

"Was a good result; five–nil to us," said Nic.

"It's an away game next. West Bromwich Albion. So I'll watch that on the box wiv Frank Bough. Then we got some big ones coming up. Arsenal, Livahpool and Man City."

"I fink we'll stuff 'em all," said Nic, noisily slurping up his gravy with a tablespoon.

"Nicholas, stop doing that. 'Ave some table mannahs, please," said Nan.

"Why, Nan? I does this every Sunday. It's not like I'm drinking out the gravy boat. I wasn't finking of doing that today."

"What 'bout Man United next momf?" asked Victor, spearing a carrot with his fork.

"Reckon we'll stuff 'em. Goddard's on fire. Lyall 'as got a good line-up. Bonds 'eading up the team. You can't go wrong. Give it a couple of years, be taking Charlie to the matches."

"You're not taking 'im into the chicken run. I won't 'ave it, Nic," said Debbie, pouring herself another glass of wine, who unlike Lisa was more than willing to get stuck into the cheap vino.

"Yes," piped in Lisa, "don't you think you should go and see to your child?"

"Charlie's fine. 'E's 'aving a nap upstairs."

"Anyone for a bit more meat, and there's a few roasties left in the pan," said Nan, hoping to divert the conversation away from Debbie and Lisa descending into a spat.

"I wouldn't say no," said Debbie, holding up her plate.

"I can't believe you want more after what you just put away," said Lisa. "Don't you think that's just greedy."

"Nic likes curvy girls. I can take full advantage of all the French cuisine when Nic takes me to Paris wiv all those lovely bistros. 'Ave you been to Paris, Lisa? Nic is booking that soon, ain't you, babe?"

"Uh, yeh," said Nic in a noncommittal tone.

"You've been going to Paris now for years, and it hasn't happened."

"I've 'ad a baby and Nic 'as been busy wiv work."

"Mat will be taking me to Paris, and when we go, I'll be buying clothes from all the designer boutiques. French women are chic and slim, so the clothes will be a perfect fit for me. I don't think La Samaritaine do overstuffed-sausage size. Did you get what you're wearing today from Geekay Styles?"

"I don't shop there, you cheeky cow," said Debbie.

"That's enouf. Cut it out," said Mat. "Nan 'as gone to a lot of effort to do us a nice Sunday dinnah and you're acting like kids."

To this Lisa studied her long, red fingernails. Debbie took a large gulp of her wine, wondering why once again Nic hadn't stepped in to defend her.

"You two grab a table, and me and Nic will get us drinks, and be'ave yourselves."

The girls walked in uneasy silence, all eyes in the pub on the Hunter women.

"Ad a good gawp, 'ave ya?" slurred Debbie to nobody in particular.

It was then that all hell broke loose. Debbie, wobbling in her stilettos, tripped, and in the process grabbed onto Lisa to steady herself.

"You bitch. You grabbed me," yelled Lisa as she reciprocated by pushing her roughly back.

"You stuck-up cow. Who the bleeding 'ell do you fink you are," screamed Debbie, who reached out and yanked at Lisa's hair, pulling out a bloody clump. Letting out a scream, Lisa retaliated by grabbing a bunch of Debbie's hair while spitting in her face.

"Debbie, you're a fat bitch who Nic can't stand the sight of."

"That's a lie," said Debbie as she punched Lisa full force in the stomach as Lisa's gob slid down her face.

Winded and gasping for air but not going down without a fight, Lisa retaliated with a right hook to Debbie's cheek. Wincing in pain and tasting blood in her mouth, Debbie went to punch Lisa back, but she swerved quickly, leaving Debbie stumbling to the ground. Debbie seized the opportunity to grab Lisa around the ankles, catching her unaware and tugging her to the floor. Debbie, propelled by momentum, jumped on top of Lisa, clawing at her hair as Lisa tried to defend herself, arms flinging around in a frenzy.

"You bitch," shrieked Debbie, pulling both of Lisa's arms down behind her and pinning her to the floor, returning the insult by spitting in her face. "You fink you're too good for 'round 'ere. Well, I got news for you. Everyone 'ates you." Her body pumping with adrenalin, Lisa pinned to the floor did the only thing she could and head-butted her assailant. Debbie released Lisa and cried in agony as her nose started to bleed heavily. Clutching her bloody face, Debbie felt strong arms lifting her into the air.

"What the fuck is going on?" yelled Nic as he manoeuvred his wife so she was standing up. At the same time Mat picked up a hysterical Lisa. She hadn't realised how much it hurt when you head-butted someone. Mat and Nic made it look so easy.

“It was her, Mat. That fat cow started it.”

“The bouf of you are a fucking disgrace, fighting like a couple of dock-dollies.”

Whereas the packed pub had been all eyes on the delicious spectacle, relishing in the Hunter women knocking seven shades of shit out of each other, once the brothers turned up, all eyes turned to their pints.

“Taking you ’ome, disgracing us like a pair of ’arpies,” said Nic as they manhandled their dishevelled other halves out of the Crown. As they left, the pub became animated again. They would be gossiping and dining out on this for the next six months. In the corner, bent over his pint and sucking on a roll-up, Hissing Sid had a sly smile on his weaselly face.

THE COMPANY OF WOLVES

McBride woke up with a start and felt a fart coming on, pushing it out. It was a hot smelly one. The trouble was he followed through with a thunderous spray-shit. Cursing himself, he ran to the bathroom, took off his soiled underpants, wiped the liquid shit with a crusty towel then threw it aside on the bathroom floor. This was an affliction he'd endured since moving to the Met and being introduced to the Hunter fiefdom. His bowels hadn't been the same since. Pulling a pair of skid-marked Y-fronts out of the overflowing laundry basket, he put them on. He pulled on a pair of dirty cords from the floor and grabbed a shirt with dark rings of sweat under the arms. McBride lived at 62 Brookhill Road in Woolwich. He'd made a conscious decision not to live in Dalston. The last thing he needed after a hard day's work was to bump into a Hunter at the local. Woolwich was a shithole, but it was Hunter-free. Not the most picturesque part of South East London, when he looked out the front window, he could see the Connaught Estate, complete with its phlegm-green paintwork. But he quite liked the area, having a pint down the Kings Arms, where he propped up the bar, or even on an occasion, he took himself to Flamingos nightclub to once again prop up the bar.

He made his way downstairs and walked into the unfitted kitchen with its orange lino flooring, the shade of orange invented in the 1970s. He made himself a breakfast of beans and eggs stuffed into a couple of doorsteps. He walked into the living room and sat on his battered sofa and stared at the walls. Taking a massive bite, the egg yolk, bursting, dripped down his beard. Munching away, he swallowed the food in large greedy gulps. McBride's walls were more his life's work. The Hunter family adorned the walls. Various mugshots of them and newspaper articles. Felt pen was scrawled next to the photos with insights he had on this pack of wolves.

He'd been so naive when he'd made his way from Cardiff Central to Paddington. The Met, the finest police force in the world, or so he thought. It had ended up being a viper's den of corruption. They seemed not to want to tackle the real evil. Never mind nicking people because they'd done a runner with a jerk-chicken butty from Johnson's Café. God forbid a black person was seen flying a kite in public, a despicable crime under the Met Police Act 1839, or worst still be caught gambling in a library, an abhorrent crime under the Library Offense Act 1898. Then there was the police's 'interpretation' of the SUS laws, which basically meant that they could stop and search anyone looking suspicious, which basically meant they could stop you if you were black. Even if you hadn't done anything incriminating, they still had powers to arrest you and charge you with a Kafkaesque crime. So-called confessions known as 'verbals' were fabricated to suspension-of-disbelief levels even Hans Christian Andersen would struggle to make up. But the Met saw this as progressive legislation. The Suspected Person Law was a stop-and-search law created in the 1824 Vagrancy Act, giving the police powers to arrest anyone they suspected of lurking with the intent to commit an arrestable offence. It was fact, was it not, that black people spent their lives lurking down dark lanes, shadowy alleyways and in broad daylight on the High Street. Not to mention Operation

Swamp, where Thatcher thought it was needed to reduce crime should we be swamped with people of other cultures committing felonies most heinous. Well, try looking at the Caucasian spiv entrepreneurs you've created, Prime Minister.

Dalston nick had its problems, but Stoke Newington station nearby had outdone itself. McBride had to hand it to their Chief Superintendent Roy Clark for his continual commitment to anarchy and his selfless contribution to the breakdown of law and order. It took the bloke an hour in the morning, when he got out of bed, to straighten himself out, he was that bent. The locals called it the Stokey Cokey as they joked unhumorously that some full-time drug dealers had part-time jobs as coppers there. A police station where bags of evidence, which always happened to be drugs, went missing at an alarming rate.

Many rotten officers fraternised with the very people they should've been putting behind bars. No more so than at Briefs Wine Bar. Pint in the right hand, and the left extended in a salute their four fingers separated. In league with the Knights of the White Camelia. All having their place and status in the pack, the Imperial Supreme Grand Wizard, Klaliff, Klokard, Kludd and Kligrapp. 1979 – the year Den Hunter and his brothers decided to up sticks to Spain, which just happened to be after a robbery and the murder of a policeman – stuck in his mind for another reason. A young teacher called Blair Peach from Hackney was smacked over the head while protesting against the National Front. The party didn't do as well as they had predicted in the general election. This was wildly thought of as pertaining to Thatcher's increasingly restrictive stance on immigration. People were also put off strangely by the overpopulous in the National Front's membership of skinheads and football hooligans. Peach was assaulted by an officer from the Special Patrol Group (SPG) and died from his injury. As part of the police investigation, they uncovered in a search of SPG lockers knives, crowbars, whips, a three-foot wooden stave and a lead-weighted cosh. These weapons were not deemed to be a police issue, but no one could accuse the SPG of not being properly tooled up. The Met brushed Peach's death under their already-stinking carpet. Commander Mitchell dealt with the paramilitary SPG operating in Hackney – with no consultation with the council – with great sensitivity by saying, "I don't feel obliged to tell anyone about my policing activities."

When pushed by the press about the white conical-hooded suit that had been found in the house of SPG Officer Grenville Bint, that was simple. Even though it was April, it was in readiness for the Met's Halloween party where he was going as Casper the Ghost. With regard to the book penned by former Democratic Governor of Mississippi Theodore G. Bilbo – *Take Your Choice: Separation or Mongrelization* – found next to his toilet, this was due to his short-sighted wife picking it up by mistake at the library.

Then there were the bloody riots that took place all over London. In Dalston, shops had been boarded up as looters descended, Mr H. Menswear pillaged down to the last buckle and button. There was anarchy on the streets; angry mobs threw firebombs. The atmosphere – *High Noon.* Johnson's Café had its windows smashed. And that was just by his work colleagues. He'd never quite understood what they wanted to achieve there. This unusual police course of action just flared the flames of the already-acute police-hatred-incited riot. McBride wondered, was it too much to ask for that the Met caught more criminals than they employed? The Hackney Black People's Association demanded a public inquiry into the conduct of the police. This never happened.

Mopping up runny egg with the crusts of his bread, McBride muttered under his breath, "*Dygaf di I lawr.*" Leaving the plate on the sofa, he got up and retrieved his car keys from the sideboard and made his way to his car.

"So, Dickson, where yew from, like?"

"Holt in Norfolk. Do you know it, guv?"

"No, can't say I do. Why the Met then, boyo?"

"It's the best police force in the world. I just wanted to make a difference and help the community."

"Well, that's commendable of yew, but this is yewer first week, like, on the job, so yew may rethink that in a bit, yew may. See, we got a bit of an issue going on yere, we have."

"What's that, guv?"

"Well, see, back in Holt yew probably don't have them, but we got lots of blacks around yere, we do."

"I've seen quite a few since I arrived, but never in Norfolk. Protecting the community and seeing that law and order is upheld, it makes no difference to me the colour of the person's skin. I intend to arrest the law breakers and protect the lawful. In the eyes of the law, we are all equal."

"Well, see, yere's the thing; the Met see 'equal' more in the Orwellian sense. Let's just say they aren't as forward-thinking as yew. Nowhere near in fact. They've put all their time and effort into making black people public enemy number one. Don't get me wrong, there's plenty of them around yere who're breaking the law, but some want to pretend it's just them. There've been some unfortunate incidents just up the road in Stoke Newington nick."

"What incidents, guv?"

"Death, Dickson. Black death for want of a better term. Started back in the seventies. Aseta Simms went in there and never came out alive. Death by misadventure. But the whole thing was dubious, to say the least. Then Michael Ferreira, a young black lad, got stabbed by some white boyos, so his mates took him there. They were desperate, and they thought, very wrongly, they would find sanctuary there. Instead of taking him to hospital, when he was bleeding all over the shop, they questioned him as a suspect while he was literally dying on their watch. When they finally decided to take him to hospital, he died from his fatal wounds."

Dickson had now gone white as a sheet digesting this information.

"Then a few months back a twenty-one-year-old called Colin Roach, not wanted by the police, walked into the foyer of the station, took out a gun and for no reason blew his own head off. The coroner's jury decided it was suicide. But this is the thing: even though there was a public furore, our Home Secretary Leon Brittan decided there was no need for a public inquiry. Would he have accepted it if it were his own child? Mind yew, that Leon, there's more than a whiff of bad business about him. There was that 1967 alleged rape of a student in his flat, but we never had enough evidence to arrest him, like. Then there's a 40-page dossier of alleged high-power paedophiles he may or may not be able to get his paws on. But he was the one who had the power to decide if we had a public inquiry or not. Just painting yew a picture, Dickson. Just hope yew're taking notes."

"Yes, guv," said Dickson, who hadn't been expecting this baptism of fire.

"But the Met, see, they had this special way of dealing with these suspicious deaths."

"What was that, guv?"

"They pretended none of it was happening, mun. Hoovered it under the carpet with all the other *ych y fi* they don't want anyone to know about. Needless to say this special protocol they got going on won't end well when is collides with reality. Let's just say some believe Colin's was heavily assisted suicide. See, here's the thing: what the Met should've done is made policing a more attractive career choice for their kind. Get blacks in the force, so they could feel like they could approach us, not think of us as the enemy. But forgive me for talking way too much common sense yere for a Met police officer. It would make certain elements of the community more trusting of the police seeing one of their own in uniform. That's the thing, Dickson; you have to actually be in the room to read it. But no, mun, they're taking from their never-ending Aryan Brotherhood pool. Say, if Sparky and Flint hadn't aggressively pursued their chosen vocation, the Met would have welcomed them with cross-burning open arms."

"Strange names, Sparky and Flint."

"Well, they're not yewer usual types, unless yew think compulsive pyromania is normal human behaviour. See, Dickson, they've got it all wrong. We've a much bigger menace around yere, we do. A major threat to law and order. But sometimes, see, the facts and the truth are just inconvenient."

"What's this menace?"

"Ones that are walking around in diamond cufflinks and designer suits. The Hunters are the real problem. I'm talking serious organised crime."

"Who are the Hunters?"

"It's lunchtime, butt what yew got planned?"

"It's eleven-fifteen, guv."

"Yes, as I said, lunchtime. I think yew and I need to have a bit of a chat, we do. Yew can buy me pie and mash at Arthur's. I'll get yew up to speed."

"Have you spoken to the powers that be about your concerns?"

"I have given them my opinions, strangely based on fact. But that's the thing, see, Dickson; most like the idea of freedom of speech until yew tell them something they don't like."

WHO CAN IT BE NOW?

"Debs, get the door."

The incessant ringing of the doorbell was doing Nic's head in.

"I can't, babe. Still in bed not feeling well. Can't you?"

"Yeh, will do, you lazy bitch. Like, I gotta do everyfink 'round 'ere."

Not expecting anyone, he thought it must be McDick about to expose him for being the Phantom Flan Flinger.

Opening the door, Nic was confronted with a young man with floppy, dark hair and a moronic toothy smile.

"Hello, my name's Tony, and I'm canvassing for the Queensbridge Branch of the Hackney South Labour Party. I'm a local residing in Mapledene Road. Could you give me just five minutes of your time, please?"

"You ain't from 'round 'ere wiv that accent," said Nic, more that annoyed that some posh twat was on his doorstep.

The trespasser was obviously used to this sort of less-than-happy-to-see-him response and continued undeterred in his smarmy voice. "We've been made to feel very welcome here. It's a wonderful area, full of community spirit and pride. I can't see us ever moving. We're dedicated to the area. Cherie and I call it home."

"Who the fuck is Cherie?"

"My wife. She's a human rights barrister. I've always thought you only require two things in life: your sanity and your wife."

"Well, I ain't got eivah of those, mate."

Ignoring Nic's comment, rhinoceros-skinned Tony continued. "We really are living in unprecedented times. What you must understand is that I love the Labour Party and all it represents. Do you realise ours is the first generation able to contemplate the possibility that we may live our entire lives without going to war or sending our children to war? But we still have problems in the guise of social injustices. Have you ever thought about that?"

"Not really, mate. There's no way you'd catch me voting for Worzel Gummidge. I'd kick 'is stick away wiv me size-firteen boot. I like Fatcher. Not like I'd do 'er or anyfink, she's minging, but I like what she's dun for the country, like shutting down 'em trade unions who was taking 'em lazy cunts out on strike cos their cup of tea weren't the right temperature. The bird's got balls; she don't back down to no cunt. And as for nukes, the more we can get our 'ands on the betta, just in case the Russians start somefink. We need to be fully nuked up. In fact, let's bomb Russia, get in there before they do us and send all the immigrants ovah there before we do. Kill two birds wiv one bomb."

"Well, that war would be illegal. I can see you have somewhat moderate political views, and I'm possibly sensing some microaggression here. Do you not care about the people living on the Holly Street Estate? I can see you have a lovely house, but in the name of community and my own unique idea of socialism, some of your neighbours are living in squalor and fear. You see, by nature I am a builder of consensus. I don't believe in sloppy compromise. But I do believe in bringing people together."

"What's your point?" asked Nic, genuinely confused.

It was full of scumbags. Surely it was a place to keep people like that.

"My point is, surely you care about this fine community you live in. The conditions some people are living in are abhorrent, and organic regeneration needs to be promoted. I quake at the imbecility of not taking this action."

"Can't say I've fought about it, mate. I 'aven't got the foggiest what you're banging on 'bout. You're talking bollocks. Illegal aliens committing crimes like mugging people and raping children and getting away wiv it. Bringing the whole area down. These backward freeloadahs coming ovah 'ere in their banana boats. The last fing we need is some bleeding 'art cunt telling 'em they can stay cos they 'ave got civil libidos. If it weren't for Maggie, I'd be frowing me support be'ind the National Front. They've got quality policies."

"We must seek to end unjustifiable discrimination wherever it exists. We must be tolerant and kind. What of their human rights?"

"I'm dead against 'em 'aving any of 'em," said Nic, hoping this twat would fuck off before he'd have to lamp him one.

"But immigration is good for the country. It brings fresh energy."

"Like fuck it does. I've got zero tolerance for it. They just scrounge off the taxpayah. And we don't need Spear Chuckahs "R" Us on the 'ighstreet."

"Be a doer and not a critic. Join the red cause and let's make this area better for all. Human progress has never been shaped by commentators, complainers or cynics. We live in edified times. Let's not become a nation of foolish, irresponsible nincompoops."

"Right, mate. If you don't fuck off in the next two seconds, I'll be exercising me 'uman rights and I'll stuff that clipboard so far down your froat it'll come out frough your arse'ole," said Nic as he lunged at him.

Tony ran for his life, making a mental note not to canvass at that address again. Even though he professed his love for the area, Tony and Cherie, some years later, moved to a Georgian townhouse in Bayswater, West London, with a price tag of £3.65 million. The Holly Estate was demolished, all save one tower. It became a pet project for Tony's political party – a do-gooder crusade to rid England of failed municipal architecture. One tower remained, as many refused to move. They liked their view from the sky and didn't like being told what to do by a vainglorious clown. The area went through heavy transformation. Some saw this as a good thing; others not so much when they were unable to afford a garden shed in the area they were brought up in. Perfidious Tony the future Prime Minister's optimism about his generation not going to war or sending their children to war was a ludicrous falsehood. When Joe Public was asked after his tenure ended if they would miss the Prime Minister, most answered that they hadn't been given the fair opportunity to aim at him and welcomed the chance.

ACT 3

GLITTERING PRIZE

The object of torture is torture. The object of power is power. Now you begin to understand me.
– **George Orwell, *1984***

There can only be one king.
– **Pablo Escobar**

"Right, gotta drive ovah to Baff to see Palmah."

"Oh, yeh, '*Goldfingah*'," said Nic.

"Yeh, Palmah knows gold, and we've got the gold, so we make the rules. 'E's got this timeshare fing in Tenerife 'e wants to run past me, and best fing is it's legit. Well, more or less legit. Could bring in ovah two mill a year."

"Smelting all that gold in 'is barn. That a good idea, ya fink?"

"It's in the middle of nowhere; besides, 'e works in the trade, so no reason 'e wouldn't 'ave a smeltah. Old Bill did come 'round a few weeks ago cos some busybody was trying to cause 'assle. Asked 'em in, all friendly like, made 'em a cuppa and showed 'em the smeltah. Said it was the tools of 'is trade, as 'e's in the gold business. Baff Old Bill nevah even wrote it up."

"Fuck's sake, I fought the Met were fick as shit. Surprised

McDick 'asn't come up wiv somefink. Don't trust Palmah or Noye."

"Why's that?"

"They're not from 'round 'ere. Palmah, 'e's from up norf."

"Nah, 'e's from Birming'am."

"Yeh, like I said, up norf. And Noye, 'e's from Kent. Anyways, they're both tight cunts. You evah seen 'em buy a round of drinks. You won't, cos when it's their turn, they do one. Tightah than Brooke Shields' snatch."

Mat was making a big impact in the underbelly of London. He was making vast sums of money that he was laundering into real estate by way of the Docklands Development and then into cold hard cash when he sold on to the LDDC. He was an untouchable, a new breed of criminals that had evolved who were highly financed and connected. They were a super league of organised criminals allied through a global underground network to the rapidly expanding drug business. Mat, at the helm, had taken the Hunter firm further up the underworld ladder. The UK being a member of the EU since 1973 was a godsend to Mat; the international barriers were melted like snow. Thatcher's unbridled free market should be working without any interference. And it was. Money launderers were spoilt for choice. There were now many more chances for the unscrupulous to make easy money. Financially, it was hard to see what was crooked or legal.

It was because of his reputation that Mat had got word to Micky McAvoy, aka Mad Mickey, who was currently serving a twenty-five-year sentence at Long Lartin Prison. McAvoy and five other armed robbers had broken into the Brink's-Mat warehouse at Heathrow Airport, expecting to make off with £3 million in cash. Instead, they got a cache of over £26 million, including 6,800 bars of gold. McAvoy had appeared in the doorway brandishing a 9mm Browning automatic pistol and snarled, "Get on the floor or you're fucking dead!" The guards were handcuffed and their legs bound with duct tape. Security guard Peter Bentley was pistol-whipped by McAvoy. The blood gushed down his face. Cloth bags were tightened over their heads. The senior guard, Michael Scouse, had his genitals doused in petrol and was then threatened with being set on fire and putting a bullet in his head unless he disarmed the alarms. Under duress, he complied. The five henchmen then walked into a treasure chest which was far beyond their wildest dreams, which they forgathered with glee, their very own El Dorado.

"Merry Christmas," yelled one of the gang as they left; it was 26th November 1983. The gold was packed into their stolen Transit, which buckled under the enormous weight. The band of thieves, having no idea how big the haul would be, now found themselves out of their league in getting rid of the gold. Without the right contacts, it was as good as fool's gold. None of their fences had the contacts to smelt the gold and convert it into cash – monetisation – which was the ultimate goal. Lloyds of London offered a £2 million reward for information leading to the recovery of the refiners-stamped gold. Commander Frank Cater of the Flying Squad, aka the Sweeney, led the hunt for the thieves; he was under immense pressure to get results. MI5 were ready to pounce on organised crime, having informed the Home Office of this. They'd grown bored of monitoring subversive left-wing politicians and trade unions. The dossier on Militant member Derek Hatton was now reading like *War and Peace*. MI5 were geared up to kick arse big time and get their fangs stuck into serious gangland activity. Albeit, they weren't willing to share their confidential finds with the police, who weren't to be trusted at any cost.

It was the crime of the century and the biggest robbery in British history. Its perpetrators needed to be caught before turning the Met into more of a laughing stock than they already were. Scotland Yard were just about intelligent enough to deduce that it had to be an inside job. Anthony Black, aka the Golden Mole, was a security guard at the warehouse. He also happened to be the brother-in-law of one Brain Robinson, aka the Colonel, a career criminal who'd served several prison sentences and was on the Flying Squad's list of London's twenty most prolific armed robbers. It was a no-brainer, even for the Met, who got Black in for questioning. Black buckled and went on to not just sing like a canary but give a full-blown opera, *Die Meistersinger von Nürnberg*-style. A detective spent eight hours taking down his twenty-one-page statement.

Most of the robbers decided to stay under the radar until things cooled down so as not to draw attention to themselves. But McAvoy decided it was a good idea to leave his council house in Dulwich and buy a big fat mansion in Kent. He also got a couple of Rottweilers that he named Brinks and Mat. Strangely enough, with these developments and Black's lengthy monograph, it wasn't long before he was arrested and subsequently sentenced at The Old Bailey to twenty-five years in jail. This was alongside Brian Robinson. Tony White, aka the King of Catford, another one of the main gang, was acquitted. The other smaller players were still at large, trying to flog their contraband. There were whispers that Scotland Yard had an unsigned statement from White in which he not only held his hands up to the heist but asked whether he could take the £2 million reward if he gave them his share of the gold. This statement, as lore would have it, said that White had read the Golden Mole's statement and told the police, "I agree wiv the fucking fing, but I can't remembah who dun what, or where. Can't we leave it at that?"

In the years before The Police and Criminal Evidence Act 1984 (PACE), the police weren't required to tape-record interviews, so White alleged this was something the police had fabricated. When the Yard were asked to hand over the admission to see if White had left his sticky fingerprints on it, they said they had unfortunately lost it before, then had clear recollection and admitted they had to eradicate it for security reasons. This being classed as above top secret. The COBRA meeting was imminent. McAvoy had reluctantly, now well and truly banged up, left Mat to dispose of a large quantity of gold. Mat placated him by sending Sid to visit him, when he told him, "Mate, course there's a pot of gold waiting for ya. But, like, you got a lenfy stretch to fink 'ow you're gonna spend it, ain't ya."

"Sid, I feel like I am being seriously fucked up the arse 'ere."

McAvoy knew that Mat had the means and contacts to smelt the bullion, sell it and launder the money through a series of convoluted financial transactions and property purchases. Mat turned to John Palmer, an associate of his father. Palmer could smelt the gold through his gold and jewellery company, Scadlynn Ltd, in Bristol. The higher-grade gold ingots were melted down and mixed with copper to disguise the quality. It was then ironically sold back to establishments in Hatton Garden, to dodgy jewellers, like Solly Nahome, and legitimate dealers, including Johnson Matthey, to whom it belonged originally. The Assay Office in Sheffield, which was in control of handing out hallmarks to jewellers and gold retailers, had unintentionally conspired in the laundering of the gold by endowing Scadlynn a seal of endorsement, which meant the tarnished gold was given a clean bill of health. Mat's accountant Jonathan Steerpike and Michael Relton their solicitor moved and hid the money via offshore front companies, in a myriad of bank accounts with the help of Panamanian law firm, Mossack Fonseca, in secrecy jurisdictions such as Switzerland, Jersey and Liechtenstein.

"I got plans on what to do wiv the revenue off this earnah. Just gotta make the right connection."

"Yeh, Mat. When you do, make sure me and the twins are in on the action. You're not the only one in this firm."

"This'll be a nice earnah for all of us. Been meaning to speak to ya 'bout somefink that needs ironing out. Some cunt is flooding the area wiv crack from Darkie Town."

"What's that, bruv?"

"They're boiling up the coke wiv baking soda."

"Nah, I meant Darkie Town. Is that Brixton?"

"Jamaica, bruv. These coons gotta be fucking up the formula. If they want to distribute this bollocks, they come to us, and we get a substantial cut."

"'Ow they getting it ovah 'ere? Frough Tilbury?"

"Nah, I've 'eard they're using these birds ovah there who's, like, swallowing it, then shitting it out or somefink when they get ovah 'ere."

"Is that why they call it crack?"

"What you on 'bout?"

"Well, like arse crack if they're shitting it out."

"No. Funny fing is, Nic, I don't fink that's why they call it crack. We gotta nip this one in the bud. I've got Sid on it. We gonna pay this pair of cunts operating on Sandring'am a visit. See where they're getting it from."

NEAR DARKE

Tommy Costello was up early. He needed to do some fly-tipping, and the best place was a secluded alleyway behind the bottom end of Sandringham Road. He'd borrowed his mate's van and parked on Birkbeck Road. He couldn't chance Sandringham; even at this time of the morning he'd probably come back to find it deprived of its wheels. Tommy started unpacking the gas cannisters. He was huffing and puffing heavily, but the near heart attack would be worth it. There was no way he was paying for the council to take them away. You really could see anything here. He'd once seen a fish tank full of goldfish discarded. So Tommy wasn't surprised to see what looked like a mannequin's hand sticking out from a pile of bin bags. A rat scurried past him towards the black bags. Tommy moved forward. The cold weather made his large frame walk in unusually quick paces. He peered over, and the sight in front of him was horrifying. It was a woman, or what was left of one. Tommy bent over and violently brought up last night's dinner. The rat, now curious, but not perturbed by his human visitors, both living and dead, proceeded to feast on blood and vomit.

"Who reported it, Dickson?"

"Tommy, the landlord from the Crown. He's in a bit of a state and a bit embarrassed. He'd been down here fly-tipping."

"That's the least of his worries. Where's he to now?"

"He's been driven back to the station to make a statement, guv."

"Do we have an identity on the body?"

"When we first got on the scene, there was a tramp sitting on a thrown-away sofa. He told us the victim's name was Stacey Tubbs, a drug addict and prostitute. He said she lived in a squat on Sandringham with her boyfriend. He offered to formally ID the body if we slipped him five quid. We took his statement and sent him on his way."

"Is Fish yere?"

"Yes, guv. The pathologist is with the body."

They moved towards the hive of police and forensic activity. A uniform lifted the police tape to let the pair through. McBride surveyed the slaughterous scene before him. The young woman's body was contorted into a spreadeagle. Blood gushed from every conceivable orifice, the wounds deep and ferocious. The victim had suffered every painful indignity before death. There was no place on her emaciated body that hadn't suffered some barbarous act. The woman had been decapitated; her head was lying next to her body. Her face showed the horror of the death she had endured. Her eyes bulged out of their sockets. The top of the detached skull had been bashed in. Pink and grey brain matter had squirted onto the rubbish-strewn road. Her vagina had been completely hacked away, now nothing more than entrails degraded and brutalised beyond recognition. But all McBride was drawn to was the initial 'N' that had been carved into her forehead.

"Fish, butt, I assume yew have concluded life extinct, not

too much for even yew to deduce. I don't suppose yew can like enlighten us yere."

"This is a very dead one. I can safely say there's no breathing, no pulse and no heartbeat," said Fish smirking as he sucked on a sherbet lemon.

"What's that moving bu there? It can't be maggots this early, can it?" asked McBride as he pointed to what was the victim's vulva.

"I'd hazard a professional guess that the victim had a venereal disease. I think you'll find that they're genital crabs. They feed on blood, only they've hit the jugular, so to speak, and are drowning in their host's haemoglobin. I'll send you the full post-mortem report shortly. Right now, I'm off to Arthur's for breakfast. The best black pudding this side of the river. Until we meet again," said Fish smirking as he walked to his car, not noticing the 'Master Thread the Tailor's Son' card that had flown into his wellington boot.

The last twenty-four hours had been difficult, to say the least, for Jimmy. Yesterday he'd been found unconscious, overdosed, on Ridley Road. Jimmy had been rushed to hospital, where on arrival he'd flatlined. Doctors were able to resuscitate him and brought back to life. He'd been pronounced dead for thirty seconds. When he awoke the next morning, against medical advice he'd discharged himself. Jimmy had blagged his way out by telling staff he'd seek help from his GP and start a methadone programme. His druggie manipulation skills intact, he'd leaned heavily on the mercy of the hospital staff and begged for some coins for the bus fare back home. He was given 30p and bundles of drug-addiction pamphlets. Jimmy had promptly left Homerton Hospital and deposited the leaflets into the nearest rubbish bin.

He arrived home and was taken in for questioning over Stacey's murder. But for once in his miserable life, he had a cast-iron alibi – he'd been dead. While kicking off at the station about wrongful arrest, not once had he enquired how Stacey had died. He'd expected her to meet a grisly end one way or another. But right now he had more pressing things on his mind, like getting his next fix. He was seriously clucking, and he needed something to take the edge off. He picked up an open bottle of Strongbow and took a swig, then swiftly spat it out again, remembering he'd filled it with piss. The squat having no plumbing, they'd taken to using the floor as a toilet. Jimmy always found a stash of bog roll, courtesy of the newsagent's; every day you could find a stash of slung-out copies of *The Guardian*. Jimmy could have kicked himself that he hadn't made a contingency plan for when this happened. How was he going to support his habit now she was dead? He briefly thought, if things got really bad, he could try to sell his own arse. But on further reflection, he'd tried that and had been given a quid in shrapnel for his time, which wasn't given but thrown at him after the event. Jimmy had something of a light-bulb moment when he decided to go through Stacey's possessions. He ransacked her sleeping bag to see if the sneaky bitch had been hiding any gear. Going through her sodden bedding, Jimmy found the elixir he craved stuffed into a hole at the bottom. The deceitful shitbag. Jimmy made haste to his work and set about swiftly shooting up. He took the needle and plunged the point into the bubbling fluid, which was absorbed up the tunnel. Taking the syringe in his hand, he unbuttoned his jeans. He tried to steady his hands to puncture his dick with the needle, but it took a few goes as he was shaking involuntarily due to withdrawal. Eventually, he clumsily made a hit in his dorsal vein, avoiding the open, bloody abscess. He pushed the needle deeper, the opioid flooding into his body. As he withdrew the needle, nirvana engulfed him.

CLOWN WORLD

"What's going on in *The Sun*, Rosie?" asked Victor as he bit into a slice of lardy cake.

"Well, a law student in Glasgow called Nicola Clownfish 'as staged a one-woman protest outside the council 'ouse 'er mum and dad was able to buy undah the Tory govahnment's Right to Buy scheme. Says 'ere she's a nationalist, finks the Scots should rule 'emselves. A proud Scott from Ayrshire, she was dressed in a tartan kilt. She believes she's been forced into politics as she 'ates Fatchah and everyfink she stands for. She's dead against Maggie putting Trident nuclear missiles in Clyde, as she's a CND supportah and regularly chains 'erself to stationary objects. Nicola finks that when they're free of the shackles of Westminstah, SNP can ride roughshod ovah any litigation they wish. She'd keep upstanding laws, such as making it an offence to drunkenly ride a cow undah the Licensing Act 1872, and implement uvahs, such as making it mandatory for farmahs to encourage foxes into chickens' coups to protect their rights. If you disagree wiv 'er, you're cou-lro-phobiac. Oh, that is a big word. *The Sun* 'as gone a bit 'ighbrow. It's this new journalist, Piers Morgan."

"They're nufink wivout the Union, Rosie. See 'ow long they last wivout us."

"That's not the end of it. It was a windy day and 'er kilt flew up and it was a bit of surprise what was undah there – it was full meat and two veg, excuse me language. What is the world coming to? Nicola is one of 'em transylvanians. That reminds me, you'll come to Sunday dinnah, won't you? Got the twins getting me a nice side of beef."

"I wouldn't miss it for the world. Too many of these notrights out there these days. Any uvah news?"

"There 'as been a kafuffle in parliament. Two innocuous Labour backbenchahs, Robert Michael Silk and Jeremy Bernard Corbyn, 'ad fisticuffs. Astonished colleagues watched on as Silk grabbed Corbyn by the lapel in a face-to-face row. You'd fink they'd know 'ow to conduct 'emselves. What does innocuous mean?"

"Means they're not important. I mean, be different if Kinnock and Foot 'ad a punch up."

"Corbyn said Silk took umbrage wiv 'is choice of 'at and tore 'is budenovka from 'is 'ead. Silk commented, 'I didn't 'it 'im. If I 'ad, 'e'd 'ave stayed down.'"

"Bit of a non-story really, Rosie."

"This is a bit betta. In separate incidents, two sexologists 'ave been found dead in Germany. 'Elmut Kentlah at the University of 'Annover and Volkmar Sig-us-ch at Goefe University. Bouf tortured to deaf by the blood eagle."

"What an earf is that, Rosie?"

"Says 'ere it's what the Vikings used to kill their enemies. They separated their ribs from their spine wiv a scalpel, pulling their bones and skin outward while pouring salt onto the wounds to form a set of wings, all while they're conscious. A terrorist group 'ave taken responsibility for the executions, but as yet the police 'ave not formally named 'em, but it's speculated to be a splintah group of MAF."

"Gordon Bennet, not 'em again. I fought we'd seen the back of the Men's Abolition Front. Anyfink cheerier in the *Gazette*?"

"No. It's awful," said Nan as she picked up the paper.

"What's 'appened?"

"Young girl found 'acked to deaf last night be'ind Sandring'am. A Stacey Tubbs. Not much of a write-up to be 'onest."

"What a wicked world. Shocking what goes on right on your doorstep."

"She was one of 'em streetwalkahs, but no one deserves that, do they?"

"The wickedness of some people."

"And the city farm we got 'ere on Goldsmifs Row; someone 'as been decapitating animals there. They 'ave found the 'eadless bodies of chickens, pigs and goats."

"Who'd do such a fing? It's for the kiddies."

"I know, Victor, and it's not like we're in a war, where you 'ad to live off the fat of the land."

LIFE IN THE FAST LANE

By mid-1985 Mat could see that drugs were changing and cocaine was the way forward. He just needed to make the right connections to be a player with the large lucrative shipments of cocaine. The police were still chasing their tails looking for wacky backy. He'd just switch products. The cannabis market was already overcrowded. The narcotic was more cumbersome to handle, so it was harder to smuggle, whereas cocaine, worth millions of pounds, could be smuggled in compactly a lot easier. Coke wasn't a widely used drug in Europe, it was thought of as a rich man's drug, but it was gaining momentum. Cocaine was a very lucrative commodity that had surpassed coffee as the chief Columbian export. The cocaine business was the sixth largest private enterprise in the American top 500 companies, ironically topping The Coca-Cola Company and PepsiCo. The biggest crime lord in the world, Pablo Emilio Escobar Gaviria, was closely watching the European hash-smuggling operations. The Columbian authorities were under immense pressure from the US to rid the country of the drug smugglers. Pablo realised that this would be a major complication in his profitable North American trading place. America's Teflon president had decided that the reds weren't the only evil in the world. Reagan had been good as gold when he was chasing the commies, but now he was sticking his nose into his business with his rent-a-gob wife, Nancy, spouting all this "Just say no" *mierda.* If he'd just put all his resources into the real threats like M-19 and FARC, pinko nutjobs seeking some sort of crazy distribution of wealth – more importantly, as the seventh richest man in the world, *his* wealth. No fucker living in the jungle wearing army fatigues and sporting mass-murderer, Che Guevara-style berets was spending his hard-earned dinero. They could cut that out when they liked. But Pablo couldn't rule out the possibly of working with these commies in the future due to their blind-faith commitment to their ill-fated crusade, his calculating mind always working overtime to get an angle. Everyone had a price; the important thing was to find out what it was. Once they had served their purpose, he'd stuff *Das Kapital* down their throats until they choked to death.

His own government was now scrutinising him like a laboratory rat. Didn't they realise how much time and effort it took to make Columbia a narco state? The total dedication and commitment it took to have to annihilate politicians, policemen and hippopotamusphobiacs each day? No one was fucking with his vision. I mean, how much more could he do? He'd offered to pay off Columbia's national debt to the tune of $10 billion. Couldn't they turn a blind eye to some of his business activities? But no, it had been thrown back in his face. Didn't they realise that actions have consequences and his business would suffer, which meant a school in a favela in La Candelaria may not be built? His people loved him. They called him 'Robin Hood Paisa' for all the work he did for good charities like the homeless, the illiterate, pension entitlements for narco-terrorists, and hippos' lives matter.

How he hated Belisario Betancur. The president of Columbia's slogan was "Yes we can", only not where Pablo was concerned. Betancur had a long-running conflict with leftist guerrillas. Again, like that B-list actor, why couldn't he just wage a war with the Revolutionary Armed Force of Columbia and keep his beak out of the work of a hardworking plutocrat? He had the impudence to call the cartels "bad sons of Columbia". The bare-faced cheek of the *coño*. Betancur had declared that Columbia's national dignity was held hostage by the traffickers and solemnly promised to extradite the traffickers to the USA. Well, two could play that game, and as far as Pablo was concerned, if he wasn't careful, he would be going the same way as Rodrigo Lara, his Minister of Justice, who was shot more than twenty times in Bogota by a motorcycle-riding assassin.

In the USA the crackdown was potentially crippling, with Regan cutting off a large portion of their cocaine supply routes through the Caribbean. This resulted in the product shipments having to go through Mexico to reach North America. This wasn't cost-effective to Escobar, as they would now have to pay the money-grabbing Mexican cartels' shipping costs to facilitate their supply passage. Quite frankly Gallardo could go do one. No one would out bandit him. By diverting the product in a major way, to Europe, Pablo believed he could stick two massive fingers up at the Mexican bandits and the United States government. Ronnie could stick that in his crack pipe and smoke it, and hopefully, *Dios* willing, choke on it. With his stupid mantra, "Make America great again", no one was going to catch on to this, were they?

Eurotrash were the way forward, and these yuppies he'd read about in *El Espectador*. In Europe there was a full-blown market waiting. Escobar now hoped the DEA would back the fuck off with their spiteful vendetta to bring him down. Couldn't they cut him some slack and try looking into the activities of General Noriega for a change. Even if he'd not had his wings clipped by the petty American authorities, he was tired of doing business with the psycho bitch they called 'La Patrona', one Griselda Blanco in Miami, where 70% of his cocaine came through. She was obviously unstable; who in their right mind calls their child Michael Corleone? Dumb, fat, ugly, bitch with no dress sense.

The Columbians were highly suspicious of outsiders, so Mat needed someone to personally vouch for him. A Scottish associate with a speccy schoolteacher appearance called Brian Doran, aka the Professor, was a Glaswegian multilingual university graduate and the first man from the UK to be endorsed by the Medellín Cartel. Escobar, who already had the UK crime lord in his sight, had been convinced by the Professor that Mat was the ideal aqueduct to move Pablo's product into Europe. This fitted in well with Escobar's vision to exploit the European market without being directly involved. Pablo liked these London gangsters' loyalty to their family and the only time you grassed was when you were smoking it.

The gangland boss flew from Heathrow to El Dorado International Airport. He was driven in a Toyota Land Cruiser to Pablo's abode, the Hacienda Nãpoles, in Puerto Triunfo. The compound boasted a large Spanish-style colonial house, a zoo, a sculpture park and a private airport. Mat had been greeted warmly. "*Qué pasa, hombre?*" said Escobar while sucking on his obligatory joint. Over shots of Aguardiente, El Doctor deduced Mat was a calculating man capable of making life-and-death decisions in him. A man just like himself. Escobar saw something else him – the cold, hard deadness and ruthlessness behind his eyes. They called Mat the *guapo gringo* – the handsome outsider.

"Your UK connection will be Santos Gomez. You'll need to assemble a trusted team of ambassadors in Spain and Holland."

"That can be dun. I 'ave the right people in mind. In the UK we can bring it in frough Tilbury Docks. They 'ave their own police force there, but that ain't gonna be a problem."

"In Spain possibly you've thought to use your family. I've heard about them."

"Yeh, I will get 'em on board. As you 'ave dun your research, you'll know they know what they're doing."

"It's good that we speak the same language. It's a shame the sons of bitches, my government here, do not."

"Same wiv mine. They don't get we're just providing a service. Just simple economics – supply and demand. If we didn't do it, someone else would."

"Tell me, Mr Hunter, do you like hippos?"

"Uh, yeh, like, as much as the next person."

"I have four of my own. I shall show you on your stay. I connect with animals. I speak to them, and I know they understand what I'm saying. It is fact that the hippopotamus is the most intelligent of all animals. It is with them I share my deepest thoughts."

"Uh, yeh, it'll be the 'ighlight of me trip."

Mat was given a blank cheque of Medellín cocaine. Escobar believed he could make Mat the godfather of European cocaine trafficking. The pipeline was now officially open. Mat negotiated a four-year agreement to supply Medellín cocaine on a massive scale into Western Europe. On his trip he was tightly chaperoned by the man they called 'Popeye', a man responsible for executing many of his boss's enemies. He made sure no one fucked with him, but Mat was also wily enough to know he was sussing him out. He didn't put a foot wrong. This wasn't a relationship he was willing to mess up. It would take his firm into another stratosphere. On the final day of his trip, Pablo said, "Mr Hunter, sell the product; don't use the product. Once you start to use the *cocaína,* we have a problem. *Entender*? This," said Pablo signalling to the joint he was smoking, "is okay, but the *coca* will kill you."

"You 'ave nufink to worry 'bout on that score. I plan to sell it all and make us loads of money."

"Ahh, yes, the *deniro*, I will take payment in *oro* too."

"No idea what that is, mate."

"Gold. From what my sources tell me, I believe a deal can be struck."

"That can be arranged."

"*Bueno*, as I have something special in mind." Pablo for some time had been hankering after a solid-gold bathroom suite. He'd been quite miffed when he found out that the Sultan of Brunei had one. It had given him sleepless nights, whereas he usually slept like a baby.

"One last thing, Mr Hunter. If you're a *estupido gringo* and work with Gilberto and Miguel Rodríguez Orejuela and Chepe Santacruz, you'll be a *múerto gringo. Entender*?"

"You 'ave me word," said Mat, being shrewd enough to know he was referring to the Cali Cartel and a slow painful death, the Cali Cartel being Escobar's main rival, who, like himself, did a lot for the community. They went above and beyond in their social duties, performing social cleansing where they sent out, completely at their own expense, paramilitary forces to kill prostitutes, the homeless, homosexuals, street children and beggars.

"One last thing. Tell me, Mr Hunter, have you ever thought of growing a moustache? It's the making of a man."

"Nah, mate, but who knows in the future?"

Mat and Pablo had shaken hands before he was escorted back to the airport. Mat took a flight to the Hague Airport. In the Netherlands he contacted a man called Klaas Bruinsma aka 'the Preacher', a global drug smuggler in Rotterdam. The city, in a prime location, boasted Europe's largest active port. It was an epicentre for the distribution of narcotics. The Preacher had a reputation for being unmerciful and a very dangerous foe. He was also an established drugs baron and a cold-blooded killer. Mat met him at Bierhandel De Pijp. The meet was successful. They spoke the same language – that of cold hard cash. Spain was a no-brainer time to get the old man and uncles out of Charlie's Bar.

UNION OF THE SNAKE

"Yeh, mon, '*pass di kouchie*,'" said Rattlesnake, cackling with gold-toothed laughter. "Lambie, mon, dem Musical Youth, wot di fook dem on 'bout, pass di dutchie? Like, who pass di cooking pot? Jeezum peas, Ise dead wid laugh."

"Mi nuh know wot dem on 'bout," said Mark Lambie as he ingested the heavy-duty ganga. It was a fact at that precise moment that Lambie's drug-addled mind understood very little. "Yeh, mon, but be brawta ting if dey pass di curry if yuh have di munchies. Some SpudULike be nice now, Daadie."

"Yeh, mon, yuh talk truth," said Rattlesnake, half listening and not quite sure how potatoes had come up in the conversation.

"Rattle, mi gonna start petition, make SpudULike have goat curry filling."

"Lambie, do your ting, mon."

"Mi wonda if yuh can smoke di potato peel like di banana and it get yuh high doobs."

"Mi nuh overstand wot yuh're talking 'bout. Fook, dis shit's strong," said Rattlesnake as he took another large toke on his Kush joint.

"Dem bones dem bones," Rattlesnake muttered under his breath.

Neville Brown was at his flat on the North Peckham Estate. Neville had reinvented himself. The six-foot-five Yardie now had bleached-blonde dreadlocks and only answered to the name Rattlesnake. He'd taken himself on a life journey back to his Jamaican routes. He'd discovered Voodoo and then Hoodoo and then added into the mix his own syncretism of his enlightened beliefs – mainly made-up beliefs. A murderer from the day he was born, having killed his *mudha* as she gave birth to him. Born at twelve pounds, his *mudha* had bled to death. Rattlesnake ripped through her and practically cut her in half. Coming down her birthing canal, he gushed out of her. As he let out his first yell, she died in agony. Haemorrhaging severely, his *mudha* let out her last.

Rattlesnake was also known on the estate as the devil man who had juju powers. He'd been suspected of the murder of PC Ken Loveluck, who'd been brutally mutilated with a machete during a riot at the estate. It happened in broad daylight, but the police struggled to get any witnesses to come forward. The constabulary believed they had his girlfriend over a barrel to supply incriminating evidence against him. She was fatally gunned down in a drive-by shooting, but again nobody saw anything, even though it was outside the Post Office on benefits day.

The flat was stark and in disrepair, but the Yardmen were dressed in Moschino and Jacob Marley-style twenty-four-carat gold chains. Inconspicuous was not a word in the Yardies' vocabulary. You needed to flaunt your wealth, or pretence of wealth, to make a mark in this gang. The reality was that even the police didn't formally recognise the Yardies as serious organised crime – more like disorganised. With no central control or identifiable hierarchy, they were rudderless, with few affiliations or loyalties. Yardies had a keen radar for anyone disrespecting them or in their alter universe called firing shots. But make no mistake, they were ruthless and terrifyingly violent. Life had been cheap for Rattlesnake, surviving day to day on criminality, his mantra, "You can kill mi today; you can kill mi inna di morrows." That was until he became a devout Voodoohoodooist, his mind now lucidly alert to injustice. One morning he'd woken up from a dream where his soul had drifted from his body into another dimension. He'd been told by Bondye the Gran Maître, the supreme creator god, that he was immortal. That day he started his journey on his reptilian metamorphosis.

Rattlesnake could've excelled as a mortal as a professional athlete he was that fast. He was highly regarded as someone with potential at Peckham Youth Athletic Club. Unfortunately, by age twelve Rattlesnake had got heavily into drugs. But he was still fast by anyone's standards, which was fortuitous in his life path of crime when he needed to do a runner. He was kicked off the athletic team at age thirteen. Not long after, he quit school, managing to be at the bottom of every remedial class he was in, leaving school not even having the reading and writing ability of a three-month-old embryo. Various stints in borstal did little for his edification.

"Mi sista, Nyoka, she live wid Rasta mon in Dalston, Delbert. She on di pipe and selling di rock deh for mi, mon. So, di ting set. Ise expanding and infiltrating into di East militantly. Dem Hunter wastemen need to small up demselves. Dem craven licky licky. Mi beat dem real bad. Been hanging out Four Aces, Dalston Lane. Lambie, can see mi performing deh. Memba mi tell yuh?"

"Yeh, mi been deh, mon. Seen Prince Buster deh. He was maad. Kicked up a rumpus. Bob used to hang deh back in di day."

"Mi artist like Bob, speaking to mi people. Mi sent tape to big mon at Bog Records – he'll feel mi shit. Doops gonna make loads of cheddar as rapper. Until mi get mi record deal, di people want di rock and Ise got di rock. Got it coming in from di Yard. Got mi poom-poom swallowing it in Jamrock. Come by plane. Dem just sick it up, mon. If dey caught, dey nuh know mi. Ise make sure of dat. Nuh blabba mout. If a dirt, a dirt."

"Do yuh ting, Rattle. It sweet nuh chacka chacka turn up di ting. Dem squeako Hunters should bi taken out of di equation militantly."

"Mi spirit nuh tek to dem. Why, dey tink dey rule London. Dis is mi place now. Mi gonna take good care of dat. Dey inna big chubble. Mi annihilate dem. You feel mi doops."

"Zeen talk truth. Mi a go, mon. Mi puppy on di promise wid mosquito net. Hotta dan ten fiyah side. Lickle bit Rattle, mi gaan," said Lambie as he got up and headed for the front door and out into the plenilune night.

"Go get di poom-poom stulla, lover. Bless up," said Rattlesnake as he took another toke on his joint, blowing the white smoke out slowly.

Rattlesnake got up and walked to his sacred room. The room was pitch black, the walls and window painted with thick paint. The disciple moved towards his alter adorned with the skulls of goats, chickens and pigs and lit up with candles. The votives were carefully chosen – black to invoke a hex and purple to gain mastery over a person. The incantation pedestal cluttered with amulets, talismans and the gris-gris, a potent charm wrapped in red cloth, to bind harm on mortal enemies. Inside the charm were a human tooth, graveyard dust and a chicken's wish bone. He stripped naked, the scars a constant reminder of when he was mortal, when one of the devil's spawn burned him.

"How mi Marley?" asked Rattlesnake to the cobra that had slithered over to him. He heard a muffled whimper from a corner of the room. His head snapped around aggressively. The woman was chained to the wall, emaciated and naked. She'd been there for days. Her captor had given her water to drink and occasionally some brown fish stew. She was left to soil herself. She had no concept of time or of day and night. She just watched and counted the snake slithering from one end of the room to the other. Ball-gagged, she tried to plead with her eyes to her incarcerator as tears flowed from them. But he showed no sign of mercy. Her name was Jessica. He'd picked her up through the guise of helping her as a volunteer from the Peckham Park Road Baptist Church. He soothingly told her they could save her life. The woman was a runaway. No one would miss her. He moved slowly towards her, his eyes twisted and cruel. He roughly pulled her legs apart and sunk his head into the woman's vagina licking and biting hungrily at her pearly juices and the exquisite curse blood, his eyes rolling back into his head, lapping like a wolf. Rattlesnake started to feel the power flow through him. The Voodoohoodoo power. Jessica bucked in pain, the terror grotesquely etched on her face. He violently flipped her over and thrust his dick in her. Rattlesnake thrust and thrust while he tightened his grip around her neck. As he came to a climax, he broke her neck. The sickening snap reverberated around the room. Marley slithered across the floor to the cadaver. Later he would dismember her body with a machete, as he had done before with the other disposables. Then as his forefathers of the Secte Rouge, he would devour the sweet meat. Scooping the mixture of leukorrhea, blood and ejaculation which was dripping down the dead woman's inner thighs into his hands, the disciple moved scrupulously to the altar, careful not to spill a drop of the warrior's brew. Taking a goblet, Rattlesnake proceeded to pour from his cupped hands the pheromone mix. In a trance, Rattlesnake brought the sanguine concoction to his lips and slurped it greedily. He chewed and devoured the ethereal coagulated blood using the power of the woman's shredding of her uterus. The biological woman, Rattlesnake both hated and worshipped in equal measures. Their power boundless, he must show caution and administer extreme trickery to get the better of these cervical goddesses. He would digest the immense power of Maman Brigitte and Ayida-Weddo. Blood magick and a full moon he knew could be the death of any mortal man, but he wasn't mortal. Rattlesnake could feel the power flowing through him. He started to flicker his tongue in and out, at first slowly then he quickened the pace, his heartbeat now rapid. He emitted a faint hissing sound. In tandem he drummed on the alter the cha-cha rattle adorned with a child's skull while he myopically stared at the goat skull lit up with a purple votive.

The dead child's torso had been found in the River Lea. He was around four years old. He'd been trafficked from Nigeria for a muti-ritual. He told the witch doctor he needed the skull after the muti-killing. The boy's tummy held a small amount of Calabar beans known as 'Doomsday'. The autopsy concluded that the amount of Doomsday in him would've paralysed him but not prevented pain. He would've suffered an excruciating, slow death. Rattlesnake had at least five illegitimate children. He had nothing to do with them. But they were still his blood. He couldn't use them in his divine rituals. There'd been one born severely disabled that he thought of sometimes. The boy died at three days old. Nyoka and he never talked about it.

He slowly opened a wooden box and gazed at the four Voodoo dolls. The crude dolls were imbedded with pins. The multiple pins were stabbed savagely over and over again into the stuffed bodies, the Spanish-moss stuffing spilling out like bloodless guts. In a shamanic trance he prayed incoherently in a tongue only known to him. Rattlesnake waited for Paba Legba to enter his body to let the possession begin, Legba being the intermediary between the lwa spirits and him, the emissary between the human and spirit world. He felt Legba possess him. He was the chual to be ridden. His body started convulsing frantically. Now he was ready for Damballa the serpent lwa to enter him. The disciple dropped to the blood-and faeces-covered floor. Crazed by the serpent, he started to slither and hiss, darting out his tongue. He stayed in this frenzied state for hours. After Damballa left his body, Rattlesnake lay on the floor comatose.

AT CLOSE RANGE

"It's Mat, Dad."

"All right, son. 'Ow's the weavah in Lundun?"

"Shit. Same old fing. Got a good fing going wiv the Columbians, but, see, I 'ave been finking. The middlemen; we don't need 'em. So I'm gonna iron out a deal to get you to oversee the product from its drop-off."

Mat deducted they were wasting money transporting the contraband across Spain using middlemen. They were taking a large portion of the profit when it arrived in Galicia, when all they were doing was taking care of the logistics of moving the cocaine.

"Yeh, get rid of surplus. One 'undred percent in on this."

"I gotta fly out to Norven Spain and speak to this bloke, Carlos. 'E, like, controls these inbetweenahs, then I got to 'ammah out a deal wiv ETA."

"What's ETA? They some firm?"

"It's the Spanish IRA. They wanna be separate from the rest of Spain. I'm sure I can talk 'em 'round soon as they know 'ow many guns they can buy wiv me deal. ETA are political fanatics, but they're interested in money. Everyone is interested in money. That's the funny fing. I 'ad this American bird called Crystal on the blowah a couple of weeks ago. Said she got me numbah from an associate. Asked me if I could get 'er a Challengah 1 tank. Said money was no object. She wanted to take out some Bildahberg Group meeting in New York. Kept banging on 'bout it being a good result to get rid of loadsa problematic people."

"Fucking random, son. What ya tell 'er?"

"Told 'er I couldn't 'elp 'er. Said she was the foundah of somefink called Cad. Nevah 'eard of 'em. Even if I could, I'd need to check 'er out. Make sure she's a propah bona fide terrorist and not undahcuvah Old Bill.

"Do me a favour. Old Bill getting a bird wiv an American accent to call you up and ordah a tank? They ain't got the charactah to fink up somefink like that."

"That was the uvah funny fing. She said if I could source one, could I send a female associate."

"Gotta be a windup, like. A bird in the firm. Leave it out."

"Probably is, but Nic finks if she's legit, it could be a nice earnah if we can get 'old of one."

"You can get 'old of anyfink if you 'ave the dough and the contacts. Right, bell me when you 'ave the details. Gotta go. Taking your mum to Red Peppah for lunch. I 'ad Nic on the blowah the uvah night. Seems the clubs doing well. When do you fink he can 'andle more?"

"Not at the moment. As soon as we start getting the consignments frough Tilbury, he can offload some of it at the clubs. Be in touch."

Mat flew to Santiago de Compostela Airport. Galicia was the main European entry point for Colombian cocaine. The Columbians delivered their wares to Spaniard fishing boats which met cartel vessels in the mainstream of the Atlantic Ocean. The boats headed to the rugged coastline of Galicia, where the Columbian motherships would be welcomed by fishing boats positioned offshore to collect the spoils. The connector between the Galician buccaneers and the Spanish champagne-swilling and cocaine glitterati was a *beau monde* Lothario called Carlos Goyannes. Mat hammered out a deal with the affable Carlos, which was mutually beneficial to them, at Casa Solla over glasses of Godello wine. Mat went on to meet ETA head honcho, Josu Urrutikoetxea. They dined at Parador de Santiago de Compostela. Josu was all but rubbing his hands with glee when he realised how many CETME Ameli and Llama Super Comanches he could buy. Mat negotiated a deal with the paramilitary to get the drugs across Northern Spain with a monetary payment per cargo.

TWO TRIBES

"I can't believe fucking 'Ackney Council putting up that load-of-crap peace painting."

"What's that, Nic?"

"Was down Dalston Lane at the nick this morning cos that piss-taking cunt McDick said 'e needed to eliminate me from their inquiries of that coppah that got 'is 'ead decapitated ovah Broadwatah Farm Estate. Like, why the fuck would I travel to Totten'am to take out a pig when I could do one 'ere? Anyways, I come out, like, and in front of me is this piece of shit. Some cunt 'as dun a big painting of people in a brass band banging on 'bout peace and banning the bomb. And all that CND crap. Like, I ain't even got any fucking idea what that stands for. It's somefink to do wiv us not being fully nuked up. They got these birds chaining 'emselves to railings. What the fuck is that gonna do? I don't get it. If you tie a bird up, some of 'em get propah bent out of shape, but it's okay if they do it to 'emselves."

"I ain't seen it, Nic. I stopped trying to work out birds a long time ago."

"I 'ave nevah really bovered, to be 'onest. I'm telling ya,

only fing we can do now wiv the Yanks is to get as many bombs as possible and nuke Russia. Then, like, we'd 'ave peace, cos every cunt in Russia would be dead. I fink they should put me in charge of the world. I got a lot to offah. There's this plaque saying 'Ackney Council paid for it, when there's people down the 'Olly who's chopping up furniture so they can light a fire to 'eat their flats. Not like I care 'bout 'em. Goes wivout saying, zero fucks given. The 'ole place could go up in flames, which, come to fink 'bout it, wouldn't be a bad fing. I'm just making a quality point. I'm pissed as fuck 'Ackney Council is pissing away taxpayahs' money on a load of bollocks."

For a moment Flint didn't respond, his thoughts lost on the tantalising, towering inferno he was conjuring in his mind, complete with charred bodies hurling themselves, burning alive, out of the windows of the Snake Block before he regained himself and said, "Yeh 'Ackney Council's all anti-war for some reason. I read in the *Gazette* that it tried to stop the trains carrying nuke waste passing frough 'ere but failed."

"And rightly so. We got trains going frough 'ere glowing like 'em kids on the Ready Brek advert. The only fing I liked on the painting was the skeletons."

NOT LIFE AS WE KNOW IT

Greta Myrtle was at Dalston Job Centre. After moving to the area six months ago, she really needed to get a job. She was living with her boyfriend, Nigel Kermit, in a bedsit on Beechwood Road. He had a job in Dixons as a sales assistant in the PC department, but his hours had been dropped, so they were struggling to make the rent. Nigel was a keeper, so she was putting her all into finding local employment. Greta from Farnham had met Nigel at a Star Trek convention in Scunthorpe. It was love at first sight, or rather love at first alien. She was standing by the Klingons display, and he was standing by the Talosians exhibition. Their eyes had locked and there was almost a mind-meld telepathy between them. They'd walked in tandem towards each other, both signalling the Vulcan salute. That day they'd been inseparable; not only because they were Trekkies, but also devoted Dungeons & Dragons disciples. Nigel was so sweet as he escorted her back to her coach. He'd presented her with a figurine of Worf even though Greta hadn't seen them for sale at the convention, just on a display. She was giddy with love for this lanky lad with receding, long, carrot hair and a beaky nose.

Their twelve months together had flown by, living in geek heaven. They were happy in their own world. Quite unexpectantly, on a daytrip to Forbidden Planet on Tin Pan Alley, they started to chat, in a socially awkward fashion, with Tarquin and Gwilbob, lads who were so far up the spectrum they'd fallen off. The four social hand grenades fast became besties who were now members of their D&D clan – the Abimelech Crawlers. Nigel had left her that morning with the inspiring words, "Adventurer, you must use all your abilities and skills to secure employment", while working his ASD level-3 face to the max.

At the Job Centre Greta browsed the cards fastidiously and was really disappointed; they all wanted years of experience. She was about to give up hope when she saw a card saying 'Assistant wanted for local business. Must be computer literate for data entry/word processing. Tea-making essential.' She prided herself for her computer prowess, due to Nigel and her being the proud owners of a Commodore 64. This was perfect, thought Greta as she grabbed the card and proceeded to hand it to the assistant.

"I would like to apply for this," said Greta in a monotone, ending the sentence with her mouth open like she was catching flies, an unfortunate habit she'd had since childhood.

The lady looked at the pitiful vision in front of her wearing a Pac-Man T-shirt, wondering what she was applying for.

"Take a seat, dear. I'll just get the details up for you. So you're computer literate?"

"Yes. I have a Commodore 64 at home. Nigel and I do stuff on there for D&D."

"D&D?" asked the assistant, looking bewildered.

"Yes," said Greta. "Dungeons & Dragons. We put all our ideas for campaigns into the computer. Nigel's a Dungeon Master," said Greta proudly.

"I see," said the assistant, none the wiser. "What are your tea-making skills like?"

"It's not really difficult, is it? You put a teabag in the cup and pour in water."

"Well, this sounds perfect for you. Let's just see what company it is, and we can set up an interview for you. It's… Oh dear… I say… Hunter & Sons."

Sensing her trepidation, Greta asked, "What's wrong with that?"

"Oh, nothing, dear. Nothing at all," said the assistant in a tone not really convincing Greta. "Shall I fix an interview for you?"

"Yes, please."

"Anything else you would like me to add when I contact them? Something to whet their appetites."

"Well, Nigel tells me that I have loads of charisma and roll high dice scores on that ability."

"Righty-ho," said the assistant, again having no idea what this strange girl was talking about and noting she had all the charisma of a lettuce leaf. Besides, maybe it would be better if she didn't find employment at this particular establishment.

LAND OF CONFUSION

"Come frough, Victor. I was just 'aving a cuppa, reading the newspaypahs. Got a nice fresh pot going."

"Fanks, Rosie. Could murdah a cup of tea."

"Make yourself at 'ome," said Nan as she sat down and poured herself and Victor a brew.

"They look nice, Rosie," said Victor, pointing to the cakes on the plate.

"'Elp yourself. They're almond slices."

"Don't mind if I do," said Victor, taking one. "Anyfink of interest in the *Gazette*?"

"I was just looking at it before you got 'ere. You'll nevah believe it. Someone 'as only gone and painted ovah the CND Peace Mural in black, and I can't say what else they've sprayed on it," said Nan as she turned the newspaper to him, showing him the photo on the front page: **FUCK HACKNEY COUNCIL SUPPORT NUKING.**

"Whoevah would do such a fing, Victor? I mean, there's a picture of it before it was vandalised, and I can't say it's to me taste, but you can't just go 'round vandalising fings, can ya?"

"Fing is, I got some sympafy for whoevah dun that, but not the bad language. No need for that. All this CND cobblahs. These youngstahs nevah 'ad to fight in a real war. I mean this Cold War. What's that all 'bout, Rosie? We was in the real fing."

"We must 'ave been in an 'ot war, where fings really did 'appen."

"We 'ad to 'ave, the bomb as collateral. Back in '45 we didn't 'ave a choice. The Krauts, they surrendered to us on 7th May 1945. We'd seen off 'em and the Italians. Japan was the only fing left fighting for the Axis powahs. Us Allies, we 'ad to sort out the Pacific War cos the Japs would fight until the bittah end."

"I know, Victor, and it's not like we didn't warn that emperor what's 'is face. Nevah remembahed 'is name. I just used to call him Ming the Merciless."

"It was Emperor 'Iro'ito, and 'e wouldn't accept defeat. We'd already bombed Tokyo to smivahreens. We 'ad no choice to fire the atomic bomb. Japs nevah 'ad one. Course we 'ad that Man'attan Project wiv Roosevelt and we developed atomic bombs the little boy and the fat man. We will nevah 'ave a leadah like Churc'ie again, and 'e was right not to trust Stalin, even when the Russian's was fighting for us. Churc'ill knew what game Stalin was playing. 'E 'ad 'is numbah – a gigantic menace trying to spread communism all ovah Europe."

"Communism don't work, Victor. Look at 'em people trapped be'ind the Iron Curtain and those trying to fling 'emselves ovah the Berlin Wall."

"It's these left-wing lunatics, Rosie, that cause all the problems in the world if you ask me. Just look at 'Itler and Mussolini. They realised people would fight for their county but not their class, so they just added a big dollop of nationalism to socialism. A big scam. 'Itler, Mussolini and Stalin, like free peas in a pod. Not that we didn't ave one we 'ad that Labour

MP Mosley who started the British Union of Fascists. Trying to infect us wiv national socialism. Course MI5 got 'im. Was talking to me old China Malcom I used to work wiv in Clarnico. 'E's now living in Islington Norf. They've got one of 'em commies as an MP. 'As no self-respect; walks 'round dressed scruffy like a tramp."

"You'd fink 'e would dress propah and 'ave some decorum, Victor."

"This MP is one of 'em 'ipocrite preachy types. 'E's a vegetarian."

"Remembah when we fought Lisa 'ad caught that."

"'E was seen outside 'is 'ouse in Finsbury Park stuffing 'is face wiv Kentucky Fried Chicken, gravy smovered 'round 'is mouf and gnawed chicken bones all ovah the floor. When one of 'is constituents brought 'im up on it, 'e said 'e was channeling 'is idol, Castro, and it was a momentary lapse of reason. Anyfink in *The Sun*?"

"Well, says 'ere in New York KAD 'ave taken responsibility for the execution of Gy-ör-gy Schwartz, not sure 'ow you pronounce that, a billionaire found dead in his Fiff Avenue apartment, gassed to deaf by 'is state-of-the-art Zyklon B oven along wiv his children who'd been executed wiv a Sauer 38H pistol. KAD was unavailable to comment as to why they'd nailed the newborn baby, who is believed to be called Alex, to the wall and scrawled in blood 'Magneto' next to 'im. They said they was finishing off a job that should 'ave been dun in 1944 'Ungary by a misguided amateur group. Crystal Lake, who's the foundah of KAD, which stands for Kill All Dudes and is a splintah group of the defunct MAF– she sounds a right one – she wants to bring down patriarchal govahnments and 'ave the male sex obliterated. She called for all women to march ovah their male leadahs' vile faces in the dead of night armed wiv Thompson submachine guns. She describes 'erself as a UVRF, that's an ultra-violent radical feminist, who actively encourages misandry. What the bleeding 'ell is that?"

"Sounds nasty, like some sort of severe diarrhoea. This Crystal sounds like a right charmah."

"Victor, 'ow is it possible for 'em to get 'old of guns so easy ovah there?"

"Anyone can go into this place called Walmart and buy a gun as long as they can prove they're sixteen and they got somefink wiv their name and address on. It was on the front page of *The Guardian*, not that I read it, just seen it at the newsagents. I like a more factual paypah."

"'Ave a butchahs at what Crystal looks like."

Nan turned the paper around, showing a voluptuous woman with flowing caramel hair, cheek bones you could cut yourself on and cat-like, amber eyes. Armed Amazonian female guards of all ethnicities flanked her.

"She wants all bepenised creatures to do the right fing, and until they can be totally exterminated, they should perform self-penectomies. In a moment of uncharactahistic kindness, Crystal said KAD are willing to supply cleavahs to 'elp 'em out, setting aside $5 million of her $600 million fortune to assist. Crystal is the only daughtah of deceased Jason Lake, the multimillionaire ownah of Lake Media, who made 'is money as a smut peddlah wiv popular magazines *Fur Burgah* and *Readah's Grandmuvah's*. Lake was found dead five years ago. 'E'd been disemboweled, be'eaded and quartered. It's still being investigated as to whevah the suicide note was aufentic or not."

"Is this that Piers Morgan again? I'm not cutting off me todgah. I feel really strongly 'bout that."

"I don't blame you, Victor. Anyways this billionaire Schwartz was the foundah of The Murky Society and Rent-a-Mob who was bankrolling this gang called AFA, Anti-Fascist Action. Their leadah Alessandro Pavolini 'as stated that they 'ave now folded 'as since 'e popped 'is clogs no ovah God complexed hypocritical duplicitous entity had come forward to fund their reactionary lunatic app-arat-chik cult. M17 masks didn't pay for 'emselves. Alessandro 'as now joined the Temple of Set 'as they 'ad the same deranged principles."

BLACK NIGHT

It was midnight at the abattoir in Dagenham on a moonless night. The butchery stunk of death, the walls and floors covered with blood stains and sprayed animal shit. Carcasses hung from metal spikes on the ceiling of bovine, porcine and ovine. Mat and Nic had driven their captor over from 150 Sandringham Road, otherwise known as 'The Shop', where the inhabitants were selling crack. His accomplice hadn't been there, but they would sort that problem out in the very near future.

"You diabolical fucking libahty-takah. 'Ave I got cunt written on me fore'ead. I control fings 'round 'ere," said Mat as Nic dragged Delbert into the urban dungeon.

"Who's been supplying you wiv the crack?" asked Nic as he lifted him, piercing the back of his neck onto a meat hook, his skin ripping, the slicing sound eerily echoing through the slaughter hall.

"Mercy, mercy. Ise beg yuh," murmured Delbert.

"I'll show you mercy," said Mat as he punched him repeatedly, full force with his fists, in the face, the gut-wrenching sound of his nose and eye socket being broken. Blood freely flowed down his green, yellow and black T-shirt.

"Who's supplying you wiv the crack? Don't tell us it's that bent pig Roy Lewandowski. 'E's small fry, and 'e will be dealt wiv. Who is flooding the area wiv this shit?"

"Yeh," sneered Nic, "the Scousah wiv the blond poncy 'air, just anuvah of Stoke Newington's finest who finks 'e's a dealah. We've got plans for Blondie."

Delbert struggled to speak from his bloodied mouth, "Yuh dun know he run road. He not Babylon. Ise beg yuh, lef mi. If Ise loud up di ting, Ise dies a million deaths. You can only mash mi up once. He di serpent, di zombie master. Mi nuh bag o' wire."

"This fucked-up drug that you coons created 'as fried your brain. The only good fing you've brought ovah 'ere is Um Bongo. I 'as that wiv Frosties for breakfast, but that's nufink to brag 'bout. Just giz us a name. Stop talking Voodoo bollocks. You come ovah 'ere and can't even be bovered to learn propah English."

"Do you wanna end up like 'em?" asked Mat, pointing at the carcasses rippled with fat and bloody flesh.

"He not mon; he Baka. Ise beg for mercy, purlease."

"You two are shitty arse-feedahs. We need to know where you're getting the supply from."

"Mi nuh biznizz. Ise can't. He comes from di udder side. Papa Legba guides him."

"What's the uvah side. Is that, like, Norf Lundun? And who the fuck is Papa Begba?" asked Nic.

Mat grabbed the impaled man's right hand and forced it against the wall. Taking a saw from a shelf, he started to saw through his right arm above the elbow. Delbert screamed in agony, passing in and out of consciousness. Mat carved through nerves, muscles and the humerus bone until it dropped to the resin floor, the stump gushing with blood. Delbert's body swung from the meat hook, but he was faintly alive, making imperceptible breathing sounds.

"Party ain't ovah yet, mate," said Nic as he chucked a bucket over him that held the offal organs and entrails of the slaughtered stock.

Delbert's body bucked back to life again, like he'd been administered with a shock-paddle dose of electricity.

"Ah, nice to 'ave you back wiv us. Now speak up. I'm asking really fucking nicely," said Nic.

It took all Delbert's strength to speak. He mumbled incoherently, "Mi drop out now, beg yuh, Bondye, take mi and protect mi from di serpent."

Nic took out his Stanley knife and drove it into Delbert's face, cutting and hacking from the corner of his mouth to the top of his cheek, which was now hanging off grotesquely and gushing with blood. "You fought Freddie Kruegah was an evil bastard. Fink again. This is what a real 'orror show looks like," said Nic as he plunged the knife, slitting Delbert's throat, severing his carotid artery and jugular vein. The venous bleed to death would be rapid. Blood squirted uncontrollably as Delbert took his last breath.

"Twins are on their way to get this cunt ovah to that moody crem. We'll get that crack whore Nyoka, but first it's your birfday."

"Too fucking right. Got an epic one planned."

"Still gotta tell Lisa. She's gonna 'ave a coronary. Just take it easy on the powdah. Fine to 'ave a bit every now and again, but keep it in check. You're 'oovahing the stuff up."

"It's all undah control, bruv. Like I say, it sharpens me up."

MONEY FOR NOTHING

On Derry Street, Kensington, Rattlesnake was buoyant. He was on his way to meet Seb Slick, the man who would make him the next rap superstar. The small thing was that the Grand Poobah at Bog Standard Records didn't know it. He was dressed to impress, wearing a Moschino silver tracksuit teamed with Nike gold Vandal trainers. Crucifixes the size of electricity pylons hung around his neck. As he walked, in the bouncy swagger with faux limp in a trance-like state, he periodically stopped to do an impromptu rap while drumming on rubbish bins with his car keys.

Seb Slick, real name Bernard Pilkington, was born in Shitterton, Dorset. At the age of eighteen he was accepted into Thames Polytechnic. A puny guy at five-foot-three, Seb had an enormous ego fuelled by short-man syndrome. He'd enrolled on a degree course in the performing arts and criminology in the Woolwich campus. The freshman found student digs in St. John's Terrace, Plumstead, with likeminded students doing similar nonsense degrees. It was here he reinvented himself as Sebastian Slick. He felt the name fitted him perfectly, exuding dynamism. This transmogrification included cube heels and a rat ponytail. The next three years had been an eye-opener for Seb, putting the world to rights at the student union bar. There really was nothing that couldn't be resolved over a pint of snakebite and a Rothmans.

After graduating with a degree no good to man nor beast, surprisingly he couldn't find a job for love nor money. He'd been laughed out of Woolwich Job Centre. The jumped-up employee had tears rolling down his face when Seb proudly announced his qualification. The jobsworth even had the cheek to tell him he had to go out the back to get a form, obviously to compose himself and try to act with some degree of professionalism, the belly laugh having totally taken over his body, the sound of sniggering deafening.

"We don't really have much cause for profilers who work through the medium of dance in here," he managed to just about get out in between involuntary giggling, making his whole-body shake. The cheeky twat.

But then a slice of luck came his way while nursing a pint at the Rose Inn. He bumped into a kindred spirit, Wayne, who he'd met seeing The Buggles at Goldsmiths University. Both lads enjoyed the student union band scene. They'd spend hours discussing which of these bands could be the next big thing. Wayne was understanding of Seb's predicament. He'd been surprised when after graduating with a third in sociology and basket-weaving, he hadn't been able to secure employment. Wayne was working as a runner for Bog Standard Records. It was hard work, but it was also a coveted role, as it was your first step on the ladder in the cutthroat world of the music industry. You even got to rub shoulders with stars. So far Wayne had provided a bucket when Pete Burns had been violently sick after a night at the Astoria and given tissues to Boy George when he had a nosebleed. He'd been up for three days at a house party at Steve Strange's flat. Seb, like Wayne, started as a lowly runner, but due to his obnoxious personality, which was held with high esteem in this industry, he'd risen the greasy pole with ease. He wasn't CEO yet, but he was head talent finder. The name made him chuckle. I mean, Bog Standard. Come on. That was obviously ironic unless you were a complete moron. They signed the crème de la crème. His recent signings included Falco with his breakout track, 'Rock Me Amadeus'. He'd singlehandedly launched the first Austrian rap superstar. No one knew what the fuck he was rapping about, but it didn't matter; this artist had pizzazz. Not to mention Men Without Hats people all over the country were doing 'The Safety Dance', albeit most had mental health problems. But a schizophrenics' money was as good as any others'.

The money in the artists and repertoire department to find and develop new artists that was thrown at him was mind-blowing. It was a constant high-speed train of drink, drugs and sluts. Last night had been raucous. It had started at 5pm. He and some colleagues had downed a bottle of Hennessy Paradis Cognac in the office, smoked a couple of joints, then on to The Cross Keys, Chelsea, for cocktails. Once halfway inebriated, they headed to Annabel's nightclub, then, completely monged out, to a house party. The whole affair fuelled by copious amounts of coke. He vaguely remembered a game of nude twister. At about 10am he decided that he should make his way to work. Stumbling out onto the road, the daylight quite brutal, he went to put on his Cartier sunglasses but realised he'd lost them. Hailing a cab, he made the Pakistani cabdriver make a pitstop to Brewer Street, where he picked up a brass who looked passable, but then in his completely fucked-up state he would've fucked a watermelon. Grabbing her into the cab, he directed her down to his 2-inch, throbbing cock, ignoring the weeping cold sores around her mouth, imaging that Sam Fox was giving him a blow job, not some toothless sixty-year-old with frazzled bleached hair. The cab driver had been incensed. "You white people are all the same. You disgust me."

As the cab moved towards his offices, a now-frantic driver swerved to a halt, desperate to get his white trash cargo out of his car. Seb, meanwhile, came hard and fast into what he thought was Sam's mouth. Pulling up his Armani trousers, he yanked the prostitutes head roughly away from him and attempted to get out of the cab. This simple task was difficult, as he was seeing double of everything. It took him five attempts to successfully open the cab door before falling out of the cab with the brass and tumbling to the floor. He left 'Sam' struggling on the pavement. The taxi driver was now beyond infuriated, so to deal with this inconvenience, Seb did what anyone else who earnt a packet would do: he threw two £50 notes at him. The taxi driver yelled "Dirty white pigs" as he put his foot on the gas and screeched off.

Seb staggered through the doors of Bog into the minimalist reception showcasing a black glass reception desk with the Bog Standard logo, an old-fashioned lavatory, where the lid was a record player. He passed the pretty receptionist, who he completely ignored, and proceeded to literally fall into his office, where he had a stash of 'emergency' coke and a bottle of Domestos to stick his dick in, as it killed all germs DEAD. Most adverts were lies, as his friend Ludwig, an advertising executive at Segaiolo Productions, was responsible for making many of them up, but on this one he agreed whole-heartedly – it did what it said on the bottle. It would save him a trip to the clap clinic. Rattlesnake was at the same time striding, yet with one leg purposely debilitated, to the record company. He pushed his way through the bubble-glass reception door.

"How can I help you, sir?" asked Hayley, the receptionist.

"Call mi Rattlesnake. Ise here to see Seb. Tell di mon Ise here and he see mi now."

"Of course, Mr Rattlesnake. If you take a seat, I'll call Mr Slick."

"You fine poom-poom," said Rattlesnake as his gold-toothed grin turned into a menacing sneer.

Pimp-rolling to the plush sofa, Rattlesnake sat down and made himself at home, settling back and spreading his ridiculously long limbs. Hayley Baxter had been the receptionist for eight months. So far it had been a dream job, coming to work looking like she'd stepped off a Paris catwalk. Today she was dressed in a red leather pencil skirt with matching jacket, teamed with stilettos boots. Hayley made the call to Seb, a man she thought was a sleazebag, but she was hell bent in carving a career out in the record industry, so she remained professional. Her mother had told her that the colour of her skin would make it three times as difficult for her to succeed in life. This had only made her more determined to thrive.

"Mr Slick, there's a Mr Rattlesnake in reception for you. I don't think he has an appointment, at least it isn't in your diary, but he said you'll see him."

Seb told the receptionist he'd get back to her and hung up. Rattlesnake. Why did that stick in his mind, and how dare he just rock up here without an invite to see him. Seb tried to remember. Had he in his inebriated state told someone last night he would see them today. Was this person a real talent or had this been some muppet he'd just been bigging himself up to? Admitting it was probably the latter, he wondered how he'd tell the dollybird to get rid of the talentless mongoloid. Then, in his narcotic-hazed mind, he had an almost crystal-clear recollection, the rap so hideously bad. Seb could hear Rattlesnake's thick Jamaican voice:

Di FEDS, dey inject mi wid MKUltra
Den like abracadabra I finks Ise Cleopatra
In di pyramids of Peckham

FEDS mind control tinks Ise in a jam.

Now Seb found himself in a state of hysterics. The tears started to roll down his eyes as his belly started to ache, he was laughing so hard.

Bluds fink Ise a bit of a nutter
Rapping is mi bread and butter
Mess with mi and yuh be in di gutter
Dead like di black Dahli... er.

Then there were intermittent sounds, like someone was clanking keys on a bit of metal, interjected with guttural banshee wails, the rap so bad it was an insult to the word. If you wanted genius lyrics, look no further than one of his signings, Half Man Half Biscuit. It made him beam with pride when he thought of the sheer brilliance of 'All I Want for Christmas is a Dukla Prague Away Kit'. The genius of Nigel Blackwell's sardonic, gnostic, and yet moronic, lyrics. Even Dylan would struggle to come up with verse like that. There was only one thing for it, thought Seb. More drugs. Then he'd laugh in the face of the fuckwit. Spilling a load of blow over his desk, Seb proceeded to hoover up a monster line. Boy, this Rattlesnake was so going to get it. He couldn't help but smile at the thought of him showing his male prowess off to the receptionist, who was a dead ringer for the singer Vanity, all coffee skin and flowing, black hair. Probably by lunchtime he'd be balls deep in her over his desk. Seb's brain was now in Max Headroom, self-admiration overload. He needed to get rid of Rattlesnake pronto. He had a megalodon to fry. Information had come to him that Pat Sharp was about to hit the recording studio. He'd gone straight into battle, and Seb was at the cusp of signing him. He made a mental note to look into this Nookie mullet that Pat was showcasing. This trend had been picked up by the gays of Earl's Court. Gays tended to pick up on trends before anyone else; they had an inbuilt radar. He wondered briefly if this Nookie could sing. Not that it mattered; he could still get a record deal.

Seb swung his office door open straight into a six-foot-five brick shithouse. Rattlesnake had manoeuvred his way over to the door that was marked 'Sebastian Slick'. Hayley had decided not to confront him.

"Wah gwaan, mon?" asked Rattlesnake with a sneer.

A startled Seb looked up at the Rastafarian and said, "Mr Rattlesnake, so pleased to meet you at last."

"Call mi Rattlesnake, mon. Ise tink we gonna bi good doops. Make yuh loads of cheddar."

"Yes, Mr Rattlesnake—I mean Rattlesnake."

"What deal you doing wid mi? Mi shit's gonna sell millions, mon."

"Come into my office. I'm honoured you're here. I have this stupid PA who failed to set up an appointment to get you in here ASAP. After I heard your demo, I was, well, blown away. Women, huh. Only good for one thing. She'll be getting her P45 later. To think if you hadn't had the good sense to turn up here today, Universal or Sony could've signed you, something I would've regretted for the rest of my life. I listened to your demo. It's real food for thought. There's nothing out there like this. We at Bog like to nurture our talent, give the world something to wait for. Let them wait!"

"Ise guided by the lwa. Mi be tinking a multi-million-pound, ten-album deal."

"Rattlesnake, YOU are not some public-school boy who lives in a mansion in Richmond rapping about how dangerous his hood is. YOU are the real deal. YOU are the voice on the street. YOU aren't a manufactured one-hit wonder. YOU are an artist like Reed, Morrison and Minogue."

Rattlesnake was now lapping this sycophantism up like a man lodged between Traci Lords' legs.

"This is thinking-man's music. The world isn't ready for this," said Seb in a hushed conspiratorial tone.

"Nah aks Chrise. Yurh're witnessing di strength of street politricks. Which one yuh like best, mon?"

"Uh, well, that is one tough question. It's too hard to pick just one. With this level of genius, it would be impossible to choose. Would I insult you if I told you your work is haunting in a postmodernism sort of way." Every track was garbage, and he had no idea what any of the abortions were called. "Do you have any thoughts on the name of your first LP?"

"Me was tinking 'Straight Out of Peckham'. Yuh feeling mi, mon. Ise no idea what you on 'bout post. Mi nuh writing a letter. Mi rapping to mi people."

"That's a thought-provoking album title. This isn't throwaway bubble-gum pop. Over my dead body will I let Stock Aiken Waterman anywhere near you. It's just that I don't think the world is ready for this level of genius right now. Look at the pop charts. We have Madonna; give it a year or two and no one will remember her. She's just a pop tart. No staying power. She's selling units now, but I know her record company aren't taking her seriously. Believe me, I know my stuff. You need to hone your skills. You're an artist like, uh, Pink Floyd. Yeh, you know the Floyd, Waters and Gilmour. 'Several Species of Small Furry Animals Gathered Together in a Cave and Grooving with a Pict'. I mean, do you think Waters came up with a concept like that overnight? No, that was years in the wilderness living like a hermit in the Himalayan mountains to get that level of genius."

The snow-white boy was losing Rattlesnake here. "Yeh, mon, wi talking 'bout mi here, not dis Floyd ting. Dis furry animals ting, me knows nufink 'bout dat. Stop yuh blabba mout. Mi no like bumbaclaat."

"What I mean is you need time to hone your skills like some

Tibetan monk in isolation and then come back guns blazing in say a year, when people will appreciate your music. It's too before its time. Trust me on this. The world isn't quite ready for it. We'll of course keep very loosely in touch. I wouldn't want to cause any noise pollution when you're weaving your craft. You'll be my most exciting signing since Sigue Sigue Sputnik. Are you *au fait* with them they're like Joy Division but without the humour."

"Yeh, mon. Ise see dis going global. Fiyah bun, Ise not impressed wid rappers, like di message don't do drugs from Grandmaster Flash and Melle Mel. Like, doops, dey got dat wrong. Ise influenced by stuff fink be big. Got bootleg tapes from across pond. Public Enemy in New York and NWA coming out of LA."

"NWA?"

"Yeh, mon, Niggaz wid Attitudes."

Seb stifled the urge to laugh, instead taking a deep gulp to stop himself.

"Yeh, like when Ise established, dese are di acts mi want to collaborate wit. Yuh feel mi."

Niggaz with Attitudes. What the fuck? And Public Enemy. Between the three losers, they'd be lucky to sell one record, and that was because they'd all clubbed in together.

"This is the start of a beautiful relationship, with me overseeing your artistic development. I can see us here at Bog offering you a record deal. The normal process would be for me to manage all aspects of the recording procedure. But you're different. We're going to give you free reign, take a totally different approach. I can't tell you how excited I am to be signing you at some time in the future. But I will be administering a strict non-interference policy."

"Yeh, mon, big tings ahead, and you do dis militantly for mi. Ise bi your number-one priority."

"We're singing off the same hymn sheet. I need you to do something for me. I need you right now to go home and look at the body of work you've submitted to me, and really listen to it. It's already out of this world, but I think you could up your game and perfect it, take it to another level. I also want you to start working on a second LP, then a third LP, then we could do something that's never been done before – release them all at the same time. Before which I'll have every music journalist in the world talking about it, get you write-ups in *Rolling Stone, Billboard* and *Woman's Own*."

"Wot 'bout mi cheddar, mon?"

"We can discuss that in the future, when we officially sign you. I mean, you're as good as signed. It's a trivial thing really, just a few bits of paper. But we're talking seven figures here. Now, Rattlesnake, keep up wid di good work, mon," said Seb, taking on a Jamaican accent. "I drink di Lilt wid di totally tropical taste. Keep loosely in touch, mon. While you're doing all the hard work, just think of me as passionately working away for you behind the scenes. Now, if you call me in say twelve months, or even longer – I don't in any way shape or form want to contaminate your genius – and let me know how your masterpieces are going. In the meantime, I'll be working up a promotional campaign frenzy, getting you on *Pebble Mill at One* and *TV-am* being interviewed by Roland Rat as a world exclusive."

Walking out of the offices, Rattlesnake was in deep thought. He could solve through mediation the problem between his *breddas* on the East and West Coast in America. He alone could make them see they were all on the same side – all *breddas* in arms. Even unite the Crips and Bloods in East LA. Then his master plan would come into play to annihilate the real enemy – *the Buckra*.

Hayley was never rogered over the desk by Seb, but five years later she was CEO of Bog. On a Wednesday night, with nothing better to do, she had tagged along to a Women First seminar called 'Is it a Girl or an Abortion?'. That evening she joined a powerful, highly influential sisterhood that brought together women from every creed, colour and religion, united in any differences for the one true cause. She dedicated her life to KAD. The speaker, Valerie Solanas, had blown her away, her most memorable quote being "Every man, deep down, knows he's a worthless piece of shit."

A CONVENTION OF DUNCES

Greta had an extra spring in her step as she walked to Hunter & Sons. She'd been working there for the last few months. All in all, she liked her job, doing everything from making endless cups of tea and general office duties. But what she really liked was being able to work on the Commodore Amiga 1000 computer. Not the prettiest girl in the world – with her coke-bottle glasses, behind which she was heavily cockeyed, with a boyish figure and lank, mousy hair – many thuggish men came in to see the brothers, but they barely looked at her, which suited Greta just fine. She found the data entry easy, so she had all the time in the world to be lost in her imagination. Daydreams of Eberron, Ravenloft and Mordenkainen.

Heading to the kitchen, she fished in her Klingons backpack, a present from Nigel, and unloaded the shopping. Teabags, milk and biscuits. Greta always wondered how Nigel managed to save up and buy her special gifts, as money was always tight. There was only one problem with the job: Mat's girlfriend. She turned up dressed to the nines carrying bags from designer shops, making a point of treating Greta like shit. Making the cups of tea just like her bosses liked and plonking them on a tray with the biscuits, she made her way into Mat's office.

"All right, darling?"

"Not bad, Mat."

"What's this, Greta?" asked Nic, pointing to her Scunthorpe 1985 Star Trek Convention T-shirt.

"Nigel and I are going to a Star Trek convention this weekend."

"What, like, to dress up as Spock and shit like that?" asked Nic, dunking his Bandit biscuit into his tea.

"No, I'll be Saavik and Nigel Sarek. But we're alien fluid at these events."

"Beam me up, Scotty," said Nic.

"Captain Kirk didn't actually say that."

"Uh, you what, darling?"

"He actually said *In the Gamesters of Triskelion* and *the Savage Curtain*, 'Scotty, beam us up'."

"Yeh, whatevah. What do you do at these conversion fings?"

"At the convention we'll watch *The Wrath of Khan*. There'll be discussions on *Arena* and *The Empath*. We'll see a Hero Type 2 Phaser and a space suit used in *The Tholian Web*. Then a meet-and-Vulcan-greet with Mark Lenard."

Mat got up and reached into his back pocket and brought out a roll of notes. "'Ere we go, darling. Somefink for the train fare."

"Thanks. Mat. I'll bring you back some Romulan biscuits."

"Fanks, but what they made of?"

Before she had time to answer, Lisa came thundering through the door.

"A pigeon has just shit on my car window. Get a cloth and clean it up, Greta," said Lisa as she made her grand entrance wearing a fuchsia peplum dress accessorised with a Yohji Yamamoto bag and Valentino high pumps.

Mouth agog, Greta scurried out to the kitchen to get a cloth and water.

"I need more money, babe," said Lisa as she plonked a lipgloss-stained kiss on Mat's cheek.

"I gave you a wad a few days ago."

"I know, but there are good sales on at Harvey Nichols, and you know I like to look good for you," said Lisa, putting on a little girl's voice and pouting, which never failed to get her her own way.

"You need to be'ave yourself. Stop ordering Greta 'round. She ain't 'ere to clean your car."

"It's not like she looked busy. She can earn the money you pay her."

"She is seriously weird. 'Ave you viddied 'er bloke. Fucking tragic," said Nic.

"Say what you want 'bout Greta; she's a good workah. She causes no aggro. 'Ow's the girls at your clubs?"

Nic didn't answer this but had the urge to smack Mat in his face, something he wanted to do more and more these days.

FADE TO GREY

"Shitty, foggy day for your birfday," said Mat as they left the Dog and Duck.

"Makes no difference to me. I intend to 'ave it large. I call this Jack the Rippah wevah. Jack was one of 'em social reformahs, you know, in 'is own way, like. Read it in *The Sun*. 'E was misundahstood."

"Social reformah? What you on 'bout?"

"I know 'e cut up a few brasses, but, like, in 'em days, who wasn't? But cos of that, rich people up West started looking at the way people was living in Whitechapel. Back then it was so bad the 'Olly would've looked like Bucking'am Palace."

"I'm sure there was an easier way to get their attention, like setting up a community group and petitioning parliament."

"Nah that's far too simple a solution. I'm finking that Jack, 'e, like, dun more good than 'arm. At the time it wouldn't 'ave seemed like that, cos they was finding dead brasses everywhere, but in the long term 'e changed fings. Not that 'e probably 'ad that in mind when 'e was carving up birds, not that it bovahs me eivah way. Goes wivout saying. 'Nuff said. You gotta give the geezah credit. Everybody brings somefink to the table."

"I fink the jury is out on that one. Try not do too much gear today. It'll addle your brain, and you really don't need that, Nic. You're stuffing more up your nose than you're selling."

"Calm down. It's just a few livenahs. I got it all undah control."

"Nic, you spent more time in the bogs than 'aving a drink wiv me in there."

"It's not a problem. Just letting me 'air down. It's me birfday. Lighten up. Stop being such a miserable cunt, will ya. Fuck me! Look at the state of it. Looks like that weirdo Steve Strange," said Nic as he saw the puss-in-booted, frilly shirted figure walking towards them on Bateman Street.

"Yeh. One of 'em gendah bendahs."

"What the fuck's a gendah bendah?"

"Fink it's some cult like the Moonies, or sometimes they call 'emselves New Romantics."

"I, like, 'adn't even 'eard of the old ones. Steve 'ad that crap club down 'ere, The Blitz. Didn't last long. Probably cos they was playing all that Kraftwerk Nazi shit. Forgettable, not like the Love 'Ole. That's gonna go down in 'istory."

As the figure moved closer to them, Nic said, "Fuck, it really is Steve Strange. Whatevah you do, bruv, don't make any eye contact wiv 'im. 'E's confused and may get the wrong idea."

But it was too late, as Steve had already caught eyes with the duo as he walked towards them, giving them a bashful smile.

"All right, mate," said Nic while diverting his eyes to the floor.

"Fuck me! More make-up than the tarts at the club wear. Weirdos are taking ovah. At the Swiss Tavern they've got this drag queen act calling 'imself Antonia LaVey. Gets up on stage dressed in stockings and suspendahs, wearing dildos for earrings, singing 'Tiptoe Frough the Tulips'. Imagine what it must be like going frough life not knowing if you're a bloke or a bird. A complete 'ead fuck. When they fink they're a bird, do they stuff their cocks up between their arse cracks on 'em days?"

"No idea, Nic. Not really fought 'bout it. Don't really want to. It's disturbing as fuck."

"Yeh, well you won't find any transylvanians at the Love 'Ole."

"It's transvestites."

"Same fing, innit. Bearded, 'airy-bollocks blokes dressing up in frocks fooling no cunt. Not even Stevie Wondah. Nufink but real birds at me club, wiv all singing and dancing fannies," said Nic as the brothers approached the door to the club.

Making sure Steve hadn't followed them, Nic gave a furtive look backwards over his shoulder, but Steve had faded into the grey fog of Soho.

"Am 'oping the twins are already 'ere. Best fing is, as it's me gaff, I don't need to go in the bogs when there's tits I can snort off."

"All right, Boss," said Dexy as Mat made his way out of the Love Hole.

"Yeh, going 'ome before I get too much earache from the missus. Not seen Nic and the twins, been in 'em private rooms for ages, so let 'em know I've gone, will ya?"

"Will do, Boss. I fink birfday boy is 'aving fun."

"Yeh, like he does every night, mate," said Mat, thinking Nic was mixing business with pleasure way too much but letting it slide for tonight. Earlier at the pub he'd been pushing Mat to be a bigger cocaine wholesaler, but Mat had high reservations about this. As he made his way across the street to his car, he saw a flash of blond hair in his periphery vision. A wild shriek and a searing hot pain, Mat fell to the ground clutching his stomach, which was spurting blood furiously, the warm sticky fluid saturating his hands as he grabbed at the laceration. Staggering, he stumbled to the floor. Blood trickled down his face, spewing from his mouth. Seconds later blackness engulfed him. Rattlesnake ran down Dean Street, his gangly legs going like the clappers, shrieking like a banshee, the sacrificial dagger dripping blood held high above his head. The blood of the firstborn who murdered his *fahda*.

LIVE TO TELL

"We've identified who stabbed Mat," said Dexy.

"Who's the diabolical libahty-taking cunt?" asked Nic, who was actually outraged that anyone thought they could mess with his family but also more than happy to be taking the reins of the firm. Nic was slouched back on Mat's chair, legs on his desk.

"It's a Yardie from Peck'am. Jacko on the door recognised 'im."

"Got a name?"

"Yeh. Snake."

"Snake? What the fuck kind of name is that? Get as many men on it as possible. These Yardies are clueless cunts. Fink there's no rules. Well there are rules. The cunt is going to find out the 'ard way."

"That's anuvah fing. I fink Snake's the one who's supplying that crack whore on Sandring'am. Sid's onto it."

"I want 'im found, pronto. I got the twins sorting out that Turk who's been pushing brown on Queensbridge. When will they learn?"

"Yeh, I'll get the men onto it now. You okay?"

"Gutted 'bout Mat, but the firm goes on. Not like I'm flatlining wivout 'im. It's all running like clockwork."

"'Ow you feeling, son?" asked Nan as she plonked herself down on the chair next to his hospital bed. "Brought you some Trio biscuits and your post. I keep forgetting to give it to you."

"I feel like I've been stabbed, Nan."

"But are you all right in yourself?"

"Yeh, I feel just great, Nan. Nevah betta. Doctors say I should be discharged next week."

The only reason Mat was alive was due to the quick thinking of Dexy. He'd seen the shadow jump out from the night and stab him. Dexy had run over to Mat, yelling at the other doormen to call an ambulance. Ripping his shirt off, he'd wrapped it tightly around the gushing wound into a tourniquet and applied pressure to stop the loss of blood. The head doorman had stopped him haemorrhaging and bleeding to death. The wound was deep, and it had nicked the abdominal aorta towards the back of the spine. If it had been any deeper, his circulatory system would have immediately collapsed, and his life span would have been minutes, perilously in danger of dying by exsanguination. Mat suffered both external and internal bleeding, losing four pints of blood. Once he got to hospital, he was put on life support, where medics pumped blood into him. It was three days before he regained consciousness. Nan held a vigil over his bed. Lisa, unable to cope with the situation, broke down in hysterical tears and generally caused a scene.

Propped up on a pillow in a private hospital room, Mat was churning things over in his head. He'd told his men just to monitor Rattlesnake but not to touch him. This was personal, and Mat would be the executioner on this occasion.

As it transpired, no one had seen hide nor hair of him. He'd disappeared into thin air. He hadn't been to his flat or any of his associates. The only reason any of them were still of this earth was that at some point they believed Rattlesnake would contact them and lead Mat's men to him. His men would find him in time. They'd turn over every stone in the Smoke if they had to. Still in considerable pain and discomfort, Mat was thankful for the morphine drip, although against doctors' orders he was weening himself off it. He would rather be in some pain than not in control.

"Well, you're on the mend, son. That is the main fing. And in the meantime, Nic is running everyfink for you, so there's nufink to worry 'bout; you just concentrate on getting yourself well."

That was a problem for Mat. He had no choice, lying in hospital, but he had reservations about Nic taking over the reins. The sooner he got them back the better. He was the boss. Nic and the twins had been in and out to see him, but he'd been in a daze with all the medication.

"Who's outside, Nan?"

"Dexy and that lad. You know… Can't fink of his name… Wiv a crew cut and big nose. Is it Brian? Or, no, could be Billy. I gave 'em a flask of tea and some custard creams."

Mat had had two men outside since he'd been admitted. This hadn't gone down well with the hospital staff, but they were soon made aware that they had no say in the situation. For all the Hunters knew, Rattlesnake may come to the hospital and try to finish Mat off. Both looked at the door as Nurse Latimer came in to check his vitals.

"How are we today, Mr Hunter?"

"Can't complain, really, darling. 'Oping to be out soon. I don't really do 'ospitals." Nurse Latimer was the antithesis of the sexy nurse. She was about six feet tall, stocky and had an unfortunate face resembling Les Dawson. The nurse started to check his respiration rate.

"What's the 'ospital food like, son?"

"Can't eat it, Nan. It's disgusting."

To this, Nurse Latimer tutted, her face morphing into an ugly grimace, which was ignored by Mat and Nan.

"I'll start bringing you in a plate each day. Do you a nice steak and chips tomorrah."

"Fanks, Nan. It's not like Lisa would fink to do that."

"Where is Lady Muck?"

"To be 'onest, Nan, I would ravah be stabbed again than see 'er today. She's doing me 'ead in. But lucky me, she's coming in."

Since Mat had regained consciousness, Lisa had been nothing but a giant pain in the backside, making everything all about *her*. If a visitor asked Mat how he was, Lisa elected to tell everyone how *she* was coping with the situation, as it had been so difficult for her. She insisted on showing Mat signs of her love by jumping on him to cuddle and kiss him, making Mat wince in pain as she nearly dislodged his many stitches.

"Oh, Mat, I thought I'd lost you. It's been so awful for me. You really should take me to New York when you're better so that I can have some me time and recover."

Now that Mat had finally taken Lisa to Paris, all she talked about was going to New York, shopping on Fifth Avenue and staying at the penthouse suite at the Four Seasons. Nurse Latimer continued to take Mat's blood pressure, earwigging the conversation. She'd met Lisa along with all the other doctors and nurses. She was universally disliked. She had this rude habit of clicking her fingers if she needed their attention.

"Maybe in her own way she's just trying to cheer you up, son."

"Cheer me up, Nan, by spending fousands of pounds

shopping then complaining about this, that and the uvah. Leave it out. At least when I was unconscious I couldn't 'ear 'er."

"Well you need some cheering up, son. 'Ow 'bout a nice game of 'Appy Families. Always did the trick if you was off school unwell."

"Nah, you're all right, Nan. Been told by the doctors, wiv all the painkillers I'm on me brain can't take anyfink too mentally challenging, like."

"Okay, son. Be somefink for you to look forward to when you're betta."

"Just the fought of it is making me feel betta, Nan."

"Mr Hunter," said Nurse Latimer in her abrupt tone. "I'll be back in a few hours to check your vitals again and change your dressing. Is there anything else I can do for you?"

"No, fanks, Nurse." Mat just wanted to get rid of the monstrosity. She wasn't exactly doing anything for his mood.

Mat watched the whale stomp out of the room as Lisa strutted in, practically barging into her. Without an oops or sorry, Lisa made her entry, dressed to the nines in a cerise ra-ra dress, black fishnet tights and Mui Mui heels.

"I've had a mare of a time up West. First Sid couldn't find a parking space near to Harvey Nics, then when he did it was a good five-minute walk to get there. Then they didn't have a pair of Manolo Blahniks in my size that I really wanted, so I had to compensate and buy three pairs of Gucci shoes. I was fuming, and I made sure the sales assistant knew. Then I went to Harrods, and I was just about spent, so I stopped off at the a champagne bar there and had a few to cheer myself up. I picked out six dresses I liked. I was feeling a bit better; that was, until I saw the queue. There must have been about half a dozen people in front of me. I had to wait ten minutes to be served. I was so annoyed when I got back in the car, I told Sid to drop me off outside the Ritz and wait for me while I had a late lunch. I just about managed to calm myself down because I had to come over and see you to cheer you up."

"That sounds like an awful day, Lisa."

"I know, babe. While we're on the subject of me, for once don't send that creepy man again to drive me. He makes my skin crawl. I keep telling you, don't I?"

Mat had made a mental note a long time ago of always sending Sid to drive her. He took perverse pleasure in it.

"Get anyfink for me, did ya? Seeing as I'm lying 'ere in an 'ospital bed. Like some Opal Fruits?"

"No, babes, I really didn't have time today. Didn't even get half the stuff I wanted. I'll need to go back in tomorrow. I've seen this lovely bag in the window of Chanel. Anyway, I think I'm due a bit of pampering. Good thing I've booked a spa day at Sanctuary on Saturday. Nan, can you make sure you get Mat some Opal Fruits. Just because you're in hospital doesn't mean it's all about *you*. I've been suffering too with all the stress."

Not quite believing what Lisa was coming out with, Mat and Nan stared at her in abject disbelief.

"Lisa, somefink I 'ave been meaning to say to you, and more important now since I was attacked. When I send one of me blokes out to mind you, that's what they're doing. Looking out that nobody messes wiv ya. They're not there to carry your shopping. Undahstand? They work for *me*, not *you*. Can you imagine someone started giving you aggro? What they gonna do? Smack 'em over the 'ead wiv an 'at box. They ain't your servants. If you can't carry all your shopping, don't buy so much."

Perching herself on the bed, Lisa took Mat's hand and stroked his forehead. "Ahh, Mr Grumpy, got to get you better, haven't we? So we can fly off to New York. When we're there, we must make sure we get a booking at Dorsia for dinner."

"Can't wait for that," Mat said flatly. "All these fings I got to look forward to."

Not in the slightest picking up on his frosty tone, Lisa said, "Nan, any chance you can come over later and do some cleaning. I haven't had time, what with being here and the worry."

"'Course. I can get everything shipshape for Mat coming 'ome. You sure you don't want to come and stay wiv me? Nan can look aftah ya. Get ya betta."

Before Mat had a chance to speak, Lisa piped in, "Just as long as you get the flat ready and, say, come around every other day to clean, Mat will be fine with me. We can just get takeaways. I'll get Greta to do a shop in Harrods Food Hall. I won't have time. I'll be looking after Mat."

Nan was once again rendered speechless but kept her mouth shut. The last thing she wanted was a scene with Mat now on the mend.

"One thing that did make me smile today. I got approached by a scout called Mike Diamond from the Samantha Bond Modelling Agency. He said I could make a fortune as a glamour model. It's the second time. Remember when I got approached by a scout from Yvonne Paul?"

"Ovah me dead body, Lisa. No way are you getting your tits out on page 3."

"Lisa, don't get Mat all worked up. 'E 'as been frough enouf."

"I didn't take his card," said Lisa. "I'm just telling you I could if I wanted to be one."

"I'm feeling tired now, so fink it's time you went so I can 'ave a kip."

"Okay, Mr Stroppy," said Lisa, planting glossed lips on his. "Nan, we'll go back to Mat's. You can make a start on the flat, and I can try on my new stuff. It's a bit of a tip at the moment. Just been too upset to do anything. Mat, I'll need a top-up in my bank account this month. I'm running a bit low, and you have to keep your princess happy, don't you? See you tomorrow. Can't come in until late. I need to get my hair and nails done."

Later that afternoon Mat had an epiphany. He'd come close to death and survived. This was a new lease of life, and things were going to change. Lisa's days were numbered. She was nothing but an albatross around his neck, albeit it a very pretty one with a killer body. He'd had a long-overdue wake-up call following recent events. Lisa was only good for one thing, and he didn't need to be in a relationship with her to get that.

"It's not working, Lisa. It 'asn't for me for a long time. It's ovah," said Mat.

"After everything I've done for you. Been by your hospital bed day and night. Stuck by you through thick and thin."

"Frough fick and fin. You're 'aving a giraffe. Babe, you breeze in and see me when you feel like. You ain't been there for me day and night, and when you are 'ere, you fink it's all 'bout you."

"Mat, you're not feeling well. The medication is obviously making you say things you don't mean. We're good together. We're going to get engaged."

"Lisa, it's nufink to do wiv the meds. I know exactly what I'm saying, We ain't getting engaged, we ain't getting married and I don't give a fuck if I evah see ya again."

"You dirty, rotten bastard. I gave you everything."

"You what, Lisa? You're an emotional and financial vampire who 'as practically sucked me dry. Well, no fucking more! And don't fink this is like the uvah times when we 'ave an argument and we finish. This is it, darling. No more cash 'andouts, and the car is going. You're on your own."

"What about New York?"

"There's no New York. I should 'ave 'ad a medal for not strangling you wiv me bare 'ands when we went to Paris."

Lisa narrowed her eyes and said, "You'll regret this, Mat. I'll make sure of that. I'm the best thing that's ever happened to you."

With that, Lisa flounced off with a face like thunder. She tried to mentally tell herself they would get back together like all the other times they had split up, but something at the back of her mind was telling her that this time he meant it.

"Darling, just make sure you leave the car keys at the flat and all your stuff is gone when I get 'ome. If it's not, it's going to the tip."

RUTHLESS PEOPLE

"All right, mate? That Santos?"

"It is. I assume this is Mat's brother; otherwise, you wouldn't have this number."

"Yeh, that's right, mate. It's Nic. Mat's in 'ospital. 'E was stabbed by some darkie foreign bastard."

"Oh, those darkie foreigners," said Santos drolly. "Yes, we are aware of the situation, Mr Hunter."

"So Mat said you wanted to meet up today at the Lanesborough at two, but somefink 'as come up, like, and I can't make it, so, well, fought I could swing by tomorrah at say four-ish. 'Ow's that sound?"

"Ahh, I see, you're too busy to meet with me at the arranged time," said Santos in a controlled voice. Nic was too hungover to pick up on the underlying menace.

"Yeh, like I said, mate, but can do tomorrah."

"It must be, Mr Hunter, of the utmost importance if you are proposing to rearrange. I shall look forward to our meeting tomorrow."

"Yeh, like, me too, mate. Will try be there as near to four as I can. Just in case, say any time between four and four-firty.

I should be able to do that, but if it's any latah, I'll try and get on the blowah to ya."

"As you wish, Mr Hunter, and thank you for giving us a window to meet you that is convenient for you," said Santos as he terminated the call. Santos straight away made another call.

"Are you fucking mental, Nic? I just 'ad Santos on the blowah. You cancelled the meet-up."

"I just rearranged. Said I could meet 'im tomorrah. 'E was fine 'bout it."

"No, 'e wasn't fine 'bout it, and why exactly can't you meet 'im today? Anuvah 'eavy night on the powdah, was it? Just get your 'ead togevah. I got to go to the Lanesborough to smoov fings ovah. Stay away from the fucking coke and sort yourself out. You're becoming a liability."

"Bruv, you're getting bent out of shape 'bout nufink. Besides, while you 'ave been out of action, I 'ave been running everyfink. Not that I'll get any fanks for it."

"Nic," said Mat through gritted teeth, barely able to control his anger, "you nevah rearrange a meet wiv the Columbians. I 'ave spent time building a relationship wiv 'em. You don't fuck wiv 'em evah. Escobar can be like Santa-fucking-Clause and keep the snowfall coming, or he can just as easy cut us off. That doesn't mean *we* don't work wiv *'im* any more, bruv. *'E* gets rid of *us*. Undahstand?" With that, Mat terminated the call on his mobile.

Back at his house, suffering from the mother of all hangovers, Nic was thinking, who the fuck did Mat think he was, talking to him like that? He had it all under control. He'd more that been a stand-in boss. He should be the boss.

Mat winced as he got up out of his hospital bed. The pain was now somewhat bearable. He was still taking the strong painkillers, but only a quarter of what they were giving him. Within the next day or two he would wean himself completely off. Mat dressed himself and made his way out, whereupon he took car keys from Dexy. He needed to do damage control. It wasn't lost on Santos that Mat was making his way over to the hotel from his hospital bed. He wouldn't make a big deal of this with Mat. He was professional, and business was business. But he would be making it clear in the future that he would have no future dealings with his sibling. The brother was obviously a liability, and that wasn't to be tolerated in their operation. Every cog of their billionaire enterprise had to run in tandem. They'd had no problems with the *guapo* gringo. In fact, Escobar held him in high esteem.

RISKY BUSINESS

"Nic, on what fucking planet did you fink it was a good idea to take out the Turkish cunt's family?"

"'E was moving serious weights of brown and needed to be taught a lesson, and any uvah slags who fink they're dealing 'round 'ere wivout coming frough us."

"Let me get this straight. You took out a whole Turkish family just cos 'e was dealing on our manor. You got the twins to drive past 'is 'ouse, spray it wiv bullets from 'Eckler & Koch MP5s then frow a Molotov cocktail frough 'is window."

"Yeh, well that more or less sums it up, like. When you was in 'ospital, I 'ad to make all the decisions, and, like, no fuckah was gonna fink the firm was weak. It was touch and go wiv ya. That's when libahty-taking cunts sense weakness. They smell blood. I 'ad to send out a clear fucking message."

"You dun that, all right. You took out 'is wife and two kids – free civilians."

"Nah, bruv, was four. 'Is old woman was there as well. Twins done a propah job, like. No cunt was getting out of there alive."

"Nic, you should 'ave just dealt wiv the cunt by torturing 'im for days wiv an electric saw, then shot 'im at point-blank range, but left the civilians alone."

"Mat, not sure where you stand on this. You need to come off the fence. And innocent? That's, like, debatable."

"Debatable?"

"I've been told the old woman and 'is missus been seen buying tin foil in bulk from Safeway, so was 'ardly innocent, was they?"

"And the kids, Nic? They were four and seven years old. You 'ave fucked up this time, 'aven't ya?"

"Can't really tell, can ya? I mean down the 'Olly they start 'em young. They got newborns who's smuggling drugs in their nappies. Don't fank me or nufink for keeping it all togevah when you was out of it."

"Keep it togevah, bruv. You 'ave probably started a war wiv the Turks. They're all fucking related to each uvah. Last fing we need is the Arifs starting a war. You 'ave potentially brought a lot of trouble to our door. We nevah start a war unless we 'ave to."

"Nah, they won't. You missed all that, like, when you was in 'ospital. Deniz and Mehmet, wearing Ronald Regan masks, 'eld up a Securicor van in Surrey wiv shootahs. Tried to get away wiv seven 'undred large. They'll be doing a long stretch now. Old Bill shot Mehmet, but 'e, like, survived, unfortunately. Even though they was tooled up, they didn't get a chance to take out any Old Bill. Probably for the best, like, cos they ain't got a good track record on shooting straight, 'ave they? Anyways, the bruvahs still knocking 'bout. They're too caught up wiv their spat wiv 'em Brindle bruvahs. Like I said, nufink to worry 'bout."

"Just cos they're banged up doesn't mean they can't give ordahs, like. Use your 'ead. Look 'ow many times the old man controlled fings when 'e was doing a stretch. It's as easy in there as it is out 'ere. If this cunt 'as got some connection wiv the Arifs, there's loads of bruvahs, like that Bekir, the one they call the Duke, and Dogan. They're pushing brown in quantity down souf."

"That's me point. This cunt was pushing it right on our doorstep. Ovah me dead body was that 'appening. A situation occurred; I 'andled it. We'll 'ave to agree to disagree."

"Nic, the bodies were so badly burned they 'ad to identify 'em from their NHS dental records."

"That really fucking wound me up, freeloading foreign cunts getting an NHS dentist. The state of fucking Englund. But if you're gonna get bent out of shape 'bout it, I could go see Dogan. Make sure 'e knows the score."

"No, Nic. Fink you 'ave done enouf."

"Good, cos I could murdah a cup of tea. Bell Greta to get us one."

Feeling the need for a drink, preferably a whisky, Mat called Greta and gave her their order.

Five minutes later Greta came in with two mugs of tea and a packet of 54321 biscuits.

"Fanks, darling. You can finish early. You've worked really 'ard this momf, and it 'asn't gone unnoticed."

"Thanks, Mat. Nigel will be happy, as it gives us more time to play Alcazar: The Forgotten Fortress."

"What's this Alcatraz fing all 'bout?" asked Nic.

"Alcazar is a castle. To get there we must go through hostile castles with many rooms, traps and doors to retrieve the stolen crown, trying not to get lost in the castle's dungeons, with all their resident evil," said Greta as she turned and left the room thinking that Mat and Nic were no patch on her Nigel. They'd be totally out of their depth in one of his D&D campaigns. With that thought, she even afforded herself a little smile. And to think they had been so skint, so it was fortunate that Nigel had told her he'd won employee of the week for his interpersonal skills with customers and was given a voucher for WHSmith.

APPETITE FOR DESTRUCTION

"As you know, I will not answer to he, him or Nigel. I'll only answer to Dungeon Master or DM."

"Understood, DM," said Greta, who was honoured that she'd hear the new campaign before its launch on Saturday evening. "I've called Tarquin and Gwilbob, and I've told them to bring a family bag of chutney Space Invaders and eight cans of Quatro."

"Silence, Adventurer. We'll now commence my campaign, one that I have spent the last two months moonshining," said the DM, giving a theatrical pause. "The Citadel of the Shadow Warriors; it's a masterpiece and something far more superior than Gygax could ever come up with." Nigel then began to talk in a nasally whispering voice. "For centuries, the denizens of the town of Wishbourne had lived in both terror and wonderstruck awe of the immortal warlock Zoltan Skull. His dwelling is a citadel 100 miles away called Ravencrow, in the Kingdom of Blacktoad. His sorcerous powers are feared throughout the nine kingdoms of Necrobutcher. The citadel looms above Firestorm Mountain. To infiltrate the Gormenghastesque castle, you must cross a moat where Wastriliths and Aboleths swim. The fortress stands fifty feet high, with bulwarks of smooth, seamless limestone. The speckled arrow slits are carved into high towers, revealing only a faint flicker of candlelight. An iron portcullis covered with rust blocks the entrance like a jaw full of jagged fangs. Machicolations jut out from walls re-enforced with the bones of Dire Trolls. The semi-circle bastions encase the stronghold of the watchtower.

"Zoltan's army of Shadow Warriors guarded the citadel. These combatants are ghostlike under their cloaks and boots. They wear beaked plague masks and carry war hammers. The few who infiltrated the citadel never came out alive. Rumours spread that they were turned to stone, their faces etched in eternal agony. Or worse, they were captured and sent to the dreaded oubliette, deep, narrow and confined dungeons that offered no chance of escape, sending the captive into a spiral of extreme mental anguish where they'd claw their faces into bloody ribbons. Some weeks ago a squad of Shadow Warriors descended on Wishbourne. Word had spread of the beauty of Mayor Thyme's sixteen-year-old virgin daughter, Dalphere. Zoltan coveted her for his wife and to bear him children. To live trapped with him forever. She was taken by force in the lunar light by Shadow Warriors and taken to Ravencrow. The Mayor, devastated by the loss of his only daughter, a fair maiden with hair like spun gold, offered a reward of 500 gold pieces for her safe return. Swashbucklers from the nine Kingdoms of Necrobutcher descended on Wishbourne to try to claim the handsome reward.

"You adventurers are gathered at Ye Ole Crusty Beaver Tavern, a squalid lodging in a pernicious area of Wishbourne called Morbidsoul, an area full of cutpurses and vagabonds. You've been brought together by your sense of justice and love of gold. And there is coin to be had here. Over feasting on behemoth ale and black parrot pie, you three strangers have decided it would be wise to work as a team and then split the gold. The quest ahead is perilous. Even before you get to the heavily armoured citadel, there will be many behemoths you will need to vanquish before setting foot in Ravencrow. The Bonegore Forest is doom-ridden with living vines that can tie a man up and strangle him to death. Once past this deathtrap of horrors, you must then navigate the hostile terrain of Molech, inhabited by Carrion Crawlers and Umber Hulks. Firestorm Mountain is guarded by Aizagora, a great dragon with seven heads. You'll need all your abilities, strength, dexterity, intelligence, wisdom, and charisma to successfully navigate this quest. Until Dalphere is saved, she is chained up near naked to her master's bed. She will stay there helpless, wearing only a gossamer-like gown, until Sunday at midnight, when Zoltan will forcefully start using her as a vessel to bear him children." The DM smiled smugly to himself, pointing at Greta, giving her the signal that she was now permitted to speak.

"Ni—I mean DM, we're in for an all-nighter here. As you have been narrating, I've been thinking about my character and backstory. I shall be Hardaker, a Paladin Elf. Rare, I know, but I feel drawn to this race, as this campaign has aroused my otherkin identity. I come from the Kingdom of Nightmourn. My family has all but perished, save for my younger brother Grator. We live in fear of the tyrant ruler, Htebazile Effilcdar. The gold will mean we can start a new life in Shadowmire. There I can buy a small holding and breed Mastodons."

But the DM's thoughts were elsewhere, as he remembered the clan's meet-up last week while playing the Tieflings' Curse of Minkhollow, where Tarquin had questioned him. The impertinence and disrespect he would never forget: "I can use the wood elf magic spell that I found in the scroll of the Sorcerer Shazarra to run away from the Cloud Giant at lightning speed," said Tarquin in his guise as Satroville, the Dragonborn Cleric.

"No, you can't," said the Dungeon Master.

"Why?" asked Tarquin incredulously.

"Because you have webbed feet, and you can't run very fast."

"But they are the rules as stated in the *Player's Handbook*."

"Do not question the DM. My decision is final."

"What about the Avariel wings potion I have in my backpack that I found in the clawfoot chest in the abandoned hovel in Crumpador. I can use that levitation spell to fly away from the Cloud Giant."

"No, adventurer, you can't use that."

"Why?" asked Tarquin even more incredulously.

Tired of the smart alec, the DM barked, "Because an Orc who'd taken an invisibility potion stole your backpack."

"I feel that I'm being railroaded here, Nigel."

"You don't call me that ever. I'm the Dungeon Master."

"Okay, can I call you IT?" asked Tarquin petulantly, who was met with a truly withering look of narrowed eyes and twisted lips. Deciding it was best to backtrack, he said, "By IT, I of course mean in the sort of celestial and transcendental sense."

"I shall think about being referred to as IT." Nigel was actually quite liking this pronoun. It was original and different. Just like him. Yes, he could identify with the Deadlights able to break a creature's mind, because one look at the Deadlights will make a person go insane, due to it not being able to be comprehended by a subordinate mind. And the Dungeoneers were vastly inferior to the Dungeon Master. The DM was shapeshifting a truly trans-dimensional being.

Nigel knew that Tarquin wouldn't make it past the classic-start tavern scene. The true Game Masters know that they don't need any rules. A disgruntled gnome cook, Giggbert Flimp, would take a dislike to the squinty-eyed adventurer. He'd mix toadstools and ghoul saliva into his stew. Guzzling it down, Tarquin would begin to vomit uncontrollably. His skin violently erupting with boils, an intolerable itching of his whole skin would make him want to claw it off, while at the same time suffering an excruciating pain in the intestines. It was an agonising death that took five hours of merciless pain. He died quite literally screaming in agony.

THE LITTLE FAGGOT

"Queen, you haven't mentioned my new fabulous addition," said Jeffrey, playing with his cross earing.

"It looks choc. I can't stop finking 'bout college this aftahnoon," said Suzie.

"Well, I for one can't wait to get my hands on the models for perming."

"I just wanna do a perfick corkscrew, but it's so difficult."

"Suzie, baby, the models may not be Cindy Crawford – more Hilda Ogden – but we'll make them all fabulous. Glamour costs, and right here is where you start paying, in sweat and noxious fumes."

"The smell of perm lotion, it's disgusting. You'd fink they'd make it smell nice."

"We must all suffer for beauty, queen," said Jeffrey, reapplying his pineapple Chapstick.

Suzie Satori was at the Crown & Castle with her best friend, Jeffrey Nookie. It was her first time there, as she was new to the area. Suzie was seventeen and blessed with a heart-shaped face, big blue doe eyes, a button nose and full sensuous lips. Petite, Suzie was dressed in a raspberry jumpsuit that hugged her curves.

Jeffrey was a fish out of water, a gay man living in Dalston. The abuse he received was unrelenting, but Jeffrey rose above it.

"Suzie, one day the Neanderthals will understand my unique ways."

He had no real friends, just a string of boyfriends whom he met at Bromptons in Earl's Court; that was, until Suzie came into his life. Suzie was a rare find. She didn't have a bad bone in her body. But this had only made other girls hate her with a vengeance. Suzie had been bullied to death in school because she was so pretty. Both friendless, the kindred spirits at beauty college had soon become besties who supported each other. Jeffrey's recent break up with Zac had been especially difficult for him.

"I thought he was the love of my life, and he turned out to be just another heartbreaking brute. I just fell so hard and fast for him, the tanned legs, the pierced pecks and just the perfect kissable, moustached mouth. He broke my heart into a zillion pieces and then stamped up and down on them in his cowboy boots," said Jeffrey as he theatrically flicked his highlighted feather-cut hair in homage to his ultimate heart-throb, George Michael. "The course and my dedication to making peeps fabulous keeps me focused. It takes my mind off the man whose name we won't mention again ever."

"You 'ad a lucky escape, Jeffrey. It's a good job you found out what a nasty piece of work 'e was and that it was only in the local paypah in 'Amstead 'Eath." Suzie just wished he could meet a decent fella. She wished *she* could too.

"Luckily for him, he was only cautioned by the police. George is waiting for me out there. I just need to meet him. We need to start hitting the clubs up West. I know he goes to the Wag & Limelight."

"Yeh, Jeffrey, but with one of 'is supahmodel girlfriends."

"Well, more fool him."

Mat and Nic had gone for a quick drink at the Crown. Mat was beyond miserable. He'd been more than happy to be rid of Lisa, but he missed having a girlfriend. He was really fussy with women, and they had to tick a lot of boxes. Nic had organised nights out on the lash with the lads numerous times since they'd split up, but no woman came near his standards. A one-night stand was one thing, but girlfriend material was like finding gold in a coal shed. Furthermore, they still hadn't located Rattlesnake. Striding up to the bar, Nic ordered them a couple of pints.

"All good, lads?" asked Tommy as he poured them pints.

"Yeh, not bad, mate," said Nic.

"Good win for us against Leicester City. 3 goals."

"Yeh, it was," said Mat with no enthusiasm. Even the Irons doing well couldn't raise his mood.

"You go down Upton to watch it?"

"Nah. Nic and the twins did. I watched it at 'ome."

"Yeh, Mat doesn't do the chicken run any more," said Nic, taking a swipe but falling on deaf ears.

Mat surveyed the room. It was the same old. Junkie Jimmy and his cronies huddled around a table, Batty Betty wearing an embroidered décor hat having a stout, and Sid with a pint, clocking everything. He was still smarting with Nic over his mishandling of the premiership. Luckily, there had been no retaliation from the Turks. It was a depressing scene, until he saw her. A blonde angel. Mat didn't believe in love at first sight, but this girl was something else. He'd never wanted a woman so much in his life. He stood transfixed just watching her. The annoying thing was, she didn't look in his direction, so he could make eye contact, but her faggot-looking friend kept catching his eye. He kept giving him the kind of lustful looks women normally did. If it wasn't for the fact he was with this girl, he would have had cathartic pleasure in going over and clumping him one.

"Suzie, queen, I'll get us crisps for the bus trip with the unwashed before we go back to college. We must give the people of the East End the same standard perm that Victoria Principal has."

"Just get salt and vinegar. I don't want those new 'edgehog flavah."

Jumping up from his seat, Jeffrey made his way to the bar to order. Glancing furtively to his right, he could see the Hunter brothers by the bar. They were just as he liked his men: tall, dark, handsome and rough. But these weren't the rough sort he coveted in the pubs of Earl's Court clad in leather and chains, or like George and Andrew in the video for 'Bad Boys' dressed in tight denim and white T-shirts. They really were dangerous men. He had goosebumps as he approached the bar. There was no doubt about it; they were fine specimens of manhood. As he waited to order the drinks, he was aware of how imposing they were. Their presence was palpable. The smelly old men in flat caps with a dog before him took ages ordering, changing their minds every two minutes as to which sandwich they wanted to order. Not the most patient man at the best of times, Tommy ran a hand over his bald head and glared at them. They appeared not to notice and finally decided on cheese and pickle. They incessantly muttered to themselves in raspy tones as they were being served.

"I'm starvin'. Hope its gurt lush ploughman's. That's the badger, all right. May as well gwoam after this. Walk our boot."

Nic wasn't slow to pick up on Mat's interest in one corner of the pub. Nic thought, *the cradle-snatcher. She is practically jailbait.* He took an instant dislike to the girl. Nic couldn't help but feel the green-eyed monster rising up in him, picturing

Mat and her together while he wondered what he would go home to. Debbie was getting worse. Her eating and drinking were totally out of control. She showed no real interest in their son. Yes, okay, due to work, he wasn't there that often, but for fuck's sake, she was his mum, and it was because he went out all hours working that Debbie could be a full-time one. Nic looked on with interest for what seemed like an eternity. His brother actually had a smile on his face. Mat watched as her friend walked back over to her.

"Pretty, ain't she? Not seen 'er 'round 'ere before," said Nic in an indifferent tone.

"Yeh," said Mat, snapping out of his rare daze. "Fittest bird I've evah seen."

"Looks a bit on the young side. Last fing you need is jailbait on your 'ands."

And with those encouraging words, Mat watched her and her friend walk out of the pub.

GROUND CONTROL TO MAJOR JOHN

"Bruv, send over some girls tonight 'round ten, and tell the drivah to stay outside cos no idea 'ow long I am gonna need 'em for."

"No problem," said Nic as he put down the phone. There was nothing more to be said, even though he was livid. He wasn't at Mat's beck and call. Knowing how fussy he was, Nic would have to send three of his top earners. Nic walked into the bar and surveyed the scene. Tracey was deep in conversation with a bespectacled bloke with a greyish complexion and white hair.

"Tracey, I need you in the office. Who's your friend, darling?"

"Nah then this is John," said Tracey as she ruffled the man's swing fringe playfully.

"I'm the gaffa 'ere. Let me introduce you to Scarlet," said Nic as he randomly grabbed one of his girls walking by. "She'll take good care of ya. John, you look familiar. I'm sure I've seen you somewhere, mate."

"Veeraswamy; I enjoy a good curry."

"Nah, not been there."

"Are you a member of the Garrick Club. I'm a regular there."

"Not 'eard of 'em, mate. If they was packing top gash, I would 'ave. It's in me interest to keep up wiv any competition."

"They're gentlemen-only clubs. Women haven't been permitted since the nineteenth century."

"Nah, mate, we don't catah for that kind of arse-bandit stuff in 'ere," said Nic as he walked away from the bloke, who was obviously a weirdo, but he had somewhat more respect for the gay community actually, having money-making sex clubs hundreds of years ago.

Scarlet, like most of the women who worked there, had gotten by in life with her tragic past by inventing a new persona for herself. Her real name was Edwina Rogan, a brunette from Liverpool. Scarlet, now a redhead with gigantic silicone implants, sidled up to John, saying, "I'll take extra special care of you, handsome."

John replied in a whiny Surrey accent, "Hello, dear. Play your cards right tonight and I'll take you out for a slap-up Indian later."

"Ohh, you know how to spoil a lady," said Scarlet, thinking there was nothing worse she would rather do.

"What can I get a lady to drink? Or should I surprise you? Life is full of surprises."

Yes, thought Scarlet, *you will be when you see the bill you get later*. "I'll have an Advocaat on ice," said Scarlet as she took the man by the arm of his pinstriped suit.

Looking around, Nic called Misty and Amber into his office, beckoning them by pointing at them and then at his office. Nic took a seat behind his desk.

"Tonight, you're gonna go ovah to Mayfair to make me bruv 'appy. Jacko will drive ya. You don't speak unless 'e asks you to, and you do whatevah 'e says. Undahstand?"

"I cun't even tell him me name? Say nowt at all?" asked Tracey.

"You especially say fuck all. Don't open your moufs unless he tells you to, and when 'e does, 'e probably doesn't want to chat wiv ya."

Misty, who was the most money-grabbing girl in the club, was for once quiet. Normally, it was all about the money, but being picked to go to Mat's... The thought of the explosive sex with him was enough. He could do whatever he wanted with her. The rougher he was the better. Nic continued to dead stare ahead. He was going to make sure these tarts made their money when they came back later. The three girls just nodded their heads, but couldn't resist little smiles – a night with Mat Hunter women would kill for. Sashaying out of Nic's office, the girls ran to the dressing room to flaunt this to the other girls. They would be pig sick that they hadn't been picked. Once they had crowed enough, they made their way back into the bar, where Amber asked Nic, "Can we take a bottle of champagne with us in the car?"

"I'll give you somefink if you don't get your arses in there now."

Giggling, they got into the car. They wore just lingerie under their fur coats. Normally, the three girls hated each other, as they were all in competition at the club to be the most sought-after girl. But just for tonight they left their differences to one side, acting as faux best friends joined in a united cause the other girls were not.

Mat opened the door, his cold eyes making no eye-contact with them.

"Bedroom is frough there," he said, flicking a finger to the right. "Strip off and start playing wiv each uvah. Keep your stilettos and stockings on." Not saying a word but grinning like Cheshire cats, the girls complied and headed to the bedroom, where they sprawled on the king-sized bed. Excited to be entertaining one of the most sought-after men in London, they started to kiss each other passionately, knowing they needed to get into a frenzy before Mat joined them. They started to lick and caress breasts and pussies, getting themselves fully turned on. Mat walked in as the girls' fannies were gushing. Taking off his clothes, he started fucking them all doggie style, taking out all his frustration on them, treating them like animals. He didn't kiss them or touch their faces. They screamed in pain and pleasure.

Once Mat was done with them, he said, "You need to go now." All he could think about was the blonde angel.

The girls got off the bed and put their fur coats on over their naked bodies and left the apartment giggling.

THE STAR CHAMBER

"So nice to 'ave all me boys 'round," said Nan.

"Got any more United biscuits?" asked Nic.

"Be a lovey, Sparky. You're nearest the kitchen. Go grab a packet." Giving Nic a you-lazy-git look, Sparky walked to the kitchen and did the honours.

"Stick anuvah one in me mug, Nan. Loads of moloko for me, and make sure you put six sugars in. Don't fink you did last time. Eivah that or you didn't stir it propah. Not 'appy."

"Sorry, Nic, I was distracted. I wanted you to see somefink," said Nan as she held up the front page of the *Gazette*. A man with thinning hair and hooded eyes adorned the cover.

"What's that, Nan, in the *Gazetta*?" asked Nic.

"It's really bad business what 'appened over twenty years ago. A little girl called Mary was found murdahed, strangled and dumped in a dustbin. She was two years old and 'ad been fiddled wiv and tortured with a broken bottle. Lovely little girl. She always 'ad a smile for you. Back then your backdoor was always open should your neighbour need to borrow a cup of sugar. That's 'ow 'e got in. Crept upstairs while Shirley, 'er mum, was cooking tea and took the baby from 'er bedroom."

"Sick bastard. Needs to be castrated," said Mat.

"This pervert," said Nan as she pointed to the photo of the man, "was captured and convicted. We all fought 'e'd swing for it, or at least be banged up for life. 'Is name is Reggie Knight, a real misfit who lived wiv 'is mum on Montague Road." Nan took a sip of her tea and exhaled. Placing her mug down tentatively, she fondled her locket.

"Know what I would chop off and stick down 'is froat until 'e choked to deaf," said Flint.

"Fing is, boys, your dads would 'ave sorted that problem out back then, seen that justice was served. You know what I mean – propah East End justice."

All four boys nodded in agreement.

"But Old Bill on this occasion got to 'im first. When they went to 'is 'ouse, 'e 'ad all these pictures of young kiddies being abused. Shirley, she nevah got over Mary's deaf. Six momfs after she passed, Shirley went ovah to Watahloo Station and jumped in front of a train. Mary's dad, aftah Shirley dun 'er self in, 'e wouldn't leave the 'ouse. We all went ovah to try to 'elp 'im, check in on 'im and fetch 'im food. But we ended up just leaving it on the doorstep. Old Bill 'ad to break down the door in the end. They found 'im sitting on an armchair just rocking back and forf. So, they carted 'im off to the funny farm."

"What's 'appened now to this nonce?" asked Sparky.

"That's the fing, boys. 'E's just been released on probation and moved back to live 'round 'ere."

"Ovah me dead body," said Nic, thumping his foot on the floor. "There's no way some sick paediatrician is living in me manor, especially now I got me own kid."

"It's a paedophile, Nic."

"Yeh, same fing, innit. Stop nitpicking."

"Any idea where 'e's living, Nan?" asked Flint.

"Like I said, son, 'e used to live on Montague Road wiv 'is

mum, but aftah 'e was arrested, she wasn't welcome 'round 'ere, so she dun a moonlight flit."

"Yeh, well, that can be easily found out," said Mat.

"I fink it's time for a fresh pot of tea," said Nan as she walked to the kitchen. Before she walked in, she turned and said, "You'll sort this out, won't you, boys?"

"Nan, leave it wiv us," said Mat.

"Me and Sparky got this one. We'll get Sid to track 'im down."

"Usual rules don't apply. People 'round 'ere, they need to know justice 'as been served," said Mat.

Sparky and Flint pulled up outside 18 Sandringham Road. Reggie's abode was a fetid bedsit there, the windows grimy with ripped lace nets, the front door pane boarded up. The garden was overgrown, with rubbish strewn across it. The twins walked up to the door and knocked. A woman who must have weighed 25 stone wearing a kaftan answered the door and said abruptly, "What do you want?"

Barging through the door and pushing the woman to one side, they made their way to Reggie's bedsit door. Sparky put his weight behind it and forced it open.

"Wh-wh-who are you?" stuttered Reggie, who was just about to bite into his fish-paste sandwich while watching a videotape of a man molesting a five-year-old girl.

"We're your worst fucking nightmare. Now shut the fuck up and do as you're told," said Flint.

Sparky grabbed the man off the chair. Reggie started choking on his sandwich. He coughed and sputtered, which seemed to force the offending food down his throat.

"Wha-wha-what do you want from me?"

"I fought I told you nicely to shut the fuck up."

Sparky threw him out of what was left of the door. Reggie's eyes flickered back into the room, the door swinging on its hinges.

"Don't worry. You won't be needing that again," said Flint.

Hauling Reggie out of the house, they bundled him into the back of the van. Jumping in after him, Sparky held him down and tied his arms and legs together then gagged him. Flint jumped out of the van and slammed the door shut. Reggie lay on the floor making sobbing noises and tried to wriggle from his restraints to no avail.

"You're now gonna see what 'ell really looks like," said Sparky.

Jumping in the driving seat and shutting the van door, Flint drove off, switching the radio on. Mike and the Mechanics' 'Silent Running' blared from the radio.

Flint drove the van around the back of the scrapyard and jumped out and met Sparky at the back of the van. They hauled Reggie out and dragged him into the warehouse. They threw him on a chair and ripped the gag off, causing Reggie to flinch in pain.

"Ple-plea-please," stuttered Reggie. "I di-did my t-t-time."

"You nevah dun no bird to make up for what you did. Now you 'ave come face to face wiv the devil itself. Where the government and parole board 'as failed, we 'ave stepped in and taken mattahs into our own 'ands. We 'ave reinstated the deaf penalty wiv immediate effect," said Sparky as he threw a bottle of hydrochloric acid over his face. Reggie screamed in pain as the acid ate through his skin, bubbling and fizzing, causing pustulating blisters to appear. Reggie cried out in agony. The twins put on latex gloves.

"See, I want our faces to be the last you see before you rot in 'ell," said Flint as he cut the leg-restraining rope with a bowie knife, delighting in holding it up at eye-level so that Reggie could see it in all its glory. The sharpened blade glinted menacingly. Momentarily thinking how hungry he was, he snapped back to the present; they could pick up a McDonald's later. He proceeded to undo Reggie's trousers and pants, noting he had pissed and shit himself. Flint then proceeded to hack off Reggie's cock. Reggie screamed in agony as Flint chopped and hacked through the spongy tissue and blood-vesselled appendage as it squirted blood, and let it drop to the floor. Sparky picked it up and held it in the air, waving it around like some sick trophy. Blood gushed from the laceration where Reggie's penis had once been as the child killer's bowels again gave way, the shit sloshing down his legs and mingling grossly with the pool of his blood on the floor. Flint forced his mouth open then took plyers and yanked out his front teeth. Blood cascaded from his mouth as Sparky stuffed his penis into it, forcing it down his throat. Reggie started to choke on his own dick. They watched him closely as he asphyxiated and died, his eyes bulging out of his head.

"Sparks, that was funny as fuck. Deaf by your own cock. Before we get to the marshes, stop off at McDonald's. I'm Lee Marvin."

"Yeh, worked up an appetite meself, bruv."

Arriving at a secluded part of the marshes, Flint stopped the van. The boys wiped their mouths with napkins and threw McDonald's wrappers into the back of the van, the brown paper bags sodden with fat stains and smeared ketchup. The twins pulled Reggie's lifeless body out of the van and tied him to a tree.

"Cunt can't say we didn't give 'im a last suppah, can 'e? Bit off more than 'e could chew by the looks of it, didn't ya, Reggie boy?"

Flint fetched a petrol can from the back of the van and doused Reggie's body with it. Taking out a gold lighter engraved with the initials 'PP', Sparky ignited the corpse, turning Reggie into a human torch. The flames ravaged his flesh, peeling skin from bones, his carcass blistering into blackened ashes.

FATAL ATTRACTION

"Jeffrey, that 'orrible Mrs Bishop is coming in this aftahnoon. She'll want a blue rinse and 'er 'air put in curlahs."

"I wish that bitch would back off, Suzie. She always asks for us, and we're too cutting edge to be colouring grandmothers' hair. We're all feather cuts and highlights. Talking of which, did you see Andrew Ridgely in *Smash Hits* this month? I nearly came in my pants."

"I know, but we can't really say no when we're training. But, yeh, I did see Andrew's 'air. It was choc. The fringe 'ighlights so subtle, yet really effective."

"Suzie, lets chase our troubles away, have a cheeky drink at the Crown and plan out a fabulous beauty-salon future. We'll have a no-blue-rinse policy, and we'll adhere to it religiously.

Giggling and walking arm and arm together down Kingsland Road, Suzie and Jeffrey went into the pub.

"What can I get you?" asked Tommy.

"We'll have a couple of Babychams," said Jeffrey.

Tommy didn't have that much call for this beverage in his boozer, but he'd bought a few cases in as a novelty, as that annoying Babycham advert was on heavy rotation on TV.

Besides, he had some of those yuppy types in here from time to time with their mobile phones and Filofaxes. He figured they'd be the types to buy it. Reaching behind the bar, Tommy took out two of the little bottles with the yellow reindeer in a blue bow on the front.

"Let's take our drinkie-poos over there," said Jeffrey, pointing to an empty table and chairs.

The pub was busy. It was giro day. Taxpayers' hard-earned money was theirs to be splurged. Skinheads and punks even tolerated each other as they had a quid or two in their pocket. The jukebox was blaring The Jam's 'That's Entertainment'.

"The salon. We need to take it one step further, do fabulous things no one else is doing around here."

"I just wondah, when we graduate, 'ow we'll evah get the money togevah to rent somewhere. I just know we could make such a go of it."

"Where there's a willie, there's a way. We'll have salons in Paris and Milan, just you wait. And we need to be unisex. That is the way forward. No reason why the boys can't be pampered too. Anyway, what do you think of this?" asked Jeffrey as he rummaged in his bum-bag and slipped on a pink, lacey fingerless glove. "How Madonna is this?"

"Oh, wow!" shrieked Suzie. "Where'd you get that?"

"Snob. I couldn't resist."

"I can't believe we've seen *Desperately Seeking Susan* twelve times. Madonna's perm and 'ighlights are the level we need to stive for."

Jeffrey went into an impromptu rendition of 'Like a Virgin' to drone out The Jam.

"That song could've been written for you, Suzie."

"I'm just waiting for a prince. I want me first time to be special."

Jeffrey mused, "Yes, I thought Humphrey was the one, but

then again, I thought that about Frank, Roger and Zac. But what's a girl supposed to do?"

"I don't wanna kiss a load of frogs to find me knight in shining armour."

"I will confess, I've had to kiss many frogs, even toads. This is so depressing. Queen, do you fancy a bit of fun?"

"What do you 'ave in mind, Jeffrey?"

"Let's have a game of snooker. Whoever loses has to do Mrs Bishop's hair."

"You're on. It'll be a bit of a larf."

"Yes, queen. There is something very satisfying about potting the pink balls."

Mat and Nic had stopped off at the pub for a pint and a game of snooker. Tommy clocked them coming in, poured them their usuals and followed them out the back to the snooker table. He was just about to tell blondie and Nancy-boy to move when Mat signalled to Tommy to let it go. There was the girl he couldn't stop thinking about. Suzie tried to pot a red and failed miserably.

"Ahh, such a near miss," lied Mat. "I saw you in 'ere the uvah day. What's your name, princess?"

"It's Suzie, and this is Jeffrey."

Both boys gave Jeffrey a cursory nod before turning their full attention back to Suzie.

"I'm Mat, and this is me bruvah, Nic. So, Suzie what?"

"It's Satori. I'm 'alf Italian."

"An Italian princess. Even betta," said Mat.

"You new 'round 'ere?" asked Nic.

"Yeh, I just moved from Bow. We're doing a beauty course at New'am College."

"I can do you some lovely highlights, Nic," said Jeffrey, giving him a cheeky wink, his imagination going into overdrive as he fantasised about Nic in a gimp suit roughly penetrating him in the back of a dirty workman's van.

"Nah, you're all right, mate," said Nic.

Suzie took another shot as Mat and Nic looked at her peachy bum bending over in figure-hugging Pepe jeans. Swinging her cascading blonde hair, Suzie faux-moaned, "Oh no, I missed again," and she turned to the brothers, flashing a sexy little pout. Now they had a view of her perky breasts encased in a tight jumper.

"Sorry, are you waiting to play? We won't be much longah. We've got to go to class."

"No worries," said Nic. "No doubt me and Mat will 'ave a little play latah aftah watching you."

"Darling, your 'olding the cue all wrong. Let me show you."

Mat got up and positioned himself behind Suzie as she leant over the snooker table, Mat's body dwarfing Suzie's five-foot-four one. He leant over her and pushed her gently with his body and guided the cue with his hands on hers. "Now take the shot," said Mat. Giggling, Suzie took the shot. Snuggling in a bit closer, enjoying the feel of Suzie's body, she shrieked in delight as the red ball went down the hole.

"Fancy giving me some up-close-and-personal lessons, Nic?" asked Jeffrey with a what he thought was a come-hither look.

Nic just ignored him and took another gulp of his pint. He was resigned to being Mat's wingman, but if these two didn't come as a pair, he would've choked the arse-bandit, disease-spreading cunt by stuffing a snooker cue down his throat.

"'Ow old are you, sweet'eart?" asked Mat.

"I'm seventeen," said Suzie, suddenly looking very guilty, her brow furrowed. "But I'm eighteen soon."

"Don't worry; I won't tell. Now, 'ows 'bout I get you anuvah drink."

"I'll have a Babycham," said Jeffrey, not missing a beat.

"Me too," said Suzie.

Seeing that Mat had no intention of moving, Nic got up. "I'll do the 'onours then, shall I? Can I get you a Babycham too, Mat?"

Not taking his eyes off Suzie, Mat replied, "No, get us anuvah pint."

Nic made his way to the bar, muttering under his breath, "I'm 'is fucking skivvy now, am I?"

"Tommy, get us a couple of pints of Carling and two of 'em, like, uh, Babycham fings."

Tommy had to turn away to stifle the urge to laugh in Nic's face.

"I'm expecting some jokah to come in and say in a deep voice, 'Hey, I'd love a Babycham.'"

Nic lit a cigarette and dragged greedily on it. "They're for Disney Princess and Twinkle Toes."

"Mat got his eye on 'er, 'as 'e? Pretty girl. I 'eard 'e's split up wiv Lisa."

"Yeh, 'e 'as. Mat was nevah in love wiv 'er. Was like a sex fing. Every time 'e tried to get away, Lisa's magic fanny pulled 'im back in like it 'ad the suction powah of the Deaf Star."

Nic was momentarily sidetracked by a picture of Maria Whittaker in a tight-cropped T-shirt, boobs spilling out in abandon, advertising Big D peanuts. "Giz us 'em too," said Nic, gesturing to Maria.

"Nic, mate, wish I could, but only the peanuts I'm selling."

Handing the drinks to Nic, Tommy said in a hushed tone,

"I 'eard that nonce Reggie got 'is comeuppance. Found on the marshes wiv 'is dick cut off, stuffed down 'is froat, and burnt to deaf."

"Dunno what you're on 'bout Tommy. Was that on *John Craven's Newsround*, cos I missed it yestahday."

Nic walked back to the bar holding the pints and peanuts, telling a goth next to him to bring the Babychams. Suzie and Jeffrey were now sitting with Mat, Jeffrey being largely ignored, but not for the want of trying.

"So, do you come here often, Nic?" asked Jeffrey.

Not looking at him and taking a gulp of his beer, Nic said, "It's me local."

Nic watched Mat practically devouring Suzie. After twenty minutes, now bored out of his brains, he said, "We got a bit of business we need to attend to, Mat."

"It can wait," snapped Mat, not taking his eyes off Suzie. There was no way he was leaving without her phone number.

"Darling, got a bit of business on," said Mat as he tilted Suzie's chin and gave her a kiss. "'Ow's 'bout you give me your numbah and I can take you up West to a restaurant. Lots of pukka places to eat where I live."

"You don't live in Dalston?"

"I'm from 'round 'ere, but I live up West now."

Pulling out a notebook from her jellybag, she scribbled her number down and handed it to Mat.

"Princess, I was finking Friday night. Is that good for you?"

"Sounds perfick."

"You may find some 'round 'ere 'ave got fings to say 'bout me and me family. Just don't listen to 'em."

"Really, Mat? Like what?" asked Suzie with a perplexed look on her face.

"Like really, uh, 'urtful fings. We've dun well for ourselves, and people, they gossip, make fings up."

"How awful, Mat. People can be so cruel. I know I was picked on all the way frough school. I only evah tried to be kind, but the uvah girls 'ated me for no reason."

"People can be really nasty, and, like, uh, yeh, they don't realise the effect their words can 'ave on you. But if anyone does say somefink, make sure you tell me, and I'll be putting 'em straight."

"What'll you do, Mat?" asked Suzie in a slightly worried tone.

"Nufink much. Just, like, tell 'em what they're saying is untrue and it's, like, uh, 'urtful trying to put me and me family down. We do a lot of good in the community."

"That's terrible, Mat. It must be so upsetting for you."

"It is, Suzie," said Mat, casting his eyes down, having no real idea how to look upset. But it seemed to work, as Suzie instinctively reached across and placed her hand over his. She was so unaffected. Sweet and easy company.

"Nic, let's go. We got business to attend to."

Irritated beyond belief, Nic lit another cigarette. Who the fuck did Mat think he was? Mat headed off, and Nic had no choice but to walk behind him. Following his older brother out, Nic thought things were really going to change around here. He'd clocked something today he hadn't seen before – a semblance of light behind his brother's eyes.

"You need to be careful, Suzie. They're ruffians. They look like Adonises, but they're bad boys."

"What do you mean?"

"They're gangsters."

"Gangstahs. Mat told me 'e's a businessman."

"What business is that exactly?"

Suzie, thinking that Jeffrey was just being overly dramatic, said, "There's no need to worry. 'E's only taking me out for dinnah. Did you see 'is eyes? Such a beautiful blue, I could've stared into 'em all day."

A killer's eyes, thought Jeffrey. But seeing as Suzie had obviously made up her mind, he lightened his tone. "Pinky-promise you'll be careful," said Jeffrey as he raised his little finger to Suzie's.

"Pinky-promise," said Suzie, touching his little finger.

"This ain't The Cross; this is an 'igh-class establishment."

"It's not as bad as it looks, Nic. I can put make-up on. Punters won't know."

"If your Gary shows 'is face 'round 'ere, I'll rearrange it for 'im. Taking diabolical libahties wiv me top earnahs. No puntah is gonna want you looking like that. If 'e was going to smack you one, it shouldn't 'ave been your face, cos you can't work like that. You're no use to me now. Fuck off and come back when you can make me money."

Knowing that there was no point in arguing with Nic when he was in this mood, unless she wanted the other eye to match, a defeated Amber left.

"And you," said Nic, pointing at Tracey, "when you finish your shift you can go 'ome wiv Sparky. This one's on the 'ouse, undahstand?"

"I like Sparky. He's uh dead-nice lad. Uh reyt good laf."

"Trace, 'e don't give a flying fuck what you fink of 'im. You just make sure you make 'im 'appy."

"All right, mardy lad, keep thee's hair on," said Tracey as she left the room.

"Dozy brasses fink I give a fuck. They're nufink but grief.

I already got constant aggro from Debbie. Should be easy, but no, I got Ambah wiv a face like she 'as just done ten rounds wiv Bruno; one of Lexi's tit implants exploded on a flight back from Majawca; and Sonietta's old man just went away for a four-year stretch, and she can't get a sittah for 'er kids. These slags ain't worth it. Then Tiffany gave me a serious case of the clap. It felt like me dick was being mangled frough a combine 'arvestah."

"You gotta be careful, Nic, who you're sticking your dick in these days. That Aids fing is going 'round."

"You can only get that if you're a dirty faggot. They'll stick their dicks in anyfink. They got this fing called a glory 'ole. I'm now on 'igh alert. When I go to the bogs, if a random dick pokes frough any 'ole when I'm taking a shit, I keep a Stanley knife stuffed down the back of me jeans and I will cut the fuckah off."

"What's this new bird look like that Mat's seeing?"

"Like 'er. Mizzi," said Nic, pointing at the Bardotesque blonde on the Page Three calendar. If it wasn't for the tits and arse, she looks 'bout twelve, but if that's what Mat's into these days, who am I to comment. I know every momf on the calendar, but I gotta wait till Decembah for me favourite."

"Who's that?"

"Maria Whittakah. I'll 'ave me cock out before I've even flipped the page ovah. It's cos of Maria I've started 'aving these deep foughts. Say in the future I walked into the Blue Anchor and cunted some F-Troop to deaf wiv a crowbar, but in the future they've brought back the deaf penalty, which I get, but your allowed to choose what mefod you're dun in by. That's what I've been finking 'bout."

"'Ow would you be dun in, Nic?"

"I'd be suffocated to deaf between Maria's tits."

"I mean, if you 'ad to go, can't fink of a betta way, mate.

What would you 'ave as your last suppah? Mine would be T-Bone steak wiv all the trimmings."

"Goes wivout saying, Dex. I'd be sucking on Maria's tits like a bloke 'bout to be suffocated to deaf by a pair of massive knockahs. It would make the public fink betta of me too cos I'd be saving taxpayers' money."

"Do you fink Maria will be up for it?"

"Wiv these looks, mate, she'd be dead up for it, and there's no reason why *The Sun* can't be involved. I can see the 'eadline now: '**DEAF BY MARIA WHITTAKAH**', wiv a massive picture of me boat stuffed between 'er tits. Fink you'll find murdah rates will go up large aftah that."

"Do ya fink it would take long to suffocate like that?"

"I'd 'ang on in there as long as I could, mate."

LONDON CONFIDENTIAL

McBride, in an unmarked police car, opened the door to his informant. Some months ago he'd received a call from Dickson, who'd collared a shoplifter in Woolworths nicking a Chewbacca figure. As Dickson started to drive back to the station, the man started babbling, "I've never done anything like this before. I need to pick my girlfriend up from work. She'll be expecting me. I've promised her a night of playing Sword of Fargoal."

"We'll sort this out at the station. You can call her from there," said an understanding Dickson, thinking the lad was having a meltdown. He just hoped at the station he would have his knuckles wrapped and then be released without charge.

"My girlfriend will expect me at Hunter's Scrapyard at five-thirty."

It was then that Dickson's ears perked up.

"Your girlfriend works there? What does she do?"

"She runs the office."

Dickson didn't hesitate to gift Nigel to his superior. Nigel had been treated harshly for a petty first offence, but that was the idea. McBride told Nigel, "There'll be no caution yere. Yew, boyo, have committed a very serious crime and yew need to be made an example of. Do yew know all those Labour do-gooders like yewer own MP Ernie Roberts will have a field day that a white boy has been arrested for practically grand theft. It would be like all their Christmases have come at once, it will. It will show them that the SUS laws are for all and the swamp contains white scum too. I could arrest yew right now, boyo, under section 1 of the Theft Act 1968, but I can help yew yere, save you from a possible life sentence in a maximum-security prison with no chance of parole. Yew could be sent to Wakefield – 'the Monster Mansion'. Do yew have any idea what it would be like for yew in there. Take the hardest disturbed men who are locked up for twenty-three hours a day. In the one hour they're let out, they become the *Diafol*."

"What'll happen to me?" whimpered Nigel.

"Let's just say you'll be in nappies for the rest of yewer life. They'll love fresh meat like yew. All that long hair yew got going on there will go down very well. Well, not, like, for yew, obviously. Yew'll be in high demand, being passed around from cell to cell. I just hope for yewer sake Maudsley doesn't escape from his bullet-proof cage. I can help yew yere, like. I can straighten this out with Woollies. I need a favour from yew, then all this stuff can go away – the high-profile trial at the Old Bailey, the media frenzy when yew have to be hooded when yew get out of the police wagon, the rabid crowd having to be held back by armed police as they shout "Bring back the death penalty" and then the interminable sentence. The judge will need to make an example of yew due to the hard-hitting 'The Met Hate All Niggers' opinion poll that's been running in the *Mirror* after a police officer from Stoke Newington, who wished to remain anonymous, told the rag that on the night Colin Roach died he overheard a colleague saying, "I shot me a nigger." This arrest will be seen as evening out the playing field and will get the public back on the side of the Met. When yew are serving yewer life sentence, I'd make sure the screws knew yew had previous; yew'd been caught doing a depraved sexual act in Mothercare."

"What do you want from me?"

"Yewer girlfriend; she works in Hunter's Scrapyard?"

"Yes, Greta works there."

"She can access their computer system?"

"Yes, the men she works for haven't got a clue. It's only because of their stupidity that they're able to be so sure of themselves."

"I think yew and I can work together and get tremendous results."

Since the DI had secured Greta as his snitch, it had all gone downhill. She'd been his most useless informant to date. She was in the thick of it. How could she keep coming up with nothing?

"What yew got for me?"

"I took one of Mat's cufflinks to be fixed. Nigel came with me. He said it looked like it was made of Kryptonite."

"*Annwyl Duw*, is that it? I need more. I saved your boyfriend's skin. Yew need to come up with the goods, like."

"It was all a big mistake. He meant to pay for it. Nigel had a lot on his mind. We'd had a heavy session of D&D the night before. We'd managed to escape the cavern of the Gibbering Mouthers deep in the caves of the Sibriex."

"Greta," interrupted McBride, "I don't want to know what kinky stuff yew and Nigel get up to, and anyway, he had Chewbacca stuffed down his Y-fronts. When we got Chewy out, he had sprouted ginger pubes – the Wookiee will be traumatised for life, mun. Yew've got to have seen or yered more than that."

"Like what?" asked Greta.

"Talk of extortion and drugs."

"Yes, I do," said Greta.

McBride nodded his head encouragingly while stuffing a handful of Treats into his mouth, some missing and landing on his humungous stomach then rolling down on the floor.

"Nic, if he's had a heavy night, asks me to get him Panadol, says it's the dog's bollocks when you're as hungover as Sue Ellen."

"Well, that's very interesting indeed. Is there anything else yew can give me? Something I can actually use, like."

"Mat gave me extra money."

"For what, *cariad*?" asked McBride in a softer tone.

"For the convention."

"The convention?"

"He gave me the train fare to go to the Star Trek Convention—"

McBride cut her off abruptly and reached over to open the car door, signalling for her to get out. "This isn't going like I thought it would. I need yew to bring me something incriminating, or I may need to reopen the investigation into Nigel. I don't care how yew get the information, just get it."

HAND OF DOOM

The figure stood stark bollock naked behind the grave of Thomas Cutbush at the abandoned Nunhead Cemetery in Southwark. Rattlesnake had been laying low there, connecting with the lwa and smoking copious amounts of crack. He'd not slept in days and was delirious with hallucinations. There'd been a nameless woman. Her dead, naked, half eaten body, was left to rot behind the Ripper's final resting place. He would know the time was right to go home when the spirits told him. Finally, Baron Samedi came to him in a whirl of smoke in skeleton form, top hat on head, cigar jammed in his mouth and a skull-topped stick in his bony fingers. The head of the Gede family came from the crossroads between the world of the living and the dead. He told him in a deep nasal tone that the firstborn of the badminds that killed his *fahda* was dead. It was time for him to take all that should rightfully be his. Rattlesnake had tried to offer him a hit on his pipe, but in a puff of smoke he disappeared. There was nothing stopping him now. It was time to destroy the remaining offspring. He picked up a grotesque effigy and started frantically digging in the soil with his long fingernails. Once he had burrowed deep enough into the earth, he buried the blue-eyed Voodoo doll.

DEVIL'S ADVOCATE

Nic walked into the Crown. He'd arranged to meet Sid. Walking over to the bar, Nic glanced and saw Suzie and Jeffrey. Catching Suzie's eye, Nic mouthed, "You wanna drink?" while completely ignoring Jeffrey.

"No, fanks. Me and Jeffrey gotta go back to school. We're doing facials."

Jeffrey wanted so much to declare he'd love a drink, and anything else that Nic was offering, but kept his mouth shut, instead settling for the heavenly vision of Nic's muscular butt walking over to the bar. Nic saw Sid nursing a pint.

"Whatcha, gaffa," said Sid. As Nic was about to answer, he noticed Lisa was by the bar with her mate, Casey. This was too much of a good opportunity to miss out on. "Sid, be wiv ya in a sec."

Nic walked over to Lisa, "'Ow you doing, darling?"

"I'm fuming with your brother. Who the hell does he think he is?"

"Lisa, 'e's making a big mistake. You and Mat belong togevah. Just can't believe that tart 'e's seeing 'as the balls to be in 'ere right now."

"Mat is seeing someone, and she's in here now?" screeched Lisa as she rose from the stool, craning her head.

"Sorry, I didn't realise you didn't know. Yeh, ovah there. Bold as brass. Can't believe the front on some people."

"Who is she?"

"She's the blonde piece wiv a guy – well, that's debatable – dressed in pink. She's 'bout fourteen."

"Right, the bitch is getting it."

Lisa stomped in her stilettos across to the other side of the bar and headed for her prey. Seeing Suzie, Lisa slightly faltered. She hadn't expected her to be so beautiful. She gave herself a mental dressing down, as Mat would lose interest fast. She was just a plaything to be tossed aside when he got bored.

"You, slut. You keep away from Mat if you know what's good for you."

Not quite believing this very angry woman was shouting at her, Suzie had to do a double take, but yes, there was no mistake about it, this verbal assault was aimed directly at her.

"Uhh, wh-what do you mean?" stammered Suzie.

"You bitch," screamed Lisa as she aggressively stuck a red talon nail in her face, so close Suzie thought she was going to lose an eye. "You've been messing about with my boyfriend."

"Mat told me you'd finished. It's ovah between you."

"No! We're on a short break. You're nothing to him, just some tart he wants a quick shag with before he comes running back to me."

Suzie could feel tears forming in her eyes. Had Mat lied to her? Jeffrey sat silent, shitting himself, white-knuckling his Malibu and pineapple.

"Mat promised me you'd finished for good."

"He lied to you just to get into your knickers," said Lisa as she grabbed Suzie's drink and threw the liquid into her face, the alcohol splashing her face and ricocheting over Jeffrey's tank top. Tears and Babycham running down her face, Suzie fled from the pub with Jeffrey straight behind her. Lisa stomped back to Casey. Her job was done. She'd seen off the bitch as she'd seen off the others.

"Princess, calm down," said Mat down the phone to a weeping Suzie.

Between uncontrollable sobs and trying to catch her breath, she said, "She frew a drink ovah me. Said you're still togevah."

Now on high alert, Mat replied, "Who frew a drink ovah ya?"

"Lisa. You said she was your ex-girlfriend. She was in the Crown and started shouting at me, warning me off you, and said you and 'er were getting back togevah. It was 'orrible, Mat. I was really scared."

Beyond furious with Lisa, Mat said, "Suzie, we're not getting back togevah evah. I'm wiv you now, and I'll be telling 'er so. I'll sort this out."

"What you gonna do, Mat?"

"Nufink much," lied Mat. "Just gonna 'ave a little word wiv 'er, make sure she's propah aware that we're ovah. You wiv Jeffrey?"

"Yeh, at 'ome."

"You stay there, and I'll ring ya when I've spoken to Lisa."

Mat pulled up outside the Crown and thundered into the pub. He could see Lisa and Casey laughing and drinking by the bar. Mat grabbed her from behind, pulled her off her stool and dragged her through the pub out the door.

"Ow, you're hurting me. Stop it, Mat."

"Me and you are gonna 'ave a little chat."

Throwing Lisa up against the wall, Mat grabbed her cheeks tightly with his finger and thumb, staring straight into her eyes. "Get this into your 'ead. We're ovah. I'm wiv Suzie. I'm being nice now, but I'm at the end of me tevah wiv ya, so take this as a warning. Next time I won't be."

Lisa's eyes stared back petrifyingly into his. Never had Mat been this angry with her. He'd never laid a finger on her. He had her cheeks grasped so roughly she was close to tears. Yes, they'd had huge verbal rows all the time, but this only ended with great make-up sex. Knowing this wasn't the time to be feisty, Lisa just nodded her head, tears flowing down her face. Mat let her go, leaving red marks on her face as she slumped to the floor.

LAST EXIT TO PECKHAM

Steering into the North Peckham Estate, Mat brought the Transit to a halt. It was close to midnight on a moonless night. The balaclava-clad men got out of the car dressed in Zegna overcoats that concealed their Remington Model 870 shotguns. Flint carried a battering ram. Rattlesnake had finally been located by Sid. The North Peckham Estate was the largest and most notorious of the Southwark council estates. It was a typical London sink estate – burned-out rubbish bins, overflowing skips and boarded up windows completed the malodorous scene. Graffiti adorned the walls: 'GRIFFIN AND PEARCE ARE THE FINAL SOLUTION. ACT NOW. SUPPORT NF. IRON LADY, RUST IN PEACE.'

Rattlesnake lived on the ground floor. They moved, synchronised, to the flat. There were children playing outside. They saw the men approaching with suspicion. These men were trouble. Even at their ages they were streetwise enough to know that. They ran off to play in one of the abandoned deathtrap flats that the estate entertained. Flint forced the battering ram into the door and broke it down. The four filed in.

"Nobody fucking move," shouted Mat as he aimed his

shotgun at Rattlesnake. The rest of his family aimed their guns at the two other inhabitants. "Wot di fook!" said Rattlesnake, who was in mid-motion of taking another hit on his crack pipe. He had burns and blisters on his lips, and his fingers wept pus. With him were Nyoka and Lambie. There was a three-bar electric fire, with only one bar working. On the peeling wall hung a portrait of Baby Doc the Haitian President proudly holding his motivational recipe book *You can Barbeque Anyone.* Crack paraphernalia lay scattered: glass pipes, rolled paper and foil. Nyoka started incoherently babbling, "Yuh unleash di Obeah."

"Shut the fuck up," said Flint as he hit her over the head with the barrel of the shotgun, causing a sickening crunch as the cranial bone shattered. But even with half her head caved in, she still kept mouthing gibberish. Although she was swaying unsteadily on her feet, the crack gave her momentum. Flint bashed her again violently. There was no surviving the second blow. Pink, grey-brain-matter-like lumps of gristle dripped onto the floor and smeared the walls as Nyoka crashed to the floor dead.

"You, cunt, are gonna die tonight," said Mat.

"Yuh should bi dead. Yuh di zombie. Di lwa guide me. Nuh romp wid mi. Dis is big mon ting. Yuh kill mi sista."

"You will fucking wish I was dead."

Lambie looked on with diluted pupils, his crack-addled brain unable to quite process what was going on. He wondered, as he'd been up for days, was this a hallucination like that time when he thought he was having a meaningful conversation with Professor Squawkencluck? Without warning, Sparky blew his head off, the shotgun jolting his shoulders back as the orange cartridges fired out. Blood sprayed around the room, covering the walls. An eyeball slid down the peeling paint. Mat kept his gun close to Rattlesnake's face, watching as what was happening sunk in.

"Yuh should bi drop out. Don't touch mi Marley. Now yuh mash up mi bredren and mi sista. Fiya bun pussyclaat."

"Keep your mouf shut. Take a look. Ya mates, they're the lucky ones," said Mat.

"I duppy conqueror. Yuh badmind. Yuh not know what ting you mess wid. Yuh not run road. Papa Legba come soon. He invoke Bosou Koblamin. He protect mi."

Grabbing him, the boys dragged him out of the door and bundled him into the back of the van. One of the kids who had scarpered earlier was now hiding behind a skip. He'd come out when he heard the gunshots. It was just as DeAlbert thought. These men were trouble. To go into the flat that everyone around here was scared of. The devil man lived there.

Rattlesnake wrestled with them as they stripped him naked and bound his hands and legs with coarse rope, cutting into his skin. Still protesting, uttering hocus pocus, Nic gagged him with duct tape. Mat and Nic jumped in the front of the van, while Sparky and Flint stayed in the back, crouched down with their guns pointed at their victim. Rattlesnake was about to see Peckham for the last time.

As they drove away, DeAlbert snuck into the flat and took Marley, who was slithering through the banquet of blood. The snake now belonged to him, as the devil man was his *fahda*.

Mat pulled up to the entrance of the scrapyard and brought the van to a halt. He and Nic jumped out. Walking around the back, Mat opened the back door. Rattlesnake was still wriggling around trying to escape his bonds. Now desperate, Rattlesnake summoned the Bakulu Baka, the horned one, that no one dare conjure. He prayed to the spirit and promised him all the black roosters, goats and sacrificed virgins he could get his hands on. Unfortunately, Bakula Baka was having a night off and was unable to help him out of his tight spot.

"You still fink you will survive this?" asked Mat as he grabbed Rattlesnake roughly out of the van and onto the floor, bashing his head down onto the concrete. The dogs could be heard barking loudly from inside the warehouse. They could smell their masters had brough fresh meat for them. Sparky and Flint dragged Rattlesnake's naked body into the warehouse and threw him on a chair and tied him to it. The dogs were tugging violently on metal chains, their fangs viciously snapping in their salivating jaws. Now they were in the lighted warehouse, Nic noticed his back and buttocks were covered with burn marks.

"I know you, don't I? You're that cunt I served bird wiv and burned. Tonight you'll wish you died then."

Rattlesnake, unable to answer due to his gag, hung his head, his eyes closed as if in prayer. In one corner there was a table, upon which lay the tools of the Hunters' trade. Nic nonchalantly walked over to the table, taking his time picking up the deadly wares, turning around holding them up, toying with Rattlesnake.

"I fink this will do," said Nic as he picked up a power drill. Moving towards his prey, Nic powered up the drill and grabbed Rattlesnake's sovereign ringed finger. He bore through it with the drill while relishing the sound as he hit the bone. Crimson and gold flecks spurted from the deep wound. Rattlesnake tried to scream through the gag, but all that came out was a low guttural sound. The appendage dropped to the floor in a pool of blood, leaving just a stump where broken bone protruded. Nic then drilled through a further three fingers. The dogs viciously drove forward on their restraints.

Sparky moved towards the victim with a Smith & Wesson 459. Rattlesnake moaned, his head nodding impalpably.

Sparky aimed at the hostage's right kneecap and pulled the trigger, followed by the left. Rattlesnake's body jolted as his patella bones exploded. Blood, bone cartilage, ligaments and tendons spewed from the grisly wounds. The Yardie passed out.

"You're gonna miss all the fun," said Flint as he threw cold water over Rattlesnake.

Gagging and spluttering, Rattlesnake was once again back in his worst nightmare.

Mat took the drill off Nic and aimed it straight at Rattlesnake's forehead. The Yardie looked into his executioner's eyes as Mat drove the drill into his forehead. All he saw was deadness – Michael Myers had more going on. The skull punctured and made a mushy mass of brain matter squirm up the drill's blade. Gouts of blood flooded from the deep wound. Rattlesnake's body jerked violently. Mat kept drilling even when Rattlesnake's body had slumped in the chair motionless.

"Fink the cunt's dead now," said Nic.

Mat finally turned the drill off as he handed it, dripping with blood and brain tissue, to Nic.

"Giz a look at the drill," said Flint.

"It's a quality bit of kit. It's DeWALT," said Nic, handing it to him.

"Game changah, cuz."

"Who fancies doing a Levahface?" asked Mat.

"Yeh, I'm up for it," said Nic, "but first I gotta change. No way I'm messing up Armani on that cunt."

Nic changed into a forensics plastic suit. Picking up the chainsaw, he fired it up and started to saw the body up, the chainsaw gouging and tearing through flesh, bone and tendons with its rotating sharp teeth, the floor drenched with blood and guts. Once he was done, he removed the plastic clothing and threw it on the floor. Moving towards the dogs, who were now beyond rabies crazy, he unleashed them. Their powerful bodies bounded with gusto into the meat feast.

MATERIAL GIRL

Casey Davis was worried about her friend. After repeatedly trying to get hold of her on the phone since the incident at the pub, she'd been met by excuses from her mum that she was sleeping or not feeling well. It had been five weeks since Lisa went underground, and Casey wasn't going to accept this any more. Lisa needed her, so she was making her way to her house on Wilton Way. A woman who sweated heavily, Casey wiped perspiration from her forehead into her fizzy hair. Making her way up the drive of Number 3, Casey's sausage legs wobbled in her teal leggings, the weight of her cankles making her heels buckle as she waddled along trying precariously not to lose her balance. She got to the door and rang the doorbell three times without any answer. She was just about to walk off, thinking she'd just have to come back tomorrow, when she heard the door opening. The girl who greeted her was unrecognisable. She looked like a vampire who had just seen daylight for the first time, squinting at the sun.

"Lisa, OMG, is that you?"

"Look, you coming in or what," said Lisa as she disappeared behind the front door. Casey followed her friend and walked into the living room. Lisa slouched on the sofa in one of Mat's T-shirts. Casey couldn't believe the transformation. Her friend had always been a slender girl, but she was now skeletal. Her once-beautiful hair was lank and greasy. Lisa's face was ashen and her eyes puffy with black circles underneath. At 3pm the curtains were still closed.

"You finished gawping?" snapped Lisa.

"Sorry, Lisa. Just not used to seeing you like this. I mean, not your usual self. How are you feeling?"

"How do I look?"

As this was a rhetorical question, Casey asked, "Have you seen Mat?"

"No, I haven't seen or heard from the bastard. Have you? And was he with that blonde tart?"

"No, I haven't," lied Casey, as only yesterday she'd seen him holding hands with Suzie, looking completely loved up, going into the Rio to see *Weird Science*.

"He's probably keeping a low profile after what he did to me. See, Case, today it really hit me. I've been wallowing in self-pity. I've not left the house, and most days I don't get out of bed. Then my mum said to me, 'Are you going to let that no-good cad get the better of you? I thought you were made of stronger stuff.' This got me thinking, and guess what?"

Casey stared back in confused silence, not knowing what pearls of wisdom her mate was going to come out with.

"I always knew I was too good for Dalston. I was born with looks that will get me far away from here. I can make something of myself. I was born to travel the world and stay in five-star hotels."

Casey tried hard not to show how bad Lisa looked, but failed miserably; but Lisa, back to her self-absorbed self, didn't notice.

"This is all going to change. The bastard has taken away my Porsche. I loved that car. He thinks he's destroyed me, but he hasn't. I'm made of tougher stuff. I have big plans."

"What you gonna do?"

"I'm going to be the biggest glamour model in the UK, bigger than Sam Fox, and then go into acting, like Linda Lusardi. She was in pantomime last Christmas. *Dick Whittington* in The Grand Pavilion, Porthcawl. She played the cat. He'll rue the day he finished with me and made a fool of me in public. They say revenge is a dish best served cold. Mine will be frozen."

"What's your plan, Lisa?"

"I'm giving it a couple of weeks, just to get myself back in tip-top form. I'm going to have a sunbed and facial every day. When I'm looking my best, you're going to take some pictures of me."

"On what?" asked Casey, not really liking the sound of this potential pressure.

"My dad's polaroid. Once we have pics of me looking really hot, I'm going to send them to a professional photographer, and they'll obviously want to get me in ASAP for a photoshoot. I've seen one first-class photographer advertising, who has studios behind Fleet Steet. He took the first professional pics of Linda. Well, that's what he says anyway. I think he'll capture something in me. I mean, more than my natural beauty. Then I'll send them to the Samantha Bond Agency."

"But what about, Mat? He's dead against you doing glamour modelling."

"Mat can go to hell. I should've done this ages ago. He's been holding me back with all his possessive ways. If anything, this has been the wake-up call that I needed. Besides, he's so jealous, he goes nuts if a guy so much as glances at me. Once he sees the whole country is looking at me, he'll be grovelling to get back together. But I'll make him work for it."

"Lisa, when you're a supermodel, you won't need Mat. Rich, famous men will be begging to have a date with you, like Nic Kershaw and Rick Astley."

“I know what you mean. I’ll be able to have anyone, even Rob Lowe, but Mat and I were meant to be together. We have amazing chemistry. Our sex life is off the chart. Once you meet someone who can give you that pleasure and, well, obviously money, you don’t give them up.”

Casey tried to be positive, as she wanted Lisa, her only friend, to get out of the bad funk she was in, but there were alarm bells ringing that told her that this wasn’t the way to get Mat back. However, one thing Casey knew was that when Lisa made up her mind and set her heart on something, there was no stopping her. She was happy to have her friend back. She had been indoors with her mum since Lisa had gone underground. Being Lisa’s friend had given her a whole new lease of life. They’d met at school, the most unlikely pair to be friends. Lisa had bagged the most handsome boy in school, but Casey noticed that Lisa didn’t exactly warm to other girls. Anyone remotely pretty was a threat to her. Casey posed no threat at all. She’d bitten the bullet and in the girls’ lavatories, washing her hands and watching Lisa preen in the mirror, she’d started talking to her, buttering her up, telling her how beautiful she was. Lisa, loving the praising and noting this girl was physically disgusting, had invited her over to her house to listen to the new Abba album. After school she had gone to Lisa’s for tea. It was the most exciting evening of her life. Over listening to *Arrival*, Lisa had talked about herself, mixed up with impromptu trying on of her vast collection of clothes and shoes, using her candy-cane decorated bedroom as a catwalk. Casey was in awe of Lisa’s bedroom, the total antithesis of her threadbare one. She was on the periphery of Lisa’s life, living it through her viscerally. Casey got to know all the gossip about the Hunters. She especially liked hearing about Linda, Mat’s mum, who was the personification of glamour, driving around in her Aston Martin Lagonda and wearing Diane Von

Furstenberg. In the years they had been friends, Mat had barely said two words to her. Casey doubted that Mat and Lisa would get back together. She'd seen the way Mat was looking at Suzie. It was the look of love. She hadn't seen that look on his face with Lisa. Lust, but not love.

"Who's this photographer?"

"His name is Jacques D'Souza, and he told me over the phone he does high fashion and glamour, like *Vogue*, *Elle* and *Playboy*. He's very particular about who he takes pictures of because he's an artist, so these polaroids have to be perfect. Do you understand, Case?"

Feeling pressure mounting on her like never before, Casey mumbled an uncertain, "Yes, of course I do."

"Anyway, Case, what are you wearing? You look a right mess. Go and get me a can of Tab from the fridge. We've got plans to make for me."

WEST END GIRLS

Glancing in his Hollywood-lighted mirror, Jeffrey adjusted his hair for the twentieth time. Fumbling around for the perfect scent, it came to him by the power of persuasion. He cranked up the volume of his portable TV as his favourite advert came on. The husky woman's voices belted out the song 'Remember My Name'.

Jeffrey reached for his body spray. The advert in Jeffrey's mind was 'iconic', a cartoon, barely legal nubile blonde sprays herself liberally with Limara. In a forest, for some reason naked, she bounces along, awakening plants, wildlife and even a stone-statue lion. Such was the power of this elixir. Slipping on a see-through white dress hugging her pneumatic breasts and bum, she then sexually assaults a sleeping man. He briefly went into a flight of fancy about kissing a sleeping Nic dressed in a white tuxedo, just like the Suzie look-a-like in the advert, but he had something a little extra that she didn't.

Jeffrey was on his way up West with Suzie tonight dressed in hot pink leggings, leg warmers topped off with a cerise duster coat. The icing on the cake was his Boy Toy belt. When he found out Macey's New York had a Madonna Land, he sent a letter to his ex-boyfriend Frank, who'd relocated there, begging him to send him one. The vision in pink made his way downstairs and flounced into the front room where Mr and Mrs Nookie were having tea.

Face agog, Mr Nookie asked, "Are you going up West to one of those ga—clubs you like?"

"Yes, Daddyo, but first I'm meeting Suzie at the Crown. We're going to the Limelight, Shaftsbury Avenue."

"The Crown? Dressed like that?" asked his dad as he stifled to stop choking on his Ovaltine.

"Yes, Daddyo, I'm dressed to impress, baby. This club we're going to, loads of stars go there, even George."

"Well, he'll probably be with his girlfriend. Is this the same one you went to last month?" asked Mrs Nookie.

"No, Mummyo, that was the WAG. Tonight I could be buying a drink by the bar with Paul Young or standing next to Boy George in the urinals. It's a converted church, so uber-trendy."

"Well, just be careful, son," said Mr Nookie, not liking the sound of this place at all and taking a bite of golden syrup cake.

"Don't wait up. Suzie and I will be boogying on down till the early hours of the morning," said Jeffrey as he adjusted his bum-bag to just the right position at the back so his new belt was on show. As Jeffrey left, Mr and Mrs Nookie just stared into their mugs of Ovaltine.

Heading out of the living room and into the hall, he opened the front door. He stepped out onto Tottenham Road and headed onto Kingsland. Walkman at the ready, he turned the volume up full blast to Madonna's 'Lucky Star'. Cindy Crawford had nothing on him. Watch and learn, baby. As he worked it along the high street, he was queen of all he surveyed. Yes, it was freezing, but no pain, no gain. He was completely oblivious to the aghast looks he was getting as he strutted down the street. He came out of his *façon de parler* when an old man in a pork-pie hat muttered, "Wot di fook?"

"Girlfriend, you wish you looked like me," quipped Jeffrey, flicking his hair theatrically.

Jeffrey was at serious risk of getting beaten up but managed to get to the pub unscathed. Dramatically throwing the doors of the pub open, Jeffrey saw Suzie and did a theatrical twirl, completely oblivious to the fact he had a serious brass monkey thing going on in his Lycra leggings. He pulled his earphones from Madonna, and his ears were now subjected to the cheery sounds of the jukebox – The Specials' 'Ghost Town'. Jeffrey saw Nic sitting by Suzie and Mat. Nic, without missing a beat, made violent motions to Flint, who was standing by the fruit machine, to sit down on the vacant space next to him.

"You look fabaglamourous. Totally choc, queen." Suzie was wearing a black, lace, calf-length bodysuit with a gold ra-ra skirt, teamed off with a huge gold hair bow.

"I love your outfit too, and that blushah shade is so, well, um, subtle but effective."

"I'm loving myself silly in it. It's Max Factor Dayglo Ultraviolet."

"Mat, look 'ow amazing Jeffrey looks."

Mat muttered something inaudible under his breath, but Suzie was too excited to notice.

Jeffrey was just waiting for Nic's reaction, but he was otherwise engaged, watching MTV playing Sabrina's 'Boys', for some reason mesmerised by Sabrina's very ample bosoms jumping up and down in a bearly there, wet bikini. Frustrated that he hadn't got the reaction from Nic he wanted, Jeffrey said loudly, to make sure his unrequited love interest heard, "Shall we get a cab up West now, Suzie?"

Giggling and giving Mat kisses on his face, she said

distractedly, “Yeh, Jeffrey, in a mo. We don’t need a cab. Dexy’s taking us. ’E’s gonna stay wiv us so we’ve got a lift ’ome.”

This nugget of information didn’t sit well with Jeffrey. He felt like they were going to be watched all night, something Mat seemed to be doing more and more of. Suzie seemed oblivious, but he’d seen the men hanging around them. He wouldn’t mind if beefcake Nic was chaperoning them, but Dexy wasn’t exactly eye candy.

“I’m just popping to the little girls’ room, queen. I’ll be back in a twirl of a magic wand.”

“Okay, Jeffrey. We’ll make a move when you get back.”

In the gents’ Jeffrey took a hit of poppers, an instant alkyl nitrites high, which worked on involuntary smooth muscles like the throat and the anus by increasing the blood flow. Jeffrey conceded if he could just get Nic turned on to them, things would be very different. Jeffrey’s mind went into overdrive imaging Nic dressed in leather chaps and waistcoat, like Fabio, brutally penetrating him. Nic just needed to take a walk on the wild side, then he would see the light and never turn back. Adjusting his belt in the mirror, he walked back into the bar.

“I’m so excited, I may wet myself. Zac said when he was there he saw two-thirds of Bananarama, which was made up for by seeing one third of Fun Boy Three.”

“Now, Jeffrey, we’re not gonna mention the ‘Z’ word, pinky-promise.”

“Pinky-promise,” muttered Jeffrey unconvincingly as he took one last look at Nic. But his mantra was one of patience, step by step, day by day and, more importantly, inch by inch.

Mat signalled to Dexy, who made his way over from the bar fastening his coat up.

“Right, princess, Dexy will take you up West then bring you ’ome. Call me when you get there and when you’re leaving. I’ll probably give you a call a few times when you’re there as well, see 'ow it's going. Then you're staying at mine, so Dexy will run Jeffrey back to Dalston."

"Mat, can't wait to spend the night wiv ya. It's gonna be really special. I can't believe I've met someone as lovely as you. When I wake up in the morning, I could pinch meself."

"Me too, princess," said Mat, although he really didn't think Suzie had any comprehension of what she'd put him through these last months. He had to give it to himself, the restraint he'd displayed. He had no idea he had it in him. Only last week he'd given her a Bulgari bracelet, and in her excitement she'd jumped theatrically onto his lap and hugged him. He had relayed it to Nic.

"I 'ad to drive 'er 'ome straight away, cos, like, I 'ad promised 'er old man I'd 'ave 'er 'ome by eleven-firty. It took everyfink in me will-powah."

"Was you mistaking your nob for the gear stick, bruv? Sounds fucking brutal."

Nic then relayed the conversation to the twins.

"Got to give 'im some credit. Didn't fink 'e 'ad that much restraint in 'im, but 'ere's the fing. It disturbs me. 'E's changing before our eyes. Mat's losing his edge. See, I got this feory, Mat ain't in control of the firm no more."

"Who do you reckon is?" asked Flint, looking confused.

"Suzie, cos until Mat gets down 'er knickahs, I'm telling ya 'e can't fink of anyfink else. Mat is powahless, so in a round 'bout way she's the boss. Until 'e gets in 'er tight fanny, which is probably made of fairy dust, 'is mind is consumed wiv nufink else. Let just 'ope for all our sakes 'e gives 'er one soon so 'e can get back to running fings. 'E's taken 'is eye off the ball."

But it would be worth it. Tonight he was going to devour her. He had waited so long he thought his balls would burst. Her nubile innocent body was all his. Mat was in pure ecstasy every time he touched her unexplored virginal body. And Mat was going to explore it all tonight. Mat had so far been the perfect gentleman with Suzie, only engaging in some very passionate kissing. He wanted to make sure Suzie completely trusted him and took it at her speed. It had practically killed him, but he knew if he touched her too much, he didn't think he'd have the self-control to stop.

Dexy dropped Suzie off at Mat's at 2.30am. Jeffrey, who was beyond rat-arsed, had plagued Suzie to let him stay over at Mat's.

"We can have a sleepover, queen, a slumber party like they have in America, but not like that film Zac made me watch, *The Slumber Party Massacre*, all those scantily clad schoolgirls being killed by a beefcake psychopath in double denim with a giant power drill. Zac seemed to get quite a thrill out of it. I still have nightmares. I'm sure Mat won't mind."

"I fink Mat will mind; you know it's a special night for us. Pinky-promise we'll go and see the *Breakfast Club* at the Rio next week."

"Ooooooh, chocky choc, I love the Brat Pack."

The evening had gone in a blur, doing synchronised dancing to Five Star and Mel and Kim, although Jeffrey had spent the night rubber-necking like a demented owl, saying, what seemed like every ten minutes, "Is that George over there?" There had been a slightly unpleasant incident by the bar, where Jeffrey was making a bit of a nuisance of himself with Nick Rhodes. As Suzie got out of the car in Mayfair, Jeffrey said, "Now go forth and get rogered within an inch of your life, but as you're not being good, queen, you must be careful – your fairy godmother knows about these things."

As Suzie walked through the door of Mat's flat, he picked

her up and took her straight to his bedroom. Suzie hugged him tightly. She trusted Mat implicitly. She was slightly scared and also excited for him to make love to her. He carried her to his bed, caressing and kissing her passionately. Suzie instinctively responded. He threw her down on his bed with unbridled passion, tearing her clothes off, and started to kiss every inch of her body. Suzie responded with sighs of pleasure. Mat sucked greedily on her breasts. Her nipples now erect, he worked his way down to her virginal pussy and opened her legs roughly, then slowly massaged her with his hands. He lost himself, licking and kissing her, relaxing her inner thighs to open her pussy while Suzie got lost in sheer bliss. Grabbing her peachy bum, her juices flowing, Mat inserted a finger into Suzie. He finger-fucked her, getting her ready for him. When he couldn't take it any more, Mat rammed his rock-hard cock into her dripping wet vagina and started to fuck her like he had never fucked any woman before. He spread her legs wider as she gasped with pleasure as he pumped into her. Suzie instinctively responded by locking her legs behind his back as he thrusted harder. She moaned in pleasure and pain. Mat manoeuvred Suzie so she was sitting on top of him, still fucking hard her newly opened pussy as they both passionately kissed each other, blood from her virginity, now very much lost, dripping down her leg. Mat ran his hands passionately through her hair, kissing her deeply. They came hard and fast together in a shuddering climax. Suzie clung onto Mat as he embraced her, kissing her and caressing her softly as she lay contentedly on his chest. Her beautiful body was now an open vessel to him, and after such a long wait Mat was going to take every advantage. Breathing deeply after the explosive exertion, Suzie melted into Mat's arms. There was no doubt in Mat's mind that Suzie was the one.

"Was it all okay, Mat?" asked Suzie innocently.

"I'm in love wiv ya, and practice makes perfick. I want to

fuc—make love to you morning, noon and night." It was the first time in his life he had told someone he loved them and actually meant it. If anyone so much as touched a hair on her head, they would pray for death. He felt euphoric, but also something else, a weakness. A feeling alien to him.

Mat awoke in a cold sweat. The dreams were always the same. He was being held underwater by an assailant, fighting to get his head out of the water. When he did manage to fight the restraints, the assailant started to fade. He couldn't see the face, which was obscured, but it wasn't a black man. The apparition was white. These dreams had plagued him for months now, since he'd been stabbed. There was something afoot. He just didn't know what. Rolling over, he could see Suzie was fast asleep, breathing lightly, with her hair cascading over the pillow.

PRETTY IN PINK

"I'm so excited to show you the salon premises," said Suzie as she stood outside 497 Kingsland Road.

"I can't wait to get inside, queen. One is all atremble."

Putting the key in the lock, Suzie said a theatrical "Ta-da" and let them in.

"Wow," squealed Jeffrey. "This is totally choc. We can do sooooo much with it, Suzie. Attention to detail is the key. All the PINK possibilities," said Jeffrey. "This will be the most fabulous beauty salon in East London. They'll be queuing up for miles to get in here."

"I didn't fink at eighteen I'd 'ave me own salon. Mat's given all this to me, so I feel the pressure to make it work so much."

"Queen, with your mind and my body we'll carry this off with great aplomb. We'll live and breathe the salon until it's open."

"Mat 'as so much faif in me making a success of 'Ot Cherry it's ovahwhelming. But 'Ot Cherry was the right choice."

"It's divine, and we were unanimous on the name. Hot Cherry has that special oomph. Now, no time like the present to get things started. The first thing we need to look at is the colour scheme, and we're talking here PINK."

"Yes, and let's 'ave fairy lights everywhere. I also want neon-light signs all ovah the place, like of lipsticks, palm trees and flamingos."

"I agree. That's exactly what I thought, Suzie, baby. We're just so on the same wavelength. Flamingos are so hot right now. Very uber-trendy."

"One fing. As the salon is unisex, Mat 'as put 'is foot down. 'E doesn't want me doing any beauty treatments on uvah blokes. Mat said it weren't right and 'e may not be able to contain 'is jealously. 'E's just being protective of me. Mat probably wouldn't do anyfink. 'E would just go ovah and explain to 'im that I'm taken."

To this nugget of information, Jeffrey pulled an are-you-for-real face but quickly changed it into a smile and said, "I'll take care of all the boys' needs. Mind you, it's your loss if Nick Kamen walks through the door stripped down to his boxer shorts."

"Best friends forevah, pinky-promise," said Suzie, holding out her little finger.

"Pinky-promise," said her partner in crime.

THE MODEL

"You can't park 'ere. You be bovering our boot, Shep. Making im joppety, you be. 'Ee don't like all that car revving," said the old man in a flat cap to the smartly dressed man sitting in his Bentley Continental. The man wearing Ray-Ban Wayfarer sunglasses was blocking the gate to the scrublands by Hunter's Scrapyard. "How are we zupposed to get our Shep in. Move your gurt big car. Don't be spuddling now and gurt noodling around." The barking dog was craning its neck to get in, pulling on his makeshift lead. "Our boot wants to go up tuther zide a field."

Mat just ignored them and checked his emerald Patek Philippe watch. Hopefully, Nic would come out of the office soon and they could be on their way. They were dressed funny, like farmers, with some sort of orange string tying up their jackets. The scruffy dog's lead was also made of this. They smelt funny too, a cloying stench Mat couldn't decipher.

Brothers Angus and Jethro Ploughers were up early taking their dog for a walk. Shep wasn't a sheepdog but a mangy whippet from the pound that they insisted on calling Shep – a dog whose birthname was actually Hank – but due to a bad problem with flatulence and excessive leg-humping, this was his fourth forever-home. Angus and Jethro loved their 'bootiful' boy. The brothers had been farmers in a former life. Their farm had been repossessed due to an outbreak of foot and mouth disease. When Midland Bank foreclosed on their fifty-acre holding, they didn't go quietly. Off their heads on their home-brewed cider, Angus had chained himself to his Massey Ferguson tractor and Jethro had threatened a PC with his pitchfork. The pair were given a term in the Bridgwater Asylum. When they were released, the farm and their sheepdog were long gone. They weren't welcomed back in their village. The Ploughers brothers, with their eccentricities, had never been embraced by the villagers. Before the incident, they were at the stage of last chance saloon when, at a Wurzel's gig at the village hall, they'd started to throw their underpants Tom Jones-style at the stage. With no money or prospect of jobs, they were forced to take refuge with their Aunt Charlotte in Dalston. They hadn't been near a farm in years, but they still managed to stink of silage. Nic finally came towards the passenger door, dragging on a cigarette.

"You be wiv 'im? 'Ee needs to move his gurt big car. Is 'ee cakey in the suede? Our Shep needs walking."

Mat continued to look straight ahead. The sooner Nic got in the car, the sooner they could get on with business and get away from the godawful smell.

"What language you speaking, mate?" asked Nic, opening the passenger door.

"We be from Zuhmuhset. What language you be speaking?"

"English, I fought, mate. No need to 'ave a coronary. Me bruv, 'e only passed 'is test last week, like. I told 'im not to park 'ere. I mean, there's a massive sign saying 'NO PARKING'. 'E'll move now and I'll 'ave a word wiv 'im. 'E needs to brush up on 'is 'ighway code." With that, Nic got in the car, closed the door and Mat floored it out of the gas chamber.

"You took your time, Nic."

"Keep your 'air on. Was trying to get 'old of you all last night. No answah. Where was ya? Anyways, don't bovah to fank me. I just defused that situation. They was just 'bout to tell you they was in a war. Killed one of 'em Krauts wiv their bare 'ands. If fings turned nasty, you would 'ave been way out of your depf."

"You got somefink on your collar."

Nic looked down and saw the large teardrop red stain.

"Yeh, must 'ave nicked meself shaving."

The offending car now gone, Angus and Jethro were doing what they did best: moaning.

"Lucky for them I didn't have my scythe with me. I could've lopped one of their heads off the betwaddled ramshackle," said Angus.

"Bloody wazzock ninnyhammers" said Jethro, turning to Shep, who was now physically fighting to get off his lead and farting at the same time.

"Our boot can't wait for his run. You go and have a run now, Shep," said Angus, letting the dog off his length of baler twine. The whippet ran straight towards a clump of hawthorn bushes.

"Where's 'ee going? 'As 'ee seen zummit? 'Ee be tugging on zummit. What you got there, boot?" asked Jethro as the brothers walked closer to the bush. "What you found, clever boy?" Now Shep was really tussling with his find, swinging the cream object in his teeth rapaciously. "Ee's got something. Ee's doing a prapper job. What you got there, 'andsome?"

It was only when they walked nearer, they could see it was a woman's leg.

"What do we know of the victim? Was she a *puteiniwr*?" asked McBride.

"Sorry, sir?" asked PC Dickson as the duo walked from the police Rover to the crime scene.

"Was she a prostitute?"

"No, guv, the victim has been identified as Lisa Alexander, the ex-girlfriend of Mat Hunter. Her bag was found near the body. We identified her from her driving licence. Her purse was in there stuffed full of £50 notes, so I think we can rule out robbery."

"*Duw helpa ni*," said McBride as he sucked a long breath in through his teeth. "Not gonna lie to yew, like. She was a right piece of work, not liked by many. But, still, to end up dead so young on wasteland used for dogs to *cachu* on. Anything else in the bag of interest? A pager or one of those new mobile phones?"

"No pager or mobile, guv, but there were some polaroids of her in various stages of undress."

"Right, well, Dickson, yew'd better give them to me, like. What I mean is, make sure yew give me the bag so I can take a good look to see if there are any clues. Make sure uniform don't contaminate it."

"Yes, guv," said the uniformed PC in a slightly dubious tone.

McBride and Dickson walked towards the gruesome discovery, where Dr Fish, uniform and forensics were already attending the scene.

"All right or what? What we got yere, butt?"

"Well, it's a woman. A very dead woman. I followed all medical procedures, but it wasn't really necessary to take her pulse."

McBride surveyed the grisly scene before him.

Lisa's body lay naked and mutilated on the dirt floor. Her once-beautiful face was frozen in a grotesque grin, as the killer's blade had slit her mouth from ear to ear. Crimson fluid saturated her hair and pooled around her head. Her eyes showed no peace in death, just the agony she'd endured as she had slowly and painfully died. Or eye was the case, as one of them had been gouged out. Her nipples had been cut off from her breasts, the wounds oozing with blood and pink tissue. Her whole body was inflicted with hundreds of viscous wounds. The remaining breasts had been stabbed almost beyond recognition. All that was left were bloody pulpy orbs. The blood tricked down to where her vagina would have been but had now been frantically carved out. The stabbings were crude and frenzied. Blood and flesh were scattered around her like a gruesome collage. But the most glaring thing was the letter 'N' carved in her forehead.

"This is some sick *cythraul* we got yere," muttered McBride. "Any idea what the weapon was?"

"The weapon could've been anything: a knife, scissors, scalpel, razorblade, sword, dagger. Pardon the pun, but I'll take a stab in the dark here and say a stab wound probably killed her. You'll have to wait for the results of the autopsy. I just can't be conclusive at the moment," said Fish, stuffing a Kola Cube in his mouth.

"This is a sensitive one. A mam and da have to be told their daughter will never be coming home and died in the grisliest circumstances. I need someone with a sensitive manner to deliver the news to the family. Fish, yew can sit this one out. Boyos, make sure yew search the area with a fine-tooth comb. There's got to be something yere the perp dropped," said McBride to the group of policemen. "Anything found, no matter how small, yew report back to me immediately. I'll be tamping if yew miss anything. This investigation doesn't go beyond this crime scene. Understand?"

McBride gestured for Dickson to walk back to the police car.

"Do you think it was Hunter, guv?"

"Not really his MO. The body has been found, for one. It doesn't make sense for it to be him. This'll bring too much heat that they won't want."

"Guv, the dog's walkers who called it in said that they had something of an altercation earlier with two men who fit the description of the Hunter brothers."

"Yes, Sherlock, the scrapyard they own is just there, mun, so not exactly strange they were around yere is it? Anyhows, we got a big problem yere, Dickson, we do."

"What's that, guv?"

"Something that's as welcome yere as an Irish Catholic walking into the King's Arms in Woolwich. We got one of them serial killers on our hands."

"How have you worked that out, guv?"

"Engage yewer brain, Dickson. She has 'N' carved into her forehead like Stacey Tubbs, information that was never released to the public. It's the same perp, all right, and he has to be found. The last thing we need is the hacks getting hold of this and creating mass hysteria. This one has to be put to bed, tidy, like."

"Like the Yorkshire Ripper, guv?"

"Yes, like Sutcliffe. See, these days serial killers, they got to get noticed, like it's a one-upmanship thing. They can't just violently defile a body; they've got to leave their mark, get themselves noticed, so to speak, like leaving some satanic marks on the body or a leek stuffed up their backsides."

PC Dickson opened the passenger door of the Rover and got in. He didn't notice he had a card stuck to his foot. It was 'Miss Stain the Dyer's Daughter'.

"I can't believe it, Victor. I mean, who would 'ave fought it?"

"What's that, Rosie."

"Mat's Lisa. She's been found murdahed by the 'ands of a serial killah." Turning the front of the paper to him, the headline read: '**THE HUNT FOR THE HACKNEY HACKER**'.

The front cover showed a picture of Lisa looking radiantly beautiful. It was a holiday snap, a colourful beach blanket in the background, a muscular arm around her slender, bikinied waist, with the figure cut out of the frame. The juxtaposed shot showed a grainy picture of the crime scene dotted with policemen and barricade tape.

"Gawd bless 'er, so young and all. I mean, she 'ad 'er little ways, but this is just tragic."

"We nevah really took to 'er, but no one deserves this. I wondah if Mat knows. I 'ad best give 'im a bell."

"Do you remembah, Rosie, in the war we 'ad that Blackout Rippah? 'Is name was Gordon Cummins."

"I do. Terrible business. 'E 'ung for that. We should nevah 'ave got rid of the deaf penalty."

"You can blame that on 'Arold Wilson. 'E got rid of it for a more civilised society. 'Ow does that work, 'ey? If they're dead, they can't commit any more crime, can they? Always fought 'e was a bit fishy. Some of the lads in M15 fought 'e was a KGB agent, and they was plotting against 'im to bring 'is government down. It was called the Clockwork Orange Operation."

"Nic knows all 'bout that clockwork fing. 'E's always talking 'bout it. I nevah really knew what 'e was on 'bout. I'll take more notice now. I'll go and put a fresh pot on and give Mat a quick call in the kitchen."

"'Course it was a shock, bruv. She was me bird for years. I 'ated 'er in the end but wouldn't wish this on 'er. I just 'oped she would emigrate somewhere like New Zealand."

"It's like a real tragedy," said Nic distractedly.

"It's a problem, Nic. This as 'appended before. Snout down at the station told me that druggie they found dead, she 'ad carved in 'er face a lettah 'N'. Pigs kept it undah wraps cos they didn't want nutjobs calling in and saying they dun it. We need to find this cunt. We don't need 'acks and 'em Rippahologists flocking 'ere. Dead bodies make a lot of noise."

"When it was that junkie, 'acks weren't really interested, but now they are. It's clevah, mind, the paypahs calling 'im the 'Ackney 'Ackar."

"Yeh, Nic, must 'ave taken 'em ages to come up wiv that. We need to find 'im before 'e kills again."

"Get Sid on it. Old Bill won't catch 'im. They wouldn't find their own arse'ole if it was stuck to their nose."

At Lisa's funeral people turned up out of respect for the Hunters. Mat made enquiries – no matter how much he despised Lisa, she was his ex – but nothing was turned up; for once even Sid came up empty. "The trail's cold as a witch's tit, gaffa," said Sid, shuffling his feet, eyes downward in a grovelling stance. "No one knows nufink."

Mat had spoken to Casey at the funeral. She told Mat that Lisa had been trying to get into modelling, but little else, as they had fallen out weeks ago and Lisa had refused to take her calls. Debbie, on the day of the funeral, had taken time over her appearance. At the church she held Charlie's hand and didn't touch a drop of alcohol. Nic had been as near enough proud of her until she uttered loudly, "Such a shame she couldn't 'ave an open casket, ain't it?"

McBride and the force came up with nothing but dead ends. This was unchartered water for the Met. Serial killers were still quite rare in Blighty. They asked for intelligence across the pond from their counterparts, the FBI's Behaviour Science Unit (BSU), where serial killers were popping up all over the shop. In a recent poll, one in ten Americans identified as a serial killer regardless of whether or not they'd actually killed anyone. So these boys really knew what they were doing. Didn't they? The report from BSU concluded they were looking for a man between the age of eighteen and eighty-eight who had a bad relationship with their mother. A poor achiever at school, who struggled with the alphabet and only got up to the said letter, this triggering post-traumatic stress disorder, cultivating into homicidal tendencies. When McBride had seen the analysis, he'd commented to Dickson, "This is like searching for needle in a haystack. It could be 80% of the men around yere. Benny from Crossroads would've been more insightful."

THE PINK PALACE

"I can't believe we're ready to open," said Suzie. "All our 'ard work 'as really paid off."

"Queen, it's been months of blood, sweat and tantrums, but we did it."

Standing in what Jeffrey referred to as 'The Pink Palace', Suzie and Jeffrey squeezed each other with delight.

"It's beyond fabulous. Hot Cherry is going to bring magic to Dalston. Give it a month and Cher will be begging for an appointment for a backcomb."

The salon was painted head to foot in pink. Large mirrors adorned the walls opposite the workstations. There were feathered chandeliers hanging from the ceiling. Neon signs lit up the walls. In the reception there was a sofa shaped as lips, with matching cushions. The workstations were in frosted glass with overhead hair dryers. The reception desk of gold chrome, which Suzie and Jeffrey had painstakingly decorated by hand with silk roses, stood ready for the cash till to start ringing. Facials like the 'Cherry on Top' and 'Knickerbocker Glory' were advertised on elaborate boards showing the list of treatments.

"The launch party 'as to be out of this world. Did we get an RSVP from Madonna?" Suzie giggled.

"Not this time, but once we open our first up West, she'll be begging to come in. And the Nookie mullet is ready to be unleashed on Dalston since it has been road-tested up West. Thank goodness the Earl's Court guys were game. Well, I shouldn't have been surprised; they usually are. And it made me brave, Suzie, going into the Coleherne and the Philbeach Hotel. I was emboldened. If I bumped into Zac, I'd look him in the eye and tell him not to touch what he can't afford."

"Jeffrey, who could resist the Princess Diana cut on top and then long, shoulder-lenf sides?"

"Word is spreading on the street. Soon everyone can look like Pat Sharp. Let's take a moment to let that sink in. Pat Sharp is sporting the Nookie. The only thing that comes close to it is the Limahl – I mean the spikey blond mullet with the playful dark bits. Do we dare to dream we can get George in for a feather cut?"

"Mat saw 'im at 'is barbahs in Mayfair. Said 'e kept smiling at 'im. Such a friendly bloke."

"I don't see why we can't have Wham on the walls."

"It's not in keeping wiv our feme, unless you can find a postah of 'em sipping cocktails wiv cherries on cocktail sticks."

"Or covered in black forest gateau," said Jeffrey, practically drooling and a faraway look in his eyes. "Let's get our pinkies together. We're going to rock this opening party. Do you think we can get Nic to do security on the door?"

"Jeffrey, I don't fink that's gonna 'appen. We'll be safe as 'ouses."

"It looks professional and pretentious to have door security. It's the look we are going for, surely. I'll be schmoozing with the guests. I can't be the door bitch as well. I can just envisage his buff body in a tuxedo."

"Jeffrey, you need to stop 'aving crushes on red-blooded men like Nic and George. Why don't you go to the Copacabana this weekend? Go sailing."

"It's called cruising, Suzie. I'm not sure I'm ready to go back into the cruel world of dating. I'm fragile. Nic is just the eye candy I need. It's his chiselled, masculine looks and buns of steel, not to mention the large package he has," said Jeffrey trailing off.

"You should see what Suzie 'as done wiv the salon. Mat is dead proud of 'er. I don't bovah going to Reids down the Roman any more. I got Jeffrey doing me 'air. I 'ad me reservations at first, 'im being one of 'em, well, you know. But 'e's a real wag. Finks the world of Nic. 'Elp yourself to a jam tart."

"I'm not gonna let 'im get 'is 'ands on me 'air wiv one of 'em funny 'airdos. What's in *The Sun*?" asked Victor, helping himself to a tart.

"Dire Straits 'as sold ovah a million copies of their CD *Bruvahs in Arms*."

"What a stupid name. I nevah 'eard of 'em."

"Me neivah. Sometimes the paypahs get it wrong, but normally *The Sun* is bang on the money. Been me go-to paypah since '79. Mat is gonna buy me one of these CD playahs and then get all me Chas and Dave on these discs. But then I was talking to Den. 'E said there was no way 'e was swapping 'is vinyl. It wouldn't sound the same. Mind you, 'im and 'is bruvahs used to listen to some awful stuff. Purple Sabbaff."

"Chas; when 'e touches those piana keys, it's like God 'imself give 'im 'em fingahs. Anyfink else?"

"KAD in Stockport 'ave taken responsibility for the deaf of Owen Jinx, a one-year-old boy. The baby was abducted when 'e was left unattended while his parents joined the picket line wiv the striking minahs at Barrow Colliery. A picketah at the scene who wanted only to be known as Arfur S said nobody could take to the whining bairn, not even 'is muvah, who described the baby as an odious runt and forbade that 'e called 'er muvah. Owen leaves be'ind a twin sistah, Eleanor, and two bruvahs. Owen was found with his arms and legs ripped off when he was tied between two cars. Reports 'ave said it was an Austin Allegro and a Triumph TR7. KAD 'ave claimed the execution was because 'e would be problematic in the future."

"They're worse than the IRA, Rosie."

"There's more. In Baltimore KAD said they were be'ind the deaf of John Money, a psychologist working at the Johns 'Opkins Clinic. 'E's been found dead, force-fed cyproterone acetate and KAD also took responsibility for bombing the clinic, killing a furvah free 'undred. Leila Khaled, KAD's second in command formerly of the Popular Front for the Liberation of Palestine (PFLP), gave a rushed statement as she was on 'er way to 'ijack a private jet on its way to Bo'emian Grove Monte Rio California armed wiv an al Nasirah rocket launchah carrying transhumanist nut jobs, Martin Rothspunk, William Sims Basketcase and a robot called BINA48. The robot wouldn't be 'armed just deprogrammed."

MAD WORLD

"I wondah what's on the news today," said Nic. "Always somefink cheery."

Mat was too caught up in snuggling up to Suzie to care. Trevor McDonald was on TV reading the *News at Ten*. He was doing a piece on the devasting effects of drug addiction that was sweeping the nation. His broadcast cut to an anchor.

"I'm in Hackney, East London, on a street they call the frontline, Sandringham Road. There is one just like it in Brixton called Railton Road and All Saints in Notting Hill and many others all across the UK. Sandringham Road is highly affected by the misery the drug trade brings. A notable landmark on this road is the Lord Stanley pub where drugs can be bought day and night."

The poverty porn scene behind the anchor didn't fail to disappoint in all its stark deprivation. The producers had made sure they had filmed in the worst part of the road. They'd been spoilt for choice but settled on a part of the road, which was slightly more squalid. It was the two burnt-out cars that finally swayed their choice. They'd hoped to find a dead body on the street, but they were out of luck. That had happened last week.

The anchor continued, "What the government and police are really looking to do is to stop this evil trade at the source. Each year kilos of cocaine and heroin are smuggled into the UK from South America and Afghanistan, with a street value of multi-millions. These illegal drugs are passed down the drug-dealer food chain, where they then flood our streets. It is the high-level, so-called untouchable drug dealers whom the authorities want to catch. To cut the supply at the source. To stop the Brahmins from passing the narcotics down the distribution chain right the way down to the Dalits. It is somewhat of a viscous circle, as these street-level dealers are usually addicted to the very drug they're selling. These street pushers are living hand to mouth and, yes, sometimes quite literally dealing straight from their mouths." The camera cut to a shifty-looking man who looked like a chipmunk.

"I feel so sorry for these poor people," said Suzie.

"Got me mini violin out 'ere," said Nic.

"Oh, Nic, your 'art doesn't reach out to these people?" asked Suzie.

"Yeh, sorry. I don't know 'ow to 'andle these, like, sensitive subjects. Us blokes, we're not as in touch wiv our feelings like you birds. It really does get to me. It's, like, what 'ave we become as 'uman beings?"

Suzie looked at Nic like he was speaking the words of the gospel. Underneath all the wide-boy persona, he obviously had a big heart.

The anchor continued, "The police have their work cut out for them at an unprecedented scale, as it's hard to fight the invisible. These untouchable drug lords use their vast wealth and contacts to hide behind, living almost above the law."

Mat let out a laugh, but seeing Suzie's hurt face, he disguised it with a cough.

"It's awful for these poor souls," said Suzie. "These drug dealahs, they must be animals."

"Yeh, princess," said Mat, rustling up as much sincerity in his tone as he could. "Really bad people. They should, like, give 'em really 'arsh prison sentences; life wivout parole."

"Fing is, Suzie," said Nic in a serious tone, struggling to keep a straight face, "some say that drug-dealing is, like, good for the community."

"What do you mean?" asked Suzie, looking bemused.

"Well, it brings money into the community, see. 'Ackney is a what they call a deprived area. For some there's not much employment. Even Lesney Matchbox Toy Factory 'as closed down. Was propah gutted 'bout that. I always seen meself working there when I was oldah when I was a kid, like."

"I fought you and Mat was gonna work for your dad," said Suzie, looking at Mat.

"That was just the back-up plan, weren't it," said Nic.

"Princess, it was a sensitive subject. I don't feel comfortable talking 'bout it. Even now it's 'ard. But, yeh, me and Nic, when we was kids, we always wanted to work there," said Mat, hoping Nic would now change the subject. He wasn't finding this funny.

But Nic wasn't half done. This was way too much fun. "See, Fatchah, she wants us all to be entrepreneurs. You know, like your business. See, some may fink they don't 'ave too many choices so they deal drugs. Then they put money back into the community cos they can buy fings from local businesses like your salon."

"'Ot Cherry!" gasped Suzie.

"Princess, of course not," said Mat, shooting Nic a shut-the-fuck-up look. "Nic is just saying that some will deal a few drugs to make a few bob. Probably more the type to spend their dough at the pub or the bookies. Like Junkie Jimmy."

"Who's Junkie Jimmy?"

"Just some guy me and Nic went to school wiv. Went down the wrong paf. Ended up a drug addict. Anyways, bit depressing this. Ain't there somefink betta on telly. Isn't *Moonlighting* on? You love that."

"Oh, you went to school wiv 'im. 'Ave you tried to 'elp 'im?"

"Uh, yeh, princess, of course we 'ave. We've tried everyfink wiv 'im – rehab and ferapy – but 'e doesn't wanna know. The drugs 'ave got 'old of 'im badly. Didn't we, Nic?"

"Don't recall that at all, bruv, but if you say we did, I guess we must 'ave. Just 'artbreaking, innit. These drug dealahs got a lot to answah for, and so 'ave the people who front businesses off the back of drug money. It disturbs me, and like these rufless people can't go to their bank and say, ''Ere's one 'undred large I got from selling crack to school kids. Bung it in me savings account, will ya?' So do you know what I've been told they do, Suzie?"

"What, Nic?"

"They set up businesses that seem, like, propah enouf, but what they're doing is pushing the money frough there to make it look like the money is legal. Cleaning it up. Like putting it frough a washing machine."

"Do you think that's going on 'ere in Dalston?"

"I fink it may be. You know Geekay Styles on the 'Igh Street? Let's just say I got me suspicions. I'm finking there's more than frocks in the stockroom. We're talking pushing serious weight 'ere. Disturbing, innit, the depfs some people will go to make money?"

"Recap Erdoğan, the ownhah, 'e does a lot of charity work for the RSPCC and Refuge"

"People can be deceiving. Just keep your eyes open; that's all I'm saying. Ask yourself this: why does 'e keep going back and fore to Turkey?"

"That's where 'e's from, and 'is family live there."

"All a bit convenient, innit. It's like that's what 'e wants you to fink. Turkey; that's where a lot of 'eroin is coming from. I watched this *World in Action* fing on it."

"I won't be able to look 'im in the eye again, and 'is wife Emine comes in for a Morello facial."

"It's like there 'as been a complete breakdown in law and ordah, and that's mostly due to the police."

"What do you mean, Nic?"

"It's like this. There's Old Bill who're as bad as the criminals. They're taking back'andahs so these dealahs can continue pushing drugs. I've even 'eard some Old Bill are dealing."

"In Dalston, Nic?"

"Let's just say I 'eard that is 'ow Mr Erdoğan can continue being a serious dealah. 'E's giving moody Old Bill a serious bung to turn a blind eye. Even frowing in a few frocks for their missus."

"Princess, what Nic means is there's a few bad Old Bill out there. It's nufink to worry 'bout."

"Bruv, I fink it's important, as law-abiding citizens, that we're aware of what's going on in our community."

Mat, eager to finish this conversation, said, "So 'ow's the wedding planning going?"

Mat, knowing Suzie was the one, had proposed to her at Langan's on Stratton Street with a platinum and diamond ring from Garrard after just three months.

"It's going really well, and Jeffrey I fink is coming to terms wiv not being a bridesmaid."

"One fing, mind, princess; I don't want 'em spuds Chas and Dave anywhere near me wedding, so you'll need to let Nan down gently on that one. Tell 'er they're on tour in Cambodia or somefink like that. Suzie nodded in agreement. She already had her heart set on a Wham tribute act called Freedom, two lads from Barking.

DRESSED TO KILL

Jonathan Steerpike was a creature of habit. He left his accountancy offices on Eccleston Place in Belgravia each day at 1pm to walk to Ebury Street, where he bought a baguette from Donato Bilancia's Deli. Today was no different, save that Jonathan had a lot on his mind. Jonathan held the bridge of his Cutler and Gross-spectacle-adorned nose, as he could feel a migraine mounting. Jonathan was an average man, five-foot-nine, with a slim build and forgettable face. But it had been indoctrinated into him from his privileged cradle that he was loftily above the average person. He'd been educated at Eton then Oxbridge. The little people didn't exist to him; unlike them, he was a card-carrying member of the establishment. By the devil, he was a paid-up member of the Tory party. What he looked like meant nothing; he had breeding, and that shone through. The street was busy with cars and pedestrians, a flurry of ballyhoo. Usually, Jonathan liked this – it made him feel alive – but today, like some foreboding omen, it felt different. It was almost like he was a man walking to the gallows. Jonathan scolded himself on these dark thoughts and encouraged his brilliant mind to think of the mess he'd got himself into and how, more importantly, he could get out of. He walked past Ken Lo's restaurant. There was a delivery van parked outside unloading delicacies. The van's radio blasted out Talking Heads' 'Road to Nowhere'.

Jonathan's father, Egbert, had established the business – Steerpike & Sons. Papa, a man who had built the firm up from scratch. The son of landowner in Sussex, he'd grown up on a 5,000-acre estate. His grandfather Archibald had believed heavily that a man had to make his own way in this world. Using a tough-love approach, he gave him just pocket change, a mere £100,000, to start his own venture. He was then brutally cast out into the abyss. When the firm really took off, his Papa had firmly believed he was a self-made man. Jonathan had spent many a happy hollibobs at what Grandpapa called the small holding. It began for him a lifelong love of all things farming. After his Papa had passed away, Jonathan had taken over the accountancy firm, a firm he was soon to find out was in dire straits. Egbert had the firm heavily mortgaged and in debt up to its eyeballs due to his nefarious gambling addiction. He'd spent many nights at the illegal gambling dens in Knightsbridge frittering away his money with the likes of Aleister Crowley. The occasional smoking of opium hadn't helped matters either. Crowley, with his do-what-thou-wilt mantra, had a lot to answer for; a man so depraved Benito had expelled him from Italy, fearful of any competition in the lunatic stakes. Crowley, a rampant individualist, was everything that Il Duce despised. How dare someone think and do for themselves and not for the collective cult of the state. But let this be a lesson if you choose to keep company with a Cantabrigian. Mummy had been left alone at home with just a cook, nanny and maid. Such a torrid affair. Egbert needed money fast, so Den Hunter had been a godsend, an East End gangster who had money that needed to be cleaned up pronto. Den was an intimating individual, but Egbert had seen pound signs when he came in. He could clean up his money and at the same time be paid handsomely. He could pay off the gambling debts to the Triads. The threat of *lingchi*, which was a slow death by slicing a body into a thousand cuts, was enough for Egbert to realise they meant business. From time-to-time Den asked to see the balance sheets, which were all completely to the letter.

But now Jonathan was in deep shit. A sure-winner property deal that a couple of MP pals had brought to him – fellow Eton and Oxbridge alumnus, Boris and Jacob. Foppish Boris, who'd studied the classics of Literae Humaniores at Balliol, a degree that covered many subjects from literature history to philosophy – literally, you became an expert in everything. If you didn't have any competency in advising in matters, you were a master of mendaciousness. If challenged on anything, he would reply with the word 'floccinaucinihilipilification', deeming the questioner worthless. If in doubt, bring the Latin out. At the Bullingdon Club at Oxbridge the old rascal Boris had once told him voting Tory means your wife will have bigger breasts and you'll drive a BMW. So far, one of these had come true, and it was terrifyingly on the cards how long he would hold on to his BMW M3. And Jacob, such erudite chats at the Athenaeum Club. I mean, the Victorian era and the level of poverty was just a preposterous conspiracy theory. Those photographs that Horace Warner took of the Spitalfields nippers, those disingenuous paupers with spindly legs and gaunt cheeks, they were obviously doctored. The conspirophile Dickens really had a lot to answer for. I mean, how could they afford flat caps and good waistcoats if they were so poor?

His chums had sold him a deal to build a block of flats in Thamesmead, which had turned very sour. It was supposed to make multi-million pounds of profit. Thinking he was onto a winner, he invested heavily, taking out huge loans on his business and house. The property was now £4 million over budget, with an end date nowhere in sight. Added to his woes, conservationists had found that a rare breed of bat, classed as an endangered species, were homing there, putting a stop to the proceedings. The rabid pro-bat activists were unrelenting. They came in their droves, confused white men with dreadlocks spewing biodiversity. He should have taken it as a forewarning when Kubrick the legendary director filmed his 1971 dystopian classic there.

His father died of a heart attack and Den Hunter was on a forever holiday. Jonathan now dealt with his sons. After a business meeting with Nic, he'd told him to head down to his club in Soho. One Saturday night, propelled by Grey Goose at the French House, he walked over to the Love Hole. Jonathan was married to Camilla, a Sloan-ranger with a grey bob who favoured a twinset. She had borne him a daughter, Sophia. Over the years, Jonathan had his indiscretions with women, mainly at the discreet brothel he used in Ambleside Avenue Streatham that Boris frequented. Jonathan had needs his wife wouldn't understand. The whores who worked at Madam Cyn's understood. There were no taboos; anything went. In the garden, slaves toiled naked. They paid their Superior Mistress £40 a week for the honour of trimming her prize bush. If you wanted to strap on a bullyboy king-cock dildo and shove it up the backside of a vicar's arsehole, this was welcome.

Walking into the club, Jonathan was impressed. He looked at the stage show; two identical twins pleasured themselves. Their faces were poised in practised throws of ecstasy. Scantily dressed women were draped over gentlemen and sucked seductively on cocktails. The DJ blasted out Scritti Politti's 'The Word Girl' from Braun L46 speakers.

Walking over to the bar, Jonathan saw Nic talking to a beautiful girl with flowing chestnut hair. "All right, mate?

What you 'aving to drink? I recommend the Moloko Vellocet."

"My friend Stephen tasted the delights here. He said it was like asphyxiation eroticism. He had a cocktail with an orange segment at the bottom."

"Yeh, that's the Ludovico. Pure firegold. It's whisky-based. Well, it's, like, all whisky, innit."

"What's in the Vellocet?"

"Vodka, Campari and Absinthe. No mixer. Just warming up meself. I'm on me eighf."

A pretty barmaid took his order. Ever so slightly taken aback by the dearness of the drink, but not wanting to show it, Jonathan took out his wallet.

"This is Tracey," said Nic.

Now a bit closer, Jonathan was even more impressed. Tracey had sultry green eyes and rosebud lips with a willowy body and large bosoms which were incased in a black basque. She wore little else other than a G-string and sky-high heels.

"Tracey is gonna take good care of you tonight, ain't you, darling?"

Jonathan had imagined that Tracey, when she spoke, would have a high, breathy voice. He wasn't expecting, "Eye up, duck. Owt thee wants, just ask. Why don't we go get comfy over in't booth. Bob in't there. Chuffing 'eck, be glad tu sit down. Me shoes is reyt killing me."

"I thought you looked like a West End girl," said Jonathan as he took a gulp of his drink and wished he hadn't; it was like drinking paint stripper.

"No, duckie. Yarkshire lass."

Tracey Braithwaite was a runaway from The Buttershaw Estate in Bradford. At fifteen she'd arrived at King's Cross train station with nothing more to her name than a bag packed with her meagre belongings, her diary and £20. Anything was better than being forced into sex with her stepdad as her mother watched, egging him on. As someone who classed herself as a streetwise girl, Tracey was shocked to find how much darker London was. After getting out at King's Cross, Tracey realised the £20 she had hidden had been stolen. Despondent, Tracey had crumpled into a pile and started to sob her heart out. A man called Malachi had taken pity on her and brought her back to his flat in Birkenhead Street. He stroked her hair and told her everything would be better and that she could stay with him as long as she needed until she got back on her feet. The irony of those words. Malachi had made her lie on her back for anyone who could pay to fuck her. Tracey walked the red-light beat of the Cross to put money in her pimp's pocket day and night. A chance encounter at an ice-cream parlour with another working girl called Clara had changed her life's path. Clara told Tracey of the 'City of Gold' that was the West End five-star hotels. The duo fled one night and took a tube to Green Park and entered the Ritz hotel. They were thrown out by the manager, as they looked too commonly dressed to be patrons there. A wealthy Arab had watched them being chucked out and asked the concierge to bring them back in. Before long Tracey was frequenting the Savoy, the Dorchester and Claridge's. At the Guinea Grill on Bruton Place, Mayfair, she began chatting to a working girl called Monica, who told them of the profitable trade at Shepherd Market. You could meet all sorts there – Harley Street doctors, hedge fund managers and even MPs. She confided in her that she had one herself. "Darling, Jeffrey. Such a sweetheart, but so light-fingered."

Away from Malachi's clutches, at the Beaufort Bar in the Savoy, a tall, dark, handsome man wearing diamond cufflinks had approached her and asked if she wanted to dance at his club. It sounded too good to be true. The charismatic man told her she could make lots of money just dancing and stripping. With his cheeky smile and mischievous green-blue eyes, Tracey had fallen for it hook, line and sinker. He had her really thinking she could come off the game. That meant she could put more energy into launching her modelling and acting career. Tracey's reality was that life was now better than on the cold harsh streets of the Cross or the streets supposedly paved in gold in the West End, but it wasn't idyllic by any means. Tracey worked long hard hours servicing punters. Nic was more than happy to give a girl a backhander if she stepped out of line, and he expected you to service him any time he wanted, having his very own special take on oral sex, where he grabbed you by the neck and stuffed your face down on his large, throbbing cock repeatedly until you were practically choking to death.

"You birds love a man taking control. Not like I give a shit. Goes wivout saying. 'Nuff said. Now fuck off back in the club and make me money."

The night had flown by for Jonathan. Tracey had been attentive, making sure she listened to his endless boring tales as if she'd just heard the most enlightening story. Only once, when asked about herself, did she tell him she was working there until she got her acting and modelling career going. All the while the champagne flowed, which was all being put on Jonathan's ever-increasing tab. Tracey conferred to him that she'd started her acting career starring in blue movies under the name of Zandaline Moon. She'd made two: *Muff by Moonlight* and *One Night in the Moon*. When closing time came, Tracey had suggested he come back to her flat on Frith Street for a nightcap. Feeling more than a bit tipsy, and high on the heady sex-fuelled atmosphere of the club, Jonathan hadn't hesitated to say yes. After settling the hefty bill, he'd escorted Tracey back to her flat. She'd opened up a bottle of Concorde and filled a couple of glasses with it. There was something so down to earth about this girl, someone he believed he could trust. Before long, when she cracked open a second bottle, Jonathan spilled the beans he'd formerly only ever told those understanding ladies that worked for Madam Cyn. Giggling like a schoolgirl, Jonathan asked if he could try on Tracey's lingerie. He was very much in touch with his feminine persona and preferred to be called India. Tracey, sniffing a way to make a bob or two here, had duly complied. "Don't worry, India, now't surprises me. Not like I'm gonna terf thee owt or nowt. India, that's dead exotic, in't it?"

Tracey noticed his eyes were staring at her hamper basket full of lotions and make-up. It had been bought for her by a wealthy American, Robert Durst, and had been filled with champagne and chocolates. "Aye, go on, India, fill thee boots with all thu lotions in thu basket. Do you want me tu make thee up? Thee would look dead good with some blusher and lippie. Eee, by gumb, thee would."

There'd been one upsetting incident when Camilla had found *Cocks in Frocks* in his briefcase. She'd been most disturbed at the content. Never in her life had she seen such abominations and bulging knickers. When she confronted her husband, he'd acted mortified and explained that he hadn't had his spectacles on and had inadvertently ordered the magazine, when what he was trying to order was *Vintage Tractor* magazine, explaining to her there was a two-page spread on John Froelich who invented the tractor. He wasn't expecting to get a full spread of a man's hairy arsehole.

While India lounged on satin sheets dressed in an aqua lace camisole, Tracey suggested they make this a regular thing. They discussed money, and high on thinking he looked like Kelly LeBrock, Jonathan had agreed. She took out a polaroid camera she'd been given by a high-ranking Met officer who liked to take pictures when she was going down on him. Egged on by Tracey, Jonathan had preened and posed 'seductively' while she took pictures, making sure his face was clear in every one. "Chuck, thee is a natural at this," said Tracey, unable to get Frank-N-Furter out of her mind. Tracey wondered why anyone would wish to be born a woman. They'd only need to walk a mile in her shoes and see why. It was food for thought when she wrote her diary – something she had done since childhood. It was a way to try to make sense of all the demons she lived with as a beautiful woman. Tracey told him she'd keep the pictures safe until next time they met, and they could have some fun looking at them. Completely turned on, Jonathan had wholeheartedly agreed. After paying Tracey handsomely for her time, the accountant left on cloud nine. Days later an envelope was delivered to his offices marked 'PRIVATE AND CONFIDENTIAL' for his attention. Opening the envelope, he'd been confronted with a selection of polaroids of him, a hairy-chested vision in blue lace, and a typed note asking for £50,000 to be deposited into the bank account of Tracey Braithwaite or the pictures would be sent to his wife. Already up to his eyeballs in debt, there was no way he could get his hands on that kind of money, and there was no way his wife could find out. Camilla would file for a divorce, and he sure as hell couldn't afford that. The last thing he needed was the astronomical matrimonial lawyer fees. I mean, charging extortionate fees for his accounting skills was one thing, but handing it over to solicitors was just daylight robbery. There was a reason that lawyers were cast into the third tier of Dante's *Inferno* in which they would spend eternity trapped inside a burning metal coffin. Jonathan, over a large Graham's Port at the Oxford and Cambridge Club on Pall Mall, had put his brilliant mind to work. How could this frightful strumpet think she could stitch him up? He gave himself a mental dressing down and convinced himself that his level of anxiety was disproportionate to the problem at hand. Then, like an epiphany, the answer came to him. It was, in a roundabout way, the Hunter brothers' fault he was in this predicament. If he hadn't gone to the club that night, at the behest of Nic, this horrid situation wouldn't have happened. Yes, this was their fault, and they would provide the solution. He would skim money off their accounts. He'd to date only skimmed smallish sums from them. Mat's biggest account was the Newman account, named after his favourite actor. There were millions of pounds in that account, and vast sums went in and out. He'd cleverly extract the £50,000 from there. Heck, why not £100,000? He could then top up his Coutts bank account which he was nearly close to losing. He had heard rumours of a faction called the Rainbow Shirts that they deployed to deal with problematic customers.

He turned up at Tracey's flat and agreed to give her the £50,000 within a week, provided that she gave him half the photos now and the other half when he gave her the money. Tracey made good money stripping and doing extras at the club, but 70% went to Nic, which was financially crippling. After paying her exorbitant rent on her flat, Tracey was struggling to make ends meet. The girls tried to circumvent this by making their own more lucrative deals in the private rooms, but Dexy had started to get wise to this. Nic had made it very clear what would happen if they tried to put one over him again.

"You scheming slags, let's get fings nice and fucking sparkling clear. Anyfink you earn in this club, I get 70% of."

Coming back to his none-too-bright present, Jonathan continued to walk down Ebury Street. He just needed to get the money he'd taken from the Newman account to him so he could pay Tracey, and then he could breathe easily. Hopefully, in just twenty-four hours it would all be over.

Jonathan didn't see the 900 MHR Ducati motorbike gaining speed in front of him, neither did he notice until it was too late the helmeted passenger on the back take out a sawn-off Remington 870 from his jacket. The driver slowed down. The passenger pulled the trigger. It was a crack shot that took off most of Jonathan's head, leaving just a partial bloody orb. The blood spatter saturated the pavement as passersby looked on with horror. A young mother retched in disgust as she saw her baby in its pram covered with pulverised brain. Sparky released the throttle, and the false-plated Ducati rocketed forward – leaving just exhaust fumes as it sped off down the street. The twins dumped the Ducati at a lock-up in Pimlico. From there they took a Ford Orion and drove back to Nan's, who was making their favourite, beef wellington, for tea.

"'Ello, Nan," said Flint as she opened the front door, and he planted a kiss on her cheek, soon after followed by Sparky.

"Oh, lovely to see you, boys. Food be ready in ten minutes."

The boys followed their nan into the kitchen.

"Right, who wants a cuppa?"

"Yeh, Nan, that be 'andsome," said Flint. "I just gonna pop in the front room and call Mat."

"All right, son. Make sure you tell 'im I picked up 'is post and took it 'ome again. I'll pop it 'round tomorrah."

"Will do, Nan."

Flint made his way into Nan's parlour. Slouching down on the chintzy sofa, he picked up the phone and dialled Mat, who picked up on the second ring.

"It's done, cuz."

"Right, and 'e's deffo brown bread."

"Yeh, unless you can live wiv only a fird of your 'ead."

With that, Flint cut the call and went back just in time for Nan to plonk a cup of tea in front of him. "Now, no going in the biscuit tin until you 'ave eaten your tea. I don't want you spoiling your appetites. Dun us a lovely steamed jam pudding for aftahs. We'll 'ave that wiv a bit of custard."

Mat was watching the news. The cuntless diabolical liberty-taker had had his comeuppance. You don't steal off Mat Hunter and expect to live. He already had an equally creative accountant lined up. Pouring himself a Dalmore whiskey, he lit a cigar and flicked the TV off.

In her flat, Tracey was painting her nails thinking of all the ways she was going to spend the £50,000. Her ears pricked up when she heard the newsreader utter the name Jonathan Steerpike. Hurling herself off her bed, nail polish splashing everywhere and making the room stink of Pear Drops, she turned the radio up. She let the news sink in. Two men on a motorbike had gunned him down. He was pronounced dead at the scene. All Tracey's dreams vanished into thin air.

Two years later Maggie Smith was cleaning the offices of Steerpike & Sons. Jonathan's room was now occupied by his daughter, Sophia, who'd taken over as managing director. She could see something almost imperceptible poking through behind the walnut bookcase. It looked like a corner of a brown envelope. Pulling it out, she opened the envelope. What she found enclosed was a very lucrative eye-opener.

The next day the headline of *The Sun* newspaper read: '**TRANNY JONATHAN GOT HIS HEAD BLOWN OFF BUT KEPT HIS BALLS**'. The *Daily Star* followed with the more subtle headline: '**THE HEADLESS CHICK WITH A DICK**'. Jonathan stared out of the front pages in technicolour glory.

WHITE WEDDING

"It's just been a perfick day. I can't believe I'm now officially Mrs 'Untah," said Suzie, admiring her platinum wedding ring.

"I've nevah seen you look so beautiful, princess. I can't wait to get you to the 'oneymoon suite as me wife."

The day for Suzie had been a fairytale. The only thing missing were Suzie's parents, who'd relocated to Lido di Jesolo. They couldn't leave Suzie's elderly grandmother, who was very sick. The newlyweds would leave in the morning to fly to Italy for their honeymoon, where they would meet up with Suzie's parents. They'd lease a Ferrari Testarossa and stay at the Danieli Hotel in Venice. The wedding was held at St Mark's Church, a magnificent monastery in the early English Gothic style. The church was filled with flowers from Moyses Stevens. Suzie walked down the aisle a vision in white silk. Nic was best man and Debbie had reluctantly been bridesmaid, squeezing herself into a dress made of pink taffeta. She thundered down the aisle behind the bride and her Uncle Alessandro, who was giving her away. Nic, at the front of the church, saw the potential car crash coming towards him.

After the nuptials, they went to the Savoy for the wedding reception, where guests ate a six-course wedding breakfast. Debbie still complained loudly that she was hungry, but consoled herself until the evening buffet by knocking back copious glasses of champagne. The reception buffet was stacked with delicacies such as prawn and avocado *vol-au-vents*, Oysters Kilpatrick and *croquetas de gambas*. There was a table dedicated to puddings, laden with everything from *crème brûlée* to *tiramisu*. The Cristal champagne fountain was twenty tiers high. Nobody could quite believe how much Debbie got on her plate. Not the first nor the second time, and the only reason she didn't have a third was because, drunk, she'd tripped and gone flying, the plate, sailing through the air, nearly decapitating Victor before it crashed to the ground. Nic had manhandled Debbie back to her seat.

"Can't ya go anywhere wivout making a scene? For fuck's sake, Debs; this is me bruvah's wedding."

"I can't 'elp it if I tripped, can I? I nevah wanted to be Miss Perfick's bridesmaid, did I? You made me!"

"Tripped? You're drunk."

"It's your fault I drink so much. You treat me like nufink. I'm your wife, and the muvah of your son."

"Son? You what? The same son you 'aven't looked at all day," said Nic without any irony, seeing as he hadn't either.

"Charlie's wiv Nan. 'E's more than fine," said Debbie as she got up unsteadily and headed over to a passing waiter, snatching two glasses of champagne from the tray he was carrying.

Charlie had been happy to be with Nan and Victor for the day. Nan had been delighted. He looked so handsome in his little suit. And little it was. He was wearing clothes for a child one year younger. Not that Nic had taken him to the fittings. That had been left to Mat, who had been very proud to introduce his nephew to his tailor.

"Posh up 'ere, ain't it, Victor? Can't see meself why they couldn't 'ave it in the Crown. Tommy always puts on a good spread."

"I fink it's all 'bout who's there, not where it is. I'm 'appy wiv a bit of pie and mash than all that fingah food."

"'Ave you 'ad a good day, Charlie?"

"Yes, Nan," said Charlie, his face covered in chocolate and cream from the profiteroles. "Can I come and stay with you tonight?" he asked as he glanced over to his parents on the nearby table who were animatedly arguing.

Nan looked over and tutted before saying, "You leave it wiv Nan."

"Debbie's a bleeding disgrace, Victor. I don't know what 'appened to 'er. She's a terrible wife and muvah. Nic works all the 'ours undah the sun and 'e gets it all frown back in 'is face."

Victor decided to change the subject. He personally thought Nic was the root of all of Debbie's problems. Batty Betty had filled him in on the things that went on at his so-called gentlemen's clubs. "Who's the girls the twins are wiv?"

"No idea, Victor. To be 'onest, they go frough so many women I stopped asking their names. Mind you, wiv the way me memory is I probably wouldn't remembah. Ohh look. It's the first dance. Let's make a move."

"I've picked a really special song for us, Mat," whispered Suzie as they held each other's hands walking to the edge of the dancefloor. It was then that Mat's nightmare started as he heard the opening bars of Glenn Medeiros's 'Nothing's Gonna Change My Love For You'. Mat wanted the ground to swallow him up, and momentarily his feet were paralysed. He tried, but he couldn't walk onto the dance floor. He furtively glanced around. No one would dare laugh. All Mat saw was a sea of tight smiles and stiff postures. That was, apart from Sparky and Flint, who didn't attempt to hide their rising smirks, and Nic who was clutching his belly laughing. Suzie gently nudged Mat onto the floor, and he found, with mind over matter, he could once again move his legs. Now he had to muster all of his reserve to get through this ordeal and more importantly keep some semblance of dignity.

Suzie tenderly whispered in his ear, "I knew you'd love it, Mat. This song is special. It's our song."

"Course it is, princess," said Mat while thinking how he would like to stuff Glenn's greasy face through a meat grinder. It was the longest three minutes of his life.

Wanting to get as far away from Debbie as he could, Nic had headed for the bar. He could see his cousins ordering.

"All right? 'Ow's it's going?"

"Good, cuz. Blinding idea, bringing a couple of birds from your place. Easier than 'aving to go to all the effort down the pub and pull 'em. What's their names?"

"Got fuck-all idea. Where've they gone?"

"To the bogs. Said somefink 'bout eating too much. Mat looks 'appy, apart from, like, the dance. That was funny as fuck. Glenn fucking Medeiros. 'E's nevah gonna live that one down."

"I'm gonna make sure 'e won't live it down. Wedding dance to some greasy spic's shit-cunt's crap song. Not sure why 'e 'asn't 'anded the reins to me when 'e's on 'is 'oneymoon. But no, Mr Control 'as to be running fings in Italy. Fing is 'is 'ead isn't gonna be in it. It's gonna be too messed up wiv Disney Princess banging on 'bout 'airspray and curlahs."

"Don't fink he plans doing much talking wiv 'er."

"Yeh, well, that's the fing, see. Birds always find a way to run their moufs off, like, unless you gag 'em, which goes wivout saying. 'Nuff said. I'm all for. Uvahwise they just go on and on talking shit. Mat's 'ead 'asn't really been innit since 'e met 'er. Fink 'e's losing 'is grip, and I don't like it. You must 'ave noticed 'e's changed."

"Dunno, Nic. 'E seems to be on top of it all to me. 'E played a blindah wiv that land 'e bought and sold down the docks. Looking back, we should 'ave put dough into it. Moving more into drugs seems like sense to us. We got a sweet fing going on in Kent. They can't get enouf of it."

"Yeh, well, 'e may 'ave 'ad a few lucky breaks, but there's more to it than that, being the boss. There's no room for weakness in that slot. I wouldn't 'ave any bird getting in the way. Trust me on this; she'll make him weak. Now she gets to 'im, that means 'e can be got to. It's a problem. I can see it plain as day. 'Is armour is cracking, and that's what always gave me bruvah the edge. No one could get to 'im. Anyways, betta go back and see what the missus is up to. 'Oping she 'asn't stuffed the 'ole wedding cake down 'er gob."

Letting that information sink in, Nic walked off muttering, "She's a sitting duck."

Suzie and Jeffrey were pulling some moves on the dance floor when Mat moved in and picked Suzie up and carried her off to the bridal suite. Jeffrey, clutching the bride's bouquet – which he had pushed guests out of the way at the church to get when Suzie had thrown it – barely noticed, shaking his booty dementedly then making jerky thrusting movements with his skinny hips. How could Nic ignore this? He was totally irresistible dressed in saffron leggings topped off with a mint tank top and denim fringed jacket.

Mat carried his bride through the doors of the royal suite. All he could think of was getting her into bed and fucking her as his wife. Throwing her down on the bed, ready to devour her, Suzie's babydoll face looked at him so trustingly. Mat pulled up her wedding dress and roughly ripped off her white, lacy knickers. Mat started to lick and kiss her tight fanny. Suzie gasped in ecstasy, her juices flowing, her body responding to his perfectly as she grasped his body. Mat was in seventh heaven as he roughly explored her body. He literally could not get enough of it. Suzie, who he'd broken in now, fucked like a rabbit, every pore of her eager to please him, squeezing her legs tightly around his waist as he pumped into her as they came together explosively. They wildly fucked every way possible until dawn when, exhausted, Suzie fell asleep in Mat's arms.

"Nic, what a beautiful wedding. Suzie looked like a princess. Do you know she even wanted to put me 'air in curlahs on 'er special day? She just finks of uvahs, that girl."

"I don't fink Mat will want to let 'er out of 'is sight. Keep 'er locked up from now on."

"Ahh, will 'e 'ave 'er in a gilded cage, son?"

"No, like, they'll be living in the flat in Mayfair," said Nic, thinking it was time to get Nan tested for dementia. "But, yeh, Nan, good day, weren't it," said Nic, looking at his wife, who was slumped on a chair.

"I was finking Charlie could come and stay wiv me tonight. I tried to ask Debbie, but she's sozzled and weren't making any sense."

"Nan, that's just normal for 'er, but, yeh, good idea. You 'ave Charlie tonight."

"You need to take Debbie 'ome, son."

"I will, right. See you tomorrah, Nan." With that, Nic went back to get his wife, but not before he made a quick trip to the gents' for a livener.

ACT 4

RISKY BUSINESS

I follow him to serve my turn upon him.
– William Shakespeare, *Othello*

The very first essential for success is a perpetually constant and regular employment of violence.
– Adolf Hitler, *Mein Kampf*

"You 'eard 'bout Noye?" asked Nic.

"Yeh, 'e'll do loadsa bird for that," said Mat.

"What's the tight git dun?" asked Sparky.

"Gone and dun in some pig who was in 'is garden."

"One less then, innit. Why was the pig in 'is garden?"

"Undahcuvah Old Bill was watching Noye. C11 and C8 got a tipoff 'e 'as some of the gold," said Mat.

"What the fuck is C11 and C8."

"C11 is the specialist surveillance unit and C8 is the new name for The Sweeney."

"'Ow did 'e get 'old of the gold?"

"Little Legs needed someone wiv clout who could convert 'is share. Noye's mate Mickey picks up a gold smeltah in 'Atton Garden in 'is Rollah, where it's so big, 'e can't do the boot up. Drives up Kent to 'is gaff, but Sweeney for some reason, as they're fick as shit, finks it looks suspicious. Anyways, Noye saw someone crawling 'round 'is back garden. Bloke's a keen gardenah, like. No cunt is messing wiv 'is shrubs. This geezah is dressed in a webbing scarf, balaclava and camouflage 'ood. Brenda, 'is missus, is in the 'ouse, so finks it's, like, a rapist or burglar or even SAS crawling 'round in his garden, cos shit 'appens in the badlands of leafy Kent. This pig clumped 'im one, so I 'eard Kenny stabbed 'im eighty times in self-defence. Can't blame 'im. Any cunt creeping 'round me garden, I would 'ave dun the same," said Nic.

"Told Old Bill when they turned up 'e 'oped the pig died, shouldn't 'ave been on 'is premises. Old Bill started a search of 'is 'ouse. They fought the gold was 'idden beneaf it, as there's a World War Two bunkah there. But, no, Noye decided to 'ide it in a gully by the garage wall. They found eleven gold bars, and, like, no idea what was going frough 'is 'ead, Noye 'ad a copy of the Guinness Book of Records wiv a circle drawn 'round Brink's-Mat as the largest British robbery evah. Noye 'as just brought more 'eat on us. 'E should 'ave just let 'is Rottweilers take care of the cunt. They got this new bloke 'eading up the investigation, one of 'em 'onest coppahs, Brian Boyce, 'e's Sweeney, and someone from C11, Phillip Corbett. Got me snouts all ovah it," said Mat.

"Noye wanted Kent Old Bill on it and not Scotland Yard. Too many there out to get 'im, ones 'e's not giving a bung to," said Nic. "When 'e was being interviewed, 'e told Kent Old Bill to get Commandah Ray Adams to affirm 'im cos 'e knows 'im from being a Mason at the 'Ammersmif Lodge."

"This ain't good. One of their own 'as been taken out. They'll be gunning for blood."

"Who's 'is brief?" asked Sparky.

"Same as ours. Relton. And 'e's instructed John Maffew QC, propah quality. If 'e can't get 'im off this pig deaf, no one can. Met is taking no chances. The jury will 'ave round-the-clock protection so they can't be intimidated."

"I 'ave faith that Kenny will get to most of the jury, tell 'em it's best a not-guilty verdict unless they want their families tortured to deaf then slung in the Thames," said Nic as he took a slurp of his tea. "Are there any more biscuits?"

Mat picked up the phone and dialled and Greta answered.

"Darling, bring us some biscuits in."

"No problem, Mat. I was wondering, would I be able to work through my lunch break and finish at four-thirty? Nigel and I want to go and buy a new computer game, Barbarian: The Ultimate Warrior. It comes out today. It's—"

Before Greta had a chance to tell him about it, Mat said, "No problem, sweet'eart. Why don't you shoot off at four."

"Thanks, Mat," said Greta as she hung up the phone and proceeded to the kitchen.

"Sparks, George Francis may be finking 'bout shooting 'is mouf off to Old Bill. 'E's got 'is 'ands on some of the gold. Old Bill fink 'e was one of the gang. The last fing we need now wiv all this aggro Noye 'as brought on us is 'im grassing."

"You want me and Flint to pay 'im a visit?"

"Go ovah to 'is pub. It's the 'Enry the Eighf in Kent. No need to take 'im out. Take a shootah and maim 'im. Once 'e's got a bullet in 'im, 'e won't be so keen to grass. Take the bike wiv Flint. In and out job. No need to set 'im on fire on this occasion."

"We'll go ovah tomorrah, but I don't fink we can rule that mefod out in the future."

Greta came in with a packet of Jammie Dodgers and plonked them on the desk.

"Fanks, darling. Leave at four, so you can go get that game."

"It's Barbarian: The Ultimate Warrior."

Nic glanced up, his interest piqued.

"Is that the game where Maria Whittakah is on the cuvah all oiled up in a gold bikini?"

"You play as sword-wielding warriors fighting the forces of darkness, trying to save Princess Mariana of the Jewelled Kingdom from Drax, an evil sorcerer. I don't know who Maria Whittaker is," said Greta. Her face never changing in emotion, she proceeded to leave the room.

NOVUS ORDO SECLORUM

"Anyfink that 'appens 'round 'ere, McDick blames me, Mat or the twins."

"That's cos it probably is one of ya," said Nan, half listening, reading *The Sun*.

"That's not the point, Nan. It's, like, next I can see it, we'll be down 'ere on a Sunday 'aving a chicken dinnah when armed Old Bill from Scotland Yard's Swear Crime Squad, tooled up wiv MP5s, raid us cos some twat 'as reported me for calling 'em a cunt down the Crown. Old Bill arrest me under Section 900 of the Crimes Against Fucking Up the Queen's English Act. Telling ya, that's what it's gonna come to."

"Less of that language. You're not down the scrapyard now, but, yeh, son, world's gone mad. Your grandfavah would be turning in 'is grave," said Nan, still with her nose in the newspaper.

"What's going on in the paypah?"

"Well, James Prickskah, a twenty-five-year-old army officah serving in Kelley Barracks in Stuttgart, 'as been found dead, 'is body found severed in 'alf in the lion enclosure at Wil'elma Zoo. KAD 'ave taken responsibility for it, citing that 'e would be problematic in the future. Says 'ere the zookeepah managed to save the top 'alf of the body. KAD were unavailable for comment when asked why aftah they severed 'is penis they 'ad crudely sewn it to Prickskah's fore'ead. The lion 'ad to be put down. And at 'Arvard University KAD 'ave napalm bombed the campus where students was protesting for toddlahs to 'ave the right to eufanasia if they can't identify as suicide bombahs. 600 students died 'orrifically burned to deaf. But KAD fanked 'Avard for developing the quality incendiary. Road tested for 'em in Vietnam. Their reason cited was you couldn't reprogram those suffering from profound retardation. Shove the TV on, son. It's too depressing. *Top of the Pops* is on. I nevah miss it."

Nic took the remote and turned the TV on.

"Gordon Bennet, who's this bleeding article?" asked Nan, watching the pontifical 'artist' badly playing the guitar vocals untuned. Billy Balls-Dragg belted out 'Blanche Kittridge's Tears'. "This is awful. What's 'e banging on 'bout?"

"Fink, like, not to bash your bird in. 'E's taking a stand, sticking up for birds whose been given a back'ander. Wants women to 'ave safe spaces or somefink."

"What a shifty-looking fing. 'E's a propah no-good. I know one when I see one."

"Bloody 'ate 'im, Nan, whining, labour-voting twat. Been told 'e supports the 'Ammahs. If I see him down Upton, I'll gladly clump 'im one. Probably doesn't even know who's on the team."

"Well, someone needs to do somefink. I wish Chas and Dave would come on. Are they coming on, son?"

"No idea, Nan. 'Opefully not."

"You gonna stay for tea? Could do you some cheese on toast."

"Can't stay tonight, Nan. I gotta get down the club."

"You do work 'ard, Nic."

"Always rock 'ard at the club, Nan. You know, working 'ard is what I mean. I'll be 'round 'ere for breakfast Fursday. Debbie don't bovah getting' out of bed until teatime."

"It's awful, son. I mean, it's what she was put on this planet to do. A woman's place is at 'ome, cooking, cleaning and looking aftah the kids. All that bra-burning malarky these feminists do. In the war elastic was in short supply. The idea of burning 'em, well, it's just beggahs belief."

"You was in a war, Nan? You nevah mentioned it."

"Debbie's a lazy mare wiv you out all 'ours working so she can 'ave everyfink but keeps your 'ouse like a pigsty. I popped 'round yours Saturday. It was teatime and Charlie was still in 'is pyjamas. Charlie was telling me 'e wanted to go down the bafs like his pals and learn to swim."

"No idea what 'appened to 'er, Nan," said Nic, half listening as he clicked Ceefax on to check the football scores. "'Course, I'd like to take me son swimming, but I got to keep a roof ovah our 'eads. Anyway, Nan, wouldn't be fair to the birds down 'Aggerston Bafs if I went there in me vulture smugglahs. Birds couldn't 'andle it. It's the reason they 'ave 'em signs up saying no 'eavy petting, cos of blokes like me. Birds would lose all control of 'emselves, their fannies going into spasms, causing fanny battah floods. Be dangerous, like."

"That reminds me, I'm out of self-raising flowah for the Yorkshire puds on Sunday. I'll put it on me list. I mean, when was the last time she cooked for you? I taught her to cook. Seems like a lifetime ago. Shame she couldn't be a bit more like Suzie. Mat's found a goodun."

"Yeh, love's young nightmare, ain't they. Don't forget me breakfast, Fursday."

"Okay, son. What do you want?"

"Don't go to any trouble, just a full-cooked breakfast, and make sure you get Frosties in."

"Will you want toast?"

"Nan, goes wivout saying, and fried bread too."

"I'll get a nice loaf in of Muvah's Pride."

"Yeh, do that, and make sure its fick sliced and not fin like you dun last time. It ruined me breakfast."

"Sorry, son. Shall I walk down Ridley Market and get you some of that blood pudding."

"Yeh, you do that, Nan, and get us some Um Bongo as well."

"Um Pongo? What's that when it's at 'ome?"

"It's this fruit juice I like."

"Can I get it at the market?"

"No, Nan, you'll 'ave to walk all the way to Safeway."

"All right. I 'ope I don't forget."

"Yeh, Nan, and make sure it's on the table at eight sharpish, as I got to get ovah to 'Arlow. The fried egg needs to be runny, cos last time you dun us a breakfast it weren't. Not 'appy. I like to dip me toast in it."

"Nan got to make sure your eggiweg is right, ain't she. You sure you can't stop?"

"Nah, you're all right, Nan," said Nic, getting up and taking his car keys off the Welsh dresser and planting a kiss on her cheek. "See ya Fursday."

BURN

"So, you gonna buy it?" asked Nic as he took a drink from his pint.

"Be a bit rude not to. These private crematoriums don't come up for sale that often. Me and Flint will 'ave to fink 'ard 'bout 'ow we run it, as we don't want no 'assle. Take a back-seat approach in dealing wiv the public. Can't be 'aving the agg wiv being nice to cunts cos their loved ones 'as kicked the bucket. 'Course we'll get a funeral director in that knows 'ow we work. Dave Sconce is up for it. 'E done a degree in mortuary science when 'e was doing a stretch. We're supposed to follow this code of cremation practice, but like fuck we reading that."

"Yeh, got sent down for clumping some geezah down the Cutty Sark boozah wiv a spiked knuckledustah. Bloke lost one of 'is eyes."

"That's 'im. Fink 'e'll be a real asset."

"Be'ind the scenes, like, we'll be fully 'ands on. We'll employ some old dear front of 'ouse, one who knows 'ow to keep their mouf shut. Then there's the ashes that nevah get picked up. We're supposed to 'ave some duty of care and keep 'em in storage.

"What you gonna do wiv 'em?"

"We'll bin it all. We've a duty of care to no cunt."

"Goes wivout saying. 'Nuff said, Sparks."

"These cremation ovens get up to like one fousand and free 'undred degrees."

"Gets rid of all evidence then."

"Nah, it don't. The ashes then 'ave to go frough a cremulator that turns leftovah bones and teef into powdah."

"Yeh, but aftah it's been frough that terminator, or whatevah the fuck it is."

"Not sure Old Bill can get DNA out of ashes, but we'll dump 'em in the Thames so they'd 'ave fuck all. The ownah said that some relatives ask questions like does the dead body feel pain when its being burned, which is just fucking stupid. But I can explain to 'em in serious detail 'ow a body reacts when they're alive and set on fire. Wiv this venture there's loads of uvah ways we can make dough. Families who's too upset to take the ashes 'emselves, we're gonna offah a personal service where we do it for 'em. We can charge 'em for sprinkling their ashes down Epping Forest, or wherevah, like."

"You're really gonna take 'em down Epping?"

"Be'ave. They'll be dumped straight in a binbag, no fucking 'bout. And it don't stop there; quality jewellery they forgot to take off, anuvah sideline. We won't give the puntahs the option to 'ave 'em back. They'll be lucky if they 'ave all their loved ones' ashes. We plan to do mass cremations, cram in as many per day as we can. Even keep it open twenty-four hours if needs be. If ashes get mixed up, they'll nevah know. Flint's 'ad this blinding idea buy one cremation get one free. Like make 'em feel betta say like when most of their family 'as been wiped out in a car crash."

"Sounds like you got it all worked out."

"Yeh, but one fing we'll 'ave to iron out is dumping the

coffin into the oven. Me and Flint will 'ave to take turns so it's fair, or it could get a bit nasty and I'd 'ave to chin 'im one. The puntahs, they don't see the good stuff when the flames burn frough the flesh and organs. For some reason they don't want to."

"Yeh, strange, Sparky, innit."

"Anyways enouf 'bout deaf. Mat's made up now 'e's gonna be a dad to twins."

"Yeh, made up for 'im," said Nic flatly, glancing to his side as he saw Junkie Jimmy take a seat, itching uncontrollably, tearing into fresh and old wounds with his filthy fingers. Nic suppressed the urge to get up and lamp him just for breathing the same air as him, but had an idea that fitted in with his agenda.

"Sounds like a good earnah. Talking of which, Suzie's salon is doing blinding business. Mat keeps telling 'er not to keep so much money in the till. She keeps saying she forgets cos she's so busy," said Nic loudly as he gave Jimmy a furtive glance and noted he was all ears, his mashed-up junkie brain processing the information and now unashamedly clucking so badly, clawing at his ball sack.

"Yeh, she should, cos there's lots of shit-cunts 'round 'ere. You want anuvah pint?"

"Yeh, go on shove anuvah in there," said Nic, handing the glass to his cousin.

TWISTED ANIMATORS

"How are we today, boys?" asked Dr Peter Potts, the twins' psychiatrist.

"We're all right, Doc. Going away on a camping weekend wiv our cuzins. Somewhere called Cirencestah. I fink it's anuvah country," said Sparky.

"Oh, dear boy, Cirencester is still England, such a charming part of the country. It takes me back to my childhood, the joys of going camping with the Boy Scouts, setting up camp, fishing and cooking on a campfire."

The twins were bored to tears and stared down at the floor, swinging their legs, slouched on the plastic chairs. Bringing himself back to the here and now, Dr Potts said, trying to make his voice as stern as possible, "Of course, only the Scout leaders were allowed to light the campfire. Matches aren't toys to be played with."

Both boys just sat there smirking at each other. All they cared about was getting through this ordeal so they could go on their boys' weekend. Their old man let them play with big-boy guns. They got to shoot real things like foxes and deer.

"You see, with actions there are consequences. Let's take

the fire at your school. You caused thousands of pounds worth of damage, and it's only by some miracle that there were no fatalities."

"Yeh, but, Doc," said Flint, "all the kids 'round our way fink we're legends, cos the school was shut down for momfs."

"You must understand, boys, what you did was wrong. Did you think about what would happen after you started the fire?"

"We finked we'd be like supah 'eroes, and we was," said Sparky.

Softly, softly catchy monkey, thought Dr Potts. They were obviously developing a bond and opening up to him.

"I'll share with you a story. I had a patient some years ago, a nineteen-year-old boy called Duncan. He too had a fascination with fire. His downfall came when he broke into a disused warehouse and set it alight. What he didn't realise was there were homeless people sleeping in there who perished. Duncan was subsequently caught red-handed after leaving a petrol can with his fingerprints on. Duncan will be in prison for a considerable time."

"Our old man dun a stretch at the Scrubs. You got to share a bog wiv someone and take a shit in front of 'em and you gotta eat food called slop. But sometimes it was okay when the screws let 'em beat up the peados," said Sparky.

"Good," said Dr Potts, delighted that he was making a breakthrough. "You see your dad did something wrong and was punished."

"Yeh," injected Flint, "'e 'ead-butted a traffic warden."

"Boys, ask yourself what made your father do this."

"He was legging it; Old Bill was coming, and 'e got in the way. 'E 'ad to nut 'im one," said Sparky.

"No, boys," said Dr Potts, feeling he was slightly losing them here. "What made him decide to do a bad thing?"

"Dunno," said Sparky, looking around the room to see if there was anything he could pinch when Potts turned his back.

Trying to put to one side the cavalier tone of the boy's

revelations, Dr Potts continued with his superior mentoring. "If you break the law, you're punished at Her Majesty's pleasure. This surely isn't what you want, boys..."

HER NAME IS RIO

Terrance Pickering had been in his element all day. It was 7pm and he'd no idea how time had flown by so quickly. Standing outside the Rio Cinema, he took one last look before he made his way back to his guesthouse. Since arriving in Dalston, he couldn't wait to get his camera out and start taking pictures. As an Art Deco cinema buff, he was travelling around the country documenting them. It was an avant-garde celebration, as so few of these exquisite structures were still left standing. Terrance was writing a book that he was sure would take the literary world by storm. With his prize possession, a Minolta Maxxum 7000 camera, he'd spent the day taking the perfect shots and making notes in his reporter's notepad.

The Rio was refurbished in Art Deco style by cult architect F. E. Bromige in 1937. The exterior had remained almost unchanged since the 1930s. The cinema was situated on Kingsland High Street, a cream and red candy-cane structure. It was probably one of the best examples of *Arts Décoratifs* he'd seen. He'd toyed around with the idea of seeing a film there, but the film showing today seemed highly unsuitable: *Betty Blue*, a French arthouse risqué piece. The lead actress, Beatrice

Dalle, a raven-haired sultry beauty, stared down from the poster. No, that would never do. Terrance suffered from high blood pressure.

This trip was a treat for Terrance, a forever bachelor living in Wiltshire who spent his days looking after his elderly mum, Mavis. Every few months he had respite when his sister came down from Port Talbot, where she'd relocated with her steelworker husband, and took care of their mum for the weekend. Terrance savoured every precious moment. Tipping his Panama hat to a passerby, he was surprised when the gentleman stuck his fingers up at him. *Probably a bad egg,* thought Terrance. This was the East End, where real, genuine, down-to-earth people lived. They'd probably be impressed by a debonaire out-of-towner who was writing a book. Walking down Kingsland, he was enthralled by the hustle and bustle. He noted this area was obviously where artistic creativity flourished, judging by the graffiti: 'SOCIALISM IS DICLINISM. IT WORKS FOR NO FUCKER.' The good folk here obviously had a good sense of humour, as someone had sprayed in purple paint: 'HELP THE POLICE - BEAT YOURSELF UP'. Not that Terrance was in any way, shape or form endorsing graffiti, but youngsters in these parts needed an outlet for their frustrations through artistic expression.

It was a warm, balmy night as he walked further down the high street savouring all the shops: Mr H Menswear, Arts Wallpaper, Mr Music and Geekay Styles. He successfully ignored the newspaper stand for the *Hackney Gazette*: '**HUMAN REMAINS FOUND AT ROADSIDE.**' Walking cheerily along, he fondled his beloved camera. He'd taken a full film and placed a second one in he'd half used up. He planned to use the rest later when he was on what he liked to think of as a meet and greet. Terrance intended to go out for dinner and meet some of Hackney's finest. At the Old Bell he'd been greeted kindly by the receptionist, a woman in her fifties with grey, curly hair. He was a bit taken back by the 'NO BLACKS, NO IRISH' sign sellotaped to the front window. You didn't see that in Shrewsbury, but then again, you didn't see any black or Irish people. As the historian walked past Arthur's Café, he realised just how hungry he was. Terrance reached the door of the Old Bell and walked in.

"Good evening, my good lady," said Terrance to the receptionist, doffing his hat. "Could you possibly be so kind as to direct me to a good watering hole?"

"You what, treacle?"

"A place to get a refreshing beverage and a morsel to eat."

"Well, me and Dave like the Lord Stanley just down the road from 'ere. Just turn right onto Sandring'am, back up towards the cinema you visited today."

"That sounds just the place. Do they do some excellent local fare to eat?"

"Well, me and Dave sometimes share a packet of pork scratchings."

"How charming," said Terrance, thinking the receptionist was having a bit of sport with him. "I bid you good evening." And with that Terrance, still clutching his camera and notebook, headed to the door humming merrily to himself. As he was about to turn the door handle, the receptionist said, "Just 'ave your wits 'bout you."

Not quite knowing what she was inferring, he concluded it was just a bit of cockney fun. He stepped out onto the street and made his way to the pub. He headed into the Lord Stanley. The air was thick with cigarette smoke. There was a gang of punks huddled together in a corner, occasionally gobbing on the floor. Doffing his hat to them, Terrance was greeted with menacing stares from the Mohican-clad group. Moving further into the pub, over by the juke box, two skinheads dressed in red braces and drainpipe Lee Rider jeans debated what to spend their money on. Madness seemed to be winning. He was slightly dismayed to see no food signs, just one outside the men's lavatories saying 'NO SKID MARKS, GENTS, PLEASE'. Terrance approached the bar chuckling to himself. These cockneys were almost feral, but good souls nonetheless. As he got to the bar, he waited until the bleached-blonde barmaid took his order.

"My fair lady, what refreshing cold beverage would you recommend for a weary traveller?"

"Well," said the barmaid with all the enthusiasm of a dead fish, "you can see what we got, can't ya?" as she made hand motions behind her.

"I'll have a half pint of Old Speckled Hen. What do you offer by way of a bite to eat in your fine establishment?"

"We got crisps, ready salted, or pork scratchings."

"I'll have a packet of your finest ready salted, please."

"We only got Golden Wondah. You're not from 'round 'ere?"

"No, I'm not. I'm here doing groundwork for my book," said Terrance, delighted that, just as he thought, the good folk of Dalston were interested in a mysterious stranger arriving into their midst. The barmaid pulled his drink. As she passed him his drink and pulled out a packet of crisps from the box behind her, she said, "Word to the wise. Just watch yourself."

Terrance took his drink and headed to an empty table. It was lovely that these strangers were looking out for him, albeit Terrance was a tad shaken by the 'watch yourself' but shook it off as him just being silly. The historian took a seat at an empty table. Behind him, near the Space Invader, was a group glancing around furtively. One had a hideous skin complaint. The figure got up to leave. As he walked past, Terrance noted that the poor soul had the skin complaint all over the insides of his arms, very aggressively. So bad, he was vehemently scratching at the sore abrasions. To his left were two gentlemen in flat caps, speaking in broad West Country accents, with a scruffy dog.

"Tell me, gents, is this your local tavern?"

"Yeh, they serve Zummerzet Zyder and they let us bring our boot Shep in. You be a grockle?"

"A grockle?"

"Not from 'round these parts."

"I am, yes. Just visiting. Staying at your charming Old Bell. I'm a historian. I've been taking pictures of the Rio. It's for a book I'm writing."

Terrance noted the mut was taking an unhealthy interest in the leg of the table.

Abruptly, the pair got up and left the pub, muttering and dragging their whippet behind them. "G'woam now. Got zummit to do."

Their sudden departure had unsettled the historian. Taking a large gulp of his drink, he proceeded to go through the copious notes he had made that day.

Sid was parked across the road from Hot Cherry. It had been an uneventful day of surveillance on one of Suzie's innovative late-night openings. Just lots of customers going in and out. The only thing of note was Sparky taking Cooper and Henry for a walk. How he hated those dogs. Cooper had attacked him once, taken a bite out of his backside, tore through his best pair of slacks. Nic had said, "Mate, 'e's just playing." The four jumpstarts doubled up with laugher.

He noted that Suzie and her accomplice rarely took a lunch break. Say what you want, the girl was a hard worker.

Not like the other one, that stuck-up bitch who got everything she deserved. This thought put a wry smile on his face. Sid checked his battered Swatch for what felt like the hundredth time. Thankfully, he could drive home soon. It was 7.35. The last client had left, and he could see Suzie by the register cashing up. She'd be shutting soon. Yawning and throwing his cigarette butt out the window, his attention was piqued when he saw a man approaching the saloon clutching something tightly in his hand. Sid's intuition told him something was going down here. The figure glanced furtively around. Sid clocked it was Junkie Jimmy. He watched him open the salon door. Getting out the car, he paced over. He got there in time to see Jimmy, armed with a garden trowel, being handed money from the till by a petrified Suzie. Jimmy, clutching the cash, bolted out of the salon, barging into Sid, half knocking him over, and ran like the clappers down Kingsland. Composing himself, Sid ran across the road back to his car and rooted around in the glove compartment. He grasped his VPI mobile and made the call. Mat answered on the first ring.

"Is Suzie okay?"

"Gaffa, Junkie Jimmy just 'eld up the salon. 'E took all the cash and ran down Kingsland. Knocked me ovah and all. 'E didn't touch 'er." Sid looked across the road and could see that Suzie, who'd been rooted to the spot in fright, had managed to get to the door and was locking it.

"The cunt did what?" yelled Mat.

"Gaffa, she's safe. She's locked the door. It's just 'er and that fairy she works wiv."

"Sid, 'e's probably gone to The Lord Stanley to score. Go after 'im. Once you know where 'e is, call me straight away."

"On it, gaffa."

"What's up, bruv," asked Nic innocently.

"That cunt Junkie Jimmy just 'eld up Suzie's salon."

"The fucking diabolical libahty-takah," said Nic, trying not to snigger.

"We gotta go sort it out. Got Sid on it. 'E's bound to be at the Lord Stanley. 'Ang on. This is Suzie calling now." Mat grabbed his Motorola.

"Mat, somefink 'orrible 'as 'appened."

"What's wrong, princess," said Mat, feigning ignorance.

"It was terrible. Some bloke come into the salon wiv a nasty weapon and took all the cash. We was terrified. It all 'appened so fast."

"Right, princess, 'ave you locked the door?"

"Yeh, it's all locked. Jeffrey; 'e's in a terrible way. 'E fainted, and 'e's lying down on the sofa with a cold towel on 'is 'ead. Shall I call the police?"

"No! Don't do that," said Mat, which came out harsher than he'd meant. "Princess," said Mat in a cajoling tone, "it's best I sort this out. No need to get Old Bill involved."

"But, Mat, 'ow will you find out who it was?"

"It's a tight-knit community. Someone will know somefink. I'll make some calls."

"What you gonna do when you find 'im, Mat?"

"I'll, uh, give 'im a good talking too. Ask 'im to give the money back and tell 'im not to do it again, cos stealing, it's wrong, innit. You stay put. Don't open the door to anyone apart from Dexy. I'll send 'im 'round to take you 'ome." Mat, now he knew Suzie was safe, was eager to get her off the phone just in case Sid was calling.

"I'll call you latah, princess, when I've sorted everyfink out."

"Love ya, and please don't put yourself in any danger. 'E's a really violent bloke. I would 'ate to fink anyfink would 'appen to ya."

"Love you too. I'll try to be careful, but sometimes you 'ave to stand up to these bad people. Bye, princess."

As he put the phone down to Suzie, Sid called. He'd tracked down Jimmy.

After alerting Mat to Jimmy's whereabouts at the pub, Sid had taken a seat at a table near to where Jimmy was sitting so he'd have a frontside seat in the theatre of pain that would shortly play out, Jimmy having no idea he'd signed his death warrant with his own blood. Nursing a pint and smoking a roll-up, he studied the *Racing Post*. A stranger was sitting on the table next to him. He was trying to make conversation with the locals, talking about the Rio and how he'd found lodgings at the Old Bell. Sid couldn't give a rat's arse, but eavesdropping was something he did on autopilot.

Mat could barely contain his temper as he brought his Aston Martin V8 Vantage to an abrupt halt outside the pub. Jimmy's life expectancy was now minutes, if he was lucky. The ride over from the scrapyard had been just as Nic had suspected: tumultuous, his brother like a man possessed. Jumping out of the car with Nic not far behind him, they made their way to the front door and swung it open. Squeeze's 'Up the Junction' was blaring out of the jukebox. Nic made his presence felt and stood against the door – no one was coming in and no one was going out. He checked his Rolex Platinum Daytona. It was just gone 8pm. It was a small pub, and Nic had a bird's-eye view of everything, just like the habitués could see *him*. Mat thundered through the pub, seeing only red mist. He shouted to Mark, the landlord, "Where's that cunt Junkie Jimmy?"

Mark gestured towards a corner of the pub near to the Space Invader. Storming over, Mat saw Jimmy with his back to him sitting down with his cronies holding court. He grabbed him and tossed him onto the floor. Before Jimmy knew what was happening, Mat's huge fists had punched him repeatedly in the face over and over again until it was a bloody pulp.

"You walked into Suzie's shop and freatened 'er, demanded she gives you money, you smack'ead cunt."

Mat took Jimmy's battered head and started to bang it forcefully against the floor. Jimmy's body convulsed as his skull fractured and blood ran gushing from the back of his head. Satisfied now that Jimmy was no longer moving, Mat gave him a hard kick in the groin with his boot. The kick so ferocious it tore through his scrotum. Mat made his way through the pub looking straight ahead. As the brothers left the pub, Nic checked his watch. It was 8.05. They'd be back at his house in two minutes. They just needed to get their alibis airtight, should someone grass on them. The locals knew better, but it was always best to have a get-out-of-jail card up your sleeve. As he followed Mat out of the pub, he was thinking that Suzie would be Mat's downfall.

Terrance was in absolute shock. What had started as a lovely night had turned into a nightmare. Who were these brutes to attack an innocent man like this? And why was nobody doing anything? This poor man was out cold. He may even be dead. Why was the landlord not calling the authorities? The bar staff were still serving drinks as if this atrocity had never happened. Terrance decided they must all be in shock, as *he* was. He concluded the police and ambulance crew would be called or had been called and were thankfully on their way. The truth was, Terrance was scared stiff to move out of his seat, just in case the thugs came back. Deciding, after waiting five minutes, to be brave and do the right thing, and more to the point, now convinced the savages weren't coming back, he got up, legs shaking, and walked over to the landlord.

Mark Butcher, the landlord, was a sinewy bloke with sandy hair. He'd been the proprietor of the pub for the last ten years. Knowing the Hunters were big trouble, there was no way he was calling the police straight away.

"I say, young man, have you called the local constabulary and ambulance service yet?"

"Just tried to call 'em, mate. Phone 'as been playing up."

"My good innkeeper, the sooner the authorities get here the better. I would try to assist the gent, but I have an almost allergic aversion to blood, and it's best left to the professionals to administer the correct medical treatment. I wouldn't want to do anything – not being a medical expert – which would add to the man's anguish."

"Yeh, mate, so until they come, do you want anuvah drink?"

"Very well, I'll have a half Old Speckled Hen."

Mark finally made the call to the police. He noticed the busybody had now vacated his seat. Terrance had finished his drink – eventually, as his hands had been shaking so much. He made his way to the gents'. He wondered how long the ambulance and police would take. But before he reached the lavatory, two paramedics rushed past him, followed by two policemen. He felt a sense of relief that the authorities were now here. *Good,* thought Terrance, *now the police can get a full description of the assailants.* Were these sadistic barbarians stupid enough to think they could get away with this? Terrance noted that the locals appeared to be giving the constabulary the cold shoulder as they moved from table to table. They were lucky if one person looked up from their drink. What was wrong with these people, rebuffing the police?

"Excuse me, sir, I'm PC Dickson from Dalston Police Force. A serious assault has taken place here this evening. Did you see anything that may help with our inquiries?"

As Terrance went to speak, he noted that the paramedics now had the unconscious man's body on a stretcher and were headed towards the door.

"Yes, PC Dickson," said Terrance, now feeling rather brave and important, and also safe in the knowledge that if the thugs did come back, the long arm of the law was here to protect him. "I saw both the attacker and his accomplice clearly."

"Thank you for your assistance. Your name is?"

"It's Terrance Pickering."

PC Dickson took his notepad out and started to take notes.

"Would you be prepared to come to the station to make a full statement?"

"Yes, indeed I would be. I'm a firm believer in law and order, and anything I can do to help. You see this is what happened..."

Sid was loitering when he noted that the stranger he'd been sitting next to was deep in conversation with a policeman. He staked a place within earshot of them and took in the whole explosive conversation. Walking outside the pub, he fished his mobile out from his jacket and dialled Mat. His call was answered immediately. Having delivered the intelligence, Sid slipped out of the pub unseen, with the camera he'd taken off the table of the out-of-towner.

PC Dickson called McBride at the station on the bar phone as soon as he'd spoken to Terrance. He didn't want to use the police radio, as the less people who knew this information the better.

"This had betta be good, boyo. I'm on my way to get a vindaloo, like now, in a minute."

"Guv, there's been an altercation at the Lord Stanley. Two guys walked in. One watched the door and the other beat the living daylights out of a man."

Yawning and fast losing interest, McBride responded, "Well, it was just a normal night at that pub then, it was."

"Guv, a witness has come forward and is prepared to make a very detailed statement about the incident and is prepared to stand up in court and testify. He said that the guy who stood by the door had a very distinctive tattoo on his left arm, one with hammers, a crushed lion's head and lots of dripping blood, and the guy who administered the beating was a tall, dark guy with very blue eyes."

"So let me get this right. Yew're saying this witness will actually make a statement, he will?"

"Yes, guv. He's a historian visiting the area. He has no idea who the Hunters are."

"Get him to the station, boyo. The sooner he makes that statement and identifies the Hunters from the wide variety of mugshots we have of them the better. Any word on the victim?"

"James Darke. A serial-offending petty criminal. He lives in a squat on Sandringham Road. Apparently, that prostitute who was found dead was his girlfriend. Darke has been taken to Homerton in a critical condition."

"Right, no time to lose. Get him over yere pronto. Bring him straight into my office and I can start to get his full statement, and, butt, make sure you don't mention this information to anyone else. The Hunters have eyes and yers everywhere. We don't want them getting the heads-up on this." McBride ended the call, smirking to himself. The Hunter brothers were as good as banged up, and he'd take the credit for their downfall. Seeing as he was going to have to put the takeaway on hold until later, he made his way to the staff kitchen to make a Pot Noodle.

"Debs," shouted Nic as he and Mat entered his house slamming the front door.

"Why did you 'ave to bang the door that bleeding loud?"

"Right. Old Bill may come 'round asking questions. You tell 'em me and Mat been 'ere since 'bout seven-firty watching TV, yeh, and Nan popped 'round as well."

Debbie raised her sore head off the sofa, mascara running down her face. "Whatevah you say, Nic."

"Debs, this is serious. Do you undahstand?

"I 'eard you the first time. I know the drill."

"Just make sure you do," said Nic, who was now livid as he looked around his living room. "Debs, what the fuck 'ave ya been doing all day? This place looks like a shit'ole. If you keep sacking the cleanah, you need to do the 'ousework. Where's Charlie?"

"Charlie's upstairs asleep. He was tired. We played wiv Lego all aftahnoon," lied Debbie. Charlie had spent a lonely afternoon in his bedroom playing with his toys. Knowing that his mum wouldn't come up to put him to bed, he'd snuggled up to Moore, his Daddy's teddy, and cried himself to sleep.

"Right, Debs. Just as long as you're crystal clear 'bout tonight."

Nic picked up the phone and called Nan while lighting a cigarette.

"Nan, it's Nic."

"'Ello, son. 'Ow are ya? Just gonna put me feet up. Me bunions are giving me gyp."

"Nan, listen. If Old Bill come 'round and start asking questions, tell 'em 'bout seven-firty you popped 'round to see me and Debs at the 'ouse and Mat was 'ere too. We was watching telly."

"Okay, son, I was at yours."

"Right, gotta go, Nan."

"Son, what did I bring?"

"Uh, what do ya mean, Nan?"

"Well, if I come to yours, I'd 'ave brought somefink to eat."

"Uhh, yeh, Nan, you did," said Nic, desperate to get off the phone.

"A cake. Did I bring a cake?"

"You did, Nan. You brought a cake. Now I gotta go. Just remembah, you was at mine wiv Debs and Mat."

"What cake was it?"

"Nan, I don't care. A cream cake, a sponge cake."

"Ahh, that's right. I brought a Victoria Sponge. Did you 'ave second 'elpings?"

"Nan, we ate the 'ole bleeding cake."

"That's nice. Shame the twins missed out."

"Yeh, me and Mat just got lucky," said Nic, losing the will to live and taking a Herculean drag on his cigarette. "Best cake we evah tasted. Right, really, really gotta go now, Nan."

"Okay, son. Cheerio."

At the same time Nic had been on the phone to Nan, Mat had been in the kitchen on the phone to Sparky, giving him full details of what to do.

MURDER BY DELUSION

"*Shwmae*, Mr Pickering. How nice to meet yew. Thank yew for coming in and helping us with our inquiry, like. I'm Detective Inspector McBride. Please take a seat." McBride had taken the witness into his room. He thought it was less formal than the interview room. He needed this bobby-dazzler to be as relaxed as possible.

"Inspector McBride, it's my civil duty to help you. This has been most disturbing to me. Never in my life have I ever witnessed such barbaric cruelty to an innocent man. I will do whatever is needed to help you in your investigation against these villainous toads."

"We value people like yew, Mr Pickering."

With a false grin on his face, McBride started to take Terrance's statement. It was more than McBride could ever have wished for. Then McBride took out a section of mugshots. Terrance identified Mat and Nic immediately.

"I'll never forget these faces as long as I live. The wretched swines. They should be behind bars for the rest of their lives. I take it they're known ruffians to you?"

"Well, they're somewhat known to us. They have some

previous form, they do. But nothing to worry about. Just common criminals."

"Yes, common petty criminals. No doubt lack of parental guidance played a part in all this. Scoundrels with no moral compass who would have benefited from being sent for a term to Gordonstoun. A short, sharp shock to the system."

"Let's just say their moral compasses have tipped over the South Pole. I agree there should be more mandatory sentences to Gordonstoun. Send them to the Scottish Highlands to do hiking and camping. Teach them teamwork. Look how well Prince Charles turned out."

"One thing, Inspector, I'm most concerned about in this upsetting event. My camera went missing. I'd taken numerous pictures earlier for my book. Would that be something you could help me with? I'd captured some quite astonishing images of the Rio."

"Mr Pickering, my men will do an exhaustive search of the area and we'll not stop until we find it," lied McBride. There was about as much chance of finding it as there was of finding Shergar. "Thank yew, Mr Pickering, for yewer services to the Met. I'm told yew're staying at the Old Bell. I'll get a PC to drive yew back there and we'll have one posted outside the front door."

"Um, well, that's very thoughtful of you, but why would I need a guard on the door. I'm not in any danger, am I?"

"*Duw, duw*, absolutely not. It's just normal police procedure in a case like this. Now, Mr Pickering, if yew'll excuse me, I have arrests to make. *Nos da*."

McBride left the room and reached for his Mackintosh on the coat stand. Dickson told him that bobbies on the beat had radioed through to say that Mat and Nic's cars were parked outside Nic's house. McBride commandeered every available police officer. This was the pivotal moment of McBride's life, and God damn it he was going to arrest these criminals, who had alluded justice for so long, in a convoy. "Get those sirens wailing, boyos." McBride rode shotgun, with Dickson driving, shouting warrior-speak, "Put your foot down, Dickson. The old boyo will get out the way when he realises we're not stopping."

Once he got out of the car, he had, in all his haste, fallen arse over tit, but eventually made it to 35 Colvestone Crescent to make the arrests he'd coveted for decades. Mat walked out and put his own hands behind his back, his face showing no expression. Once in the Rover SD1 V8, he stared ahead and said nothing. It took seven officers to get Nic into the Black Maria and handcuffed. He kicked off the whole way as they tried to arrest him, verbally and physically assaulting the officers.

"Fuck me gently wiv a chainsaw, nevah 'eard that one before. You sad cunts working on fuck-all dosh. No wondah so many of ya work for us. I've been wiv me missus all night."

A hysterical Debbie stood outside screaming, "Leave 'im alone. 'E 'as been wiv me all night."

"You know exactly what to do?" asked Sparky as he dropped Tracey off just around the corner from the Old Bell on Ashwin Street.

"Yeh, duckie, unno," said Tracey as she jumped out of the car in lemon-and-lime spandex.

"Trace, I'll wait 'ere for ya, and as soon as I see 'im running past me, I'll be out and straight into the 'otel."

"Okay, chuck. Gonna just run up and down on't spot for a while, work up uh sweat, make it look like I've been jogging. You know, get reyt into role. It's called method acting. That Meryl Streep does it."

"Trace, don't take too long. I need to get in there."

Tracey appeared not to hear Sparky, as she jumped and up and down pounding on the spot aggressively as she channelled Jennifer Beals in *Flashdance*. Then, without a word of warning, Tracey bolted down the street and around the corner to the hotel.

"Help, help! Chuffing 'eck, uh lad's grabbed me, mate."

True to Sparky's word, a lone copper was positioned outside the hotel.

"What's happened, miss?" asked PC Clutterbuck.

"'Ow do? I were just jogging down Dalston Lane wae me mate, Shelley, and owt of nowhere this lad grabs her from behind and drags her down snicket. He tried tu grab me tu, but I manged tu run away. I were so glad to see thee, duckie."

"You say he dragged her down Dalston Lane into a snicket. What's that?"

"Ohh, duckie, an alleyway. He looked proper weird. Had uh knife mark across his cheek and looked uh bit like that Larry Grayson," said Tracey, impressed by her improvisation.

"Okay, miss, leave this with me. Stay here. Go inside the guesthouse and wait for me. You'll need to make a statement. Let the night porter know what's happened."

"Okey dokey, chuck. He cun't of got far, cun't he? Ta-ra."

PC Clutterbuck fled down the street, baton extended, ready for action. If he got this collar, it could give him kudos at the station, build up a bit of reputation for himself. PC Clutterbuck had graduated fresh-faced out of the academy in St Edmundsbury and had been on the beat in Dalston for the last three months. If he had been a more seasoned copper, before leaving his post he'd have radioed it in. But a sucker for a pretty damsel, and surely this was more important – a woman had been abducted at knifepoint and dragged away by some psycho – he had to act fast. As the hapless PC bolted down Ashwin Street, Sparky got out of his car and made his way to the guesthouse.

"Trace, good job. I won't be long."

"I were reyt chuffed wae meself. When am I gonna get brass, duckie?"

"Just get in the motah. I'll sort you out latah." Sparky made his way into the hotel. The night porter was ready and waiting. No words were exchanged as he handed Sparky the key to Room 4. He walked through the door with a sign on that said 'EMPLOYEES AND GUESTS ONLY'. He made his way to the door and inserted the key.

Terrance was resting on his bed reading Moby Dick when he heard the door open. He was surprised to see a man with a snarling face standing over him.

"Who the devil are you?"

"My name ain't important, mate, but what I'm gonna tell you is. So, if I was you, I'd listen very carefully like your life depended on it."

It was then that Terrance saw the SIG Sauer P226 pistol he was holding. Terrance started trembling and thought, could this really be happening? How many brutes were there in this area, and how had he got in? There was a policeman outside.

"What do you want from me? I'm here at the behest of Detective Inspector McBride, you know."

"Mate, I know why you're 'ere, and that's why I'm 'ere. You see, it's like this," said Sparky, aiming the gun at Terrance's forehead. "What you saw earlier this evening, well, I'm sure once you 'ave fought 'bout it you'll realise you're confused, like your imagination ran away wiv ya. But right now you're gonna put all that right, ain't ya."

"Are you threatening me?"

"Mate, I got a loaded gun to your 'ead. What do you fink," said Sparky as he pressed the muzzle of the gun to his forehead.

"What do you want me to do?" asked Terrance, who was practically in tears.

"Now, that's betta, mate. Take this," said Sparky as he reached inside his jacket and pulled out a pad and pen. "All you need to do is write down exactly what I say, and aftah that pack your stuff, get in a taxi and go back to Shrewsbury, and please say 'ello to your old mum Mavis for me. Got a nice little 'ouse on Vicar's Close there, ain't she? Shame when these old dears get on. Their bones go, don't they? So much easier to break 'em, especially when they're tied up wiv barbed wire to their commode then decapitated wiv an axe. Takes a while that mefod. 'Uman necks can take up to five swings, all while they're conscious. And I bet you're looking forward to seeing your sistah again, ain't ya? Got an 'ouse on Margam Road. Convenient, like, for 'er job at the Twelve Knights 'Otel. Be such a shame if she 'ad like a freak 'ousehold accident wiv a machete. Now, do we 'ave an undahstanding?"

Terrance, now beyond petrified, took the pad and started writing like his life depended on it.

McBride was actually grinning, which was something he seldom did, as he made himself a coffee and got stuck into his second Pot Noodle in the staff kitchen. This hideous room with its bottle-green painted walls was enough to make Ken Dodd depressed, but tonight he saw everything through rose-tinted glasses. Let the little sheep-shits wait. He was in control now. After all this time, putting these despicable criminals behind bars was finally in his sight, all the years of sleepless nights and torturous days a thing of the past. Their lawyer, Michael Relton, had arrived from his offices in Westminster, more bent than a nine-bob note, albeit a very expensive one. McBride had always though their choice of lawyer strange as Relton spent a large proportion of his time getting moody coppers off with charges of corruption and misconduct. He couldn't help but think the line was thin. Very thin indeed. Mat had told them on entering the police station before being placed in the custody suite, "We'll get our brief. We don't need your duty solicitor – legal-aid crap. We don't waste taxpayahs' money. We're 'onest businessmen."

Relton was in attendance with Mat and then he would confer with Nic. Sticking his spoon into the Pot Noodle, he took a hefty portion, dribbling the juice down his chin onto his shirt. He'd leave them, wait, and then interview Nic first, the weaker link of the two. With Pickering's explosive evidence, he could put the monkey into a corner and then, in his own time, as he was in charge, interrogate the organ grinder. Taking the Pot Noodle container up to his lips, he slurped down juice, noodles and dehydrated vegetables, then mumbled to himself, "*Iechyd da.*" He could see it now, being honoured for putting two of the most ruthless criminals behind bars. When he had the ear of the Home Secretary, Douglas Hurd, he'd get to grips with the epidemic corruption in the Met. He'd be tasked with heading this up and even naming the operation. He quite liked Operation Countryman, a throwback to good, honest policing with the trusted village bobby. He would then move up the police ranks swiftly, until one day he would be the police commissioner.

Dickson walked into the kitchen. "I hope, guv, their solicitor doesn't take too long. The sooner we get on with the interviews the better."

"I've spent years waiting for this day, boyo. We don't need to rush this. The Hunters are yere as detained suspects, and they're not going anywhere. Not being funny, like; they're as good as banged up, mun. CPS will be all over taking this one now we've got to go through them to take it to court. It's in the bag – bang tidy, like."

The kettle whistled to a boil and PC Dickson poured the boiling water onto a teabag.

"You're right, guv, but I just can't help but want to get in there as soon as possible, see you tie them in knots."

"Guv," said PC Lynch as he walked into the kitchen looking winded.

"What is it, butt? I'm about to interrogate a Hunter, I am."

"Well, that's the thing. I came to find you as quickly as possible when I found out."

"Found out what, mun?"

"It's James Darke, guv. He died ten minutes ago. They tried their best, but his injuries were catastrophic. He had severe bleeding on the brain, like he'd been involved in a high-speed car crash. Maybe it was for the best. The doctor said if he had survived, he would've been a cabbage for life. You know, one of those mongs in a wheelchair drooling down their chin like Stephen Hawking. The beating was so severe they were shocked he held out for so long."

McBride tried not to smirk, but failed badly. This was now a murder inquiry.

"And, guv, Relton is now in attendance with Nic Hunter."

"Dickson, there's no need for the good-cop-bad-cop routine with career criminals of this calibre. We got mugshots of this pair through the decades, we do. So let me do all the chopsing in there, like."

The inspector let out a loud smelly fart. PC Dickson wrinkled his nose in disgust. This was lost on McBride. The only thing he had on his mind was murder and putting the culprits behind bars.

McBride, grim faced, walked into the interview room. PC Dickson followed behind him. He was greeted by a grinning

Nic and his bespectacled lawyer, who was immaculately dressed in a Huntsman suit. The officers took their seats opposite them. The inspector pressed the record button on the tape recorder and started speaking, "This interview is taking place at Dalston Police Station on Wednesday, 28th August 1986, at 11.30pm, with Nicolas Dennis Hunter, the detained suspect. Also present in the interview are Detective Inspector McBride, PC Dickson and Mr Hunter's legal representative, Mr Michael Relton of Lynn, Relton & Co Solicitors."

"'Ello, McDick," said Nic, lighting a cigarette and blowing the smoke into his face. "I fink there's been a misunahstanding 'ere, mate."

"The name is McBride. Detective Inspector McBride."

"Whatevah, McDick," said Nic, continuing to blow smoke in his face.

McBride decided not to correct him again. He wasn't going to give him the satisfaction. Besides, he could afford to be magnanimous. Nic was dressed in a Bottega Veneta T-shirt. The tattoo that would seal his fate was in plain view.

"Mr Hunter, yew've been brought yere tonight for questioning over a very serious incident that occurred this evening at the Lord Stanley. James Darke was viscously attacked there and left for dead. We have a witness who has come forward to advise us that yewer brother Mathew Edward Hunter was the person who committed the attack, and that yew were his accomplice, complicit in aiding and abetting it. Can you tell me where yew were at around 8pm this evening, Mr Hunter?"

"Well, its obvious, innit."

"What's obvious, Mr Hunter?"

"Well, what's everyone doing at eight on a Wednesday night? Watching *Dallas*, weren't we. We fucking love that JR. 'E's a real evil bastard. Me, Mat, me missus and Nan was all at mine watching it. Nevah miss it. You seen the inflatables on Pam? I could 'ave a good bounce 'round on 'em."

"For the purposes of the tape, the suspect is holding his arms at chest level and is making large grabbing motions with his hands," said McBride.

"Pam was wearing this, like, red neglijiggy."

"Negligee," corrected Relton.

"Yeh, one of 'em. You missed a right treat. It was just 'bout 'olding her knockahs in. They was seriously straining, like. You must 'ave been on some plod work. Probably trying to fit someone up for twatting Colonel Mustard ovah the 'ead wiv a candlestick down the Blind Beggah. We was 'aving a nice family evening in. Only fing missing was the twins."

"Ahh, yes, Dalston's own chapter of the KKK."

"You've lost me now. Your witness must be mistaken. I was in me 'ouse wiv me family."

"This is not the first time yewer wife has given yew an alibi. Far from it."

"We're a close couple, McDick. We like spending time togevah. I'm guessing you, mate, don't 'ave a girlfriend."

Not rising to the bait, the inspector continued the interrogation. "Yewer nan is another person who has repeatedly been yewer alibi; a woman who would probably swear on oath yew were in Narnia having tea with Mr Tumnus at the time of the incident if yew told her to."

"Narny? Tumney? What?" asked Nic. "What's this, like? Jackafuckingnory wiv McDick? Or is it sheep-shaggah language, cos I don't speak it."

"Ahh, yes, I forgot. Yew didn't have a childhood. And then we move on to yewer brother, the man who is currently waiting to be interrogated about a very grave offence indeed, a man who has been connected to a slew of murders, extortion and drug trafficking."

"Nufink 'as been proven. We're illegitimate businessmen. Like, what's your point?"

"My client means legitimate," said Relton, adjusting the Mascot glasses on his nose.

"Yeh, like, that as well. We've made a bob or two, and you lot can't 'andle it. Fit us up for anyfink and everyfink. Just clutching at straws. All like that circumcision evidence."

"Circumstantial," corrected Relton.

McBride sat back in his chair relaxed as he played what he thought was his trump card.

"Mathew Hunter, a man who is now waiting to be questioned over the murder of James Darke," said McBride letting the word 'murder' sink in. "Yew see, this is now officially a murder investigation. James Darke unfortunately didn't make it after the lethal, unprovoked attack he endured. He never regained consciousness."

"Yeh, that's, like, really sad news, innit. A man cut down in 'is prime. It's a real loss for 'umanity," said Nic, lounging back on his chair as if he didn't have a care in the world.

McBride's revelation so far wasn't having the desired effect on Nic. In fact, totally unfazed, he continued to stare at him obnoxiously cocksure, not even a flicker of uncertainty passing across his eyes. He stretched his legs out in front of him lazily, managing to kick McBride in the process.

"My witness has made a full statement and has identified yew from mugshots and is willing to take part in an identity parade. Yew see, there's the matter of yewer tattoo. It's rather distinct. My witness has described it in great detail."

"Yeh, I know. So it's obvious, innit."

"Once again, Mr Hunter, I fail to follow yewer chain of thought."

"Well, probably some bloke 'as seen me down the Boleyn wiv a tattoo that's the dog's bollocks and 'as gone and got 'imself one. It's not like there ain't many West 'Am fans 'round 'ere, is it? I mean, do I 'ave to do all the pig work 'ere for ya?"

Nic's cavalier attitude was starting to grate on McBride, but he was damned if he was going to let it show.

"Inspector, my client has just told you he has two witnesses who'll swear on oath that my client was nowhere near the pub tonight at the time in question. Your witness it obviously mistaken or highly delusional, quite possibly both. This really is a witch hunt against my clients. This isn't the first time you have hauled them in here on trumped-up charges, which have never gone anywhere, I may add. My client is just here to clear up any misunderstanding. He isn't guilty of any wrongdoing."

Nic decided to take it up a notch or two. He flicked his cigarette butt on the floor and started yawning and stretching his legs out further, hands clasped behind his head, staring at the ceiling.

"For the purposes of the tape, the suspect is feigning being asleep and pretending to snore."

"Was the victim, James Darke, known to yew?" asked McBride.

Nic replied in a bored tone, "I went to school wiv 'im. Poor sod got in wiv the wrong crowd and got mixed up wiv drugs. Could 'ave been a dealah 'e owed money to. Who's to say? I mean, I, like, don't know much 'bout drugs; me body is a temple and all that. Fing is, McDick, there's some very bad people 'round. Know what I mean?"

"Please once again enlighten us with your insights."

"Well, it's like this, innit. Jimmy probably owed dough to some people who 'e shouldn't 'ave. Reckon they came aftah 'im and gave 'im a kicking when he couldn't pay. Or the ovah fing I was finking was some community-spirited individual 'as taken the law into their own 'ands. You know, get the junky scumbags off the street. Like that Equalisah geezah on TV does. Doing your job for ya."

"Not being funny, like. My witness will swear on oath that it was yewer brother who was the vigilante and yew stood at the door of the pub making sure no one could go in or go out, intimidating potential witnesses."

"These accusations are completely preposterous. My client has tried to help you. He hasn't gone down the 'no comment' route. He's been transparent and helpful in giving you an insight and advising you on what sort of person may have carried out this crime," interjected Relton.

"Yeh, any 'elp I can be, just ask. 'Appy to serve the community. Right, can I go now? I'm bored."

Before being able to respond, a very anxious PC Lynch opened the door and interrupted the interview. "Guv, can I see you outside for a moment?"

McBride was beyond incensed that this uniform had interrupted him but decided it must be something important.

"I suggest we take a small break," said McBride. He'd leave the cocky bastard to sweat it out.

"For the purposes of the tape, at 11.50pm we're taking an adjournment from the interview."

With that, McBride got up and left the room, with Dickson straight behind him. All the time Nic stared at him, smirking.

"This had better be good, boyo," said McBride as he exited the room and closed the door behind him.

"Well, guv, there's been something of a development in the case."

"Go on, spit it out, mun." McBride wondered if the PC was going to divulge to him more hard evidence against the Hunters.

"Mr Pickering has changed his statement and gone back to Shrewsbury."

"Changed his statement to what, PC?"

"Here it is," said Lynch, who shakily handed over the piece of paper to McBride. "Maybe it would be better if you read it yourself."

McBride grabbed it from his hands and started to read it. There was practically steam coming out of his head when he finished. In a nutshell, Terrance had changed his statement to say he wasn't in Dalston as an Art Deco buff. The truth was, he was a true crime buff who had become obsessed with the Hunters after reading articles over the years in newspapers about them. He'd gone to the pub, and when a fight had started, his overactive imagination had got the better of him and he had invented that it was Mat and Nic. He further confessed to being something of a fantasist. He described himself as a weak man prone to telling fish stories. His own mother called him Pinocchio. He also confessed to being behind the Yorkshire Ripper hoax phone calls in '78 and '79. John Samuel Humble had no business confessing to being Wearside Jack. He acknowledged he had a serious problem and would look to get psychiatric help immediately, or failing that, section himself. But to try his best to make up to the police for wasting their time, he'd given a true description of the perpetrators of the crime. The attacker was around six-foot-eight with a ginger goatee and a squint in one eye and the accomplice was a dwarf with a hook nose and a monobrow.

It took all of McBride's willpower not to rip the statement up. How in hell had the Hunters got to the witness in such a short space of time, and with a policeman guarding the guesthouse? Heads were going to roll for this, make no mistake. And just like that, McBride's dreams went up in smoke.

"It all been a big mistake," said Mat to a near-hysterical Suzie the next morning.

"But they arrested you for beating up a bloke, and now 'e's dead. I was so worried. Debbie called and said it must all be a terrible mistake, as you was all togevah at 'er's watching TV. I was just finking of you at the police station alone, feeling distressed."

"Everyfink is okay, Suzie. It was mistaken identity. Me and Nic 'ave been released wivout charge and no furvah questioning. Old Bill even apologised to us. It's only cos of that we ain't pursuing wrongful-arrest charges. I 'ad gone 'round Nic's and was waiting for a call to see if anyone knew who dun ovah your salon. Then Old Bill turns up and arrests us."

"Did you know this bloke?"

"No, someone called Jeremey Darko or somefink. It's awful. 'E was just 'aving a quiet pint. I can't imagine who would've dun it."

"I'm just 'appy they released you. It must be really traumatic for you."

"To be 'onest, princess, we're really cut up 'bout it. We're going to send this bloke's family some flowahs to reach out to 'em. Show our respects. Pass on our sincere condolences."

"That's such a lovely fought, Mat," said Suzie, thinking, how could the police believe her caring boyfriend could possibly do such a thing?

"Right, princess, shall I pick you up at sixish?"

"Can we say six-firty, as Jeffrey is so traumatised by what 'appened 'e's taken to 'is bed and won't be back in work until next week. 'Is mum 'as to spoon-feed 'im chicken soup until 'e gets betta."

"Uh, right, okay, princess. See you at six-firty. Love ya. Bye."

"Greta, come in 'ere, darling. I need you to send a wreaf to this address," said Mat as he passed a piece of paper to her when she came through the door wearing a Voltron T-shirt.

"What do you want on the card, Mat?"

"RIP YOU CUNT."

Judging by her boss's steely face, she knew he wasn't joking and duly did what she was told, having to use the phonetic alphabet when she called the florists.

KILLING IN THE NAME

"Terrible business what 'appened to that young lad in the Lord Stanley. It 'appened that night I was at yours, and we watched that JR on telly. Made a nice cake, I did, son."

"Yeh, you did, Nan. Anyfink in *The Sun*?" asked Nic, swiftly changing the subject.

"Man United fans and West 'Am fans clashed on a ferry going to Amstahdam. They was on their way to pre-season friendlies. They 'ad knives and broken bottles. It left four people seriously injured. They 'ad to turn the ferry 'round. Old Bill was waiting at the port of 'Arwich and arrested fourteen people, and anuvah one 'undred and ten soccer fans were put on a train to Lundun wiv police escorts. Uvah travellahs on the ferry locked 'emselves in their rooms, they was so scared."

"Nan, was propah gutted couldn't be part of it. Too busy at the club. Anyfink on the deaf toll rising in that Russian nuke accident. Giz us some good news."

"Nufink on that, but says 'ere KAD in Glasgow 'ave taken responsibility for the castration and execution of Scottish law student Nicola Clownfish. The reason cited was 'e was deemed to be problematic in the future. They issued a statement that the 'ighest biddah got the grisly pictures. Clownfish's 'ead 'ad been chopped off wiv an axe and stuffed down a lavatory in a men's public convenience in Anderston frequented by tramps, one of which had emptied his bowels on Nicola's 'ead. This prompted a frenzied bidding war and newspaypahs was offering six-figure sums. They was gazumpted by billionaire aufor E.C. Pottah, writah of the bestselling *Mille Mermaid and the Bound Treasure Chest*. She wanted them for 'er own personal reasons. The philanfropist, who 'as given away millions to good causes, made copies and sent them to every newspaypah 'round the world as an altruistic act. Whatevah is the world coming to? These terrorists are women too."

"Can't say any of this 'as any impact on me life, Nan."

"It goes on to say that 'igh-up people in the IRA, like Kevin McKenna and Thomas 'Slab' Murphey, are getting twitchy cos they get most of their weapons from Colonel Gaddafi and they're not getting anywhere near what they used to cos a source told the paypah that Gaddafi is selling most of 'is weapons to KAD. Crystal Lake knocked back any chance of coming to the negotiating table wiv the IRA, as KAD was a real cause. Gaddafi wouldn't confirm or deny 'is involvement wiv KAD, but did randomly tell *Tishreen* newspaypah that he often found 'imself listening to Slayah's 'Reign in Blood'. Leading female IRA membah Donna Maguire 'as left the Provos. She believes she 'as been fighting the wrong cause. To show 'er allegiance to KAD, she 'as formed BIGOT."

"What's that mean, Nan?"

"Says 'ere it stands for Biological Intelligent Girl Ovah Testosterone."

"Is that what a bigot is? Nevah really knew. No idea why I've been called one. Not that I care. Goes wivout saying. 'Nuff said. Is there a picture of Crystal? She's seriously fit."

"Crystal is now in 'iding, as she's numbah one on the FBI's

most-wanted list. KAD is now believed to have influence ovah the most powahful institutions in the world and 'as infiltrated deep state. She's now fought to be in one of 'er many safe 'ouses 'round the world and estimated to be worf £2 billion due to donors. The Koch bruvahs 'aven't commented on the rumour that they are mega-donors. This is the last known picture of 'er in Monaco," said Nan as she showed Nic the picture of Crystal in Chanel sunglasses and a Dolce&Gabbana bikini.

"She's fit as fuck, I so would."

"She's not a nice person. I don't fink she likes men much."

"Nan, 'er personality means nufink to me."

VISION QUEST

"You listening, Nic?" snapped Mat.

"Not really. Just finking 'ow much I could get in me mouf, like," said Nic, showing his brother the smiling girl adorning page 3. "I reckon I could get a good fird in. I mean, deep froating ain't just for birds, that's sexist, innit."

"Not seen 'er before. She new in *The Sun*?" asked Mat.

"Nah. That's it. This is a new paypah. The *Sunday Sport*. Been buying it religiously. I wouldn't mind getting me 'ands on 'em," said Nic as he pawed the picture of Lola Dawn McKenna.

"She looks like a propah dirty bitch who takes it straight up the arse. We're talking six rubbahs 'ere," said Flint.

"See, I'm a greedy cunt, like. The more arse and tits the betta. Know what I mean? Whoevah said more than an 'andful is a waste is a mug. Says 'ere she 'as 38HHH tits."

"No idea what that means. They just look propah massive to me."

"This rag 'as got the balance just right. There ain't much to read. I always fought *The Sun* got it wrong. Just the important stuff: sport and tits. All it tells you is what the bird's name is and the size of 'er knockahs. It's just the right amount of reading I wanna deal wiv. Obviously, it goes wivout saying. 'Nuff said. There's a propah write up on the footie."

"I bet Fleet Street is feeling really freatened wiv this kind of competition," said Mat sarcastically, which was lost on Nic.

"They gotta be. This paypah is a game changah. Anyways, this Lola was, like, fifteen when they discovered 'er, so for the run up to 'er sixteenf birfday they counted down wiv pics of 'er wiv less and less of 'er school uniform on, cos it's not right to 'ave a fifteen-year-old schoolgirl wiv her tits out. But then on 'er sixteenf birfday she 'ad all 'er kit off."

"So, it's okay to 'ave, like, a sixteen-year-old schoolgirl wiv 'er tits out but not a fifteen-year-old one?" asked Sparky in all seriousness.

"Yeh, cos it's all legal and propah, like. Now she's sixteen, there's no reason why she can't provide us wiv quality wank material. May 'ave to get this picture framed and sent to Noye now 'e's doing serious bird. Won't be getting the real fing for a long time. The only fing 'e 'as got is waking up to Pat Tate's face."

"Can't believe he went down for the gold but got away wiv killing the pig," said Flint.

"Yeh, 'e fought 'e was gonna just walk out of court a free man. Old Bill 'ad uvah ideas. Wanted to frow the book at 'im. Sixteen years of bird for VAT evasion and conspiracy to 'andle stolen gold. Plus 'e's gotta pay back one million in back taxes and 'undred of fousands in court fines. And it 'as gotta 'urt just aftah 'is 'earing Patsy Adams was acquitted of importing 3 tons of grass."

"Yeh, weren't 'is best day, was it," said Nic distractedly, still looking at Lola.

"Noye couldn't 'elp 'imself. Told the jury 'e 'oped they all died of cancah. Judge weren't gonna go leniently on 'im," said Mat.

“Doing ’is bird, mind. Noye ’as dun the right fing and treated Old Bill wiv uttah contempt and kept ’is mouf shut,” said Sparky.

“Yeh, well, on a more important note,” said Nic as he turned to the back of the paper, “Lyall’s still leading the Iron army into battle. Got a quality line-up of boys this year. The Boys of ’86 – Martin captain, wiv shit-hot playahs McAvennie, Ward and Cottee. Fird place in Division One; only four points be’ind the reds ’ighest evah league position. Anyways, top geezah who runs this newspaypah, ’e should buy the ’Ammahs. ’E’s a bloke of great vision.”

CHARLIE SAYS

Debbie's head was aching and banging like a drum. Staggering into the living room in her dressing gown, she sat down on the sofa. Charlie was playing with his cars and shrieking with pleasure.

"Mummy isn't feeling well, so keep the noise down," said Debbie while she took a large gulp of her black coffee to wash down four paracetamol.

Look, Mummy, I'm winning the race. I'm a real top racing car driver. Brrrrrrm, brrrrrm, brum."

"Charlie, please be quiet for Mummy. I 'ave an 'eadache. *Transformahs* is on TV. Why don't you watch that. And close the blinds. What 'ave I told you 'bout opening 'em? Batty Betty will 'ave a field day poking 'er nose in."

Debbie took another gulp of coffee and grimaced as she realised that this caffeine infusion wasn't cutting it. Muttering under her breath, Debbie stomped to the kitchen. She switched the radio on. Duran Duran's 'The Reflex' blasted out of the airwaves. She loved this song, but today her head was just too sore to listen to Simon Le Bon, so she quickly switched it off. Debbie chose to ignore the chaos in the kitchen. There was takeaway debris everywhere: greasy pizza boxes, Indian and Chinese plastic containers. The sink was piled high with pans and crockery. Opening the fridge, Debbie took out a bottle of Vodka and poured a large measure into her coffee. Shutting the fridge door, she took the bottle with her back into the living room and slumped back down on the sofa. Charlie lined up his cars and pushed them as if they were racing against each other. The lounge was in a similar state of disarray as the rest of the house. Dust was thick on the furniture, albeit very expensive furniture. There was stuff everywhere, bags of unopened shopping. Debbie couldn't bear to open them. The frantic shopping for shopping's sake became a burden when she got the loot home. Shopping drunk, Debbie convinced herself she was a size twelve.

"Are you sure you don't want to play cars, Mummy? You can be my best car. It's yellow. It's a Renault 5TL. Varoom, vroom, vroom."

"No, Charlie, not now. Mummy 'as an 'eadache. Stop bovering me. There's a packet of crips in the cupboard if you're 'ungry. And if you're getting a pack, grab me a couple of packs of sausage and tomato. Don't make Mummy cross, or you know what'll 'appen."

"But, Mummy, you can even be the pink car if you want. I have one. Look, it's a Datsun. It's a top car. Is Daddy coming home today? We can all play together."

"Just shut up and play wiv your cars. Do you want me to give you a clip? I 'ave no idea where your dad is, but I'll take a guess 'e's wiv 'is dirty sluts. Get used to it, Charlie. Your old man is a bastard, and 'e doesn't care 'bout you. We're nufink to 'im."

Not really understanding what his mummy meant, and not wanting any more of her wrath, Charlie continued to play alone. Soaking in the coffee and vodka on the sofa, Debbie began to feel a little more human. She toyed around with the idea of going upstairs and having a shower. She hadn't had one in a few days. Maybe even wash her hair that was matted and greasy. But after she finished the coffee, she decided just to fill the mug up to the brim with vodka. Her head muddled with the alcohol and smarting about her no-good husband, Debbie mused, but as much as she tried to hate Nic, she couldn't. She still loved him. Maybe they could get back to the way they used to be; then Debbie wouldn't need to eat and drink so much and would be content again. She could lose the weight and go to Suzie's place and have a spa day. Maybe she could get her to give her a makeover. After all, she kept going on about it. She just needed to find the right diet. After the latest one, the Ethiopian, had failed, she'd all but given up until she read about the toothpaste diet. All you did for one week was consume just a tube of toothpaste and nothing else. This apparently could let you drop a stone in seven days. Then she would look like the girls at Nic's clubs. She'd gone to the Love Hole once when he'd disappeared for a week. Beyond worried and incensed, she'd been met by a girl who'd greeted her with, "Aye up, lass, is thee looking for a job. Thee's got uh pretty face, but boss will want you tu lose some pounds. He likes checking out our bodies, make sure we're in shape."

"Where is 'e?" screamed Debbie.

"Where's who, duckie?" asked a bewildered Tracey.

"Nic 'Unter, me 'usband. Where is 'e?"

"Aye, lass. No need tu get mardy. He went off t' bog."

Debbie stormed off to the gents' and flung open the door. Stepping in, she saw Nic and let vent. Nic was in mid-flow of taking a slash and turned in shock, narrowly missing his enraged wife with flying piss.

"You useless 'orrible excuse for a bleeding 'usband. Too much for ya, is it, to come 'ome to your wife and child? I 'ate you, Nic 'Unter. I wish I 'ad nevah met ya. You care more 'bout 'em 'orrible dogs than you do for us."

Enraged she had turned up at his club and barged in on him in the khazi, Nic stuffed his dick back into his jeans and grabbed hold of her, pushing her up against the wall in temper, his fist held ready to hit her, but he couldn't go through with it. There was a glimmer of something that stopped him. He felt a nostalgia, something that had been there before. Instead, he pushed her away and stormed out, shouting at her, "You're a lush. Get back 'ome and look aftah our kid. Don't evah embarrass me and turn up 'ere again. Do you 'ear me?"

What was the world coming to, thought Nic, where you couldn't even find solace while taking a slash in the bloke's bogs. It was supposed to be a man's last sanctuary, where you were safe from the incessant nagging of birds. The truth was, Debbie that day had come face to face at the club with her worst nightmare. It was wall-to-wall beautiful women with perfect bodies. She'd never felt so inadequate. And her good-for-nothing bloke – well, she shuddered to think of what his work consisted of. The thoughts of the other women made her feel physically sick, and the only thing she could do to stop the pain was to drink and eat more.

Charlie gave up hope that his mummy would play cars with him. She was always tired, grumpy and falling asleep. He flicked the four channels and started to watch *Danger Mouse.* Thinking his mummy needed something to eat, Charlie ran to the kitchen to get some food. There were slim pickings, as Debbie hadn't left the house in days. "Here, Mummy, some crisps," said Charlie as he handed her the packets. Debbie snatched them from him and proceeded to rip a packet open. Stuffing her hands in and bringing out large, greasy handfuls, she munched away. Charlie opened his Ringos. It was the first thing he'd eaten all day. He continued to play as he watched his mummy eat and drink and then lay down and fall asleep on the sofa in a drunken haze. Charlie ran upstairs and got a blanket to cover her. He would take good care of her. She just needed to rest. Charlie heard the beckoning sound of the ice-cream van outside.

"Mummy, Mummy, Mr Sidoli's outside. Can I get an ice-cream?"

Getting no response from his mum, Charlie tried to wake her by gently shaking her.

"Please, Mummy, can I have an ice-cream?"

Debbie, out for the count on the sofa, still didn't rise. Charlie decided to let his Mummy sleep. He ran up the stairs to his bedroom to get his piggy bank. Carefully shaking out his spoils, Charlie grabbed a handful of coins. He picked Moore up from his pillow and hugged him tightly. "I'll share my ice-cream with you and I'll buy Mummy one." He ran down the stairs and out the front door that Debbie had forgotten again to lock. All he could think about as he started to skip down the garden path was what he would have. Would it be a Mr Whippy or a Funny Face? He opened the garden gate, deciding on a Funny Face. He needed to make sure he didn't get any on his clothes again, as Mummy would hurt him like before. He knew she didn't mean it. She just got upset. She missed Daddy. He missed Daddy. His Mummy didn't mean to slap his face. It stung, and even more so when his salty tears ran down it. Excitedly, Charlie bolted across the road, where the van was parked playing *Greensleeves*. Charlie didn't see the Volvo approaching from his left. He stood no chance as the car ploughed straight into him. His little body was thrown into the air like a toy. His head smashed onto the road and his skull cracked open. Blood spurted onto the road, his little legs, grotesquely contorted, now saturated in vermilion fluid. His femur bone grotesquely stuck out from his pajamas. Moore lay by his side, splattered with blood. Charlie's last thought was how happy his mummy would be with her Pineapple Mivvi. He just wanted Mummy to love him and let her know he really was a good boy and would make her proud of him.

The bereft Volvo driver jumped out of the car at the same time as Mr Sidoli leapt out of the van dropping a Zoom lollypop he was holding for a girl in a pinafore dress. Both men rushed to Charlie. They knew from the state of the body that the little lad was dead, but Mr Sidoli checked for a pulse just in case by some miracle he was still alive. The Volvo driver clasped his head and moaned in between sobs, "He just ran out in front of me. I didn't have time to stop without hitting him."

As Mr Sidoli suspected, there was no pulse. Batty Betty, who'd seen the incident, as she'd been peeking out of her curtains, came running out of her house.

"I've called an ambulance. It's Charlie, such a dear little boy. This is too awful to be true." Within minutes they could hear the cacophonic wails of the ambulance siren. Soon it could be seen with its blue lights flashing as it came to a sudden stop. Two paramedics jumped out: a man in his fifties with curly black hair and a younger woman with Titian hair tied back in a ponytail. A few moments later a police panda turned up. The boy was dead; that was evident. Even so, the lady paramedic reached down and gently took his pulse. But there was nothing. She made a gesture with her eyes to the other paramedic. He seemed to understand without a need for spoken words. He went back to the ambulance to get a stretcher. Picking Charlie up gently, they put him on the stretcher and walked towards the ambulance. All that was left on the floor was a teddy bear soaked in blood and three silver coins.

PC Dickson and PC Clutterbuck were speaking to the gaggle of people who were outside and taking statements. The ashen-faced Volvo driver had been placed in the back of the panda for questioning. Both constables had felt sorry for him; this was obviously just a tragic accident. Batty Betty told PC Clutterbuck which house Charlie lived in. Walking across the street somberly, PC Clutterbuck took his hat off, getting ready to tell the parents that Charlie was never coming home again. He knocked the door, but there was no answer, so he tried again, this time knocking harder. When there was still no answer, he rapped the window gently and waited. After a few moments, a woman opened the door in a dressing gown, her eyes bloodshot, her hair bedraggled.

"What the bleeding 'ell do you want, coming 'round 'ere? If it's that no-good 'usband of mine you want, 'e ain't 'ere. I aven't seen 'im in days. Probably find 'im in one of 'is tart clubs."

"You are Mrs Deborah Hunter?"

"Yeh, I am. What of it? What the 'ell do you want? Look, like I said, the good-for-nufink ain't 'ere. Now sling your 'ook."

"Mrs Hunter, there's been an accident. I need to come in if that's okay."

"Accident," said Debbie, thinking something dreadful had happened to Nic. She now noted the somber look on the PC's face. She glanced at his helmet held in his hand. She started to go back into the hallway in a trance, and the policeman followed her into her living room. It was then Debbie started to scream.

"What's 'appened to Nic?"

"I'm sorry, Mrs Hunter, there has been an accident. Your son has passed away."

There was a lapse of seconds, where Debbie's befuddled mind tried to process the information. Then she let out a cannibalistic scream and crumpled to the floor.

It was Batty Betty who called Nan and told her of the tragic news. Rosie had broken down on the phone. Her beloved great-grandson was dead. But Nan knew she had to stay strong for her grandson. Nan ended the call by asking Betty to go over and sit with Debbie until she or one of her family got there.

Debbie had been in such a state when the constable had delivered the news, her body uncontrollably shaking and a sobbing that came from the very pit of her soul. She'd refused to get up off the floor. When he gently tried to coax her up, she'd wailed incoherently, "Find me 'usband. I need Nic. Our boy is dead."

A doctor had been called and had given her Librium, a sedative that half knocked her out. Social services were alerted by the police as protocol. Debbie maintained, in her comatose state, that it was a terrible accident. She'd been exhausted, having been up all night with Charlie, as he'd been playing up. She'd been so tired the next day, she'd fallen asleep on the sofa and forgotten to lock the front door. This was of course a lie, as most nights Charlie put himself to bed, as Debbie was out for the count after she had drunk herself into a stupor. Social services took it no further. There were no red flags. The lounge was a bit chaotic, but this wasn't a cause for alarm. The family weren't on their radar, and no previous allegations had been made against them. It was deemed to just be a tragic accident. Debbie, now somnolent, had called every number she could think of to get in touch with Nic, but no one knew where he was. The doctor had left her with some sleeping pills, Halcion, along with the tranquillisers. Before Debbie fell into a bleak, dreamless sleep, her final thought before blessed oblivion took over her was, what now that Charlie had gone, the only real thing that kept her connected to Nic, would he now abandon her, or when she awoke, would he be cradling her in his arms?

Nan had had no joy getting hold of Nic. She'd called Mat and broken the news. Mat was devastated. He'd always loved his nephew and couldn't understand why Nic took so little interest in him. He was hoping Suzie would sire him two boys when she gave birth to their twins. Mat told Nan he hadn't seen Nic today but would go out with some of his men to look for him. But it was Nan who finally tracked him down at the Crown. Tommy had answered the phone on the bar, and sure enough Nic was in there playing snooker with Dexy.

"Tommy, love, can you get 'im to the phone? Can you tell 'im it's very important?" asked Nan while trying to hold back sobs.

"Will do, Rosie. I'll just go and get 'im."

Tommy went over to the snooker table. Nic was just about to take a shot to pot the black ball.

"Nic, your Nan's on the phone. She needs to speak to you. I fink it's a bit urgent, like."

"Okay, mate," said Nic, taking the shot and potting it. Handing the cue to Dexy and picking up his pint, he sauntered over to the bar and picked up the phone.

"'Ello, Nan."

"Nic, son, I've got some terrible news for ya. You gotta stay strong. There's been a tragic accident. Charlie's been knocked down. Son, 'e didn't make it. 'E's gone. I'm so sorry."

"'Ow?" asked Nic in a dead tone as he lit a cigarette and took a large drag.

"Debbie, I fink, fell asleep and 'e got out the front door to buy an ice-cream. 'E just ran into the road."

Nan got no further response from Nic, as he left the phone dangling at the bar.

Nic didn't go home to comfort his wife. He blamed Debbie. She was an unfit mother. But something stopped him from going home and ringing her neck. He knew however much he tried to cover it up, he hadn't been there for his son either. Ashen-faced Nic told Tommy to give him a bottle of whisky. Seeing the look on Nic's face, Tommy obliged, pouring him a huge measure. Nic the joker had heard news that had silenced him. He just stared ahead and downed the amber liquid. Tommy kept refilling his glass. He didn't stop until the bottle was empty. Something died in Nic that day. Whatever semblance of conscience or humanity he ever had was now gone. All that was left was a soulless husk with a black heart, devoid of any real human emotion. A walking, ticking time bomb.

In the days that followed, Debbie was now a barely functioning phantasm, propped up on medication and alcohol. Nan had tried her best, but Debbie needed her tea and sympathy like she needed a hole in the head. Nan called incessantly. Debbie was too scared to leave the phone off the hook just in case Nic called. As soon as she heard Nan's voice, she hung up. She was ambivalent about Nic. She on one hand craved to the core of her being that he came home to her so they could grieve together. She also hated him with a burning passion for leaving her bereft and alone in a personal hell. Was he staying away because he was just dealing with his grief in his own way, or was he never coming back? Not once did it cross Debbie's mind that she was in any way responsible for Charlie's death. Her brain couldn't go there.

For three days after Charlie's death Nan had called to see Debbie with no success. She realised she was grieving bitterly, but being on her own wasn't good for her. She needed to talk the pain through with someone. So today Nan wasn't taking no for an answer. Nan knocked on the door, and as she suspected, there was no answer, so she called through the letterbox.

"Debbie, please let me in. I've dun us a Dundee cake. If I 'ave to camp outside 'ere on the doorstep, I'm not moving until you open the door. There are fings no mattah 'ow upsetting we need to talk frough. It really will 'elp, love, to chat 'bout it. I promise."

Nan waited patiently for fifteen minutes, but no sound came from the house. She was just about to knock again when she heard movement from inside the house. Debbie slowly opened the door. The sight before her shocked Nan. She'd seen Debbie looking dishevelled on many occasions, but the woman standing before her was like a living ghost, her face cadaverous. She squinted in the sunlight. Her eyes were sunken into her skull. Her grandson's wife looked like she'd aged ten years, and there were flecks of white in her hair. Debbie didn't speak; she just turned around, leaving the door open. Nan followed closely behind her, grimacing at the musty smell inside the house. Debbie threw herself down on the sofa.

"Debbie, 'ow you doing, love? I 'ave been so worried 'bout ya."

Debbie pulled her dirty dressing gown around her and just stared at the floor as Nan moved a load of empty wine bottles so she could sit down.

"I got you some Lucozade. This will buck you up," said Nan as she fiddled with the orange wrapping covering the bottle of fizzy glucose. "You 'ave to talk 'bout it at some point. You need to let it all out. It's not right bottling fings up."

"I'll let it out all right. Where the 'ell is that bastard grandson of yours? Nic 'asn't been 'ere. 'E 'asn't even bovered to call. I don't need any bleeding Lucozade or fruit cake. I just need me 'usband."

"Debbie, I promise you we'll get Nic 'ome on Fursday. Mat and I 'ave made all the arrangements."

With the mention of what Thursday would bring, Debbie broke down in uncontrollable sobs.

Nan went over to her, sat down and took her in her arms, where Debbie just flopped and cried bitter tears, all the time Nan holding her and telling her, "There, there, girl. Get it all out. Nan is 'ere wiv ya. We'll get Nic 'ome, don't you worry."

Nic had been up for days with little sleep. When he did fall into a fitful sleep, he kept seeing Charlie's face crying out in pain as he was hit by a car. His little body, as if clutched by an invisible hand, was flung high into the air and tossed violently onto the road, his body smashed to pieces. There was another face in these dreams: his brother. He hated him. Everything was his fault. If he hadn't given him those strip joints, if he had handed over half of the assets he was entitled to, he probably wouldn't have strayed from Debbie, who'd been his rock. Mat had betrayed him. Mat, with his perfect life, with his virgin bride about to give birth. Sleep wasn't a comfort for Nic. In fact, it just propelled him into a nightmare so tormented and sinister that the alternative of awake torture was preferable. Since he'd heard the news of Charlie's death, he'd been holed up at Tracey's flat off his head on drink, drugs and self-gratifying sex. He had made no contact with any of his family. Tracey padded into the lounge.

"Misty's okay. She can get uh dentist tu reconstruct her front teeth. Just got off phone wae her. Her nose weren't broken tu. Just uh bit bashed up, buggerlugs, so that's summat. Don't think she'll be able tu work for a reyt good bit."

Nic had relieved Misty of two of her teeth. She'd come over to party with him and Tracey. Nic had shagged the life out of both of them together. After he ejaculated, the slapper smiled at him. She was obviously mocking him, so he did what he thought any other bloke would've done in the situation and punched her in the face.

"Trace, I don't give a flying fuck, and I 'ope the slag doesn't fink I'm paying for 'er dental work, cos I ain't. I'll be paying for fuck all. She deserved it. She'll be no good to me now – damaged goods – so when you speak to 'er, tell 'er not to bovah coming back. Now get over 'ere," said Nic as he roughly grabbed Tracey by the head, unbuckled his jeans and stuffed her head into his crotch. Tracey dutifully sucked on his penis as Nic thrust into her, at the same time practically gagging her. It was to her relief that just before she actually thought she was going to choke, he got up, holding her and pushing her up against the wall, and started to fuck her. The violent pounding not quite releasing his tension, he thought the best way forward was to strangle her. Tracey was left gasping for breath and choking as he tightened his hands around her neck. As he climaxed, he threw her to the floor, walked back over to the sofa and did a fat line of coke. Tracey's face flushed red as she gasped in stilted short breaths. Willing herself to get up off the carpet, she forced herself up and said, "I'll just go make us some grub. Ham barm cake do yuh?"

Mat had tracked Nic down to Tracey's. Since the death of Charlie, he hadn't left the flat. But today he would be leaving, even if Mat had to personally carry him out. Mat and Nan were parked on Frith Street in his Bentley T Series Mulsanne.

"Right, son, 'e's not gonna come quietly."

"Nan, 'e is coming whevah 'e likes it or not."

They both got out of the car, Nan clutching a shopping bag and a suit carrier. Mat pressed the intercom for Flat 6 and impatiently waited for an answer. His fingers rapidly tapped the steel device. After a minute, when there was no answer, he became agitated and kept pressing the buzzer. Finally, just about when Mat was about to break the door in, Tracey answered.

"Ey up, what's wae all thu buzzing? My lugholes can't take it."

Mat cut her dead, his voice as cold as steel. "It's Mat. Let me up. I need to see me bruvah."

"Duckie, Nic's, uh, bit busy at moment, int'it. I'll get him tu call thee later."

"Tracey, let me in now before I break the door down."

"Chuffing ek, if thee's got face on, suppose you'll have tu come up."

With that, Mat heard a click and he opened the door. They walked up the flight of stairs to the second floor where Flat 6 was situated. The door to the flat was already open. Tracey stood in the doorway wearing a short kimono. She went to say something but was stopped in her tracks as Mat barged past her into the lounge. Nan followed him, eyeing the young woman suspiciously. The girl, just as she suspected, looked like a floozy. But she was sure she'd seen the girl before leaving the twins' house. The room they entered was a mess. There were empty alcohol bottles everywhere, the ashtrays were overflowing, various items of lingerie and sex toys were strewn across the floor, furniture was overturned and the TV had been smashed to smithereens. Nic looked up as he was just in the process of taking a Scarface-sized line of coke with a rolled up £50 pound note. He cocked his head as if he couldn't quite believe the sight in front of him, his eyes bloodshot, his face heavy with stubble. He wore just a pair of Gucci jeans and was barefoot. He stuck his head back down to hoover up the white powder; it was the only way he could handle the intrusion.

"Bruv, you need to get in the showah, 'ave a wash and shave."

"I've got a new suit for you to wear, son," said Nan as she sat beside him and reached for his hand.

Nic snapped it away and mumbled "I'm okay 'ere. I'll 'ave a showah latah."

"Nah, bruv, you'll 'ave one now. It's your son's funeral this aftahnoon."

Nic just stared ahead and lit a cigarette, taking a large slug from his whisky bottle.

"I can't 'andle it. I can't go."

Mat darted forward and dragged his brother up from the sofa. He grabbed the cigarette out of his mouth and stamped it out on the carpet. If Nic had been in his normal state of health, there would have been no saying who would have been the victor in an altercation between the brothers, but Nic was taken off guard, his resolve broken. The days and nights of little sleep filled with excessive alcohol and drugs had weakened him. He tried to resist, but it was a lacklustre attempt at best, and Mat held onto him, keeping him upright.

Mat turned to Tracey. "Where's the bafroom?"

Tracey motioned to the door on the left. "It's reyt through there."

Mat proceeded to haul him into the bathroom. Running the shower, Mat put the setting on cold. Nic needed to sober up fast. Mat pushed Nic clothed into the shower.

"Now, bruv, you're gonna get washed and shaved. Undahstand?"

The freezing water gave Nic some momentum. He stood there lifting his head up to the jetting water. It was strangely soothing. After a good five minutes he finally started to get undressed and wash. He threw his saturated jeans onto the bathroom floor. Fifteen minutes later, washed and shaved, Nic got out of the shower, the water dripping down his face and body. Mat handed him a towel.

"Right, bruv, dry off and brush your teef. I'll get your suit."

"Bruv," said Nic in a muted tone, "bring me stuff in – I need it. I can't get frough today wivout it."

Mat looked straight into his brother's eyes and made an imperceptible nod of his head as he left the room.

Nan was fondling her gold locket. The atmosphere in the room was uncomfortable to say the least. The girl had offered to 'mash' some tea for her, but Nan, having no idea what she was on about, had abruptly declined. She tried to divert her attention from the range of dildos on the floor. She couldn't help but notice that one was the size of her rolling pin. Nan blamed these wanton women who worked at the clubs for the breakdown of Nic and Debbie's relationship. These women were no doubt flinging their bodies at her grandson. I mean, he was just a bloke after all, and Hunter men were very red-blooded. Nic had just been led astray. He just needed to get back on the right path, and she would see to that. She needed her beloved family back together.

Relieved to see Mat, she asked, "Son, 'ow is 'e?"

"Washed and shaved and just doing 'is teef. Giz us the stuff."

Nan handed him the suit carrier and the shopping bag containing a new shirt, tie, socks and shoes. Taking it from Nan, Mat also picked up the whisky bottle, the table mat that was home to the white powder, the credit card and the rolled-up note. A frown crossed Nan's forehead at the same time as a look passed between her and Mat that she understood. Today it was a matter of whatever it took to get Nic to his son's funeral. Stepping back into the bathroom, Mat saw that Nic was seated naked on the toilet seat.

"Bruv, get dressed. Your suit and stuff is 'ere," said Mat.

After taking a long swig of whisky, Nic unsteadily got up and started to get dressed. One thing Nic couldn't do was look in the mirror; he didn't want to face what was staring back at him. Once dressed, he wearily walked back into the lounge.

"Ah, son, you look evah so smart. Dun a lovely job, 'as that tailor. We'll be wiv you every step of the way today."

Nic barely acknowledged Nan; he just did a semi-shrug, more interested in making sure he had the bag of blow stuffed in his pocket.

"Right, we'll be off then," said Nan as she got up from the sofa and linked arms with Nic.

Nic just swigged the rest of the bottle of whisky and then grabbed another full one.

"'Ere," said Mat as he tried to hand him his watch and cufflinks. "Put these on."

Nan took the jewellery off Mat and gently fastened them onto his wrist.

As the three walked towards the door, Tracey asked, "Is thee coming back tonight, buggerlugs?"

"No, 'e fucking isn't," snarled Mat. "Now get your lazy arse back to work."

Mat glided the car to a halt outside St Mark's Church. Nic had sat in the front with Mat. The whole journey he hadn't muttered a word; he just kept swigging from his bottle and lighting cigarettes one off the other. He'd ceased the need to use the rolled-up note; he was just sticking his nose in the bag.

"Bruv, you need to get out of the car now, but before you do, wipe your nose and giz us the bag."

Nic shakily gave Mat the perforated bag. Nan reached over from the back of the car with a tissue.

"'Ere we go, love. Now take a deep breaf. This'll be the 'ardest fing you'll 'ave to do in your life. But you must stay strong, son. We'll not leave your side."

Grunting in response, Nic opened the door, taking a large blow on the tissue, bringing up strings of bloody snot, and stepped out onto the pavement. It was a gloomy day. Dark rain clouds hovered overhead in the dull, listless sky. A murder of crows squawked while swooping down onto a maple tree. Nic tossed the bloodied tissue on the floor. Nan manoeuvred herself to Nic's side and took his arm. There were many cars parked alongside St Mark's Rise. Many others had walked to the sombre occasion. This was a Hunter funeral, and the locals had turned out in droves to pay their respects, along with a large portion of the criminal underworld. Most of the mourners had already made their way inside, as the funeral was at 3pm, and at just gone 2.50 they were cutting it fine. Mat led the way as they proceeded up the church's flag-stoned path to the arched, black door. He pushed the door open with a creak. There was an eerie silence inside, even though the church was packed. Walking down the main isle, Mat's eyes darted. He saw Sid, then as they neared the front, Victor, Dexy and Tommy made respectful nods. Batty Betty adorned a large black boater hat. Nan ushered Nic into the first pew to sit next to Debbie. His wife had seen him coming in. She'd hoped beyond hope he'd come. Even in her sedated state she managed a half smile. Debbie looked presentable; her mum had forced her to clean herself up and get into a black shift dress. Her mum kept her face towards the alter. She'd nothing to say to Nic; he'd ruined her daughter's life. Debbie took Nic's hand and held it tightly. Nic didn't reciprocate, but neither did he remove his hand, giving Debbie even more hope for their reconciliation. Watching as if from another dimension, his only son about to be buried, his resolve was shot through.

Mat sat next to Suzie at the end of the pew and put an arm around her and her baby bump as Father Tobias started the service. Nan had instructed him on what she wanted, as

Debbie was in no fit state to organise the funeral. Mat, Sparky and Flint had been bricks, rallying around doing whatever they could. Suzie, suffering from terrible morning sickness, had been like an angel. Such a selfless soul, trying so hard to reach out to Debbie. But seeing Suzie all glowing and lustrously pregnant was just too much for her.

The church was covered in flowers. There were wreaths shaped as teddy bears and butterflies. A large picture of Charlie wearing his football kit, with a beaming smile, was blown up on the alter step. They could hear the sound of the horse-and-carriage hearse that had led the cortege and was now outside the church. Belgian black horses dressed in velvet and plumes gently nodding as they came to a halt. Sparky and Flint were the pallbearers. They brought the tiny white coffin, adorned with a 'SON' wreath, into the church. Moore was in the coffin with him. Nan had lovingly washed him, silently weeping as she removed Charlie's blood. It was at this point that Debbie let out a wail that sounded inhuman. She broke down, crying uncontrollably and clinging onto her husband. Nic just stared ahead, unable to look at his only child's casket, unable to put his arms around his wife and comfort her. Instead he did the unthinkable and reached into his jacket pocket and hoovered up the spilled coke. His face now a mess with the white powder, Nan passed him another tissue from her bag, which he just ignored, so Nan took to cleaning his face up. Father Tobias took the service with warmth in his soothing Welsh lilt. When it came time for the actual burial, Charlie was laid to rest at the south side of the graveyard next to his great-great-grandfather and great-uncle.

"We therefore commit this body to the ground, earth to earth, ashes to ashes, dust to dust; in sure and certain hope of the Resurrection to eternal life."

The Hunters paraded past the coffin as they said their final goodbyes. Both Nic and Debbie glared at Mat and Suzie as they walked hand in hand past their dead son's grave.

Hiding behind a tree, McBride looked on as the funeral-goers left the church. A crow had shit on him. White gunk ran down his forehead. He contemplated whether this meant anything, a crow taking a crap on you. He knew that a different number of crows meant things. Superstitious things.

THE MEANS OF REPRODUCTION

"Lovely to see you, Nic. You've not been 'round for a while."

"Yeh, Nan, been busy at the clubs, trying to keep me mind off fings. Got the two up West sorted. Goldfish Jam and Strawberry Split doing a blinding trade. Just gotta get the one 'round 'ere sorted. I'm calling it the Pink Taco."

"What pretty names. 'Owevah do you come up wiv 'em?"

"It's natural, Nan. They just come to me, like. It's this feme I got going on."

"'Ow's fings at 'ome. You need to make amends wiv Debbie, son. You need a fresh start. Nan knows best, and what you need is to 'ave anuvah baby. It'll bring you back togevah."

To this Nic just stared into his mug of tea. After the funeral Nic had, as a sense of forced duty, stayed with Debbie at the house. The truth was, Nic hadn't the resolve to go anywhere else. They moved like self-medicated ghosts with no purpose around each other. After a few weeks he'd taken himself back to work and bought a place on Powis Square in Notting Hill without telling her. The lairy, gobby Nic came back bit by bit, but inside he was hollow.

"I 'ave seen too much deaf and 'artache in life, more than

anyone should, but one fing Nan knows is that life 'as to go on. 'Untah men are no good wivout a woman. As Suzie is gonna give birf soon, if you 'ad anuvah baby, they'd be close in age, grow up togevah like you four did."

"Suppose so," said Nic flatly. He'd been more than incensed when Mat had been going on about how much he was looking forward to being a dad the other day.

"I'm really 'appy for ya," Nic had lied as convincingly as he could. Mat was too away in 'Suzieland' to pick up on any undertone, or so he thought. But Mat had clocked something almost imperceptible in Nic's eyes, a flicker that didn't sit well with him. But it was fleeting, and Mat wrote it off as it being difficult news for his brother, given the loss of his son. Nic had gone on a bigger-than-usual bender after that revelation.

"Are you trying, son, for a baby?"

"Fing is, Nan, gotta be 'ome really to do that, and she is blotto most of the time."

"I know fings 'ave been really tough for you and Debbie, but time is an 'ealer. I know undahneaf it all she's the same lovely girl you met back all those years ago. The only way you're gonna get frough this is togevah."

Nic was ambivalent about how he felt about his wife. On one hand he blamed her for the death of his son, and on the other she was in a strange way the only person who was solely there for him. Something stopped him from completely walking away.

Nic continued to stare into his tea. Nan stuck her nose in the *News of the World*.

"Blooming 'eck, you seen this? Some coppah 'as dun 'imself in. Some Welsh bloke called Alan 'Taffy' 'Olmes."

"Yeh. Shame it weren't McDick. I would 'ave 'elped 'im out there."

"You always was kind. Nic," said Nan distractedly as she

further studied the paper. "It's being linked to that private investigator Daniel Morgan who was found wiv an axe frough his skull outside the Golden Lion Pub up Syden'am. I remembah that cos I fought they only 'ave 'em private investigators in 'Awaii, like that Magnum. Says 'ere it's wildly speculated that Morgan was going to expose corrupt policemen associated with villains rooted in Brink's-Mat. Why do they keep banging on 'bout that robbery. It was years ago. Like, 'ow can it be responsible for everyfink? It's just silly."

"Yeh, Nan, getting a bit boring now, like one of the old man's Sabbaff records on repeat."

"There's an investigation of corruption that goes to the 'ighest levels of Scotland Yard and also extensive intelligence-gavering on major organised criminal gangs. The current 'ead of C11 is Commandah Ray Adams. E's a Freemason and since 1965 he has been subject to 11 complaints."

"Yeh, well, good luck wiv that, Nan. Fink you'll find they will end up 'aving to sack 80% of the Met."

"Our new MP, Diane, who's one of 'em blacks, she says she's coming aftah these bent policemen. She 'as made a speech in the 'Ouse of Commons accusing 'em of planting drugs, theft and conspiracy to pervert the course of justice. She describes 'erself as a level-minded voice who sympafises wiv the IRA and finks the 'Olocaust can't 'ave 'appended, as Jews aren't black. The journalist spoke to a local who said they was rocked to the core when they found out that Diane was an MP. They just fought she was an 'ard-working, single-mum dealah, not a scum MP, and whoevah they interviewed then spat on the floor."

"I can't get me 'ead 'round the fact we've got a spear-chuckah illegal alien as an MP. 'Ow did that 'appen, Nan? 'Ackney is going to the dogs."

"Says 'ere, son, she's from Paddington."

"Nan, they probably mean darkest Peru. Paypahs get it wrong all the time."

"We got no idea who's coming into our country. Be the deaf of us. Enoch Powell could see trouble was brewing bringing all these foreigners ovah 'ere."

"Who's that? Some geezah you know down the bingo. You got any more Penguins, Nan?"

"In the biscuit tin. I'll get you one now," said Nan as she reached across and took one out of the tin that was right next to Nic. "Enoch was a politician."

"See the colour of me face? That's where I'll be voting. Anyfink else going on, Nan?"

"KAD 'ave taken responsibly for the deaf of 'singah' Billy Balls-Dragg. The multi-millionaire socialist's body was found outside 'is mansion in the conservative strong'old of Burton Bradstock 'e was in the process of selling for a 'uge profit to a Goldman Sachs executive. 'E'd been executed by a mefod called the waist-chop, whereby 'e was sliced in 'alf at the waist, and cos this missed all 'is vital organs, 'e would 'ave been in agony for 'ours before 'e died. KAD cited their reason was they couldn't let the public be inflicted any more wiv 'is rubbish music. A poll in *The Sun* concluded that 99.9% of people supported KAD's actions, most believing that Billy was now in a betta place, 'aving lived most of 'is life on Planet Fuckwit, excuse me language. The landlord of Billy's local, The Free 'Orseshoes, was quoted as saying, ''E spent 'is time making a nuisance of 'imself, swigging bottles of Bollingah, pissed as a fart, shouting out, "All wivin socialism, nufink outside socialism, nufink against socialism" then doing the Roman salute. No, 'e won't be missed.'"

"At least that's some good news, Nan."

"There's more. KAD in New York 'ave bombed the offices of BlackRock in Man'attan. They made the CEO, Larry Fink, wear a bomb belt aftah they stuck a stick of dynamite up his anus. There was no survivors. They 'ad only been an entity for a year, but KAD cited they were already very problematic and there was only room for one global terrorist network."

"Got to give it 'em, Nan, KAD get 'bout, don't they? Like, credit where credit's due."

"It's too much misery for me. Take me back to the war any day. Shove the TV on. It's *Kilroy.* I nevah miss 'im, and e's always got a lovely tan. Yesterday 'e was debating 'bout whevah Ireland is run by priests, peasants and pixies."

"Right, Nan, gotta meet a man 'bout a dog in Beffnal Green."

"All right, son. Cheerio. Try to make it up wiv Debbie, will ya? It'll be worf it."

"You're knocked up and you fink it's mine!" yelled Nic.

"Yeh, duckie, were late so took test and it were positive. I'm in't pudding club. Haven't been with nowt other lads since thee were crashing at mine."

"You're putting it about in 'ere and making skin flicks. Get rid of it! There's no way I'm 'aving a sprog wiv ya. It's not mine."

"Unno. I never thought I could have bairns. After me stepdad did what he did, doctor said I cun't have bairns. Me insides were reyt messed up. Nic, we could make this work. I know you're the dad. I've checked dates. It would be uh new start after losing thee's lad. Just think, it be reyt good if it were uh boy. I like the name Doug."

"Make this work! Make this fucking work! You're off your 'ead. You're a brass. Birds like you are a ten-a-penny screw," snarled Nic as he lurched at her and punched her full force in the stomach. Tracey doubled down in pain, instinctively grabbling at her tummy.

"Nic, no, please," whimpered Tracey, severely winded. "Don't hurt our baby."

"Listen, bitch," said Nic, "you're a wank-filling bag, and sluts like you should be grateful for it." Raising his arms, Nic pummelled mercilessly with his fists into her stomach over and over again. Tracey fought with all her might, tooth and nail, to save her baby, but her attacker was too strong and overpowered her. Nic left Tracey a bloody mess on the club floor.

Sometime later, Tracey managed to stagger out of the club, her foetus destroyed. She would painfully miscarry tonight in her flat. The physical and emotional pain ripping through her was worse than the first time, when she'd miscarried her stepfather's baby on her bedroom floor at twelve years old. She would clean up the bloody mess as she had before. The foetus flushed down the toilet. She had no choice. Girls like Tracey seldom had a choice.

Later that night, after downing a bottle of Absinthe, Nic vented his spleen on Sid, who'd called in to collect his money. "Tracey, the shit-cunt, only tried to make out I 'ave knocked 'er up. Do me a favour, 'ave a kid wiv a brass. The conniving bitch."

Sid took it all in his weaselly faced stride. He really could not have cared less. He just wanted his money and to get out of there. He wondered momentarily what a fourth generation of Hunters would be like, as they progressively got worse. Hopefully, this would be the last he would work for. But the crawling Uriah Heepesque employee answered dutifully, as he had for decades, "What a piss-taking slag, gaffa. You're gonna need to keep a lid on that. Show the tart who the boss is."

"I already did. There's no baby. I took care of that. Saved 'er the trip to the clinic. Trying to take me for a ride. She's a good earnah, I'll give 'er that, so I'll be expecting 'er back in work tomorrah night."

Sid was used to seeing highly debased things in his lifetime in the murky gangland world, but Nic Hunter was something else. Even Sid had a really bad feeling about him. This was disturbing, as Sid's base normal was below sewer-rat level.

"Right, gaffa, I betta make a move. I got a job on for Mat."

Nic walked to the safe and handed Sid his money. "Enjoy it, mate. You nevah know when it's your last day, do ya? And you can't take it wiv ya. Like, you're an old geezah; you could drop down dead at any time, couldn't ya? Make sure you're 'round 'ere early to clean up the mess next door."

"Fanks, gaffa. I'll be 'round first fing," said Sid as he scurried out the door. He might as well have been on all fours. He'd clocked the blood on the floor and the walls as he'd walked in. Trying to shake his feelings of unease, he made his way into the vibrant streets of Soho. There was no job on for Mat; he just wanted to make himself scarce. He had money to spend, maybe pick up a woman to take home – hopefully one he didn't have to pay for, but then again, he was flush tonight. He'd pulled out all the stops, splashing on Brut – total fanny magnet aftershave. Talking of fanny, the last whiff he'd had of a proper date was three years ago with a bird called Charlene. She had tits like golf balls in a sock and a face like a badger's arse after it had been run over. He'd bought her a fish-and-chips supper at Faulkners and given her a gift, a bottle of Tramp perfume. After their first date, and only date, he'd never heard from her again. If desperate, which was most days, he went down the docks, but it always went through his mind that he could be shagging his half-sister, or half-brother even – it was hard to tell these days. That fact put him off nearly 20% of the time. Walking onto Dean Street, Sid walked into a telephone box. He had a call to make. After that he would have a couple of pints at the Coach & Horses on Greek Street, see if there was any stray fanny going spare. He liked the pub, with all its scruffy nooks and threadbare carpet. The phonebooth was covered with XXX cards – 'Khloe's Spanking Fun', 'Sexy Sindy's Sinfest' and 'Mr Saw the Carpenter'.

ACT 5

CUPID STUNT

Not that you mind the killings! There's plenty of killings in your book, Lord.
– Davis Grubb, *Night of the Hunter*

All I know is that to see, and not to speak, would be the great betrayal.
– Enoch Powell, *Rivers of Blood*

"Do you want anuvah top-up, Victor?"

"I won't say no. That picture you've 'ad framed of James and Joshua makes your 'art melt."

"They 'ave captured me 'art. Where 'as time gone? They're nearly eighteen momfs old," said Nan.

"They're a credit to you, Rosie. Go on then, what's in the news?" asked Victor as he helped himself to a slice of chocolate sponge.

"There are some big stories today. The Ayatollah of Iran 'as ordered the killing of Salman Rushdie cos of 'is book *The Satanic Verses*, and Dirty Den 'as been found dead from a gunshot wound in *Eastendahs*."

"I don't watch that nonsense. It's nufink like the real East End."

"There's a big write-up on some bloke in America who's on deaf row, a murderah and rapist called Richard Ramirez who now finks 'e's a woman and wants to be moved to a female prison. Said 'e now feels like 'e's in a good place and believes that 'is suppression of 'is true identity was to blame for 'is misdemeanours. Richard 'opes people will be respectful of 'is metamorphosis from a moff into a buttahfly."

"What's 'e on 'bout buttahfly? Fought 'e wanted to be a woman. Do you fink the paypah is pulling our legs? Murdock; 'e's an Aussie. They're known to 'ave that sort of sense of 'umour."

"I don't fink it's a joke. It's not funny, is it?"

"Ramirez told Adolf Stonewall, a sympafetic journalist at *The New York Times*, 'e 'opes to live 'is best life evah as a woman. Richard, who is also known as 'The Night Stalkah', is six-foot-six and 'as gone frough puberty four times, defying medical science. 'E 'as arms the lenf of Slendah Man and 'ands like industrial shovels. Richard 'opes to betta 'imself while inside, learning needlecraft and playing competitive netball. Ramirez now goes by the name of Mable, a name 'e's liked since 1985."

"You couldn't make it up, Rosie. I'm so confused."

"Says 'ere that 'is lawyah, Jame Gumb, finks stunning and brave Mable 'as a good case to set a new legal precedent and 'opes the wheels of justice can be put in motion and that legislation can be fast-tracked frough congress. Gumb also says it's intolerable that now 'is client identifies as a woman 'e 'as to be incarcerated in a toxic male environment. Gumb admitted 'is client 'as made mistakes in the past, but this shouldn't be 'eld against 'er. Ramirez was sent down for killing firteen people, but the police fink that 'e may well 'ave killed a furvah four 'undred."

"I 'ave nevah 'eard such wickedness, Rosie. What was 'e identifying as when 'e killed all 'em people? John Christie?"

"Says 'ere 'e'll be put to deaf by the gas chambah at San

Quentin if 'e doesn't win 'is case and can't move and be dun in living wiv vulnerable women."

"Fings like this only 'appen in America. Gawd 'elp us."

"Crystal Lake, who's self-diagnosed 'erself wiv 'eterophobia, dragaphobia and transmisia, spoke to Sophie Scholl at the *White Rose Post*, where she coined the acronym SMURF, Sham Mutant Unrealistic Rip-off Female. Men finking they 'ave a right to live in this world was just a wild social contagion and virulent mind virus. Biological denialism and auto-gyn-ephilia – all these big words; it's that Piers Morgan again – were mental illnesses men were pushing on a society already inflicted wiv man-made mental 'ealth problems. She says all women must rise up and commit androcide for the Great Reset. Any woman not compliant would be dealt wiv in the New World Ordah as a gendah traitor, punishable by deaf. Crystal said that at present we are living in a dynamic far-from-equilibrium state, but KAD, as a manipulative function, were striving for a dynamic, pure-equilibrium state of the universe, where only women exist. She paid 'omage to her sistahs who'd laid the foundations for KAD, but Valerie Solanas she was critical of. Lake agreed wiv Solanas' beliefs, as stated in her SCUM manifesto, the Society for Cutting Up Men 1968, that the male is a freak biological accident – the 'Y' gene being an incomplete set of chromosomes, meaning the male was an incomplete female, a walking abortion aborted at the gene stage; maleness was in fact a disease manifesting in a deficiency, rendering them emotionally crippled simpletons – but was 'arsh when she tried to murdah misogynist and 'omosexual Andy War'ol. Solanas shot 'im, but missed any vital organs, when she should 'ave gone for the 'art or 'ead."

"No idea what the bleeding 'ell she's banging on 'bout, Rosie. Biological whatevah, they need to put it in layman's terms, don't they? I don't wanna 'ave to consult a dictionary when I'm reading the paypah. All I know is since the dawn of time a bloke's a bloke and a gal's a gal. 'Ow 'ard is that? Are we getting more stupid?"

"I fink we must be. Joe, a Delaware Senator speaking from his 'oliday 'ome Wolfsschanze in Poland, said 'e wanted to give a break to every rapist and murderah so that they can seamlessly transfer to a female prison. Male genitalia in the 1980s meant nufink. 'E proudly stated 'e 'ad 'is removed years ago, along wiv severing connections wiv 'is prefrontal cortex. Women just 'ad to suck it up. If a penis-wielding cross-dressah believed they're female, their 'uman rights needed to be respected. Joe, a formah willing and enthusiastic volunteer in the CIA-run Operation Midnight Climax is sick to deaf of rabid suffragettesque women trying to stuff down the froats of decent Democrats their rabid ideology that a woman 'as as many rights as men. It was 1989, not 1666. Joe finks you can identify 'owever you want and 'e identifies as Neil Kinnock. It was bigots who pushed him out of running in 1988 cos 'e did. Joe believes the time 'ad come to form a squadrismo to fight against reality and to unleash Goebbels' style propaganda. This had nevah failed before wiv the vegetative state of the usual jackass votahs. Intellectuals opposing this would be dealt wiv by the AB-Aktion. The Extraordinary Operation of Pacification which should be brought into law by passing the Enabling Act. As a cruddy politician he could take away the First Amendment any time he wanted."

"You what, Rosie? Give perverts a golden ticket? These Democrats are all the same: bigots. Fings like genocide, forced sterilisation, eufanasia and concentration camps, the Democrats was doing all that first. Practically gave the Nazis and Fascists a blueprint. The regressive left make out they are on the side of 'umanity, but they just want to destroy it."

"There's more, Victor. A Republican Senator in Iowa called Chuck challenged Joe on 'is deranged rantings, citing that Joe

’ad been forced to ’ave a penectomy cos ’e kept siring degenerate retards. E ‘adn’t ‘eard such batshit crazy pseudo-ideology since the Tate-LaBianca trial and wondahed was the CIA be’ind this too. Joe ’it back wiv a particularly stinging response: ‘I can’t remembah saying any of that, although I enjoy conversion. You’ll nevah see me photographed in a baving suit, unless I’m in the showah wiv me daughtah.’”

“Robert a West Viriginia Senator and proud exaulted cyclopes of the KKK defended Joe by stating ‘there was ways ‘round the ‘uman scum, imbecile, useless eater situation – Joe’s kids could be sent to an ’ospital along the archetype of Aplerbeck in 1940’s Dortmund supervised by Dr Weinah Sengenhof. Failing that a viable option was to send the simpletons to Madagascar.”

“Rosie, ’ow can these people ’ave any powah. I fought Livingstone was bad enouf.”

“It’s beggahs belief, Victor. ZZ Top then waded into the argument accusing Gumb of being a biological woman eliminator. They ’ave re-released ‘Woke Up Wiv Wood’ to raise money to legally challenge Gumb’s crusade. They furvah cited that no woman ’ad any business ’aving a beard. Their contemporaries, Slayah and Megadef, ’ave pledged to make sizable contributions to the Texan trio’s fundraising. ZZ Top said they’re willing to personally bankroll first-class airline tickets on Iblis Airlines for Gumb from the “Great Satan” to Iran – one way – where they actively encouraged ’im to preach from Mount Damavand ’is ’uman rights opinions to the Ayatollah.”

“What’s ZZ Top when it’s at ’ome? And woke up wiv wood? Did they go to sleep wiv a tree?”

“Not ’eard of ’em meself. Can’t be very popular, can they? Their managah, Seb Slick, ’as secured ’em ’eavy rotation on MTV of their deeply fought-provoking song. Supahmodels

Naomi Campbell, Kate Moss, Linda Evangelista and Cindy Crawford offered their services free of charge to appear in the video, which showed them in bikinis mud-wrestling. Linda told Rein'ard 'Eydrich at *Vanity Fair* that on this occasion she would get out of bed for less than $10,000. Seb issued a statement on their behalf stating that the band are pioneers in their commitment to the elimination of male supremacy and the abolishment of a patriarchal state – a trans'istorical phenomenon deepah than any uvah origin of oppression – and impose matriarchy wiv immediate effect. Seriously committed to KAD, they 'ad previously 'onoured Lake by penning the track 'Planet of Women' on their 'Aftahburnah' album."

"Gordon Bennet, Rosie, that's all we're 'earing 'bout these days is this KAD. Put a sock in it."

"Dave Mustaine from Megadef told Feodor Eicke at *Rolling Stone*, 'Yeh, we wanted to be, like, part of this ultra-violent radical feminist movement cos it's, like, well, radical, dude. We're super excited to be part of this cause and, well, yeh, radicalised. We're totally behind Kill all Dudes, including ourselves.'"

Another Dalston resident read the newspaper article with interest and remembered a favourite bible verse from childhood – Deuteronomy 23:1: '*No one whose testicles are crushed or whose male organ is cut off shall enter the assembly of the Lord.*'

BLOODY KISSES

Debbie glanced at herself in the full-length mirror. It was a sunny day and the mirror in this light told no lies; she was looking a million dollars. It was surprising what six months of no alcohol, a strict diet and beauty sessions could do. Now a size twelve, with curves in all the right places, Debbie's sun-tanned skin glowed and her light brown hair was long and luxuriant. After two months of her new health regime, she'd bitten the bullet and gone to Hot Cherry to see Suzie to make amends. She had nothing to worry about. Suzie greeted her with open arms. Both Jeffrey and she fussed over her.

"Girlfriend, you have cheekbones to die for. We'll have you in weekly for a Cherry on Top facial."

"I fink, as well, Jeffrey, Debbie's 'air would look good wiv golden 'ighlights."

Suzie and Debbie had become friends. Whenever Debbie approached the subject of how she had treated Suzie in the past, she wouldn't have any of it.

"Debs, the past is the past. The main fing is we're mates now."

Jeffrey insisted on going to step aerobics with them. Thankfully, the crush on Nic was over and Jeffrey was head over heels in love with his boyfriend Julian. He didn't even talk so much about George. Nic was far more attentive, giving her genuine compliments about how she looked, moving more or less back into the matrimonial home and bed. But that was the thing; since the morning of her epiphany, she'd realised something: she'd always love Nic, but she no longer felt she was in love with him. She was living a clean, healthy life, whereas Nic's continued to plunder into new destructive depths. She walked down the stairs of her immaculate house. Debbie had started a course in interior design and studied it with gusto, favouring the Scandinavian style emphasising natural and artificial light to create a bright and clean space. This resonated with Debbie; she needed a new dawn, a new start. Six months ago, she had woken up, yet again hungover and broken, but something was different. She wanted her life back. Her sleeps were plagued by nightmares, where she was holding Charlie in her arms, kissing him softly. Charlie was chuckling, giving her one of his cheeky grins, then from nowhere he started spewing blood, his body contorted as he tried to return her loving kisses, bloody kisses which covered Debbie's face. Charlie, in abject terror, screamed as he began to choke. It was at this point Debbie woke up from her grotesque sleep into her new nightmare – another day in hell. After cleaning the house from top to bottom and throwing out all the alcohol and calorific food, she'd made the call she should've made a long time ago.

"Nan, its Debbie."

"'Ello, love. 'Ow lovely to 'ear from ya."

"Nan, I fink I'm ready to go into Charlie's room. Can you come 'round?"

"Course, love. When do you want me to come ovah?"

"I'm ready now."

"I'll be ovah in 'alf an 'our."

"Fanks, Nan. See you soon."

It had been a hard afternoon, but Nan and Debbie had laughed and cried in equal measures. Charlie's room, not opened for years, was filled with dust. "We'll carefully put our best boy's fings in bags, and when Nic comes 'ome, 'e can put it all up the attic."

Debbie threw a Kiton coat over her Balmain dress and grabbed her handbag and left the house. She was meeting Suzie for lunch.

DANGEROUS LIAISONS

Tracey had left Sparky's early. She had a very important date, one that could change her life. It was 8.30am, and Sparky had been fast asleep when she'd left. Normally, this hour of the morning was alien to her; nonetheless, Tracey was dressed to the nines in magenta leggings and a black batwing jumper dress, accessorised with a pink, chunky belt and spiky stilettos. She teetered on her heels as she delved into her gold clutch bag and brought out her plum lipstick, which she reapplied heavily. She passed through the gates of St Mark's Church and made her way to the north side of the graveyard. It had started to drizzle, and Tracey cursed herself that she hadn't brought her umbrella. The last thing she needed was for her hair to frizz. She needed to look like she had stepped out of the pages of *Vogue*. Looking ahead, she saw a figure standing by the side of a gravestone. She held up her hand in a greeting gesture, but the figure didn't respond. She approached nearer and said, "'Ow do? That thee, duck? Is it Jacques D'Souza?" The figure made a nanoscopic nod of his head.

"So happy you live local and can give me uh lift up West. Funny place to meet, int'it, a graveyard? Small world, yer mam being buried reyt here. Me bloke, well, on-and-off-again bloke, lives reyt 'round corner. That yer mam's grave? It's a reyt dead nice one, int'it," said Tracey, thinking he must be one of those intellectual arty types who didn't talk much.

"Where's your car, duckie? We going downtown or summat? You said your studios were near Fleet Street. So glamourous. That's where all the rags are, int'it? Cun't you say summat? I feel like uh reyt daft 'apeth talking tu meself."

The figure stood still and made no reply.

Tracey was near enough now to have a good look at the man. He was wearing non-descript dark clothes. But on his head, he had on what was obviously a black, curly wig and large square sunglasses. Tracey, a streetwise lass, now found herself on high alert. Her fight-or-flight radar told her to run like the clappers. In that split second the figure ran at her with almost inhuman speed, a sickle held high above his head as he charged at her. Tracey went to run, but stumbled in her shoes, the floor now slippery with rain. The figure was now almost upon her, she could feel his breath on her face, but fortuitously the figure tripped on broken tomb marble and went flying. As he did, the wig fell off his head, releasing a shock of orange hair. The sunglasses slid to the floor over his beaky nose. As he splayed out on the floor, Nigel made a desperate grab with his hand and took hold of Tracey's ankle, clinging on with all his might. He was frothing at the mouth and screaming, "And on her forehead was written a name of mystery: Babylon the great, mother of prostitutes and of earth's abominations."

This wasn't like when she took a lamp from Nic or Malachi, who'd conditioned her to toe the line. Tracey knew she was fighting for her life, and fight she would. She did what any self-respecting northern lass would; she took off her shoe on her free leg and bashed the 6-inch heel through her attacker's eye. It pierced through vitreous into Nigel's brain. He slumped to the floor as blood spirted like a myopic fountain onto the hallowed ground. Tracey, being a resourceful lass, pulled the heel out, which made a squelching sound, Nigel's eyeball impaled on her heel, along with the bloodied optic nerve. The Hackney Hacker's last words were, "Mother, see you in hell. Behold, I was brought forth in iniquity, and in sin my mother conceived me."

Tracey had fled into the church clutching the bloodied heel, saying, "He fell arse over tit, so I wanged him one." A startled Father Tobias had called the police straight away.

In the aftermath of the slaying, the *News of the World* did a lucrative exclusive interview with Tracey. Crystal Lake had read Tracey's story with interest. She saw Tracey as a feminist icon and life survivor in the cesspit-filled world of men. Crystal taking time out from masterminding *coup d'états* encouraged her to publish the diaries she'd kept since childhood. So that there were no repercussions, she changed names to protect herself. Nic was called 'the man with the diamond cufflinks'. Lake showed how from the cradle she was enslaved by toxic male supremacy. Writing an introduction to the diary, Crystal made a solid case for drowning all men at birth. Lake proposed that a select few men would be incarcerated in high-security dungeons to produce sperm until such a utopian time came when medical science was able to produce synthetic semen. KAD were actively abducting sperm contraptions, their latest a half-Canadian Pretoria University student with an IQ of 160 and a 'Dan White Society' history student at Trinity College, Connecticut, captured at a Grateful Dead concert at the Forum.

Tracey signed a seven-figure deal with HarperCollins to publish her book. People identified and connected with her prose; it was brash but honest, candid but vulnerable. The *Sunday Sport* ran a week-long tribute to her using stills from her blue movies. The headline read: '**THE KILLING MOON**'.

Her book, *From the Cradle to Enslave*, was a bestseller all over the world. Tracey's misfortunes had now minted her a large fortune. As her porn alias, Zandaline Moon, her films became cult classics after the paper hit the stands. The public couldn't get enough of a beautiful actress vanquishing a serial killer.

She did a two-hour exclusive with Barbara Walters and was a regular on Johnny Carson's and Phil Donahue's shows. Tracey made the cover of *Time Magazine*, a last-minute decision by Editor-in-Chief, Jason McManus. He couldn't run with the scheduled cover, as the New Yorker billionaire entrepreneur married to a Czechoslovakian model was being held at the J. Edgar Hoover Building in Washington, where he was being questioned by the FBI, as they believed him to be the Zodiac Killer and responsible for the disappearance of Jimmy Hoffa. FBI Director William S Sessions had ordered the incarceration, on admittedly baseless grounds, to stop a potential bloodbath, be that real or imaginary. It surprised people that Tracey was resilient and not bitter by her life and the cards it had dealt her. There was a warmth that Joe Public picked up on.

"What don't kill thee makes thee stronger, duckie."

Nic was vexed about Tracey's rise to fame. He could have kicked himself he hadn't been more included in her adult movie work. He could be making a killing right now on those skin flicks. Nic did, however, hold her now in a slightly higher esteem – she'd taken out the Hackney Hacker. Who would have thought that Greta's gormless boyfriend had it in him. Both Mat and McBride were strangely on the same page. They, for their own reasons, were glad the serial killer had been caught. However, due to Greta doing a moonlight flit shortly after the news broke that her boyfriend was a deranged killer, McBride would now have to find a new snitch to infiltrate the Hunter gang, and Mat needed a new tea girl. Both men set to work with alacrity to replace the roles.

DNA testing of the sickle proved that Nigel had killed Lisa and Stacey. HOLMES (Home Office Large Major Enquiry System) identified that Nigel's mother had been found brutally murdered some years earlier. The killer hadn't been brought to justice. The investigation was ongoing.

MAKING PLANS FOR NIGEL

"You dirty, disgusting boy. Have you been peeking again while I was taking a bath?"

"No, Mother, I've been sitting here reading the bible like a good boy."

"Have you been having ungodly thoughts about those nasty harlots dancing on *Top of the Pops*? Whores from Babylon wearing no brassiere, bosoms jiggling, and in hot pants, buttocks hanging out like the tongues of the devil."

"No, Mother, I've been a reading from the good book."

"What did you learn from the book of the Lord? Don't forget the Lord is always watching you, boy."

"From *Psalms 101:3*, Mother, I learnt I will not look with approval on anything that is vile. I hate what faithless people do; I will have no part in it."

"Correct, boy. You mustn't let the filth that is unleashed by Beelzebub into you, or you will suffer under the seductive fate that a sinful succubus will bring, corrupting and violating your weak human flesh to do the devil's business, and from there cast into the burning eternal flames of hell to be vanquished for eternity, never dying but confined to Hades, screaming in pain as the fires conflagrate your weak male body over and over again."

"Mother, I will never be tempted with the sins cast by Eve. I won't be beguiled by the Serpent. The Lord leads me along the path of perfect righteousness."

"Do not lie to me, boy. I saw you playing with your growing snake watching those shameless strumpets. Your wickedness has caused me excruciating distress. That I could have given birth to Satan's spawn has caused me agonising bowel blockages. I have haemorrhoids the size of Kyoho grapes. Do you understand, boy, what you have done? From within, out of the heart of man, come evil thoughts, sexual immorality, theft, murder, adultery. You're not a good boy, You are a wicked boy, led on by Lucifer himself."

"Mother, I promise I'll stive to rid all of the wickedness out of my heart and soul. I will read the scriptures day and night. Create in me a clean heart, oh God, and renew a right spirit within me."

"I will expect that, boy. Do not defy me. Affliction will slay the wicked, and those who hate the righteous will be condemned. Abstain from every form of evil."

"Mother, I will pray day and night for the redemption of my soul."

"Make sure you do. Now come upstairs, boy, and get the castor cream from the bathroom. I'll be in the bedroom."

"Yes, Mother."

"And cut your fingernails before you come in"

"Yes, Mother."

Nigel put the bible down. He'd been reading Judges 19–21. The dismembered concubine. An Old Testament tale of a Levite and his concubine as they travelled through the Benjamite City of Gibeah. While there, the menfolk of Gibeah threatened to rape Levite, so he did what he thought to be the just and right thing and handed his mistress over to the rabid gang so they could gang rape her and not him. They raped her until she was unconscious, and left her for dead. When the Levite found her body he cut her up into twelve pieces and sent them to the Twelve Tribes of Israel. When Nigel pictured the concubine, she had his mother's face. Nigel had prayed to the Lord to get him away from his piles-inflicted mother, but his wishes were never granted. A God he believed impotent, but expected ultimate dedication and belief in him back. Why should this God be so powerful when he did nothing? Nigel hated this God as he hated his mother.

At school he was bullied and referred to as 'The Freak'. When he was just about to give up all hope, the loner came across a crowd of other social rejects, who called themselves the Intellect Devourers. These outcasts introduced him to a new world – a world of Dungeons & Dragons. He studied the proverbial trifecta – the *Player's Handbook,* the *Dungeon Master's Guide* and the *Monster Manual* – in intricate detail. The Intellect Devourers answered to a higher power than any human God. The gods they served were deities such as Bane from The Forgotten Realms, the tyrannical god of hate, and from Greyhawk, Erythnul, the malicious god of slaughter. These were real gods. Powerful gods. Nigel soon progressed to the position of Dungeon Master. He grew bored of the Blackmoor and Greyhawk campaigns and stove to invent his own campaigns, ones where evil banshees and spectre harpies died excruciating deaths at the hand of chaotically evil Gargoyles and Chimeras. These campaigns in Nigel's own words were so genius they were more moonshined than home-brewed. He took some solace from his forced-upon bible studies – he still believed in fire and brimstone. Nigel remembered one verse fondly – 1 Peter 2:18, *"Slaves, be subject to your masters with all reverence, not only to those who are good and equitable, but also to those who are perverse."*

In his first campaign, The Curse of Zuggtmoy, he made sure the adventurers tracked and found the Wench of Decay and crucified the demon bitch. He was now god of this fantastical brave new world – the master storyteller, the rule maker and enforcer. Why worship a god when you could be one?

At seventeen he'd left Berkshire for London. The City of Thieves, his mother had called it a den of vice, full of immorality. His mother was found dead in an alleyway behind Pound Lane. Her body hadn't been found for over a week, and by then vermin had flayed her face and body. If she'd been found sooner, Newbury Police would have seen the 'N' carved into her forehead. Nigel was making plans. He could now be happy in his world. The boy's whole future was as good as sealed.

WHOOPS APOCALYPSE

Sid parked his pride-and-joy spearmint Cortina Mark III on Curzon Street; he'd been summoned by Mat to his flat. He had a fleeting memory of when he had a Mark I and had come out of the scrapyard to find an eight-year-old Nic with a black marker in his hand after decorating his car with obscenities and spunking cocks.

"Mistah, what do ya fink 'bout what I've dun to your motah?"

The gaffa had a high-ranking officer who wasn't playing ball, and Mat needed some ammunition on him. Intelligence informed him Commander Drury was picking up rent boys in Piccadilly Circus, the Dilly Boys who worked on the 'meat rack', the railings around the central traffic island where the statue of Eros stood. The winged statue was surmounted on a fountain located at the south-eastern side. Sid had to pick up a Hi8 Sony Handycam from Mat and then lurk around the neon signs advertising displays, hoping to spy Drury, Mat had told him earlier, "Once you 'ave collected the equipment, keep on it until you 'ave the footage. Once you 'ave it, give the kit back to me pronto."

As he stood in the porch about to ring the buzzer to Mat's flat, Sid's head snapped to the side as he heard mufflings coming from behind him. It was dark, and Sid tended to blend into any situation. He was sure he hadn't been seen. His Machiavellian sensors homed in that he recognised one of the parties. The lovebirds were giggling, caressing each other as they made their way holding hands towards the steps to the basement flat. If it wasn't Phillip Paddock the TV presenter canoodling with someone. It sure wasn't his co-star wife Wendy, unless she'd shot up 8 inches and taken heavy-duty steroids. A wry smile came over Sid's face as his calculating mind realised that this could be a goldmine. Sanctimonious Paddock was gay. This man had even jumped the queue before Bono on self-righteous levels. All he needed was to get some pictures and he could sell them to a tabloid. Sid visualised the front cover of the paper: '**PANTS DOWN, PHILLIP AND HIS BUM CHUM. WHERE'S WENDY?**' Sid just so happened to have the perfect thing to take the incriminating pictures at home. Hopefully, he could get the photos of Drury tonight. He could then put his time into the real stakeout. Sid rang the buzzer.

"Sid?"

"Yeh, it's me, gaffa."

Mat hung up and the door clicked open. Sid wondered if he would cop a look at Suzie breast-feeding the antichrists. She really needed to experience a real man like him. A crooked smile crossed Sid's weaselly face.

At 2.30am, stiff with cold, Sid watched his prey pick up a lad who couldn't have been more than twelve. He followed them to Trebeck Street, where the rent-boy plied his trade in the doorway of a tobacconists. After ten minutes the dirty deed was done. Sid scuttled back into the darkness with the incriminating film. The close-up feature was pure genius; it was a shame he had to hand the kit back to Mat. If he could get pictures of Phillip doing the kind of sick stuff he'd seen Drury doing to that kid, he could name his price for the pictures.

NIGHTMARE WALKING, PSYCHOPATH TALKING

"Mat, I want more of the product. I wanna be part of this in a biggah way. When our old man was pushing stuff, all free of 'em was on an equal footing."

"I'm already giving you serious weight. When you stop sniffing more than you're shifting, then you can 'ave more. I can't 'ave any liabilities in me firm."

"Yeh, your firm, innit. Mat, don't fucking forget you'd be nufink wivout me and the twins. Forgotten, 'ave ya, what our old man drummed into us? We're four bruvahs," said Nic, banging his fist down on the table.

"I 'ave nevah forgotten, Nic, but you're not in the same 'ead space as me right now. I'm going to Manchestah tomorrah for the night. We'll talk when I get back."

Nic had spent the rest of the day at his club breaking in a new stripper called Mandy and downing whisky. Walking into the

Crown to meet the twins, he was in a mood of pure nastiness. Nic stomped up to the bar, where his cousins were standing. The pub was decorated in all its cruddy glory. The Christmas tree was threadbare, the decorations sparse. At the top of the tree hung a naked Sindy doll garrotted around the neck with a piece of silver tinsel. The West Ham cabinet, by contrast, Tommy had spent no expense. He'd gone to Woollies and bought lustrous red and blue tinsel, lovingly hung around the shrine.

"You all right, cuz," said Sparky while jamming a cigarette into his mouth and lighting it.

"Feeling nufink but 'ate and murdah."

"What you 'aving, Nic?" asked Tommy.

"I'll 'ave a treble Bell's seeing as you only serve shit in 'ere. Second foughts, just fill the glass up."

Tommy did as he was told, sensing that Nic was in a very volatile mood.

"Busy in 'ere tonight," said Nic, knocking back his drink.

"Yeh, we got a stag party out back playing pool. Come down from Kent."

Nic ignored the landlord and turned back to his cousins.

"Still can't believe they sacked Lyall and replaced 'im wiv that crooked cunt Lou Macari. Lyall 'as seen it all before in '78, but 'e led the club back to the top. If anyone was gonna get us back into first, it was 'im. What the fuck was the board finking? But, no, we get some ex-Man U, Celtic playah. Not fucking 'appy."

"Fucking low blow. I mean, it's Lyall's club, innit," said Flint. "And that Paul Ince, what a traitorous cunt transferring to Man U. Every game 'e plays until 'e goes, the black cunt's gonna get it from the terraces, telling 'im 'e's a traitor and we fucking 'ate 'im."

"We got McQueen, Stroddah, Kelly, McKnight, Brady,

Dicks and McAvennie, but still didn't save us from relegation. This momf, I mean, nil–nil to Stoke City. Fucking tragic," said Nic.

"You seen Mat?" asked Flint.

"Yeh, and 'e as pissed me off a treat banging on 'bout 'is firm. "'E's going up norf. Wants to buy some club up there called the 'Enrietta. No idea why."

"Fink it's the 'Acienda, Nic."

"Whatevah, the pile of shit is called; it's not gonna be legendary like the Pink Taco. Got it looking the business, barmaids walking 'round in bikinis. Been taking a lot of inspiration from that new show on telly, *Baywatch*."

"Not seen it. What's that 'bout?"

"How the fuck would I know. I watch it wiv the sound down. It's just loads of fit birds wiv big tits running down the beach in slow motion."

"Seen the new club fliers, Nic. Was surprised you could get away wiv that. You'll 'ave the Dirty Squad aftah ya."

"They ain't gonna be a problem. Most of 'em are puntahs."

"Whose gash was it?"

"Uh, Scarlet, or could 'ave been Bianca. No idea really."

"Doesn't she mind 'aving 'er gash all ovah Lundun."

"Whoevah it was didn't 'ave the option. The slags aren't at libahty to fink for 'emselves."

"Who took the photo?"

"Me," said Nic, not expanding and taking a drag on his cigarette.

"You tried these 'E's?"

"Yeh, they're not for me. You feel 'appy and start talking to cunts you would usually kick the shit out of. You find you're 'aving a chat wiv a uni student and start telling 'im where you buried 'em bodies undah a car park in Shoreditch. I've even seen 'Ammahs and Millwall 'ugging each uvah. I'll keep to the coke so I want to kick someone's 'ead in. 'E's are doing a blinding business. Got 'em coming in from the Dam. They can't get enouf of 'em at the clubs. I mean, if they was caning arsenic, I'd sell that."

"You getting 'em from Klaas, like Mat?"

"Fuck Klaas. Got me own connection. Martin Kok. Unfortunate name, like, and 'e 'as this really bad stuttah, but 'e's sound. Got a shipment of white doves coming in. Gonna make a killing."

"You making more off it than the sniff?"

"Yeh, you can easy sell 'em for twenty quid a go. It's like all the uvah stuff you can fleece 'em for, like marking bottles of watah up ten times the price, selling Vicks inhalahs for a mint. Soppy mugs; once they're on it they'd empty their parents' life savings for a glow stick. I've pinched Seb Fontaine from the Fridge and Danny Rampling from Shroom."

"'Ow you getting 'em in?"

"Frough Tilbury."

"Does Escobar know Mat is getting quantity from Klaas?"

"Fuck knows. 'E's prob cut a deal wiv the Cali Cartel. Who cares. Business is business. But only Mat is allowed to speak wiv 'em direct," said Nic contemptuously. "Cali Cartel; they're a slick operation. They keep their 'eads down; not like Pablo, who fought it was a good idea to try get elected to government. Can you imagine one of us tried to stand as an MP? Mind you, we'd do a betta job than that backward bitch Diane we've got. 'Ave you seen the state of it; seriously challenging wank material – the fought of it is fucking with me 'ead. But I, like, try to fink positive and say now we lost our contact we could ask Diane to put us in touch wiv anuvah IRA terrorist. Anyways, Escobar's got more to worry about, like serving five 'undred years in a max security."

"Not a bad plan if Mat 'as jumped ship, cos if DEA get

Escobar and they've got a massive 'ard-on for 'im, 'e can still keep the shipments coming. Cali keeping it low profile, but Escobar, 'e bombed a plane and the one guy 'e wanted dead weren't even on the flight," said Sparky, signalling to Tommy to stick a fresh pint in his glass.

"Yeh well Interpol and NCIS got an 'ard-on for Mat. Its getting 'airy ETA 'as ended their ceasefire so they want a biggah cut to arm 'emselves so they can wipe out as many politicians as possible. Escobar probably got the bomb from ETA they're quality bomb makahs."

Nic's attention was momentarily sidetracked as he saw the back of a bloke in a red football shirt make his way into the snooker room.

"Who's that cunt, Tommy?"

"It's one of the lads who 'as come down for the stag do. You clocked the shirt. I told 'im 'e was taking 'is life into his own 'ands coming in 'ere dressed in that. Soppy git didn't even know what I was talking 'bout. Ain't been any trouble, mind you."

Nic downed the rest of his whisky and made his way to the back room, followed by the twins.

"You got some fucking nerve coming in 'ere wearing a Goonahs shirt. The Arsenal don't drink in 'ere."

"We don't want any trouble. We're on a stag do. Jason's getting married. We've come down from Kent. I'm Lee, this is Jason and that's Dave."

"I don't give a fuck. The only red in 'ere is claret."

"I'm not even really into footie. It's just a top; no harm intended," said Lee. "We're down here to go to Pink Taco – it's legendary."

"You cunts ain't going in that club. It's mine. Only place you're going tonight is to 'ospital," said Nic, cracking his knuckles, about to unleash Plantagenet-level violence. Nick headbutted Lee, cracking his nose, which burst open. Blood spurted out as he lost balance and cracked his head on the side of the snooker table. As Lee crashed to the floor, Nic attacked Jason with his fists, a barrage of punches pulverising his face. Nic picked up a snooker cue and started to whack Jason with it, violent blow after blow. In the sheer madness, Dave tried to grab onto Nic's back and destabilise him, but Nic just threw him to the floor as he continued to whack Jason's skull, his eye socket broken, his ear drum perforated. He fell like a dead weight to the floor in a bloody, broken heap. Dave got back up, but Nic, too fast, headbutted him then bludgeoned him repeatedly with the snooker cue. Lee, who was badly disorientated, was rousing. Nic started to violently kick him again and again in the chest and stomach, severely winding him, the sickening sounds of his ribs cracking. Tommy watched on and dreamt of owning a boozer in Stow-on-the-Wold.

Nic woke up on the floor of his office. He had no idea what time it was or when he had passed out. Raising his head, he saw he had company: Sonietta, who was naked, asleep and handcuffed to a chair. His head ached and his body was shaking. He vaguely remembered meeting the twins at the Crown last night. Reaching for a bottle of Glendronach, he thought now that Mat was away it would be a nice surprise if he visited Suzie and his nephews.

THE NIGHTMARE BEFORE CHRISTMAS

Sid had spent the last five nights freezing his balls off, sneaking around with the camera he had pinched from Terrance at the Lord Stanley. Tonight was no different; he just needed to get the scandalous pictures. Sid waited behind the glow of the Christmas tree that adorned Curzon Place dressed in a snorkel jacket. It would take all his tenacity, as this was not the Paddocks' main residence; they just used it when they needed to stay in London instead of heading back to their main residence in Chiswick. Watching and waiting and trying to kill time, Sid flicked through his copy of that day's *The Sun* newspaper for what felt like the tenth time. KAD in China had taken responsibility for the execution of a six-year-old boy Zhang Yiming in Longyan, who'd been force-fed raw chicken and Nyquil then cooked in an industrial microwave. A Romanian faction of KAD had abducted a three-year-old toddler reported to be called Emory from the Walter Reed Army Medical Centre in Washington. The terrorists, in a statement, advised he was being held in a dungeon in Bucharest until he turned eighteen. Their leader had taken a special interest in the boy and she would be back for his baby brother. Sid just kept going back to page three: Kathy, aged twenty-one, from Liverpool, who enjoyed knitting and taxidermy. The brunette beauty stared back at him. He could feel the wetness of drool gathering at the corners of his mouth, making his faux-fur-lined jacket moist. Sid thew the paper into the nearby rubbish bin and shoved his now-cold flask of Bovril into a carrier bag. What he could do with now was a crafty cigarette. Satisfied that there was no one around, he unzipped his snorkel, took a roll-up from behind his ear and lit it, taking a drag. Feeling the nicotine flowing through his body, he felt momentarily better. A light sprinkle of snow started to fall, touching the branches of the festive tree and landing daintily on the pavement. Taking the last greedy pull on his fag, Sid threw the butt on the pavement, the butt landing on a stray fir-tree branch that had dropped to the ground, letting off a burnt alpine smell and satisfying fizzing sound. Sid zipped his snorkel back up and was once again breathing in his own foul breath. The burning mess was now just letting off a small black plume of smoke as the flurry of falling snowflakes put it out. Thinking of calling it a night, he was about to walk back to his car when he saw the figure of a man emerge from Curzon Street. He walked quickly and was dressed in a black coat, but what had really spurned Sid's attention was the baseball cap the figure had pulled down over his head. Camera in hand and ducking further behind the tree, Sid watched. The man's face, which was obscured, was fiddling with the front door of Mat's apartment block. He was wearing black gloves. There was a faint radiation from the porch light. From what Sid could make out he was picking the lock. The figure still had his face down, betrayed by shadow; his body was at an angle that meant Sid could just about make out he was using what looked like a tension wrench. The torque manipulated just right, and the lock must have clicked open, as the figure looked up before he let himself him; but it was enough time to take a picture. There was no mistaking it was Nic. What was he doing breaking into Mat's apartment block? Sid watched him go in the front door. Something was very badly wrong here. Checking his Swatch, he clocked the time as 9.55pm. Sid waited what seemed like around five minutes, when he heard what sounded like a gunshot, closely followed by another two shots. Could it have been a car backfiring? Moments later the figure walked out the front door. Sid crouched and took a few more shots as the figure walked briskly and disappeared onto Curzon Street. Was that really Nic he'd captured on film? And what the fuck had he done? Feeling the coast was clear, Sid emerged. He needed to get back to his car with his finds on Kodak. Sid did a double take as he stared at the entrance to Mat's apartment block. Was it his imagination or was there something twinkling on the floor? The earlier flurry of snowflakes had stopped, so he wondered if it was a glint of ice. Walking over, he reached out and picked up the object. It was a diamond 'N' cufflink. Sid held the precious find and had an idea. He walked to the rubbish bin he'd thrown the newspaper in. Lifting it out, he walked over to the entrance of the flat. He placed the cufflink near to the date on the newspaper. Sid took his Swatch off, displaying both the time and date, and placed it by the cufflink. Picking up the camera, he took the shot. He then stepped back and took another picture of his evidence with the door of Number 9 in plain view. Satisfied he had the goods, Sid packed all the items back into the bag and made his way to his car.

Sid got to Boots at 9am and deposited the film in the one-hour service. He had an hour to kill, so he stopped off at a newsagents to pick up some tobacco. Stepping into the shop, he was momentarily rendered motionless when he looked at the front of *The Sun*. The headline read: '**IN COLD BLOOD: GANGLAND BOSS'S WIFE AND BABIES SLAIN**'. Picking the paper up, he made his way to the counter, placed the newspaper down and asked for a pack of Golden Virginia. The shop assistant gave him what he thought passed as a smile. She had severe buck teeth, but he could put those to good use. Delighted by the attention, he uncharacteristically put some coppers into the Save the Spastics box, something he immediately regretted as he watched the money zigzag down past the two-by-two animals until it reached the ark. But there was no time to have negative thoughts. He checked his Swatch. He had forty-five minutes until he could pick up the photos. He headed to Arthur's to read the full newspaper article.

The article didn't explain how they'd been killed, but Sid knew. Little more was said, only that the police were appealing for witnesses and pursuing lines of inquiry, which Sid knew was Old Bill speak for they knew fuck all. The rest of the article was made up of all the allegations that had been made against Mat over the years. It was a grim yet highly glamourised account of murder, torture, extortion and drugs, with every other line pointing out that Mat, through his ill deeds, was a multi-millionaire, the paper even sharing with the reader that his former girlfriend had come to a grisly end by the Hackney Hacker. On the inside pages the story continued. The journalist had managed to get hold of a police-issue, crime-scene photo of Lisa with her face cut up. They had also got their paws on a topless photo of her, which they shared on page 3. Finishing his cup of tea, Sid headed to Boots and collected the photos. Scuttling out, he didn't hear the assistant call him back as she'd forgotten to put the negatives in. They were just another set of negatives that would be disposed of. Sid needed to get home promptly, but first he needed to make a pitstop at John Menzies to buy paper, envelopes, scissors and glue. Sid arrived back at his flat and sat on an armchair, pulling the spoils from the bag. He got to work cutting letters from the newspaper. After thirty minutes Sid held his masterpiece up.

I no who dun in yor wife and nippers.
Send £100,000 by SWIFT ear.
John Thomas
Bank Account 00683856
Sort Code 00-66-48
I got fotographs who dun it. Waz outside your drum on knight it went down.

Sid had a fake passport made by a bloke in Camberwell, just as a precaution. Some years ago he'd been asked to do a clean-up job at Mat's request for the Clerkenwell Crime Syndicate. Things got dicey, as the victim Claude Moseley, had been found in a shallow grave; he'd been cut in half with a Samurai sword. Gilbert Wynter, an Adams family enforcer, had been taken in for questioning. The Hunters wouldn't have his back. Sid had thought it only prudent to get a fake passport should he need to do one. He planned this afternoon to go over to North London and set up a dodgy bank account away from prying eyes. He needed to have his wits about him. Mat was razor sharp, but he wouldn't be seeing straight at the moment. He'd be gunning to get this information.

The police hadn't been able to get hold of Mat on that fateful night. He was in Whitworth Street on the south side of the

Rochdale Canal in Manchester talking to representatives from Factory Records. They'd contacted Rosie. When Nan had got hold of Mat at the Midland Hotel and told him, he had hung up then sped down the M6 recklessly and turned up at her house on Downs Park Road as if it had all been some sort of nightmare. He'd tried Suzie's mobile what seemed to be over a hundred times, but no answer. When he arrived, Nan sat him down and told him that his wife and children were dead. He started smashing everything into oblivion. Nan watched as he got it out of his system, standing back. She'd seen it all before. She would just stay there and be there for him. It was all she could do. When Mat finally exhausted himself, he went to the kitchen, took a bottle of whisky from the cupboard then sat down and stared straight ahead, not speaking, and only moving to pour and drink the Jack Daniels. Nobody could get through to him, not even Nic and the twins.

"Bruv, its fucking diabolical what 'as 'append, but we'll get the cunt. Got all our men on it. When we find 'im, 'e'll wish 'e'd nevah been born."

The police had just merely taken the human remains and any evidence from the flat. They wouldn't clean up or remove all the blood and guts. Nan had spoken to Charlie Richardson, an associate of Eddie's, who'd put her in touch with a crime-scene forensic-cleaning firm. They sanitised the flat. Mat had been swiftly cleared as a suspect, having an airtight alibi; he was in Manchester at the Hacienda with two of the owners and Bernard Sumner, the lead singer of New Order. The night had gone well, apart from Seb Slick, who'd persistently tried to get the attention of Bernard.

"As your manager, I can take you into the next stratosphere. I'm thinking a collaboration of you and Black Lace. I moved the Lace into films. They had a cameo in *Rita, Sue and Bob Too.* They played one of their original numbers – 'Gang Bang'."

He'd eventually taken the hint that Bernard wasn't interested when he was told to "Fook off, you spastic twat." Seb had duly 'fooked' off to do the cabbage patch to the Stone Roses' 'Fool's Gold'.

Mat never went back to the flat. Nan collected all their personal belongings. One day Mat may find some solace in them. She and the twins had gone over and packed everything up. She collected his post and dropped the keys off at Savills. Nan put his post on the Welsh dresser and, distracted by being asked for a cup of tea by Flint, didn't notice the letters fall down the back behind her serving plates. Comatose, Mat sat in silence, only moving to raise his glass to his mouth.

The flat was put on the market, and a Korean-Japanese real estate speculator, JoJi Obari, bought it. It was uncertain whether the new owner knew of the grisly history of the flat. Maybe this was just lost in translation, he was a horror goon or he just didn't care. After all, Mayfair was prime real estate; it was in walking distance of Green Park and Shepherd Market. The views from the penthouse of London's skyline were spectacular. So multiple gruesome deaths could be conveniently forgotten. Nan wondered how much more her family could take. Mat didn't know that Suzie was pregnant – he couldn't take that news at the moment. But one day the truth would come out.

Nan made endless cups of tea that went undrunk and chatted to him, and he remained silent. She rarely left the house for more than ten minutes, worried what Mat might do, but five days after the deaths she said, "Son, the cupboards are bare, so I'm going to Safeway to do a shop. I'll get a taxi there and back. I won't be more than an 'our. Will you be okay, son?"

Mat made no comment, just took another gulp of whisky.

"Look, what 'as 'appened is the biggest, most diabolical libahty-take evah, and this firm will get the cunt who dun this before McDick does, but Mat's not well at the moment. I'm the boss now. We're all part of this firm, but someone 'as to be in charge, right? Mat's a vegetable. Just 'ope 'e gets frough it. To be 'onest, that's all we can 'ope. Can't tell you 'ow much this cuts me up inside. We'll find who did this nastiness and crucify 'im. But this firm will survive."

"We want that cunt badly too, but Mat's just in shock. 'E's mentally strong and 'e'll get ovah it. 'E just needs time."

"Flint, that's the fing; I don't fink 'e will evah recuvah from this. It will 'ave completely weakened 'im. 'E will nevah be the same. We gotta accept the Mat we knew is gone. Nobody's 'ead, no mattah 'ow strong, could survive this. Mat's brain as dun a David Bannah."

"What does that mean even," said Flint looking bewildered.

"Like you know on that telly show at the end of the 'Ulk David always walks off on 'is todd."

"Can't say I watch it Nic. I fink that's when *Jim'll Fix It* is on the ovahside""

Nan was surprised when she got back that Mat was showered, shaved and dressed.

"Son, you feeling betta? You off out, 'ave some fresh 'air? Do you the world of good."

"Back to work, Nan. I got a score to settle." Mat took his car keys off the dresser and walked out the front door. As he left, her grandson looked her straight in her eyes, and what Nan saw scared her. She saw pure unadulterated hate.

Mat walked into the scrapyard office, which unsteadied Nic, who had his legs up on the desk, leaning back in Mat's chair. He knew his brother well. He was walking and talking, but those eyes did not betray a deadliness he hadn't seen before, one he was not expecting nor had factored into his master plan.

"I'm back. You don't look too pleased."

"'Course, bruv, just surprised. You sure you're up to it? Take all the time you need. Got all our men looking for the cunt."

"What 'ave they found?"

"No one knows nufink. Even Sid can't get anyfink. 'E said it was someone you wouldn't fink of, so I fink it's some new gang trying to muscle in. It was like 'e 'ad really fought 'bout it, cos for once 'e wasn't doing that foot-shuffle fing 'e does, and 'e was looking me straight in the eyes. Fink 'e's onto somefink."

"When I know who killed Suzie and me kids, no one touches the cunt. That's for me."

Mat moved over to his chair, and Nic took his cue and got up.

"This is what's gonna 'appen. I want the 'eads of the Turks, Russians, Albanians, Kurds and any uvah cunting gang, and their families too."

What Nic had done hadn't weakened Mat; he'd come back more ruthless than ever.

Mat had remained stoic at the funeral of his wife and babies. It was Father Tobias's first triple funeral, one he never wished to conduct again in his ecclesiastical career. He'd married the young couple and christened their babies. Rosie was such a lovely woman, full of kindness, who did everything for her family. Of course, he wasn't one to listen to idle gossip, but it had reached him that her grandsons were involved in a particularly clandestine line of work.

Jeffrey, escorted by Julian, had dressed in black, complete with a lace, veiled fascinator. He'd passed out and could only be brought around when one of the choir had given him smelling salts.

There was no wake. Nan, the four boys and Debbie went back to hers. Nan had made tea and a coffee and walnut sponge and tried to make some semblance of conversation. But the four boys sat in silence, with only Debbie making any attempt.

SOCIETY

Nan turned on the TV to watch *Kilroy* while making a mental note to give Mat his post. She glanced at the dresser, but she couldn't see it. Obviously, she must have given it to him already. She just couldn't remember. Today Kilroy's question was, will the vagina become extinct and was it really that important that a woman has one? Silk glided through the audience. Those members who didn't answer quick enough, Kilroy prompted them. "You could look at it on a scale of one to ten, one being you're not too bothered what's going on down there, five meaning depends how desperate you are, and ten being hell, yes, you expect to find a fully functioning vagina." Kilroy became more and more animated, gushing, "One that's an elastic muscular love canal with a soft, flexible lining oozing with natural muliebral lubrication and heavenly exquisite sensation, the clitoris more magical than *Fantasia*." Every audience member for once on his show was in full agreement and 100% pro-vagina. When they stood up and gave him a standing ovation, Silk, emotional with tears, gushed, "Surely, this was the most wonderous of all God's creations. Not a day goes by when I don't feel a blessed man that my wife has one.

It was a near-perfect creation. Surely, there has been a biblical mistake, and this was what God made on the seventh day."

When Kilroy was about to give his parting shot, going out live at 9am in the morning, the show was abruptly taken off air. Far from denting his ratings, they went through the roof. Off the back of this groundbreaking TV, Silk got signed to L'Oréal to bring out his own self-tan range that came in mahogany, café noir and blackfishing. He was offered a prime-time show on NBC but decided his future was back in politics. There was another matter that needed to be dealt with, that being saving the UK from the clutches of the European Union, one which he believed had more clamp-down power than the pubococcygeus, puborectalis and iliococcygeus muscles.

Switching the TV off, Nan put her overcoat on and fastened her headscarf. She was going over to see Victor. She could do with speaking to someone she could offload her problems on. She opened the dresser drawer and took out her oldest set of Happy Family cards she'd been given as a child. She opened the John Jaques vintage cards and tutted. There were four missing. Wherever could they have got to? She'd have to take a newer pack over to see Victor. A fleeting thought passed her mind as she went out the door. What she really needed was a full spring clean. She'd start with the dresser, get all the china down and give them a good clean.

Sid wondered why Mat hadn't been in touch. Had he asked for too much money? Had Mat even had the letter, and if not, where was it?

The Met and McBride were at their wits' end. Mat's henchmen were causing a hecatomb, the bodies at the morgue piling high. Only one witness had come forward in the investigation of Suzie and the twins' deaths. A few nights before the murders, they'd seen a scruffy-looking man loitering by the Christmas tree. They just thought it was a vagrant who'd made his way up from Oxford Street.

Debbie sat on the side of her bathtub as she painted her toes. She sighed contentedly to herself. She had a date later. She hadn't been looking to meet anyone; she was dedicated to working on her rehabilitation. The tryst had been so natural; her lover had needed her as much as she needed him. It couldn't have been more natural. They'd made passionate love for hours. It was nothing like sex with Nic, even when they'd been madly in love. She'd meet him later at the house he'd rented for them in Virginia Water. Just the thought of him touching her gave her goosebumps. Debbie had spent hours in La Perla looking for the perfect lingerie for their tryst. From the bedroom she could faintly hear the radio. Chris Isaak's 'Wicked Game' was playing. Putting the last stoke on her pinky toe, she reached up to the window sill and brought the white plastic object down. It showed a solid red line. Debbie smiled to herself. She was indeed with child. The only thing was, she didn't know which brother was the father.

TO BE CONTINUED...

ABOUT THE AUTHOR

Political 'liberty', it is said, is simply a bribe, a bloodless substitute for the Gestapo – **George Orwell, *Fascism and Democracy***

Blood Betrayal is Eric's first novel, he wrote whilst serving a lengthy stretch at Her Majesty's pleasure. Since leaving Belmarsh he has turned his life around and now works as a full-time specialist consultant on diversity and inclusion for the Order of Nine Angles. Eric is now working on his follow up book whilst bumper recruiting in Islington North.

This book is printed on paper from sustainable sources managed under the Forest Stewardship Council (FSC) scheme.

It has been printed in the UK to reduce transportation miles and their impact upon the environment.

For every new title that Troubador publishes, we plant a tree to offset CO_2, partnering with the More Trees scheme.

MORE TREES
LET'S PLANT A BILLION TREES

For more about how Troubador offsets its environmental impact, see www.troubador.co.uk/sustainability-and-community